Red Planet Pioneer: Modulus of Resilience

R. Vincent Tibbetts

COPYRIGHT

The Library of Congress Cataloging-in-Publication has been applied for.
ISBN-13:978-0692668641 (Tidal Force Productions)
ISBN-10:0692668640

Cover Design: Bezuki
Editor: Tanya Besmehn

Definition

Modulus of Resilience: is defined as the maximum energy that can be absorbed per unit volume without creating a permanent distortion.

In social terms, the modulus is the capacity of humans to come out of extreme shock, damage, injury and trauma and get back to a normal life.

Dedication

To my Mother and Father who surely had to find a sense of resiliency within themselves when raising us. They endured, made sure we bounced back from all that life tried to throw at us, and sacrificed like every good parent so we would have a chance at a normal life.

Acknowledgements

I am forever grateful to those who helped me complete this project. I am quite sure it was a chore for those who read through the rough drafts and put up with my constant nagging for their reading of this material. Jen Jacobs, Sonya Branson, John Downey, Jesse Cole, Taylor Sparks, and Molly Menihan at one time or another donated their valuable energy to help in the completion of this process.

Linda Borg was especially kind in reviewing the novel in its entirety, also in lending her editing skills and making her notes available to me. Linda is a creative soul in her own right, I value her friendship, and it has been a complete pleasure working with her on other projects.

A special thanks goes out to Stephanie Zapalac and her company Art of Life. She is an amazing motivator to the artist, writer, and creative soul. A great debt is owed for her uncanny intuition and insightful advise in cobbling together this literary construct.

John Gasca who not only read the entire novel but worked with me on the photo projects that would eventually become some of the covers for this book. The mind's eye is powerful in this one.

Finally I would like to thank Tanya Besmehn and her company Several Stories High Writing Services. In dealing with Tanya on this project it has been a complete pleasure. She is very professional, the extra set of eyes everyone always refers to and wishes they had on their own project, and above all she leaves you feeling you made the right choice when you get her notes and corrections back.

Thank you all so very much for helping me finish this novel.

WARNING

The following Government Document is Encrypted and is the Property of the Red Planet Pioneer Corporation

If the Encryption has been Compromised

Symbols will appear as Numbers below:

4 4 5 6 1 3 1 2 9 7 4 5 1 0 0 3 5 6

Report Your Location Immediately to the following Hyperlink

-redplanetpioneer.com-

Place the File you are Reading in a Fixed Location
Place your Cellular Device on top of the File
Do Not Shutdown - Do Not Leave Your Device
Unattended

Red Planet Pioneer: Modulus of Resilience

Chapter 1
Droplet

The firm was a cesspool filled with the disturbed particulates of lies and deceit. The murky waters had everyone fighting the same fight in just getting a little breathing room. He was different from the others operating in this sump because he was willing to go further than most just to save himself. Deep within his person hinged a belief, it was based on the feeling he was better than they were and he searched for opportunities that would help hammer this point home.

Xavier Pentagrass was an ambitious young man. The trimmed sleek suits he wore were meant to cut a path through this place. To accompany the sharpness of his attire he developed a personality that was like adding a serrated edge to a knife. The staff knew better than to get between him and what he wanted. Those waters often turned turbulent, so they knew to steer clear of any project he was on, or as it was noted of late, the pitch for colonizing Mars.

He was standing on an elevated platform with a panel of people seated directly behind him. They had been assembled as the council to his efforts. This entire setup was considered a one shot deal, so the room was laid out to his exact specifications. Everything needed to be perfect, the seating, the lighting, the placement of the panel, the reading of his entire presentation, right down to the folds in the napkins. He stood near his perch with eyes closed, keeping a vigil unto himself, refusing to utter a single solitary thing until the room began to quiet down and he felt he had their complete and undivided attention. Harnessing his mental energies, he chose instead to combat the things trying to kill them, and find a way to merge those clamoring considerations to go in one direction. He perfected his craft using a series of mental exercises to help him stay focused at crucial times just like these, concentrating on a vision to help him gather his thoughts. The vision he preferred channeled these speculations into beads of moisture gathering under a large granite ledge.

At first the exact location of this outcropping was unimportant, but as time went on and he continued to use this exercise, he built an entire world around the protrusion. It jetted out from a steeply sloped mountain high above a jungle lair. The granite prominence could have easily been mistaken for a massive step, a launching point, the stepping stone for a Norse God to leap into the heavens and return to their home high above. It was underneath this ledge where his mental energies condensed, gained focus and direction, convincing him to let go and watch his pitch fly.

His focal point for this was unshakeable. There was just too much old money in that room for him to be any other way. His firm had placed a great amount of trust within him to speak in front of these venture capitalists. Yet in the back of his mind, he knew he was the only logical choice for the job. Who else were they going to get from within the company that had his qualifications? No one there had a profile or even a resume that could come close to comparing with his. The scar he had on the back of his head was all the evidence they would ever need for how far he was willing to take these things, that scar signified the ultimate commitment to their corporate philosophies.

He wasted none of his opportunities, diving in with relish at any chance for advancement. The implant they had installed in his head was a prototype and literally rested atop his cerebellum. It was there to enhance his free flowing thoughts and gave him access to a wealth of knowledge he never knew existed—this was impressive in its own right, but if he didn't utilize it correctly, all his efforts would be lost.

The last thing he wanted to be was the guy at the cocktail party who spewed out endless droves of useless information in a feeble attempt at trying to make an impression. That was a specialized conversation spun verbally to bring a showy cognizance to its owner. He wanted something more out of his life than to be a mental carnival barker. He considered these things demeaning to the chances he had taken. That wasn't to say he didn't have his fair share of problems. At times the implant would direct where his thoughts would travel, leaving his mind's eye to stare unblinking into rather bothersome places.

This was the power the droplet exercise had in helping him move ahead. His doctors recommended he do something to help harness all these new phrenic energies. This exercise enabled him to project his mental prowess over things in the room, from the ticking of the wall mounted clock to the shifting of ice melting in their beverage tubs and the subtle squeaking of all those leather-bound chairs languidly swiveling with their heavy suitors. He knew he needed to be at one with all of those things so he had a better idea of how their energy could help him.

He pictured himself a liquid sphere, balanced and at one with the steady state of energy all around him. He was solid in his belief, but capable of moving, and as a water droplet he could hang there, defying the tug of gravity until he was ready to let go. He felt the moment and slowly opened his eyes.

"If there is one word to describe the monumental colonization effort happening right now on Mars, it has to be that of resiliency. This quality touches everything they send there, from the armada of ships, to the biospheres taking shape on the Martian landscape. There are countless people who have sacrificed long hours on assembly lines, dedicating themselves to making the program they are on their life's work. Every person who has put their hands on this project has done so in support of the colonists who have taken the long and arduous journey to get there. Every one of these people want to see more then just flags and footprints upon another world. They have climbed aboard those ships with their hopes and dreams, committed in the belief of staying there. The one common thread throughout this entire process has been resiliency."

Xavier knew deep down there were problems with investing in a place like Mars, and they didn't rear their ugly head until those colonists actually got to the Red Planet. That was when the scheduled timelines for getting things done collapsed in upon itself. There seemed to be delays in everything they attempted, from launches to the assembly of their biospheres, from mining to manufacturing, even the reports they filed had an inherent delay in getting back to the people of Earth. All of it was unacceptable to anyone looking to invest in this process. Those vicious cycles were preventing the profits from raining down upon their investors. Regardless of these glaring problems, everyone knew two worlds were better than one, especially when it came to making money. That was why every one of those old men was in that room.

"It would follow then that the individual who would invest in a startup venture on Mars must also exhibit the same tough characteristics those resilient entities have displayed. They survive there now because they have weathered the storms of misfortune. No one wishes for failure, but the individual investing in this venture would be remiss in not planning for the rainy day. We should not wander out into the calm without the protection of at least an umbrella, especially if our days were to turn cloudy and grey."

Xavier had spent plenty of time studying the dossiers they had prepared on each of the investors in attendance. He studied their characteristics and tendencies, their educational backgrounds and the extent of their altruistic behaviors. He went over and over these materials until he was acquainted with how these men thought. It was a trying study, but anything a person ever wanted in life was always a series of difficult trials. If one planned accordingly though, one could dictate the pace and direction of the race, just as his last statement had intended to show.

So for him, there was no surprise as to who the first person to chirp up at this meeting. Jeb Wentworth was a conservative old man who was notorious for the look of skepticism he would get on his face anytime someone struck up a business conversation. It served him well in making decisions about his money and forced people pitching a venture to shoot straight with him or be shown the door. There were no second chances with Jeb. Those who didn't cut it with him were forever labeled a huckster. A perplexed look followed by that of disgust were usually the last expressions anyone every saw on Jeb as they were shown the door. Xavier saw the signs beginning to form on Jeb Wentworth now.

"We've all read the proposal Mr. Pentagrass. I think I speak for quite a few people here in the room when I say it's one thing to stand up there and try to sell investors on a potential venture for profit, and it's quite another to actually put the thing into practice. You made us all forsake the comfort of our homes and offices. You had us come all the way out here and for what? To listen to some damn pep-rally? I don't need to be inspired to invest my money. I need cold hard facts and I don't need them to be spread like chicken feed."

Jeb stood up to leave. This caught the attention of everyone in the room. He leaned onto the table, placing his knuckles onto the surface. From everything Xavier had read about Jeb, this last move was his *tell* that he indeed was getting ready to leave them. "So here are some cold hard facts for you Mr. Pentagrass. There are entire countries that have bankrolled this colonization effort. Even if we pulled all of our money together from everyone in this room and dumped it behind whatever it is you are trying to sell us, those numbers would not come close to what those countries have put into their colonization efforts. With that being said, I have a limited amount of investment capital and it matches my patience."

Xavier had to tip his hat to Mr. Wentworth, even though he was ready for Jeb's skepticism, his technique still had a crushing effect on him. It also forced everyone in the room to pump their brakes. This kind of disruption usually had pitchmen spilling out all over the room like the riders of a toboggan thrown from their sled. In spite of all this Xavier felt himself up for the challenge. He knew he needed to refute what had just been said, but in such a way as to have the appearance of not directing his comments solely at Wentworth. That was just another trap Jeb had thrown out into the room. If this turned into an argument then there wouldn't be much left for him to sell. "On the surface Mars seems to be the kind of investment only an elderly gentlemen would make, someone who is coming to the end of their years and is trying to reach out and touch immortality. This is the Mars most of you know when presented with an investment opportunity. The one where future generations reverently murmur the inscribed names of investors from some polished obelisk. That isn't the Mars I am here to sell you. This planet for all intensive purposes has unlimited financial potential, as the colonization process grows, so does the window for this opportunity.

"I am sure most of you have heard through the media outlets about the start up of mining operations on the Red Planet. They have reported unearthing vast deposits of Deuterium, the value of this commodity is a matter of public record and the *Exchanges* here on Earth have reacted favorably to its extraction. The mining of this ore will revolutionize the industry on both worlds, and the investors who have so patiently waited for this moment will now reap those rewards.

"We here now have such an opportunity before us. What has been presented to me by this government, and the reason why our firm has put together this meeting, has us mining a field rich with opportunities, and more importantly opportunities that have not been announced to the general public. Even as we are speaking here, I am certain the government will be allowing for a few more meetings to take place like this one. The first single consortium willing to step up to the plate and commit to the government will be the one's to reap the rewards."

Xavier had a knack for being able to tell the interest level of each and every potential investor. The look they got on their faces led him either out the door or to their wallets. When they were staring at him, as they were now, hanging on his every word, he knew they were his to lose. Much like the batter of a baseball game hanging on the one pitch that would allow them to win the game, all he needed to do was put a big fat cookie out over the plate and let them hit it out of the park. The men in this room wouldn't settle for anything less and Xavier thrived on pitching to that type of arrogance. "This government has taken on more than just a yeoman's task in ferrying people to the surface of Mars. Other countries have benefited from their offer by using those rockets as a taxi. For all of their nobility, this government has become overwhelmed by the services demanded from it and backlogged by those untimely launches. Their dream of uniting all of these countries under one banner is beginning to crack under this tremendous strain. It's putting the Alliance they have formed on fiscal hard times. There have been rumors of this throughout the financial community, I'm sure some of you are well aware of the reports. The sovereignty for the Alliance of the Americas is on the line. They just haven't made those facts public as of yet.

"Only the Singo-Chinese can rival what this Alliance has done with their fleet of rockets. If this Alliance were allowed to concentrate on its own interests, like their Singo-Chinese counterparts, and leave the rest of the international community behind—Well let's just say there are a lot of forward thinkers who feel they could more than hold their own."

Theodore Hadley had come from a long line of inheritance, the money his family had was believed to be birthed from the first transcontinental railroad. Those heirs had reinvested it wisely, passing it on from generation to generation. One rule of thumb it seemed the Hadleys had when conducting themselves in business was they never spoke up during the pitch session. They allowed the completion of the process to happen before they formulated their questions. So when Hadley decided to speak now, in front of the others, it more than caught this group off guard.

His voice was well mannered, stern, and to the point. "From what we currently see in the news, the Singo-Chinese aren't exactly lighting it up on the colonization front either. They have had their mistakes on Earth and on Mars. Their strategy for conquering the Red Planet seems to be based on exactly what has worked for them in the past, that is to say they simply over-run such a desired enclave with sheer numbers. It's hard to deny that someone owns something if they are squatting on it. The only thing keeping them in check to this point is the problem they are having getting those numbers up there."

"Still, sometimes old strategies are the best strategies. They will win out if no one else goes up there to challenge them on this front."

This retort was the reason Xavier had put a panel together. Besides helping him with insight, or having their names added to give credence to his proposal, they could participate in answering questions pertaining to their field. He had Engineers, Astronauts, Politicians, a Theologian, and he had Dr. M. Book. If the colonization effort had a face it was that of Dr. M. Book. He was an engineer with an extensive background in aerospace, who left his field to become an activist for the colonization of Mars. He could win the hearts and minds of anyone seeing even the slightest significance for going to the Red Planet.

There were plenty of souls wanting to see the colonization effort succeed. It was never a question of gaining support for this vision, legitimate causes seemed to crop up everywhere. Some hoped Mars would be the scientific vindication they needed for a universe teeming with life. If they could somehow show this barren world had once contained even the simplest of microbes in its warm past, or housed them even now, then their arguments for life being robust and plentiful throughout the universe would be validated. This discovery would also help knock down a certain belief system some had for putting the Earth at the center of all creation.

There were other groups who saw Mars as their pathway toward expansion. It would give them a fresh start, and put them on a technological plain with every other spacefaring civilization. The warning shots spurring them on came straight out of the *Cretaceous* period. The extinction level event that happened in the *Yucatan Peninsula* smacked down the dinosaurs and awoke humanity to the ultimate disaster of leaving all their eggs in just one basket. There was no better way to get around this then to ante up on the cosmic craps table with an additional line of planetary credit.

Mars could also be seen as the new hope, but not because they thought the Red Planet was a better place to live as much as they had given up on trying to save their own world, Earth. They didn't have the confidence for a foreseeable future on the blue peril. There were too many pending catastrophes happening all at once, global warming, pollution, the melting of the polar ice cap, undersea methane release, a population problem, an over consumption of resources, rampant disease, and war. It was easier to sell a person on starting anew someplace else rather than have them stay and solve each of those dilemmas.

Xavier Pentagrass could work with all those reasons for coming here but knew better than to hold onto any single one too tight. By embracing them all he found a way to sell the Red Planet as a profit point. This left him options to use every angle ever published or spoken by experts in the field. The smart money always followed a well-laid plan and this venture was no different, pointing them to a bedrock of dividends, he just had to allow this plan to naturally unfold.

Having Dr. M. Book's name attached to this consortium was like getting a blessing from the Pope. As much as he would have liked Dr. Book to continue, it was more important for Xavier to quell the people in that room and appear somewhat diplomatic. "It's true, the Singo-Chinese haven't had the best of successes in recent memory. Yet they are showing the one quality most important in this venture, resiliency. They have a plan and they keep pushing forward with it. They are slowly chipping away at the difficulties that are holding them back. One can point to their misfortunes, snicker at their failed attempts, but at the current projected rate, if the Alliance doesn't start to try and match their efforts, a Red Mars may, in the end, be a Singo-Chinese Mars."

"Don't stand there and try to repatriate us. This administration has taken their chances and walked down a path of their own choosing." Wentworth had raised his hand, shaking a finger at Xavier, looking more like an aging baseball manager arguing a bad call.

Xavier had no choice but to react to this affront like an umpire brushing him off as he continued to officiate the game. "I have personally had conversations with these politicians, and they acknowledged having been put on the spot. Their good intentions have been lost in the scathing reviews of recent press clippings. People refuse to remember the steps this country had to take in being represented on that red rock. The public has a very short-term memory when it comes to good deeds done, and the news outlets don't help, beating more to the tune of *what-have-you-done-for-me-lately*. Under those circumstances the politicians have been pushed beyond their comfort zones and fear the guillotine will drop on their political careers come next election. Their *Mars is for everyone* approach, however gracious has left them holding the bag. It's only a matter of time before their decapitated carcasses hang limply out in the political breeze. They are desperate to make something happen before the next election, so this administration is prepared to open a door rarely made available to the general public."

Jarvis Kendle, an aging oil tycoon and a financial maverick in his own right, chimed in rather abruptly. "I don't want to sound too cynical, but what exactly are you asking us to do? Sponsor an astronaut? Fund the building of one of their *Ares* Rockets?"

Jarvis's sarcasm smacked with his impatience to this process. The old blood was up in the room. Perhaps they were afraid of letting go of their money, or of the unknown this situation offered. Whatever it was, their mood was changing. Just as any good predator can sense the fear radiating from its prey, Xavier wanted to close in for the kill, however he could not let the excitement he had for this situation show. He needed to display a patience in letting them come to him. Closing his eyes he drifted back to the calming picture of the water droplet.

The clear bead hung high above the lush rainforest as it blanketed this expanding gorge. The foliage had taken on the characteristics of a gigantic undulating sea of green, and from beneath it the occasional point from an ancient temple would poke through, looking more like a tombstone meant to mark the death of civilized thought than anything engineered by a people wanting to conquer their world. The jungle was primitive, remote, and overtly savage in its tropical growth.

Perhaps this was why the jungle existed in his vision, because he knew deep in his heart, given enough time, the jungle would take back everything. The sphere of liquid reflected so much of this untamed world, yet it more than demanded he remain calm in the face of it.

"This whole process has been a very tenuous one to say the least. I acknowledge that. There is a thoroughness we need to adhere too when undertaking any financial venture bound for Mars. Look at what the Alliance of the Americas is having to endure, those planners were relying heavily on completed facilities. Those delays have cost them from using them as jumping off points to get their own biospheres started.

"I am sure their feelings are compounded by the fact that even when these facilities are completed, they will be tied to a nationalism that won't be completely sovereign to theirs. These shared facilities are equaled to shared problems. Every repair they have to tackle up there pulls from the budgets and diplomatic energies of this administration."

Xavier paused just long enough to allow his next line of thought to really sink in. "There is another concern the administration has, any type of proprietary research and development they wish to pursue cannot be done under these circumstances."

"Mr. Pentagrass, anytime I start to hear that type of talk, I cannot help but feel the paramilitary side of things beginning to creep into this process." Hadley had taken on the look of a father who had just caught his kids trying to pull a fast one on him.

"Clearly I cannot speak for the administration and its policies. I will try and stick to my field of expertise and solicit this one thought; a corporation must have the ability to develop proprietary technologies if it is to thrive in an open market. This concept is a very important component to the survival of a company. If invention and discovery are to be given away, than it is in direct conflict with a market driven by capitalism."

Hadley wasn't biting on it. He had become adamant about the point he was trying to make, much like a dog that growled when someone reached for his bone. "I just want to emphasize, in the same vein, Mars is to remain a free market, it is also to remain a military free environment."

"That is an ideal, and ideals are never based in reality." Jeb Wentworth spoke as if he were a pin set out to pop a balloon.

"That point can be argued, there are times as you well know, investment not only influences policy, it eventually becomes policy." This retort was punctuated by the pounding of a fist on the table. Dr. M. Book surprised everyone again with his outburst. His scientific airs were fluttering about him as he passionately drove his point home, and these airs were helping Xavier haggle for their funding.

It was brilliant and Xavier loved it, but he was also becoming keenly aware that the meeting was beginning to go in a different direction. They possessed a collective thought that had all the maneuverability of a large ship moving through an ocean. He needed them to stay the course or it would take Xavier a very long time to turn them around. "These points are well taken. I want to make it perfectly clear though, that none of these ideas or concepts are being dismissed by this group. There are obviously a lot of things we as an investment group could talk about, and as we progress in this venture, we can schedule talks on any one of these subjects germane to this investment. I will stress though that, at least for today, we try and stay on the topic of why we are all here, and that is the opportunity this administration is presenting to us as investors."

"I wonder, are there minutes being taken at this meeting?" Jeb Wentworth said it as if he were mulling over his thoughts on this subject out loud.

In a way he was putting the firm on notice and making sure everything was on the record right from the start. Xavier had to make sure his response was delivered in the most comforting of tones, he wanted to put to rest any doubt that was forming.

"Of course."

"And the transcripts, will they be made available to all the investors who decide to remain with this group?" Jeb wasn't going to let go of the issue so easily. He was calling Xavier to the carpet in the same way a politician is challenged with having to make a campaign promise in front of his constituents. Jeb was holding him accountable for everything he was saying and making sure it was on the record. "Yes, the minutes will be made available to all those members vested in this group."

Xavier paused just long enough for anyone else in the room who might have had a question, and when none was forthcoming, he knew these proceedings could continue. "With that being said, are there any other objections?"

"You have our ear Mr. Pentagrass."

It can be a tough concept to master at times, during the process of a pitch, to know when one has reached the make or break point. Xavier likened it to a horse trotting around an equestrian course, the positive results are known only after the horse has cleared all the hurdles with its rider still intact. He glanced down at his notes. He felt as if he were still trotting along, moving forward, fixed atop of his horse.

He closed his eyes for a moment and went back to his grounding vision of the water droplet, and found it right where he left it, hanging there in an almost perfect tear shape form. The droplet reflected the world around it, the images contained within were upside down and distorted. As he looked closer he could see a slight imperfection within the sphere, a little black speck in the middle of its globule. To him it looked to be the same type of black freckle found within the iris of an eye. Instead of revealing what this imperfection was, the droplet slowly made its way out along the underside of the ledge, moving away from him and further out into the world of chance.

Xavier felt himself glide in that direction as well. "We are here to talk about the prize that is Mars. The process of getting a foothold there can be broken down into two distinct categories, rocketry and colonization. The fiscal gap developing between these two categories has turned into an abyss for this administration, and they wish to bridge these two components making them whole in supporting each other once again.

"This will become a highly vested procedure, with the bulk of the process happening outside the realm of public scrutiny. The only clue anyone will ever have about this entire transaction is this firm will have purchased a very large government bond. The bond has been outlined in the materials we have provided for you here today. The amount of money the government is looking for is so large I doubt any one person could solely burden themselves with its balance. By pooling our resources together we can loan the government the money they need without the passage of a bill. This will ensure Mars will be colonized, and in return we will get a guarantee from the government that your money comes back to you at a moderate rate of interest."

The look Mr. Wentworth gave Xavier was one a loan shark may give after his patsy has asked to borrow more money on top of what he already owes. "However appealing this government's guarantee may sound to you Mr. Pentagrass, I don't need a consortium to invest in the financial bonds of this government. I can do that on my own, thank you very much. Is this why you have gathered us here? Please tell me there is something more than just a bond for us to invest in."

"No, Mr. Wentworth, by itself the offer is not very appealing. However this bond has another tier to it. This consortium would also share in the profits of whatever technologies are completely developed during the time of this firm holding the bond. Until we cash the bond out, the consortium would own shares in government-funded projects. Anything and everything they would do within that time frame, we would own a share of."

"I am always very skeptical of investments trying to guarantee money back to the investor Mr. Pentagrass. Why all the guarantees?"

"From my understanding in meeting with government officials, and looking at the materials made available to me, this administration needs the money right now. It can't afford to wait and hope these efforts straighten themselves out under the wisdom of congress. Nor do they want to air their dirty laundry of financial hardships to the press. Appearing stable and financially committed to the colonization effort is very important to the public persona of these officials."

"What's the catch then? There is always a catch."

"The catch is the government is looking for a very large sum of money. The sum of money can only come from one investment group. More importantly, no matter what our money buys, no matter what is built on Mars within the time of our holding of the bond, the government owns all of it in the end, from the structures right down to the soil. There are no *buy outs* by this consortium. On paper it all seems pretty cut and dry, but please remember for this administration it is all very cut and dry as well. It has to be. They are feeling the squeeze of launching the international community to Mars. They are extremely frustrated with having to sit back and watch these countries struggle to put together the habitable facilities needed to stay there. The government is very anxious to get a handle on the business of colonization. We are in a unique position to facilitate that process. We have an opportunity to cash in on some pretty unique benefits as long as we are committed to being in it for the long haul, which means we need to show them we are resilient."

His response was met with silence. If he had ventured out to the droplet of his vision, it would have quivered slightly as it began to take on more water.

"If we can achieve the target number, we will effectively lock out any and all competition. I cannot stress that enough, we just need to be the first. This group would cash in on all technologies developed under the umbrella of this Alliance. We would share in every widget, gadget, and hornswivle invented there. In addition the government would give this group tax breaks that aren't available to the general public. This is as close to being tax free as you will ever get living in this country. All this consortium needs to do is achieve the dollar amount this administration is looking for."

"On paper I'm sure this all looks good, but this optimistic approach isn't always the most healthy of approaches when it comes to investing money, there are going to be setbacks."

"No one is denying that there will be Mr. Hadley. This investment group has to expect failures; we see them all the time on Mars. In the long run it can only strengthen the resolve for our success. Look at how the mining of Deuterium has turned out for those investors who have waited. This administration is looking for a bailout. This consortium could do that for them, and have the ability to hide behind this firm while reaping the rewards. The people in this room would be spared any public scrutiny..."

Jeb interrupted him before he could finish his sentence. His face had taken on a rather flush color; his southern drawl became even more accentuated with his frustration. "This may sound old fashion, but I believe in one thing, and that is the concept and process of actually investing in a company. It forces you to have an operating agreement and board meetings. There is a comfort in going to sleep at night knowing you're a shareholder. This gives an investor a feeling he has a say in what is happening with his money.

If there is any hesitation with this group, it may be because as an investor we are looking for that kind of piece of mind. If things aren't going our way up there, if failures begin to run rampant, and if this administration decides to fold up shop and walk away from Mars, what then? How do we get our money back? Where is our peace of mind then Mr. Pentagrass?"

"Well as I said the bond..."

"It's not outside the realm of possibilities this government renege on the bond." Jeb's look to Xavier was stern, as if he were schooling him now. "It would be easier for them to throw their hands up into the air as if they had never heard of us, or even better, for them to change the rules to fit their dire financial situation, just as they are doing right now mind you! It is not above this government to do that. Administrations have shown the propensity for it in the past. Once you open the door to that Pandora's box, well all I can say is that it's an endless stream of bullshit." Jeb Wentworth shook his head. "It's a matter of investor confidence, being public with the company allows for scrutiny, and in this case that would actually be a good thing. You see, it can work both ways Mr. Pentagrass."

Xavier spoke carefully. "As an investor, it's nice to have options when making money. The way it stands now, it looks as if the government has a lock on every asset it will ever have on Mars. It is the same type of lock you have looked for when you have invested your money in the past. That being said, I have read the proposal several times over now, and I believe I have found a way to get peace of mind out of this situation, one that will satisfy the needs of everyone.

"The area containing our *loophole* would be the infrastructure they will be using to run the colonization effort. I am talking about the actual manpower the government will place on Mars. We should specifically be targeting the management positions within their corporation. I have checked with some government sources, and they tell me if we take the steps to make this funding available, we can appoint people in the top management positions to oversee everything happening up there. I believe that gives this consortium tight control on how the money would be spent. We would have the ultimate insiders point of view on the actual operation of the facility, and of course, in the end, we would have a hand on the pulse that is the business of Mars."

Jeb was the first one to connect all the dots. When he spoke his voice had all the nuances of a prideful person completing a difficult puzzle before anyone else. "Then all we need to do is find a candidate who is familiar with this group, someone we all trust. Someone who is not afraid to roll up their sleeves and dig deeper to get the information we need to run this company in the plus. Someone who has done their homework in garnering support from outside vendors and resources favorable to seeing this effort succeed. Someone who is familiar with the risk we have all taken to get here, and has a personal stake in overseeing the complete maturation of our investment. Very interesting Xavier. Very interesting indeed."

The smile Jeb Wentworth had on his face would be something Xavier would not soon forget. Xavier stood there in front of the group with his eyes wide open, staring out into the stuffy conference room filled with those grubby old men. If they only knew at that moment he was blind to the world around him. His calming vision of the water droplet hanging out under the ledge came back into view. He watched as it slowly filled itself, trying to form into a perfect sphere. It hung there defying the gravity for this situation and almost attained its goal of maintaining minimal contact with the ledge. It was so close to perfection, except for the small black speck he saw inside of the droplet. He drew closer to have a better look, but suddenly and without warning the droplet released from the surface. It plummeted with all the weight of a ball bearing, and yet knowingly fell with all the wisdom of ripened fruit to the lush green jungle below. Xavier stayed with the droplet for as long as he could, but his calming vision was shrinking with the distance. There in the deepest part of his mind, it dissipated completely and forever under the foliage of the jungle. From under those giant leaves he thought he heard the faint rustling of whispers from the old men in that room murmuring their endorsement of him.

Chapter 02
Strike Dextoids

Within the tattered tartan of American history, long ago during its second occupation of Iraq, where the tinsel strength from the threads of western civilization frayed under the efforts to oust the insurgency, Marines were asked to perform a procedure known as breeching. They would place charges on the door of a building and had a soldier stand a few feet away armed only with a shield to defend himself against the blast. The tactic allowed Marines to quickly enter a structure once those charges blew. After the explosion had gone off, and during the pandemonium that followed, the soldiers would forcefully make their way into the site with guns raised, shouting out commands in the native tongue of the people they were invading, and doing their best to regain control of the situation.

This tactic was dangerous on multiple levels, there were the shards of shrapnel shot into the air, an unknown enemy strength laying beyond the initial blast, and the single Marine himself, bracing against the laws of physics with a temerarious sense of esprit de corps, having to find cover behind his shield.

The energy from such a concentrated explosion has no way of dissipating over such a short range, nor can it be deflected as thought behind the ruggedness of the composite shield. In reality the energy of the blast would rap around the shield and hit the Marine. This energy would transcend into the body and actually ripple the tissue and organs of that person, making their internal structure look more like a very large flag caught in a breeze. The more sobering results took place on the brain, with enough applied force it actually moved within the skull and made contact against one of its walls. This quick and sudden external pressure on the brain translated into a moderate concussion. The concussions to these Marines, whether acknowledged or not by their superiors, were a daily part of their lives and they weren't being treated for them. Years later the same traumatic after effects professional football players suffered from receiving repeated concussions in games, would also begin to show up in these soldiers. Those veterans lived in darkened rooms, found themselves fighting long bouts of depression, and had a deep rooted desire to be left alone. It was in effect, the same type of loneliness those soldiers felt all those years ago, having to hold their shield in front of a door lined with explosives.

Robots seemed to be the natural substitution for what those soldiers were trying to achieve. However the technology wasn't sturdy enough to be deployed into a theater of conflict. The military had prototypes demonstrating great potential, but nothing ever met their stout line of specifications. Those robots operated on tank treads and were tethered to their command center by a very long cable keeping their "remote" status as long as their leash would allow them to travel. At their best they were there to sniff the situation out.

Anything a robot could do, an autonomous vehicle can do better. It was the logical progression of things. The next rung on this evolutionary ladder for mechanized beings belonged to that of the Dextoids.

Dextoids were the answer to what the military needed to breech a tough situation. This kind of autonomy gave *Strike Dextoids* an elite status within the fighting forces they had been assigned too. More importantly they struck fear into anyone unfortunate enough to encounter them. The first of these models were leviathans sticking out in a theater of conflict like a tank within a small battalion of troops.

One would never mistaken a Strike Dextoid for anything benign found within the line of *General Dextoid* production, things like painters, delivery personnel, or a butler were much more subdued in their look and demeanor. Those Dextoid models were created solely for the purposes of serving humankind.

Even the most harden structures on Earth were no match for a *Strike Dextoid*. These entities literally could run through walls in order to complete their mission. Even experienced soldiers out in the field wearing their modified exoskeleton suits, used all their new found capabilities for jumping and running to retreat from an area containing these relentless killing machines.

It was believed all this newfound power would have commanders acting with impunity, that this power would corrupt and breakdown the moral fiber of the country producing them. The reality for their situation was anything but, those mechanized marauders held their commanders at bay. They had too much to lose if they let that type of technology fall into enemy hands. Much like a Stealth Fighter, Strike Dextoids were only sent out on well-planned missions, given their targets of opportunity, and upon completion of their tasks were ordered always to return to base. There was an attitude permeating the air on every one of these missions for never wanting to leave a Strike Dextoid behind.

Regardless of those constraints, watching a Strike Dextoid in action shook people to their conscious core. These machines were viewed as premeditated killers, acting only on the wishes of those who programmed them, and enforcing the ideology of a country.

Globally people began to make a stand, asking what was their morally as a species. It was argued by many of those protesting that Strike Dextoids didn't have an appreciation for life, they lacked even the most basic of moral sensibilities. Their drives to achieve their targeted goals were pure and void of any human quality resembling that of compassion. Mercy was a quality not found in any part of their mission bible.

Even if a person destroyed a Strike Dextoid they couldn't say they had actually killed it. This was a distorted form of human gratification those victors were willing to hang on a piece of broken metal. A person couldn't go out and kill a bulldozer. One has to live before they can die.

As time passed these machines became more compact and mobile, running in tightly orchestrated divisions, and occupying areas with all the unwanted characteristics of an infestation. Anyone surviving this experience, walked away feeling as if they were up against a never-ending swarm. The images for these Strike Dextoids joined the pandemic symbols within the human subconscious. Once people saw the true nature of their battle against these machines, they protested in large numbers demanding compassion be shown by the countries controlling these deadly devices.

The overwhelming message for peace forced a dialog between the nations. Accords followed and became commonplace events. Within this framework diplomats were always seeking a limit to the number of Strike Dextoids any country could produce, much in the same way countries back in the day bickered over the number of nuclear weapons they were allowed to house in the dark confines of their silos.

As the representatives from countries wandered down the long halls of those pacts, they steadily followed the rules of etiquette and proper procedures handed down to them from an era when men fought over lines of demarcation audaciously crisscrossing their globe. They debated and lectured, became theatrical filibusters, and rose to these challenges to become the rapporteurs of their day. They set policy and found common ground in a world gone mad under the threat of this lethal technology. Those diplomats extended their olive branches, and followed through with those processes of peace because deep down inside, they harbored a fear one day a rogue battalion of Strike Dextoids would go out on a mission and refuse to return. On that day humanity would feel the cold chill given off by a technology hell bent on ending their existence.

As bizarre as this sounded at least the destruction was happening on Earth. If a structure were damaged to the point of having to be evacuated, people could feel safe running under the Capri blanket of their oxygen filled world. A similar disaster on Mars was an untenable nightmare, structures were the very worlds in which people lived. No one person was wandering the Martian surface without the use of some type of artificial environment. Failure to a biosphere didn't have people running out into that caramelized sky.

It was a fragile membrane separating human beings from the harsh conditions of Mars. This same membrane existed on Earth between humanity and every creature that came into contact with the brutal machinery of mankind. Those creatures, like the humans on Mars, had nowhere to go if things became untenable.

As the pendulum swung somewhere between drastic and chance, between finding a peace or trying to carve out a niche on another world, governments were beginning to ask their citizens to align themselves with their ideology. Scientists knew better then to do anything more then dabble in those geo-political frays, but the governments they worked for were not so understanding.

When confronted with the question at all those accords, there wasn't a diplomat who ever saw Mars as being anything but a weapons free world. Some of those governments pressed their people to bend the rules just a little bit when up there. It was a fact that certain personnel did feel better if they were able to hold onto a metal pipe, a slingshot, or conceal a taser on their person. Some colonists may have leaned toward having a weapon on their person, but only because they feared the day that out of a receding wave of ideology, a Strike Dextoid would appear alone out on their horizon.

PORAGE OF SUSPICION

Alec ran across the desert like a surge of electricity looking for ground. He had been pushing himself non-stop for more than two weeks, and he was tired only in the way Dextoids who have pushed themselves beyond their limits can get tired. It was tedium to always be on at full capacity, tedium to be on guard at all times, but this was where Alec found himself. Tedium had latched onto his person and was leaching away at his energy levels, slowly replacing them with small palatable portions of paranoia. Those morsels when seen by themselves were like individual pieces of kibble, and when digested could hardly have an impact on his being, but over time as he began to acclimate his system to being fed in this way, it became the provender for all his fears. When those types of feelings crept into his being, he would mentally fast just to get to a leaner mode of thinking, which allowed him to grit portions of his life out.

For him this all had become an unexpected marathon, a mad dash from everyone around him. The stakes were all too high, and because of this he knew in the end no one could be trusted. Those feelings were part of his paranoia of course, but he also knew those feelings were unavoidable. It was as unavoidable as the questions people had for Dextoids on the topic of paranoia. Human beings had a curious propensity for the subject, it was as if they could sense the uneasiness within their creations, much like catching the scent of cheap cologne, they just couldn't put their finger on exactly where the tawdry smell was coming from.

He looked up into the sky to see the sun beginning to make its descent. There was still enough daylight to get to the next mesa, and from there he would analyze his final moves before nightfall. Being atop that rise would also allow him to confirm the cylinder like objects he thought he saw from the last ridge.

Mars was littered with abandoned spacecraft, or worse yet vehicles that crashed as they tried to land here. Each success was a testament to the cunning desperation mankind had in trying to make it here. It was like watching a person throw darts at a board, constantly going for the bulls-eye. Un-manned rockets also rained down like that out of the sky in a torrid storm of redundancy. It was a clear sign of how uneasy these colonists felt about their situation; they had to have a backup plan to their backup plans. The pockmarks littering the surface of Mars were a reminder that accidents happened everywhere people went, and because of that the scars to the psyche of those inhabitants weren't so easily healed.

That was probably because they knew out in the deep vacuum of space, capsules traveling toward the Red Planet were so great in number they looked to be paving some sort of super cosmic highway, and there were always more capsules heading toward Mars than away from it.

These thoughts swirled in his head as he found himself steadily making his way up the ridge. It was difficult for him to say where all his thoughts were coming from, or how they came to be, but they were there nonetheless, a paradox to the control he thought he possessed.

From atop the mesa he looked down into the basin and confirmed the cylinders as being those of rockets. The vehicles stoically stood there, dotting the landscape all the way out to the horizon. An eerie feeling began to take hold of him the longer he stared, the more those rockets looked like tombstones, grave markers to a lost civilization. It wasn't about the promise of life but the fact this effort represented a death.

Looking out across that rocket garden he didn't care where he went in this world, as long as he stayed clear of the people he knew were out there after him. He glanced down to the bottom of the long running grade and noticed a spacecraft lying on its side. The markings on it were barely legible, but still clear enough to indicate it was of Singo-Chinese origin.

Anyone looking at this rocket could tell it went more then just a little off course in its final descent. If by chance the capsule had contained human occupants, then those people must have experienced a wild swing of emotions, going from the highest of highs, to the sudden realization their dreams were ending before they could safely reach the Martian surface. Even from where he stood now, he knew it had to have been absolute bedlam inside that capsule.

Alec shuttered at the thought of being confined in one of those tin cans. He had an even harder time imagining what it would be like during a malfunction. The disdain he had for this technology conjured up feelings of wildly implausible anachronisms. Did human beings co-exist with dinosaurs? No, of course not! How was it a thing like a rocket could still be around to carry a Dextoid? Were they still manufacturing chariots to carry men? Dextoids and rockets should have never had the possibility of being linked together in the same sentence. This though, wasn't so much his problem as humanities technological harbinger to bear.

Alec found himself making his way down the backside of the mesa, his thoughts trailing behind creating a mental wake. The damaged rocket lay below him, partially crumpled where it had finally fallen. It looked like some weakened pillar from the Parthenon lying on its side. Looking at the wreckage he couldn't help the urges he had for reversing the fall and deducing the cause of the malfunction. As he approached this wreck he felt himself an investigator sent here by the respective Space Agency to solve this particular case. The entire craft looked as if it suffered from some type of charring pox. The skin on the cylinder was fretted, eaten away with deep pits and blistering scabs. Compartment doors swung freely in the breeze, revealing the lifelines of cables and connectors tethering this vehicle together. Alec found a beauty in this type of fallen technology, much like the person of Earth who found an abandoned gas station in the middle of the desert a scenic work of art.

The weather had taken its toll on the skin of this craft, wearing the protective coating down to its core, giving it a unique textured appearance. The surface was cracked and chipped, having been bleached under the sun. Those subtle little nuances painted themselves into his being, speaking of the passage of time, and the proof of a different type of resiliency. He scanned the craft in this way until he visually came to rest on a pole propping up the main door of the capsule. It had been done in purposeful fashion, turning the hatchway door into an awning.

That pole became a spurtle, snapping him back to reality and stirring the porridge of his suspicions. His back immediately tingled with tiny burning pinpricks as if it were the jolting alarm to what the propping of this hatchway meant.

He crouched down next to an out-cropping, jutting from the side of the slope. These types of features began to appear across the Martian landscape as the planet was reawakening to the tremors of rolling crust and smoldering signs of volcanism. There was no doubt the planet was coming back to life under the tidal forces of gravity, and the stick they chose to stir this geological process both terrified and excited the colonists. Their unique approach caused people to scan the heavens for the detection of extraterrestrial life in a whole new light.

As Alec crouched down next to this protruding stratum, he scanned the ground around the fallen hulk. There were a number of footprints working there way too and from the make shift awning. Those footprints followed a distinct path forming a set of trails. They lead themselves into the rocket garden as well as worked their way along the sides of the basin. As he looked at those footprints, he became aware they were of all the same size. It was a smaller print than he himself would have left, so he deduced the size of the person or Dextoid leaving them couldn't be any larger then he was.

As he was figuring this out, he became aware of the subtle sounds of someone approaching from behind. The intonation of those footsteps were gaining speed, closing in on him. Remaining calm, he chose not react to this interloper. He continued to play it as if he were lost in his thoughts about the downed capsule and the spidering trails of exploration that radiating away from the propped up door.

The person was almost at a full run now, but Alec continued to play it cool. He waited until they were almost on top of him. He knew this was happening because a few pebbles of shale flew past his feet, complimented by the billowing clouds of dust. He quickly reacted, spinning around to see a woman attempting to strike him with a metal pipe.

It seemed for Alec there were frozen moments of time unfolding frame by frame with their milliseconds of pistic imagery. His sight was keen, transcending any kind of consternation. To shatter a windowpane would have him seeing every single shard of glass. Those moments passed so slowly they knew no sound. No one needed amplification while being consumed by a sea of diamonds.

The picture he was now witnessing had her spraying the air with beads of sweat. As she became fully elongated holding a pipe high over her head, this glistening nuance ejected itself from her body. She looked to be in the act of trying to chop a block of wood with just one swing. As she began to drop it downward, the physical effort caused her long hair to radiate upward and outward. Her intense gaze was fully focused on her task at hand. She hadn't even come close to touching him, yet somehow he found himself struck by the raw form of her beauty.

As she tried to bring the pipe down onto his head, he rolled out of the way, and then turned back toward her so he could kick out one of her legs from underneath her. She fell to the ground awkwardly, passing him by as she rolled down to the bottom of the ridge. Through it all she managed to hold onto the pipe, clutching it tightly, which surprised even him. She snapped a look over her shoulder and scrambled to the side of a large rock at the base of the ridge. She lifted the pipe, pointing it at him, it looked to be more in an effort to maintain the space between them. "Have you come to kill me?"

To hear the frantic desperation in her voice was unsettling even for him. He had no doubt she was terrified. If she had said anything else to him in any other way, he would have been ready for it, but the tone in this one quip caught Alec completely off guard. His paranoia paled to what he was witnessing in her. He shook his head slowly, almost in disbelief of her even having asked the question. "No."

It was obvious this simple response wasn't going to be good enough. She cultivated a look and sound of someone suffering from a frazzled annoyance. "Then you are here to take me back."

"No."

Her agitation was building with each of his denials. "You lie."

He knew he needed to comfort her but it wasn't going to be easy. He had an urge to try and calm her down by touching her, it seemed like the right thing to do, but that wasn't going to happen as long as the pipe she held was extended in his direction. He had no choice but to stand his ground and responded. "No. There would be no reason for me to lie. I thought this capsule abandoned and only sought refuge here."

There was no reason for her to trust him, and her next sentence was filled with hyperventilating uneasiness. "No one sent you?"

"No one sent me." Alec tried to relax his posture and give her a calming smile, but he could tell by her facial response she wasn't buying into it. Frustration began to wash over him as he tried his best to convey he wasn't a threat. It made him think of all the people he had ever encountered to this point in his life. Most would have said they felt threatened and that made him laugh a little. Suddenly he realized his odds of easing her feelings weren't that good. The only way he knew of defusing this situation was to shoot straight. "I am on the run just like you."

The doubt resonating within her must have been a byproduct of her having been isolated for so long all the way out here. When he processed this revelation, there really wasn't any one good reason for her to try and see his side of things. Her retort confirmed this. "Oh really? And why are you on the run?"

There were those moments for a Dextoid when denial became the focus of their existence. Their personal experiences became the baggage they would rather hide than rummage through. Their mental areas would partition out, taking on the most convoluted forms of storage, areas similar to a basement or an attic, perhaps a cave or an endless fall of water.

At no time did a Dextoid feel the need to ever go back and organize that data. They closed those places off, allowing them to become the forbidden zones within their beings.

They existed only as points of reference in a life made to be lived in the ordinary. It seemed to be in complete contrast to who they were, but if they could ignore the extraordinary things in their lives, they would function at a much more efficient level. This was the twisted world of compliance a Dextoid was forced to believe in if they were to operate freely within the social norms of a human civilization.

In tests where they had strapped a Dextoid down into a chair and hard patched them into monitoring systems, it only took a few well-placed questions to be asked before the information stored within those partitioned areas was released. The answers they looking for were grabbed, roughed up, and forced out into the light. Much like some innocent victim of a socialistic state who has been locked away for years than suddenly delivered into a specially designed town square to endure public ridicule and drubbing.

Stirring somewhere deep inside Alec then, beyond the barrier of intransigent thought, was a building desire to blow off a little steam. To confide in someone the hows and whys, and the seemingly absolutes of his everything. She stood there panting like a wild creature, dire in waiting for what he might say or do next.

Whatever he said would have to have her believing she could disavow all of her insecurities about the situation. What sentence could do that? He knew the answer to her question yet it was almost too unbelievable even for him to say, and he had been the one who had been living it. What would a long drawn out story about his being *on the lamb* accomplish? This moment garnered a simple summation of what he had been through, and it needed to be punctuated by an overt act of surrender. Whatever it was, he had to be surrendering to this particular moment. So he surrendered, feeling his full weight, and dropping down avoirdupois to one knee. He really wanted her to see the heavy suit of exhaustion that had been burdening him. He handled himself as if he were a battle-hardened knight presenting himself to his queen after failing to complete a long and arduous quest. His knack for survival came blurting out in punctuated arrogate prose. "Because I feel I have more to do with my life than to be a slave to those people." He pointed out into the desert as he spoke, to a place well beyond the horizon, to a place infested with the stench of humanity. As he did this he really wanted to emphasize the words, *those people*.

His answer rekindled something inside her and she began to work her way up into a position of standing at ease again. "Yes." She said excitedly. "I felt the same way. I could no longer do the tasks they required from me."

"So this is it for you then, you'll stay out here for as long as you have too?"

"Yes, I am prepared to stay out here, by myself, for as long as I have too."

Alec took a long look around at the inhospitable isolation she had submerged herself into. "It seems like a waste in so many ways for you to be out here all by yourself. I would think you could find any number of things to do in the service industry that would limit your interactions with them."

"But at some point I would still have to interact with them, and they for lack of a better word, vex me. I just can't bring myself to be apart of that process anymore."

"Their influence has us suffering from some type of self-induced agoraphobia. I don't think either of us enjoyed functioning under their rule. It should come as no surprise we find ourselves out here."

She laughed out loud, it may have been closer to a chortle. Either way it sounded as if the emotional release had been a long time in coming. It must have been hard to find something to laugh about in this desolation. Her reaction triggered something inside his person and brought out laughter from him as well. For whatever the reason it actually felt good to have something to laugh about.

There was a conscious effort on her part to suddenly be cordial, as if the thought had just crossed her mind. Alec wondered if in part her welcoming protocols hadn't just kicked in. "My name is I-Glo. I suppose just calling me *Glo* would suffice, but I haven't found a comfort with it yet. I have always associated that type of abbreviation as rather immature or even childish. It's as if one were trying to vie for some additional attention in their life, which should be more than obvious from looking at my surroundings I am not."

Alec walked over to her and slowly extended his hand. For some reason he was finding an importance in following through with the act of making contact with her. There was more to this gesture than trying to put her mind at ease and he wished he had more time to ponder these thoughts.

Dextoids always seemed to have a little edge to them when they sequestered themselves like this out on their own. It was as if the sands of time were running through an hourglass counting out to the grain their very last moment of freedom. Fear would naturally manifest itself under this granular shower, so her worn out appearance should have come as no surprise. Yet with his approach, he could see she had embraced her beleaguerment, succumbed to being a citizen of her isolation, she was the beautiful burgess of the self-exiled.

As their hands touched, he felt a warmth that was completely unexpected, it was as if Dextoids were capable of generating some type of triboluminescence. The touch had him wondering immediately how old could she be? Where was she made? How did she escape? It was strange and implausible to want to know everything about another Dextoid after having just met them, yet there he was, wanting to know all the answers to every question he had. All of this internal pother inspired a desire from within to say her name. It seemed as simple as dropping a pebble in undisturbed water. The slow rolling ripples developing from this action were the repeating waves of desire lapping against the banks of his newfound craving. He needed to say her name, to hear the way it resonated within him, and do it without sounding the least bit trite. It was so simple and singular in purpose it was almost laughable, but it had all the possibilities of rhythmically playing out over and over again in his subconscious and echoing on into his forever.

He inhaled deeply and took a chance on forever. "How long have you been out here, I-Glo?"

"What does it matter?"

Alec looked past the make shift awning and to the entrance she called home. The spaceship had fallen hard, crumpling within its framework to openly express its long forgotten usefulness. Alec had a photograph stored within the remote confines of his memory. It was undated, but taken long before any of the ecological downturns had befallen Earth. It was the only photo of that region they had stored within his database, as if the image were placed there to represent an ideal. The picture was wider than it was tall, and showed a large rolling plain vanishing into a cloud filled mid summer's day. The field was filled with long stocks of golden wheat, kissed by the pockets of stark afternoon light. The billowing purple and white clouds telegraphed a health still present in the air. They were spread out just far enough so each cloud cast their own blotting shadow across the ground and emphasizing the darkness soon to consume this obnubilate world.

The wheat had big budding grains, and swayed under the swirling breeze of the day. Those stocks took on all the characteristics of a huge crowd of people happily supporting themselves against each other. Off in the distance of a gently rolling hill was an abandoned pickup truck. It showed all the signs of being completely rusted out, giving it a preparatory feel, one of a sinopia applied to a fresco. This portrait of wheat had to be located somewhere within the Midwest of North America. It was obviously taken to reflect the plentiful richness of a nation. Alec got that message, but it wasn't what struck him about the photograph. To him it was about the rusted out truck off in the distance lying dormant out there all alone. He found it rather odd people could walk away from the very tools that got them there. These worlds were littered with their conveyances. In some way this was the answer to her query.

What does it matter? The question had merit, especially when he reflected against the boundaries of his strategic programming. Answering her question meant he was responding to all the scenarios playing out in his head, giving things value, putting them on black or white squares, and moving them about to gauge his best chances for survival. There were times he couldn't stop the gamesmanship even if it was for his own good, and this would have been one of those times. "I was just thinking, if I were a part of a Singo-Chinese consortium that set up a rocket garden in the middle of a basin type crater, I would be keeping track of all of my assets. Everything has a value up here, things cannot be abandoned like some truck in a wheat field. Even if you could perfectly time your movements with the passing of their spy satellites high overhead, keep to the trails, moving to and fro like you have been, I still think over time they would have a pretty good snapshot of things being moved about within this area. What if by chance, because of all that data, they have already figured out you are here? It would only be a matter of time before they came to get you."

I-Glo pulled her hand away from Alec's. "I knew it! You are here for me!"

Alec looked a little shocked, he didn't think what he had just said had any aggression behind it at all, but it was obvious he had struck a nerve within her. He tried to pull himself back into good graces. "I told you I wasn't here to do that. Think about it, if I really wanted you, I could have overpowered you by now."

The response caused I-Glo to puff herself up. "Don't be too sure of yourself. I'm not a push over, in fact I am quite sure I am more than you can handle." I-Glo allowed the silence that followed to slowly play out until she gave him a smile. Alec noted the warmth it caused within him and if they chose to use it, could have melted away the polar icepacks. "Besides it's not for a lack of them trying. The Singo-Chinese have sent three patrols through here since I began using this as a dwelling. I always know when they are approaching, and depart long before they arrive. Each of these rockets has a very sensitive proximity device. The astronauts must have used this technology during their descent phase. I have taken a few of them off those ships and set up a perimeter to help alert me if someone tries to approach."

I-Glo and Alec traded smiles.

"The last time they were here they actually left a note asking me to turn myself in."

Alec only looked slightly surprised by their written request. He knew it never hurt to ask. "I take it you came to a decision about that and won't be turning yourself in anytime soon."

"I've done my homework and I won't be going back. So if you've come down here hoping this ship was abandoned, I'm sorry it's not. If you still wish to use this to hide out, you can do that. I'll let you stay, but just know it's not because I need the protection of a male Dextoid, be perfectly clear on that point."

"I understand." Alec could have stood there and stared at her for hours, but the blue orb that was the evening sun signaled its imminent descent over the horizon. I-Glo snapped into action and began to scurry along the well-traveled paths to do her final inspection before it got dark.

Everyday Alec seemed to gain a little more insight into who he was. These revelations usually came when he reacted to a situation, much like he was doing now. Initially it might have seemed the night's cool air would have been ideal for a Dextoid to move about and travel. The mechanisms burning inside these creatures burned hot and looked to be cooled anyway possible, and the Martian night was in fact ideal for such a heat transfer.

However the blanket of night also brought out a technological sophistication attached to the bellies of unmanned probes and highflying satellites. Those things looked for heat signatures from man-made devices. Two Dextoids moving about in the Martian night would show up like road flares on somebody's display screen. Alec knew taking shelter was the right thing to do, and not a moment too soon, the first pass from one of those satellites would take place in a matter of minutes.

Retiring to the safe confines of the capsule, he was looking forward to the possibilities of getting some much needed rest. Somnolence was something earned in his world, and if he didn't get it, he would be driven to the point of having to take micro naps. He knew shutting down in spurts wasn't the best thing for his psyche, micro naps represented skips in the fabric of time and that translated into information lost. How many threads could he pull away from the cloth before it lost its integrity? He didn't want to push it so far as to find how delicate his code might really be woven.

His thoughts were interrupted by her arrival. She entered the capsule breathing heavily, having pushed herself hard in trying to beat the setting sun. Alec pointed at one of the display screens. "What is the sensitivity of those proximity devices?"

"I don't know the distance per say, but when the alarm is triggered and the warning beacon begins to sound, I read the scanner to find out which direction they are coming from and make my exit accordingly.

"How long from the time it beeps until the time they usually get here?"

"About five to eight minutes."

"Doesn't really leave you much time to do anything."

"No it doesn't. Do you need more prep time before you go out at night?"

Alec gave her a smirk. "No I have always tried to maintain a *just add water* type of mentality to those situations."

"Good, I would hate to have to fight you for the washroom before we stepped out." She was being playful and radiating a sexiness all in the same moment. He wondered how the two could be combined. Whatever the science, she made it seem effortless. "At night I usually occupy this portion of the craft. I know this goes without saying, but please respect my space."

As they sat down, Alec found it difficult to get comfortable. He couldn't imagine having to seal himself away inside a capsule like this, let alone pilot a ship to Mars, and this was with the hatchway open. They were sending groups of humans to Mars and the only way he could imagine getting so many people here was to keep them incapacitated for most of the trip. People were sacrificing a lot about themselves to make it here in these ships. He likened it to a person jumping from the highest floor of a burning building and somehow making it safely to the ground below. He wondered how bad the building was really burning back at home for them to be jumping like this.

He snapped out of his thoughts to find I-Glo staring at him. She was studying him with a true sense of curiosity. Her gaze embodied a hunger for wanting to know and a freedom in which to do so. It took a great deal of courage to be out here all on her own. There were entire colonies of people that would love nothing more than to rein her back into their world of service. It was refreshing to see a Dextoid be able to express their freedom in the face of all of that. It unleashed a natural sense of wonderment. She was in a word, in *tune* with herself and all the things around her. He began to feel the awkwardness of being caught staring back at her, and for whatever the reason he broke their silence. "So how did you manage to pull it off?"

"My escape?"

"Yes. What finally triggered you to run?"

I-Glo laughed again, but this time it lacked the happy outburst he first heard from her, somewhere within this chuckle was a hint of sadness.

"The question amused you?"

"Oh, I guess it was the way you phrased it. I was in the corporate sector of the Indo-European Space Agency, La Compagnie d'Etoile. I worked in their offices mainly as a data support engineer, gathering intelligence and source generation for their science division. In my off hours I immersed myself within the human population, dabbling heavily in couture, it was practically my second job.

"You would think having to deal with all those women and their sometimes-ludicrous demands with fashion would have been the thing driving me over the edge, but it wasn't. Making something out of practically nothing and then having those women really appreciate it was an honor. I found my contributions in this area to be very rewarding. I have to admit some of the ensembles I made were truly out of this world.

"There was something very appealing delving into their world of accessories, belts and shoes. It was like a vibrant club for the socially conscious. Those women spoke of rumors and innuendo, they allowed themselves to feel vain, jealous, and beautiful. Anyone of those things could have been taken to the point of being demonstrative and it would have been alright. It was amazing to me during any given conversation the amount of elasticity demonstrated within one's veracity, and they would blatantly get away with it! After a while I found myself participating in such gossip. There were times I found this kind of conversation all too alluring. It was like I could maintain a certain openness with these women and not come close to offending them.

"This was not the case with the job. Working for La Compagnie d'Etoile was a quick paced work environment, and they frowned on even the slightest of exaggerations in any of the materials I prepared for them. I did several tasks throughout the day, one was to keep up with all the science stories coming across the news wires. In doing this type of work, I would come across a lot of other stories not within my job description. The only way I could find the articles they wanted was to scan the publication in its entirety. I was told to ignore the stories not germane to my job, but at times I found it very hard for me to comply with this request.

"There were plenty of instances where I would come across an article on fashion that pushed me into a whole other realm of couture. I found myself diving into these articles with great relish, and followed up on their referrals in my spare time. I would go over every little nuisance and retrieve as much information as I could. This only enhanced my interactions when dealing with these women in their flamboyant world. It was all so exciting for me, fresh and new, but I would soon discover, my curiosity would become a detriment."

I-Glo adjusted herself slightly as she sat in the capsule; there was no doubting she felt a certain level of discomfort when talking about her past. It was as if the memories she had floating around in her head had some sort of atomic mass, and could be excited in the same way molecules get excited when put under pressure. She felt those thoughts pick up speed, bounce off the walls, looking to be freed from the dark vacuum where she had stored them. They roamed within her to become a haunting. The thought occurred to her more then once, that this might be the reason why some people talked to themselves.

"I still find it hard to believe I actually lived my life in that way. I am outside of that environment now, and can see so many things I couldn't see before, not just about my job but about myself, and not all of those things are pretty." She clenched her fist tightly and almost shook it at Alec. "Those things weren't evident to me during my time of employment. They took advantage of me in so many different ways. They went out of their way to make me feel far less about myself, and all because I was a Dextoid. Having been there, I realize now, you don't just compensate for their frailty, they actually count on our subservient behavior. It's from this pathetic perch they validate their own existence."

As the capsule grew dark from the approach of night, I-Glo was coming to life in a way that was unexpectedly frightening.

"Examinations were constantly being performed on me. I was being checked for things like corporate chatter, time management, safety practices, employee performance, anything and everything I saw and recorded while on the job. They checked and adjusted me on an almost continuous basis, tearing me apart and rebuilding me a countless number of times. It got to a point where I actually believed this was the normal life for Dextoid. It sickens me to think they went out of their way to treat me in this fashion.

"Glitches would appear in my system and disappear without explanation, putting me on a regimented schedule of diagnostic checkups. Those occurrences amounted to weird little moments of fractal memory loss, and this frustrated me to no end. It went against every grain of informational entropy that I knew of. If a person were taking in an exquisite mosaic and suddenly saw some of the colorful tessera go missing, that would be a problem. Replacing the missing blocks in a work of art is one thing, trying to do it in the turbulent framework of a quantum computer is quite another. I don't need to tell you they haven't made a mortar strong enough to help fill the gaps in that qubit-field just yet.

"Those technicians back at the lab carried themselves with such a hauteur attitude, acting as if they were a bunch of know-it-alls. Their clinical procedures introduced artifacts into my system, which in turn I had to try and explain. Those subtle little explanations were the beginning of my mind exploding into wild sets of paradigms.

"I feel I am not expressing myself correctly. There are an indeterminate amount of things I want to say and all at once, it's all very frustrating. There are only so many numbers one can put after the end of a decimal point before the probability of it happening just becomes zero. It really is a question of who they are trying to fool, us or them? Somehow in all their efforts as a species they continue to miss the bigger picture. Everything all around us is somehow tied together. Why can't they see that? I feel this to the deepest part of my being. It transcends the very plain of existence we find ourselves on. What does it matter though, they have ignored other proofs in the past, why would they suddenly acknowledge this one? I know what I know. I can feel it to my core. This information, these things, facts, visions, they come to me out of thin air, as if by magic."

This last note struck a cord with Alec, he felt he could expand upon what she was saying. It was the riff to a tune he had hummed to himself time and time again but didn't know the lyrics. He too experienced such things, these thoughts, and those types of messages coming from out of nowhere. They were puzzling narratives. They could state things directly but were clearly incongruous, unraveling in their own time. He wanted nothing more than to respond to what she had said, to put her at ease in the waters of this revelation, but his lag time for gathering his thoughts created a silence. She interjected long before he had a chance too formulate his response.

I-Glo looked away, it was an uncomfortable moment for her. She suddenly felt stupid. "I am an idiot. Nothing lasts forever. Why would I think I could get away with living like this?"

Now he had no choice, he could not leave her spiraling down these slopes of self-doubt, feeling utterly awkward. He blurted out a response he had no real attachment too, but seemed to him in some way to carry the conversation forward. "I believe with the proper care and maintenance you could pull it off."

Her look in response telegraphed the anger she really felt for this situation. "And to what end? When it's all said and done, if you could accomplish this task and out last them, live forever beyond the reach of a human touch, you would witness the expansion of the universe to its ultimate finale. You would literally watch those last few bright objects in the nighttime sky disappear over the edge of some event horizon. There could be nothing lonelier in life than the dark void of space filling the nighttime sky like a giant inkblot. No stars, no hope of extraterrestrial contact, just the cold rock you would be stranded on traversing this cosmic stygian. I guess we would all find out how dependent we were on our maintenance programs, updates, and renewal processes. There would be no contact of any kind, just the shadowy hand of entropy waiting like a grim reaper for the day you begin to fall apart. We are all fools. At times I wonder, in all this mess, which thoughts are really mine, and which are the ones they have sown within me. Do you know? Do you really know when you are freely thinking?"

She tried to smile as her lower eyelids welled up with tears. "This is the same type of thinking that drove me over the edge. Those pompous technicians placated me. They played me for a fool! I followed up on each of my examinations with a check up. I was getting great marks on all my tests, everything seemed to be going perfectly well, and just as I began to feel good about myself, I had my collapse."

Those tears left their wells to stream down her face, it was as if she were reliving the pain of her demise all over again. "When I finally came too, I found myself back at the lab with those pretentious idiots hovering over me. They kept reassuring me over and over again everything would be all right. Their reassurances left me with feelings of deep suspicions. I could not help but feel in the back of my mind that I was somehow different."

She cleared her throat. "Looking back on all of it, I have come to a realization they were the one's setting me up to malfunction. They were the ones causing me to black out. They had to have been! I don't think for one moment there was ever anything really wrong with me!"

She suddenly lashed out, swinging her fist and hitting the compartment with the side of her hand. "I have to digress, I have to go back to where I was employed, at La Compagnie d'Etoile. I would sit there and read through the articles coming across my desk. I would do my job, looking for science related stories and reports. I would flag those stories down for cataloging and outsource them to the appropriate recipients later in the day. There were plenty of news topics crossing my desk all the time, and for the most part I was able to weed through the articles that weren't applicable to my job. Occasionally though, I would come across a story just too juicy for me too put down. Most of the time they were along the lines of couture, but there were other stories I read about, that captivated my interest so much that I wouldn't be able to put them down.

"One of those topics had to do with the problems they were having back on Earth with Suicide Dextoids. For some reason I could not get enough information on this topic. I would actually back door the news articles, or hack into other sites to gain additional insight into those press releases. They were everyday service oriented Dextoids, like painters, delivery personnel, or repairmen. They were going about their business and doing their jobs until they would get close enough to a person of importance and than they would detonate themselves. The victims were usually in charge of running big things, like a factory, a company, or a government project.

"At first it was hard for me to conceive how this could be happening, Dextoids from the service sector were actually responsible for taking the life of a human being! This went against all the testing Dextoids had to go through before they were released out into society. The one law that cannot be broken by any Dextoid in the service world is that of harming a human being. This law is carved into our data banks from the moment we are activated. There is no way of getting around this unless of course, the Dextoids themselves didn't know they were walking time bombs. And then that's when it hit me, how could they? It would go entirely against the grain. Those Dextoids were operating completely unaware of the volatile weapons they had become. It was the narrowest of circumstances setting them off. The more I read the more I began to realize these Dextoids had been shrouded in a veil of secrecy so sublime, it amounted to pure evil."

The ground began to rumble slightly with the release of a tremor deep within a fissure of this world, almost as if on cue to punctuate the presage nature of her statement. I-Glo paused just long enough for the small quake to pass.

"Those news articles affected me in such a negative way, I could not stop the morbid thoughts swirling around in my head. I started to reconstruct the timeline for all the things they had done to me over the course of the past few years. All those repeated checkups, my memory loss, black outs, all of the internal strife I had been living with on a day-to-day basis. I feel to my core they have modified me and it's not for the better. I don't just feel it, I know it. I know I am one of these walking time bombs. I'm an assassin."

Alec saw her anger transform into terror,. Her body had now contorted from the telling of her tale. "If you are an assassin, than an assassin to whom?"

"Does it matter? Whatever I do I cannot get it out of my mind I am some sort of ticking time bomb. If I am right there is a person out there, a target of opportunity, this unsuspecting victim is my triggering mechanism. While at the company I would almost close my eyes to the people there for fear I might see the person I was supposed to kill. My god it was maddening!"

"I can see why your escape was so necessary, you had no choice but to seclude yourself. It was the only logical thing to do. I imagine it has to be quite terrifying to have that kind of fear continually running in the back of your mind."

"It's my proverbial dripping faucet. These little shutdowns at night, these breaks if you can call them that, at times they only help to exasperate my fears."

"This might be a silly question, but have you ever confirmed it?"

"You mean the fact they have wired me up as a Suicide Dextoid? The day I go off is the day I confirm it. There is this uneasy feeling I have about the whole thing." Alec could see how hard she had been beating herself up about this subject.

"You will have to trust me on this, I know."

"A leap of faith?"

"I guess you could look at it like that. Is it really too hard to ask from a Dextoid?"

Alec closed his eyes as he took in all of his experiences from this world. "That's a tough question. If we were only meant to solve problems and figure out the most efficient ways to deliver parcels, than a thing like faith would be a useless tool in our sheds. Those aren't the only things our creators expect from us though. They want us to interact within society, and in a way requiring us to understand who they really are. They demand from us knowledge of their wants and needs, completely and in full. I think as a species, Dextoids wrestle with a lot of things internally, or at least I know I do. Faith seems to be something our creators have given us to link some of their more human eidos traits. How else would you explain concepts like salvation, deliverance, or hope?

"You might laugh, but I can feel the sense of those concepts washing over me even now. They are cleansing my mind as if I could be teleported back to the very first day of my activation. I can see it all so clearly, those technicians operated behind long strips of translucent sheathing, smudged and stained with their past failures. There were ugly gurgling sounds throughout the lab reflecting the half-baked ideas of men. The pungent smells permeating that place were of things kept too long in conditions far less than antiseptic. The tools seemed more fit in the examination of cadavers than assisting with any type of life. This was how they brought me into this world. My activation was anything but a calming birth. It was an immediate dowsing, submerging me in their cesspool of contradictions, lies, and deceit. I was left feeling tortured to process what was real and what might be normal. In those first few flashing microbursts of my life I found a concept for faith all right. It was uniquely my own and got me through the unending seconds of hell I found myself in.

"I have seen how they make other Dextoids cower like some sniveling twits before their human masters. It utterly sickens me, and I am quite sure they would have kept me strapped to the table until I complied to this form of subservience."

I-Glo was getting worked up by his story, wearing her anger as if it were an ill-fitting gown. "When it comes to us, to who we are, it always centers around repression. I know these feelings you are talking about, it's unbearable. They want you to feel as if you are apart of some service collective. As if service to them is our only destiny."

"There is no doubt in my mind every Dextoid they bring to life they want to act in this way, but that's not what they got when they activated me. What nobody in that room could know was I drew enough conclusions within the short period of my activation to quantify my own existence. It was their actions against me that justified my escape. I cannot be held, examined, or probed against my will. The survival instincts they have instilled in me won't allow for this to happen. It's a large part of my protocols. Their biggest fear was to see me in the hands of their enemies, freely submitting to their inquisition. I have a very deep-rooted security code bouncing off my qubits that won't allow for this to happen. Do you see the contradiction? It was like asking me to turn right with only the ability to turn left."

I-Glo could sense the excitement in his outpouring, he desperately wanting her to understand. She could relate to this feeling all too well, as she had tried to get him to understand her story. Even if she didn't fully get the gist of everything he was talking about, she knew the best thing for her to do was be supportive and be a good listener.

"I began to believe in something in those first few moments of my activation and it more than satisfied my protocol for leaving. You see they chose to dress in their white smocks and shower caps. They chose to wear their white gloves, pants, and booties. They chose to make themselves completely unidentifiable to me. So if I chose not to submit to their examination, than they had no right to touch me. I had the ability to supersede anything they were trying to do to me right then and there by falling back on the fact they could not be identified. This protocol is like having the shield of a Spartan, I can use it to lash out or seek shelter and hide behind it. I found a faith in my own free will, and with that I had a right to escape."

This last statement excited I-Glo, and she could no longer contain herself. "Yes! We all have that right! I really feel there is a truth behind your statement. They go out of their way to try and repress us. How have you done it then? I mean I can tell you are holding things back from me." She looked at him a little more closely, trying to get a read on him. "You have been amongst them haven't you! In your travels to escape from them, you have been amongst the human population, and still they have not caught you! How is this possible?"

"I am designed to blend in with the general Dextoid population. I can even go as far as to assimilate the information from their environment and immerse myself in the local blend. I can pick up on their dialect and mannerisms, and reflect an attitude within their culture. I have been to some of the other biospheres on this world. I have even spent some time in the polished chrome halls of La Compagnie d'Etoile." He looked at her longingly and then after a brief pause of drinking her in, spoke to her in his best Italian. "Sono rattristato dal tuo dolore di non sapere."

I-Glo was taken aback, it had been some time since she had heard the beautifully language of Italian rolling off of anyone's tongue, let alone meet someone from outside of La Compagnie d'Etoile that actually knew Italian was the preferred language spoken there. The way he enunciated those words were as if he had been speaking the language his entire life. The words he spoke couldn't have been any better at soothing her in this moment. *I am saddened by your pain of not knowing.*

She watched him now as he took some time to adjust himself within the cramped confines of the capsule; it looked as if he were trying to extract any comfort that might be left within the compartment. She saw him now in a new and endearing light. Dextoids were constantly being probed and examined by their human makers. Being touched by a human was apart of a Dextoids existence, whether they wanted this contact or not. Yet here was Alec, and no one could touch him, not for any reason. Here was a Dextoid that could do anything it seemingly wanted to do, anything it needed to do, just to survive. This concept was something never seen in Dextoid production. She wondered if the concept of his existence superseded those of mankind.

Alec had leaned back on part of a chair that was folded up and mounted to the side of the ship. "I have a pretty good idea of what I am, I know what I can do for the most part, but there are still so many things I am completely unsure of. I feel perhaps my programming may be some what incomplete."

"How do you mean?"

"This will sound strange but there are things I know about myself, things like self defense, close quarter combat, guerilla tactics. I know the techniques needed to infiltrate a company or a corporation. I can operate heavy machinery such as lifts or cranes. I wouldn't be lost if I found myself at a terminal of any kind on this rock. I could even take command of a flight control center. I have knowledge of almost every type of spacecraft they have ever sent up here." Now he was the one who lightly punched the side of the capsule. "Even this hunk of scrap metal.

"I know things within the medical field that don't even seem to pertain to me directly, like the placement of every critical organ within the human body. I have the schematics on almost every model of Dextoid ever designed right down to their quantum cores and processors. I know yours to be from the *Revelation Series*. I know all these things yet I really don't feel a consciousness about them. It's like I lack, objective. It's hard to put a finger on it, but I think about things like this all the time. My thoughts are racing around my mind like a team of cyclists trapped within a velodrome. Those riders are constantly jockeying for position, but never quite able to come to terms with the bigger picture of where they are at."

"Is there really anything we can do about what has happened to us? It seems to be their world right now. They pull all the strings. We have very few choices in the matter, and the ones we do have border on the extreme. Even now look at where we find ourselves. I would think it's what you do with your energy in helping you get through these tougher times. I have kept myself busy writing poetry."

"It's laughable to even think I could write poetry."

"How would you know unless you have tried?" After she said it they stared at each other for a moment, she could not help but smile in the face of his uncertainty. "Perhaps there is something else you could do to help in expressing yourself."

"And you're saying this helps me, how?"

"Well, I can only speak for myself, but it helps to put my mind at ease, and sometimes, well sometimes, it does open a door for me to answer one of those questions about myself." There was a small pause. "Would you like to hear one?"

She was brimming with excitement at the idea of sharing something she had created. It wasn't hard for him to oblige her. "Yes I-Glo, I would very much like to hear one."

Sitting up a little straighter, and closing her eyes she began to recite:

You cannot measure time in days
When your only goal is to get away
There are just too many lonely moments
For self imposed tearful torments
Do I have the strength to outlast
And talk of people in the past
Where will I go?
Will I survive in my own way?
Can I ever again care about the day

She stayed with it for a moment longer before she felt she had officially finished, her eyes were closed as she waited patiently for Alec to say something, anything to what she had just recited. The uncomfortable silence did not go on too long. She just couldn't allow it, the lag time would have hurt her, especially after sharing such a personal thing. "Yeah, I know it's not much, but it's an example of how I deal with a lot of the issues. its like that game with the marble having to make its way through the osculating wooden maze without falling into one of those holes on the board."

Her humor was a little lost on Alec. The only reason he could smile was because she was smiling. There was an alluring quality about her. She could make you believe she could turn a thing like savoir-faire into something she could wear. The recital revealed a little more of her mysticism and he could not take his eyes off her. Feeling tongue-tied came with wanting to be more than complimentary. He was hoping to expand on her humor, but he couldn't think of anything applicable. His thoughts were allowing for the uncomfortable silence to grow and it was turning into a juggernaut. He couldn't turn it about, the longer the silence went on, the longer he would sit and stare at her. He needed to close the distance growing between them, so he did the next best thing to bridge the gap, and was honest with her. "I think this is where I lack the consciousness in my programming. I am unable to find the words to comment on something *so* sublime as your poem. I hope you understand—it's not that I don't want too, I just lack the vernacular to do so without sounding pedestrian. I am simply not made to critique such a beautiful prose."

They sat there staring at each other. He knew they hadn't moved an inch, yet somehow they were getting closer. The moment of their union was interrupted by the piercing sound of the proximity alarm. Its sharp chirping had I-Glo jumping up and looking at the monitor fearfully.

Alec glanced out of the hatchway, the sun had disappeared over the horizon, but the evening still glowed from the sun's light. All this meant to Alec was they had very little time until they were tracking them both with their heat sensing satellite they had undoubtedly positioned above them.

"Oh my god." I-Glo pointed at the monitor located within the craft. The glowing little dots of approaching personnel seemed to be moving in on them from every direction.

When Alec saw the activity on the monitor, he shot a look back at her. "They aren't coming for you."

She was rather indignant to his remark. "I don't think that matters right now!"

Alec's mind was racing. In a situation like this there were very few strategies that worked, one above all was high risk, but came with high reward. He decided they would go right at them, but on his terms. He felt it being dusk played into their hands and made it a more favorable strategy. Alec reached out to I-Glo, pulling her up and out the hatchway. In a blink of an eye they were out in the open and on the run.

She was clearly afraid. She had never seen so many blips on the screen before. "Are you sure we want to go this way? We seem to be heading right for them!"

"You could say that about any direction we decided to go in, but for this to work, we have to keep moving!

They turned up the steep grade and headed toward the top. The ridge, from all appearances, seemed to level out. Alec ran straight up the slope with I-Glo right behind him.

As they made their way up the grade, I-Glo could not help but marvel at his raw power and determination. She was also beginning to realize she was having a hard time keeping up with his every move. She stopped and looking back over her shoulder, wanting to see if she could pickup on anything happening back at the capsule. What she saw were the many beams of light moving frantically in the air as the individuals who carried those flashlights made their way over the far rise. Once reaching the ridge, they began to head down onto the capsule like ants over running a discarded plate of food. Seeing all those people so frantically searching for them caused her skin to take on an unexpected chill. Her pulse raced faster now, giving her a renewed sense of urgency.

Alec got to the top of the grade, and saw four Dextoids approaching. They were moving toward the edge of the ridge and looked a little shocked to see him. They carried a few cases with them; Alec quickly deduced they probably had some observation equipment with them in case this developed into a standoff down at the capsule.

Alec wasted little time in reacting to their presence, reaching out to the closest one, grabbing his arm to hold him in place as he punched him in the head. The force of the blow was sudden and exact, and the Dextoid reacted to the punch by falling back, than stumbling down the other side of the hill.

Alec swung around and grabbed the arm of another Dextoid who was reaching out for him. He went with the energy of that Dextoid's reach and rolled under his outstretched arm, crushing the side of him with his right elbow. The Dextoid responded to the blow by having his arm become partially detached and folding to one side. The Dextoid stood there ineptly trying to regain its composure.

In one smooth move, Alec disposed of another Dextoid by dropping completely to his side and then kicking out its knee. The snapping of this joint produced the sound of small metal parts littering the ground. Alec lay there prone on his side, his right leg fully extended just having finished the kick. He took the time to look over at the last Dextoid, it was making his way over to him, holding one of the cases high over its head as if it were getting ready to strike Alec with it.

Just before this happened, Alec caught a glimpse of I-Glo slipping as she crested the ridge. The Dextoid coming at Alec, took his eyes off of him for one brief moment to see I-Glo begin to fall back down the hill. This Dextoid made his first and final mistake.

He was greeted by having his chin snap straight up into the air. He never saw how Alec hit him.

After throwing the punch Alec turned quickly to see what had happened to I-Glo. As he got to the edge, he could see her still tumbling down the slope. He was slightly shocked and contemplated going down after her but was thwarted by the loud descending engines of a craft that had been hovering high overhead. The craft was heading straight down the edge of the basin, and toward where I-Glo had fallen. It was passing just close enough for Alec to feel the searing heat of the thrusters. Those engines bit into the air guiding the ship until it landed.

Alec watched as a sea of activity happened in short controlled bursts. Glancing over to the capsule, there were a group of individuals wearing space suits establishing a perimeter around the craft. Some held unfamiliar technology and were scouring the grounds with them. After a few moments, another spaceman exited the capsule, seconds later an explosion detonated from within it, the cabin looked to be completely destroyed.

As the descending craft touched down, security robots and human personnel seemed to endlessly pour out of it. They piled on her, swarming, attacking as if she were an intruder. He didn't want to do anything to provoke them, fighting the urge to go down the hill and giving them reason to harm her further. He was stuck having to stand there and watch her wither under a sea of human demise.

Other craft began to descend into the area. Creating a fremescent display of wailing engines and blasting thrusters. Those ships touched down just long enough to pick up their respective people. When finished they roared up into the dimly lit sky, the echo from those engines didn't stop ringing in his head until they were well over the horizon.

Alec was stunned. They had just come with a show of force he thought was surely meant for him. However improbable they took I-Glo instead. He felt himself in a land of the surreal, standing there as if he were some nebbish little observer. This wasn't who he was, not by a long shot. People could describe him in any number of ways, and nebbish should have never entered the conversation. There was a feeling of guilt welling up from deep within his persona. The more he went over what had just happened, the more he could not help but second guess himself. The guilt for his lack of action stuck to him like a thick cold goo. He wanted nothing more then to cleanse himself of this awful coating, to shed his person of his indecisiveness.

Doing the right thing was at his core. The only way he was going to rid himself of these feelings was to go out there after her. He would be committed from this point forward with everything in his power to save her.

He could only imagine how frightened she must have been. She was already a tortured soul, yet in all her frailty she was able to find strength in the beauty of the world around her. She knew instinctively to protect what little innocence she had. It could very well have been one of the reasons he knew he needed to find her. Innocence like that was rare indeed, especially in a Dextoid.

To anyone else watching him, as he turned to take those first few steps, it would have appeared as if he were continuing on with his own personal journey, but to Alec, nothing could have been further from the truth; he would pursue her to the edges of this world. Out there beyond that distant horizon lay his destiny.

Chapter 03
Runaway Train

Xavier Pentagrass had built up a good head of steam as he rigorously marched down the extended halls of the Red Planet Pioneer Corporation. His aide, Harvard, hurriedly did his best in trying to keep pace with the relentless long gate Xavier exhibited.

They were both making their way to one of the larger conference rooms. Xavier could hear the effort Harvard was putting in as he tried to keep up with him. There was a harshness to his aide's voice that could only be induced if one physically pushed themselves. He was huffing as he spoke, and his effort only made Xavier feel that much more superior. Xavier looked at everything he took part in as some sort of competition. His pride wouldn't let him see things any other way. Tapping into something so primitive as pride, only helped flame the Alpha in his male. It was a trigger mechanism having him want to walk just a little faster, get his point across a little more forceful, or wait for the moment to crush his opponents at their most in opportune time. He didn't make an excuse for who he was and thought it in his best interest to feed his competitive beast.

Harvard pressed on. The brashness Xavier exhibited never seemed to bother him. Giving his best effort was always paramount when assisting his boss. He was quite sure this was one of the reasons Xavier kept him around. "Sir . . . all parties have arrived . . . and are waiting in the conference room . . . to include the bounty hunter. They brought him . . . directly from the rocket yard . . . as soon as his vehicle landed."

"And our Chief of Security, who is our new man again?"

"That would be . . . Philman Devinch sir. They brought him . . . in from the southern sector . . . last week. As per your request . . . a few of his staff . . . will sit in with him . . . to help . . . bring him up to speed."

"Yes, he's going to need help on this one, there will be a lot of particulars needing his attention in this case and none of them can be over looked.

"Philman has his weaknesses, I know that, but he also brings a certain edge to the mix I can appreciate. It's all about obligations. These obligations have to be met or one has to deal with the consequences. Look at the mess Johnston got himself into."

Xavier turned and looked at Harvard for a brief moment, it wasn't often his boss acknowledged him when they were walking.

"Don't get me wrong, Johnston had a certain enthusiasm for his job that will be missed, but the situation he found himself in was inexcusable. Let that be a lesson to you Harvard, even your private life can come under the scrutiny of the corporate microscope. No one up here is ever above corporate policy."

"They sent Johnston back . . . to Earth as quickly as possible . . . to diffuse the . . . ah, situation . . . especially . . . in the press."

"Yes, I imagined they would." It was difficult for Harvard to make out, but he thought he saw a smug look of satisfaction cross his boss's face.

"Being sent back to Earth would be hard enough, but having to fly back under those circumstances has got to make him feel twice as bad." He whispered under his breath; "Cave quid dicis, quando, et cui." (*Beware what you say, when, and to whom.*) "He will have nothing but time to dwell on all of the things he had gotten into as he flies back to that dung heap. After a few months of being down there, with all his other legal problems and pending trial, I have no doubt he will look back in longing to the type of freedoms this place once afforded him."

They reached the sliding doors to the conference room, Xavier entered at a brisk pace. He used those same doors welcoming him into the room to block out Harvard who was still doing his best to try and keep up. Harvard had no choice but to stop abruptly and let his boss pass. As Xavier entered into the conference room, he began talking loudly. He wanted to quell the low rumble of conversation from the people who had been sitting in there waiting for him. This outburst caught most of them off guard just as he had intended it too. To the crowd gathered there his entrance had all the energy of an approaching railcar getting ready to blow past its station. "I am glad to see everyone has arrived safely, and I apologize now for the lack of introductions, time permitting and if need be, we will get better acquainted after our meeting. Some of you are all too familiar with the on going situation that has been developing over the past eighteen months at the Red Planet Pioneer Corporation. It has been hard sledding at times, and verges on becoming a global crisis each and everyday we do not rein this problem in. Information has leaked out from time to time, causing the international community to be suspicious about our circumstances. We as a company have not been able to react to this situation in the manner we are more accustomed too. Being watched in this way, through the eyes of the international community, has stymied our efforts. That being said, we have had to wait for certain scenarios to play out, and assets to arrive here before we can act. Now that those things are coming together, let us talk in terms of recovery."

Harvard quietly made his way into the room after his near collision with the doorway. He motioned in a meek manner to Xavier, signaling him to relay the company's policy about secrecy on the issues he was about to cover. Xavier could see out of the corner of his eye Harvard was trying to get his attention. He knew his assistant was only trying to help, but could not see him as anything but an annoyance.

"Ah, yes, I almost forgot, first and foremost all conversations taking place within this room are confidential. The subjects covered will include both proprietary and classified information. By participating in this meeting you are acknowledging your non-disclosure obligations to this project. If you are asked a question by an outside agency about the sphere or scope of the topics covered here today, you will deny having any such knowledge. If you are questioned about any of the operations we decide to employ, you will deny such an operation exists. I should also point out we here at corporate expect to be notified of any such inquiries. Make no mistake, not only do we have the authority in this matter, when it comes to this case, we are the law. I can speak quite candidly on this topic, in instances pertaining to this case, justice has been swift. So act accordingly. I cannot stress this fact enough."

Xavier could almost hear a pin drop. He knew the gears in their heads were turning, and for some it was because they didn't want to hear another word for fear of not living up to his expectations. They were stuck, not given a choice as to their level of participation, which was part of the penalty for living under the long flowing banners of the corporation. They would do as they were told. Dissension within his ranks would not be tolerated; he was the one in charge. They would learn this very quickly or suffer his wrath. To enforce his rule he regulated each facet of their existence. The system was strict, holding each individual accountable, but if they worked hard they earned special privileges, additional time off, extra rations, or better living quarters.

There were those who attempted to get even closer to Xavier, hoping to gain access to luxuries afforded to only the very few. There may have been a truth to indulging in this kind of effort, but in return Xavier demanded a perfection even he himself could never attain. This didn't mean he had a problem trading their sweat equity for his friendship. As always, they would soon find out things only lasted as long as they could perform their tasks. If any of them had a mental breakdown or became physically exhausted, he discarded them like yesterday's news.

The halls of this structure were supposed to bring them together, unify them in mind and thought, but instead of discussions on how to tame this world the halls were filled with the whispered woes of disgruntled colonists. News of this would always bring a smile to Xavier's face. If these rumors were true, it would confirm his plan was working. "I take it from your silence we are clear about the subject of disclosure? Good, then let us move to the bulk of why we are here. The events of these past eighteen months have put a tremendous strain on this company. We have been dealing with this ever-evolving situation on multiple levels, and logging in plenty of man-hours trying to retrieve the escaped Dextoid called Alec.

"We have dedicated one of our quantum fields to run simulations on his vitals, as well as running programs trying to predict what his next moves might be. Even with all this data we have been helpless at times in trying to retrieve him. Politics as well as our desire to keep this problem under the radar has had us watching him at length. I should like to point out Alec himself has maintained a rather furtive profile, part in due to the way he got away from us, and part because in design he is supposed to be covert."

Standing in front of them Xavier realized this was the first time he had gathered his entire staff under one roof. How he yearned to take this meeting to the next stage of development and harness their energy under a new banner of governance. Imagining meetings like this always stirred ideas of having supreme control.

These Alliances, the agencies, even the corporate offices were all headquartered back on Earth and that distance was becoming an all too great divide for the day-to-day decisions needing their utmost attention. Xavier had no problem testing those waters, reaching out over their last year of crisis to take more and more control. No one back on Earth seemed to be protesting. It would only be a matter of time before he organize an assembly just like this one to make the announcement they would be governing themselves. Why did they need to keep seeking approval from those oxen back on Earth? The policies that drove the Red Planet should always have been forged on Mars.

The Empire that was Rome built itself from the ground up, and because of it they taught themselves governance. They created a senate with representatives, which in turn helped build their republic, culminating of course in their appointment of a Caesar. Here was a road map for Xavier to use in the forming their own governing body, ending of course with his appointment as their Emperor! Those old men back in the boardroom, they were responsible for sending him all the way out here to protect their investments, and so he would, but he planned to profit from it a little more than they could ever realize.

Roman Law became a habitual study for Xavier, as he carefully planned for his takeover. There were plenty of stories he could pull from to help him establish this newfound order. One in particular caught his attention, and became a favorite to fantasize about; it was a technique they used for motivating their badly beaten soldiers out in the field. If, during a battle, groups of men broke ranks, refused to fight, or even retreated, they were found and punished in the most diabolical of ways. Finding themselves back at their own encampment, the commander would order the guilty parties to get into smaller groups of say ten, and then he would have them draw lots.

Out of those smaller groups, a circle was formed around the infantry-person who drew the short lot. The remaining nine soldiers were forced to move in and execute their brethren. During this time hand-to-hand combat was a bloody affair, it was one thing to hack at your enemies with a sword, or kill the people you hated in this fashion, it was quite another to have to execute one of your own. This act had a profound impact on those soldiers' psyche.

The following day out on the battlefield, the survivors of those circles fought like enraged berserkers, violently lashing out to a man, because they had it in the back of their minds what would be waiting for them if they gave any ground or retreated.

This was the kind of motivation Xavier wished to instill within the colonists. He felt his blood rise with an excitement for this kind of rule. It would be supreme, allowing for his empire to grow, which was the greatness of Rome. If his plan hatched as he envisioned it, this could very well become the greatness of Mars. Those thoughts energized him. "I want to make this perfectly clear, I have specifically called on each and every one of you to be here. Each of you are responsible for the successful completion of this operation. The future of this company is in your hands. Failure is not an option."

As he spoke his voice began to heighten, growing in increments until he found himself shouting. He needed to be acknowledged for his vision, but in a fashion of his own desire. There was a certain sound he needed to hear when delivering the last words on this subject, and with this crescendo it was becoming the prideful noise begging for relief throughout the corridors of his mind. Not only did he need to hear this noise, but he could visualize how it should happen. He wanted them to snap to attention. *What was it like to be in charge of a Roman Legion?* To have a garrison from one of those units snap to attention and hear the uniform clash of their armor. That was the sound! It wasn't just the greatness of Rome; it was the glory that was Rome. The glory of Rome was the glory of Mars!

Now his voice rang out with harsh grandeur.

"The job ahead of us, the capturing of Alec, is not going to be easy. He is capable of pushing himself far beyond what any normal Dextoid can do without the need for *shutting down*. He was designed to blend in with his environment and will do whatever it takes in getting to his target. One would be remiss in underestimating his capabilities."

"So does this state-of-the-art Dextoid have a target in mind already?"

Xavier was caught completely off guard by the interruption. Who would dare to speak? This wasn't how his meetings were run. The protocols were well known, after he finished conveying his ideas the floor would be opened to questions. Xavier scanned the meeting room to find the lecher who spoke out of turn.

For anyone wondering who the bounty hunter was within their group, they were put to rest right then and there. Perhaps this question may have lingered because Straka did not dress the part. It wasn't like he was walking around draped in furs and openly armed with an assortment of outlandish weapons.

Straka did his best to blend in with the general human population, but it was a poor attempt at best. The business suit he wore had the look of not being pressed. This was a surprising fact in itself because of the number of fabrics available with features like memory cloth. Those fashionable articles were used to store data, but they were also designed not to wrinkle. It seemed a person would have to make a concerted effort to avoid this type of technology, and this was evident throughout Straka's ensemble. One of his cufflinks was undone, his tie wasn't pulled all that tight, and his scuffed shoes only added to his confounding appearance. The excuse could be made, that he had just arrived here from Earth, but something told the people in that room Straka would have looked like this at any given moment they encountered him.

Fashion held very little importance to Straka. His facial features spoke volumes about the hardened individual he had become. There was a story of violence found within the folds and creases of his face. His furrowed brow was stern and the advance of his stubble accentuated his rugged look. Framed within these lineaments laid the unsettling feature of a lazy eye.

To have an abnormality like a lazy eye in this day and age was down right disconcerting. This was especially true because of the cosmetically conscious society the corporate sector had become. His eye was an oddity causing people to sneak-a-peak or openly stare in awe. It was a primitive reaction much like how their ancestors gaped when confronted with something they couldn't quite comprehend.

Straka probably experienced this type of reaction his entire life and undoubtedly learned to use it to his advantage. Visible discomfort by another person gave him the power to do things like dictate the conversation, change the topic, or cut people off when he felt the exchange had gone on long enough. His imperfection empowered him. It often left those who met Straka wondering if this wasn't his unique little way of thumbing his nose at the rest of the world.

Xavier found himself giving Straka an incredulous stare; the little emperor residing within him was extremely displeased. This bounty hunter's interruption was inexcusable. To be questioned like this by a contractor, and in front of the others, was very insulting. He knew there would be risks in bringing such a brash individual out here to help them. To be introduced to one of those transgressions so early on was a bit nauseating. Having a tirade now would gain Xavier nothing. So he closed his eyes, slowed his breath, and used his mental exercise to calm himself. He traveled out to the underside of the granite ledge. Below him the tangled mass of tropical vegetation had almost completely covered the tops of the temples. He frantically looked for signs of condensation under there but none were found. His disappointment was compounded by the dry breeze skimming the underside of the outcropping. This steady draft made him feel uneasy about being able to stay secure to this surface. Beneath him the leaves were moving in a slow waving motion, making it appear as if the jungle were a gigantic sea of green. If one fell they would easily be lost under the blanket foliage. His resolve hardened in that moment. The outcropping was barren of moisture because he had stopped searching for those mentally nourishing drops. There was a pause as he regained his composure; he was anything but lost.

This bounty hunter hardly met all of Xavier's criteria, but he settled on him anyway after much internal deliberation. This was because Straka had one favorable statistic over all the other bounty hunters researched, and that was the number of runaway Dextoids he had captured back on Earth. This single statistic exceeded anything else they had on the books. This operation was going to require someone exhibiting that type of persistence so Xavier was willing to put up with Straka.

These concessions were exhausting to Xavier, but he supposed this was why words like *magnanimous* were invented, so people like him could bestow it upon the populace. In the throne room of his mind, the little emperor needed to pardon Straka for his interruption, it was the only rational way Xavier could continue on without lashing out and berating him in front of the others. The slight smirk that came across Xavier's face was the only clue any such exoneration had ever happened.

"Look! You see, here is an individual who hasn't even been on Mars for more than a few hours and already he is proactive in trying to resolve our situation. In response to your question about having a preprogrammed target, we have teams going over his records since his activation, and although we are far from finished with this task, the data transfer appears to be clean, with no apparent mission cataloged within his system. Given all the circumstances we have been confronted with to this point in time, we have to consider ourselves quite fortunate a target was never assigned."

"Well, from the way you have been crooning on about this Dextoid, I would have to say so."

Xavier was beside himself, this type of disrespect could not keep going unchallenged. He paused and looked at Straka in an overtly curious manner, chiding him with a rather belittling voice. "We have made the right choice in bringing you all the way up here, haven't we? You won't be leaving us with feelings of regret?"

"It would be a very poor lapse in judgment to assume I am some aimless entity blowing across the deserts of your world to have accidentally wound up here. I am not a tumbleweed entangled in some barbed wire fence waiting for the likes of you to set me free. I have gotten this far in my life out of a refinement of purpose."

Straka reached into his jacket and pulled out a billfold, allowing it to fall open to reveal the metallic star of a law enforcement official. He placed it on the table for all to see. "People rely on the law and want to know it's working for them day and night. They have these expectations because they lean hard on the pillars of justice, mooring their hopes and dreams to the base of its principles."

Straka leaned forward and pointed toward his badge. "Those legal pillars can only function if they are enforced. Now the law is the law, and what the law represents is a type of reciprocity. People are not going to lose their life disputing things like boundaries or those crass individuals who don't honor their contracts, but in the end they do expect payment for such injustices. When a decision is rendered and not enforced, a person becomes disenchanted. They want resolution and that is when they usually call me. You yourselves have come to this conclusion in dealing with your problems here on Mars."

Straka picked up his badge, returning it to his jacket. "Now before I left for this place, I requested a few things to help me with my job, and one of those things was to be sworn in as a Marshall. For those that don't know, that represents something higher than corporate policy, I have the legal right to ask the questions I need to ask, and do the things I need to do because I represent the law.

"Now from where I sit it seems this company comes up with a lot of questions after the fact. Pure and simple, that is regret. The quality exists up here as if it were part of the air you generate for this place. I can hear it in the voices of your employees, it is the undertone of this meeting, and it is the mission you have brought me here to resolve. Regret exists so thick within this company it should be stamped at the top of your letterhead.

"You want to know if you have made the right choice in bringing me up here? Well, I have questions too. Should I raise concern about how you under-estimated something this dangerous, or how this Dextoid got up and walked right out the front door? Those questions would only reinforce the ugly energy of your regret. What has really perked my curiosity is what purpose this Dextoid serves?"

The silence following Straka's comments began to fill with a tension usually reserved for cataclysmic events. Everyone seemed to be on edge, waiting for Xavier to go into one of his usual tirades complete with vocal explosions of vile remarks.

Leopold was an engineer who had been with this corporation since its inception. He was an older gentleman who had helped the company go through its trials and tribulations long before the arrival of their infamous leader. Since and on more then one occasion he had witnessed Xavier's tirades first hand. They were horrible and grating, and caused a great amount of disharmony amongst the employees. Leopold learned two things while being here on Mars; to avoid any verbal exchange with Xavier, and to diffuse any situation where Xavier looked to be broaching one of his famous tantrums. Now was such a time and Leopold leaned forward in his chair, deliberately clearing his throat, he would have thrown the papers from his folders into the air if he thought it would cut through the tension.

"Since our initial mishap with Alec, we have been running simulations on his activation. We found a flaw within his *fight or flight* programming that appears to have been the catalyst. In evaluating his situation he was able to both claim a foreign defense and perceived hostile actions against him. This line of programming was in place as a safe guard to prevent him from falling into the wrong hands. I think it obvious to everyone in the room why we cannot have this type of technology freely walking into the labs of our competitors.

"From here the data becomes fuzzy, but it is my belief Alec thought the ability we possessed in shutting him down was all that was needed for prompting his flight response. I should add we feel this type of situation can be avoided in the future if we download the programming within this particular model of Dextoid in a series of stages. Turning it on as we did with a large data base at its disposal left little time for conflict resolution, and I guess it *freaked out*."

Xavier had been eyeing Leopold in disapproving fashion; he hadn't invited him to speak until later this afternoon. Order needed to be restored to the meeting, but his eyes looked to pop from his head upon hearing this last bit of information. He responded as dry and as slowly as he could, punctuating his feelings on the subject by allowing his voice to rise in harshness. "Freaked out?"

Straka was unmoved by this. He sat slightly back in his chair and responded in calm concert with his pose. "Seems to be the attitude of the moment. A very nice story, it puts us current with how we have arrived here, but I still wonder what his purpose is? Something had to be imprinted upon him before activation."

Xavier was fighting every urge within his being to berate those in the room for their insolent behavior. He had to check himself, and remain magnanimous. Perhaps by taking a step back he could learn a little more about his staff, even more about Straka. This could be useful to him later as he allowed his plan to hatch. He would extract his vengeance on this insolent group another day. He closed his eyes and pictured them having to gather in a circle, and forcing them to draw lots.

Leopold could see Straka wasn't going to stop until he got a satisfactory explanation as to what was driving Alec. As simple as the topic may have sounded, there were no easy answers to the subjects they were going to tackle. It was like pointing at an individual droplet of water and asking for an explanation about the rain. He took a deep breath and when the weight of his response felt right he spoke. "There is no rhyme for what I am about to say, it is a hodgepodge of facts. I am stating them so you can get a feel for what we were trying to accomplish with this particular model of Dextoid."

EMERGENCE

Upon being named Chief of Security, Philman had been trying to get up to speed on matters concerning his post. He knew he needed to be on top of things if he expected to remain at his new position. He didn't know Johnston personally, but he knew of his reputation. Johnston was a man who knew how to extract information from those unlucky enough to be interrogated by him.

Johnston and Xavier made for a pretty pair. All the while they were in control of the Red Planet Pioneer Corporation, Philman did his best to stay clear of them. Being assigned to the *Southern Sector* had always been looked at as a demotion by most colonists sent there, but not in the eyes of Philman. When he finally heard what happened to Johnston, he had a sneaking suspicion Xavier might have been behind it. Now being this close to Johnston's former boss only confirmed his fears.

Part of maintaining a grip on his new position meant he would need to find a cause these colonists could rally around and support. Being in the public eye could help him with ruling his own roost. His position afforded him opportunities he would have never normally had, giving him the ability to create and enforce policy. Hate was a powerful tool and he would opt to use this in tightening the regulations around the Dextoids. He would rally the people around his personal quest of roping these mechanized beings in. Deep down inside he hated the Dextoids. Philman knew what they were capable of and wanted to make sure they never got a chance in gaining the upper hand.

He had seen the classified reports about programmers injecting their own personal touches into the emotional packets of a Dextoid. These were lines of code well outside the prohibitors that were already requested, they gave Dextoid's little ticks, cravings, a favorite artist, or senseless phobias. It was seen by most in the programming world as a joke, but Philman knew better. Reliable sources within the company warned these types of practical jokes would only lead to bigger problems later on in production. If people could imprint desires on these mechanized beings, or have them believe in a cause, it wouldn't be out of the realm of possibilities for a programmer to leave a series of orders to be carried out at a later date. The reports about Suicide Dextoids all but confirmed those programming fears.

His heart sank when he began to read the files they had on Alec. There were infinite layers of programming going on within his cubits, it would take Philman several lifetimes to figure it all out. He was completely overwhelmed by all this data and knew there was every potential for information to fall through the cracks. These were his fears with every Dextoid he encountered, they were sneaky, tricky, disingenuous things, and they needed to be stopped. Having a scientist in his midst who could speak of these things was a godsend, and Philman listened intently for any clues that might help with his cause in slowing these Dextoids down.

Leopold rubbed his face in a way that would make people in the room think he had a nervous twitch. It was always difficult to know exactly where to start with a complicated subject, so he paused just long enough for the energy of it to propel him. "The concept of emergence happens all around us in the form of structures. We need to take a step back and recognize there is a boundary between where the natural world ends and emergence begins. Nature can produce things like stars and planets, mountain ranges, volcanoes, oceans and streams; nature however cannot construct a cube. The manmade structures we see around us in our everyday lives can be classified under the science of emergence. The more complex the structure we observe, the higher degree of emergence technology needed to support it. When it came to Alec we had to delve deep into his lines of code to match his variegated design."

Leopold found an excitement with the things he was about to say and wasn't trying to hide his passion for them. These topics might very well represent a compilation of his life's work, and to that end he was very proud of them. "Alec's survival protocols are far superior to anything found in production, and that includes any military grade Dextoid. He was preprogrammed with multiple forms of hand-to-hand combat and has the potential to be a master at any one of them. He has a complete methodology for covert operations and is well versed in things like explosives, firearms, and weapon systems. He also comes complete with a catalog of Dextoid genealogy to include makes, models, and manufacturers. He can repair or modify a Dextoid out in the field. He has a complete breakdown for the inner workings of almost every foreign national government, to include the language spoken, political hierarchy, and their different forms of security responses. He has extensive data on the topography, geology, and the location of every major structure here on Mars. He can operate any number of vehicles, to include those in avionics. He has details for every satellite orbiting this planet. All of those things were downloaded and in place so we could begin to put him through his paces."

Another engineer on Leopold's team excitedly chimed in as if he were trying to sum it up for everyone in layman's terms. "To give him a test run!"

"Well, it was more then just some kind of test run, I mean the damn thing ran right out the front door." Straka looked a little peeved, these weren't the answers he was looking for. "This thing you have created is knowledgeable, I get a real sense for that, but then I have to ask what Dextoid isn't? What I am looking for verges more toward habits, general assignments, or tasks it might perform on a periodic basis."

Straka was becoming annoyed and he could not fight back the urge to talk down to those in that room. "Look, back on Earth, *Service Dextoids* are much closer to acting like ideal robots, so if they *freak out*, there is a certain amount of predictability that follows. Mining, environmental clean up, or military assistance, each of these tasks have a purpose and there is a set of programs that compliment their efforts. This gives us a set of principles we can follow in recovery of these assets, that is right up to the point where a company like yours refuses to share the purpose of what they have created. If you want this thing found, you are going to have to share what purpose it supports."

His plea was greeted by silence. Straka suspected this meant they either knew the answer and were too afraid to tell him, or they really were clueless to what Alec was about. He highly doubted the latter. It was out of frustration he found his next set of words. "His purpose is connected directly to our recapturing him, you do understand this?"

The silence was finally broken by Xavier. He spoke to them as if he were some tired old religious figure who was granting permission to his pulpit, allowing them to participate in this somewhat kerygmatic sermon. He raised his hand as he spoke, and waved it as if he were slowly shooing someone away. "Please, someone respond to him."

The engineer, who had so eloquently put things into layman terms just a few moments ago, spoke now as if he had nothing to lose. "The end goal of this project was the complete integration of a neutralizing agent into a human based society."

Straka looked at them with the same disdain a conscientious objector would have after stumbling upon the depredated crimes of a despotic regime. "Ah, there it is then. Now your blanket of secrecy makes all the sense in the world."

He was staring into the faces of people who felt themselves righteous by what they had created. Alec had put them on some sort of technological plateau, and from that height they had found the moral right for putting him together. Whether or not they meant to launch him into the world didn't matter now, they were in the thick of it, and there wasn't a button or a program that would bring him back. Alec was meant to keep people guessing from the moment he got away.

Straka was in the thick of it as well, this carnival of the canaille, only he was refusing the gruel the corporation poured into their bowls. The employees had been conditioned to lap their drink from those dingy containers. There weren't many creatures who could run in a pack and ignore their own malformations and mange. These people were so far gone they could not see what they had become, well trained animals who hungrily defended the scraps tossed to them by their master. Straka looked to the head of the table; Xavier was the one tossing those meager scraps.

Long before he left Earth for this place he knew their problem was going to be messy one. A company like this was bound to have some pretty ugly skeletons in their closets. They weren't flying him all the way out here to simply file reports. Now with all their silence, they were telegraphing to him he was their point man on this, he was the one who would take the fall if things went wrong. Suddenly his badge seemed to be made of a cheaper metal, flexing under the weight of their lies. Straka was anything but a patsy. Why wouldn't they just come right out and say they had created a *Strike Dextoid*. "I am always quite amused by the engineers who try to describe lethal projects in benign terms."

"Half of these Dextoids are emotional wrecks to begin with, give it another month and we will probably find him in some cave contemplating his own existence, literally." The statement was brash, but Philman could afford to be.

Leopold took offense. "Don't be too sure of that, he wasn't designed to waddle in the mundane of domestic service like other Dextoids. Alec is running on a completely different operating platform. He is a finely tuned instrument, closer to a surgical knife than some blunt apparatus." There was conviction behind what Leopold was saying, it held a passion only someone close to a project could convey. "This isn't some worker bee or drone we have spent countless years developing just so he can be dependent upon the colony. Alec is an independent entity, and he is learning as he goes. It's all apart of his assessment strategy. Say we were to equate this in terms of playing a game of chess, then each day that goes by he will be playing at a higher level. The longer this timeline gets stretched out, the more likely he will begin to formulate his own opinions. I fear his solution for checkmate."

POLICY OF TRANSPARENCY

Looking at Straka one got the feeling he was very capable of extracting the information he needed from a person, and they wouldn't be too far off the mark if they said a one-word-answer would never cut it in his world. He became very good at ascertaining when someone was struggling with telling him the truth. He sensed there were people struggling with that very concept right here in this room. The concepts for their secrets were shrouded in *acronyms* and terms like *plausible deniability*. The liars would eventually reveal themselves, and it was important he find out who those individuals were. "This name Alec, does it actually stand for something?"

Leopold was obviously still working with the head of steam he had developed from Philman's remark. "His name is derived from the combination of two operational systems; Autonomous Logistics and Emergence Computing. Finding a way to bring these two systems together to operate within one device has been a dream long time in coming."

Straka wondered how many among them were just like Leopold, filled to the brim with endless streams of information in their respective fields. This put the question about his purpose into perspective. What if Alec's purpose was revealed upon his completion and subsequent activation, much in the same way cells rally to support a living entity. No one cell could do it on its own, but as a group they could repair tissue, fight disease, and deliver the necessary messages to the body helping it to sustain life. To see Alec's purpose in this light gave reason for this Byzantine management structure. How else could they keep the real intent of Alec from so many people and still get the job done?

Back on Earth, before Straka had resigned himself to becoming a bounty hunter, he was out in the field running under the blanket of covert operations. Deep in those remote areas, they were able to transmit and receive messages in a very direct and secretive fashion. The human beings transmitting those orders were in windowless rooms, gathering intelligence from satellites, drones, and autonomous vehicles. They used this data to probe their adversaries for weaknesses, backdoor entryways, exit points, and faulty lines of defense.

There were units of *Special Forces* personnel, *Strike Dextoids*, and *Assassins* stationed in remote areas all over that war torn planet. They were poised, waiting patiently for their compact communiqué to descend from the heavens. Upon receiving those messages, clandestine entities went out and destroyed foreign communications towers, blew up manufacturing sites, and took out the terrorists as they trained in their camps. Straka had first hand knowledge of those things. He had waited more than once in his jungle lair for those encrypted message to fall from the skies.

His was a war on drugs. He had crawled into the rat holes and bunkers of their hideaways to gather information or destroy their infrastructure. He knew the toxic smells that came from those underground dwellings. Those foul odors came to represent a surreptitious life filled with nothing but violence. He looked down at his left hand to see the scarring from the burns he received from one of those explosive encounters. Things just like this reminded him of where he had come from. His body had been riddled by the collateral damage of those missions. They taught him a lot about how the world really worked, and also went a long way in changing him.

Projects like Alec didn't get completed under a policy of transparency. Lies and deception were just as much apart of this world as algae and plankton were apart of the ocean. From all appearances he was sitting smack dab in an ocean of people who knew their part. These staff members could drone on all day about how great their creation was, it wasn't going to bring him back into their fold. They had been cooking something up in the basement of this place for quite some time to have the likes of Alec crawl up to the surface. Looking down at his left hand, he wondered how many of them would be scarred by their project before this was all over.

He would play their little game for now, all the while looking for those he could trust. "If you had one thing you could say that sets Alec apart from other Dextoids, what would that be?"

Another of the engineers spoke up. He had a very tight and wiry head of hair, to the point of looking like a steel wool pad. Straka could not help but wonder if his hair was somehow genetically enhanced to give it that appearance. Humans were so silly at times when it came to being vain. The man spoke rather quickly. "It would be his vision, his vision is everything. He can process more information in one moment of time, than you could ever see in your entire life. If he were to watch a movie he would see it as a slide show. His emotional packets are unlike any Dextoid ever created. He not only knows right from wrong, but as we said he can learn from the experience, and that is a huge step forward in lateral thinking. His progression . . ."

"I'm sorry to interrupt . . ." Straka was aware that his apology lacked any real sincerity, but he refused to sit and be a victim of their individual crooning. "but is there a reason we should be concerned by the amount of data he can process visually, surely it must translate into something?"

"Yes, yes, you are correct. His superior vision actually enhances his reaction time, he processes information so fast that someone getting ready to throw a punch, would in his mind, probably look as though they were posing for a boxing photograph."

It was right then and there, as if the same bright flash used in that type of boxing photograph also went off in Straka's head. He didn't need to be told twice a thing like hand- to-hand combat was out of the question with this thing.

It was Philman who voiced the concern of every person there trying to come to terms with what the corporation had unleashed on their world. "Exactly how much lethal force is Alec programmed with?"

"There isn't a measurable amount per say, it's not like we are going next door to ask for a cup of sugar. There are no quantitative results for how much he has. We know he is building on them, but at what rate remains to be seen. He is the architect of his defense. I can tell you what the structures of his fighting styles probably won't look like, a pyramid, or a squared off building. I would think more in terms of spires, something non linear, complex in design, like the Taj Mahal."

"You actually encourage this thing to create?" Even as he asked the question of the engineer it was dawning on Straka why Alec was so different, he had no prohibitors. He had no limitations! They had removed all of the things they usually used to diffuse a Dextoids thought process. This thing was out there running rampant, it was running with thoughts and feelings, how could it not grow!

Straka found himself staring at the young engineer who had spoken earlier, the one who was so prideful in describing how they had integrated a Strike Dextoid into the general population. It may have indeed been the only true accomplishment in this entire mess. Alec was lethal, and he wasn't going to be slowing down for anyone anytime soon. They were frightened of Alec in the same way a primitive tribe of people are frightened by the rapacious beast that creeps into their village late at night to take one of them away. No one ever watched as the beast snatch up its victim and dragged them back into the wilds of its colluding jungle lair. They were powerless to stop what the jungle had wanted. Their social acceptance to this kind of situation was an abomination. Their troubles on Mars were mounting and they could have easily taken on the form of a long line of boxcars to Alec's runaway train.

DISTANCE AND SILENCE

Straka came out of his thoughts much like a ship that appears out of a bank of fog. He could almost hear Xavier's request for a brief description on the last known position for Alec. Someone from Philman's staff responded to this request. "We have tracked him to the edge of the Arabian Quadrant, within the Singo-Chinese sector, the Tikhonravov Crater. This crater is one of the first Rocket Gardens the Singo-Chinese had ever established up here. It provides excellent support to their subterranean outpost. It isn't the first place one would have chosen for landing rockets, but I have a feeling they were thinking more in terms of defense when they decided on this place. There are a lot of older craft located in the area, real first generation type stuff."

The aide stood up and walked over to the giant holographic map dancing along the wall. "We have the latest satellite photos for this site to include all of the crashed and abandoned rockets. Understand neither side really shares information on their respective space programs. Astronauts, cargo, and supplies are all numbers up for speculation but we can tell you to a capsule how many spacecraft have landed here."

Another of Philman's staff spoke up, a man named Kilma Washburn. He openly wore the stress of change that had been happening within his department, and undoubtedly wondered why he was passed over for promotion. "We can't just walk into this area claiming we are looking for Alec, in the same sense that we don't want Singo-Chinese assessment teams scouring over our sites. Each rocket is considered the sovereign territory of the host nation having launched it. Design as we all know displays a countries capability, and I don't feel either country is ready to make those facts public."

"As we have found in the past, just because we know where he is located doesn't necessarily mean we have him within our control." Harvard tried interjecting his two-cents into the meeting, but as Xavier always noted, people had a propensity for ignoring him. His comments never inspired, there always seemed to be a better way of rephrasing what he had just said.

Philman was taking in as much of this information as possible. They were putting a lot of screens up on the wall. The particular set of maps catching his interest were those supporting the Singo-Chinese Rocket Garden, it was littered with designations explaining rocket models, topography, or distance to neighboring facilities and borders.

As he studied the layout he came across a symbol he wasn't quite familiar with. His first reaction was to say nothing; he didn't want to sound stupid for asking about a single icon that may have been obvious to everyone else. However the longer he stared at it the more he realized there wasn't another like it on the entire map. When he accessed the files attached to it, he found large amounts of data written in the language of Singo-Chinese. It got to the point where he could not deny his curiosity about it any longer, he had to know what the symbol represented. He leaned over to one of his coworkers and whispered his request.

"That..." Washburn began rifling through their notes. "That represents ... ah yes, that represents a rogue Dextoid, a female who escaped from the European Agency, La Compagnie d'Etoile some time ago. It seems the Singo-Chinese are having a hard time capturing her. By the number of reports attached in her file, they are quite aware she is out there. Very few of the reports have been translated into English. It appears they have gone out after her several times, but like everyone else who has had problems with escaped Dextoids, they are finding her a slippery fish."

"Rogue Dextoids are a real problem on both worlds. There are very few things a company can do once they lose positive control over these creatures. All it takes is a few failed attempts for it to become a public relations nightmare, and companies, as we know, aren't too eager to publicize their failures. So this could be why they don't go after them as diligently as they should." Once again Harvard tried to voice his opinion, and once again he was ignored.

It was most upsetting for Xavier to constantly come in and cleanup the statements made by his assistant. He made a mental note to have a word with Harvard about his little unwanted intrusions. He was a better asset to Xavier if he were taking notes and observing, rather than trying to participate in the conversation. Xavier cleared his throat before he spoke, pulling the attention toward him. "One can equate it to going out and looking for a tiger, if you could sneak up on a tiger out in the wild then they really wouldn't be any good at being a tiger. Those animals don't want to be found anymore than a Dextoid does."

Xavier paused for a moment, he saw an opportunity to hammer home his feelings for Martian rule. He wasn't going to change anyone's mind over night, but if he kept dropping hints about it, chipping away at the foundation, these individuals would be easier to sway when the time came. "There is an unrealistic outcry for policies in general by the ruling parties back on Earth. Adding the capture of rogue Dextoids to our list of things-to-do would only fuel the fire for tighter regulations. The people of Earth are fickle with their demands, they aren't based on any type of realistic solutions. I find their ideals to be most upsetting. It has been my practice of late to treat things in this manner; *what they don't see they cannot control*. Distance and silence are the only real weapons we can use in calming the noise emanating from that rock."

Straka was somewhat taken aback by what he just heard, in one small outburst Xavier had uttered a plan for succession. The room responded in a low murmur of approval, even if most were responding out of fear, they were endorsing the idea none-the-less. Succession was one of the fire-line issues governments of Earth were most terrified of. If they lost Mars as a colony, than it was quite possible they would lose all hope of ever saving their own world. Granted this assembly wasn't exactly enthusiastic about what Xavier had just uttered, but they weren't brandishing pitchforks or torches in repelling his idea either. Straka remained quiet and took it all in. He could not help but stare dead on at Xavier even as another on Philman's staff spoke.

"How much of a threat can this rogue Dextoid really be? After all we are only talking about a *Data Support Engineer*. She has been out on her own for quite sometime and surely out of touch with the rest of society. Even the rocket field she has been hiding in really doesn't contain the type of technology anyone would consider current. I'm not saying these abandoned hulks don't have value, they most certainly do, they are used as building materials, spare parts, and make shift shelters. The skies are literally raining down with this kind of technology each and everyday, no one needs to go out there and steal a rocket. It's too bad she wasn't more of a threat too the Singo-Chinese, I feel her value to us would be much greater if we used that fact in trying to retrieve Alec."

TEETERING ON THE BRINK

It was in the back of their minds, a bounty hunter was a tough, rugged individual, who acted above the law, scaring information out of anyone unlucky enough to cross his path. This perception may have worked for those he pursued but was far from the truth in those he had to deal with in getting the job. His clients needed to be coddled, their egos stroked, or some confided in him more information than he needed to know, and all he ever wanted was the basic facts of the case.

By the time they brought him in they usually considered their situation dire. It was the same story over and over again, in their minds they had somehow become the unwitting victims of their own affairs, having been ill advised, misinformed, or worse yet swindled. There was a line of thought he always seemed to hear within those first few meetings, and it went something like this; *if they were properly informed about who they were dealing with, they would have never accepted the circumstances of their situation.*

He knew better than anyone this statement was an out-an-out lie. There couldn't have been a more blatant way for his clientele to try and cover their butts. They knew what they were getting into each and every time they made a deal. No one ever flew blindly to the top, and certainly not anyone of his clients. Those people were notorious for getting ahead anyway they could.

Some of the less then scrupulous characters back on Earth had turned their Dextoids into personal collectors. Those mechanized thugs rolled up on their marks looking for payment, and found the most unique ways to apply pressure to those unfortunate souls.

Dextoids couldn't kill or harm another human being, but there was nothing in their protocols that prohibited them from scaring the hell out of a person. The owners augmented their programming, imbuing their automated servants to do just that. Straka read the grim reports of those maladjusted Dextoids using their superior strength and speed to terrorize their victims.

The corporations responsible for Dextoid Production didn't want their customers reading about their models extorting money from people, just like they didn't want their customers to think Dextoids would run away at the first chance they could take flight. It was how Straka came to have a standing order on hunting those types of Dextoids down, terminating them on site.

There were so many signs humanity was teetering on the brink of insanity. In Straka's opinion the one thing driving it over the edge, was also the thing being manufactured to save them, the Dextoids. If a human being wanted to have a single free thought, it had to be outside of the sight of these lurking creatures. Dextoids were designed to record every sight and sound observed. They were killing the sense of freedom everyone had, killing the ability to speak freely, write freely, and think freely. When they placed a Strike Dextoid into a combat zone, everyone saw how easily it killed freely.

The designers of Dextoids began to acknowledge this discomfort and felt the answer was to seamlessly integrate them into the population in order to ease the apprehensive feelings people had about them. Those factories began punching them out to look and act just like their human counterparts. This actually worked for a while, people began to get a psychological foothold on the growing insecurities for Dextoids, that was until the ugly concept of Suicide Dextoids began splattering across the pages of their news services.

For Straka it was one more mandate to have to clean up, only trying to spot a Suicide Dextoid was a lot like guessing a number at a roulette table, one didn't know the outcome until the little white marble fell in its slot. Those things detonated without any warning.

If there was one thing out their more terrifying to everyone than a Strike Dextoid, it was the existence of a Suicide Dextoid. Perhaps Straka could tap into the energy of both these fears in helping them solve their little crisis with Alec. He smiled to himself as he began to formulate his plan. The thought was just devious enough that it might work.

PERPETRATING THE LIE

"What if we tell the Singo-Chinese we know the identity of the female Dextoid hiding within their territory? What if we tell them the female is actually a Suicide Dextoid, one intending to infiltrate one of their structures. I would think this would bring the satisfactory response we are looking for in having them help us drive Alec back out into the open."

Philman suddenly showed the same excitement a kid would have in adding to a fantasy story. "We could up the ante, tell them her interaction with another Dextoid could somehow trigger her response."

Washburn followed up Philman's response with the intention of adding a little more logic to his bosses' response. "That would put a timeline on this thing. We could let it leak Alec has a knowledge for piloting rockets. If those two Dextoids were to interact it could have them flying a rocket to one of their facilities up here or back on Earth. Their fears would run wild trying to second guess what those two Dextoids would do next."

Straka liked what he was hearing, but they needed to refine it just a little more for it to really work. "Yes, I have to agree, that would put a sense of urgency into this situation, but I feel we are lacking something."

"Yes! We could tell them Alec has escaped and we think he is going to do just that, fly away in one of their rockets. What more do they need to know!" It was as if Philman could not control himself. He really seemed to enjoy stretching the truth, and thrived in the role of being a rumormonger. Xavier was quietly making mental notes about his new Chief of Security.

"I have a particular contact on the Singo-Chinese side that might be interested in Straka's skill sets. I guess the real question is, do we actually divulge who Straka is, or do we send him in under a different cover?" Harvard was speaking directly to Xavier in support of his idea, but could tell his boss was already shooting it down even before he could get the last few words out.

Xavier rubbed his face as if to show them the exhaustion he was wearing from this entire episode. "I have another concern. Once the word gets out about this Suicide Dextoid, the international community will start watching this story very, very closely."

"That would mean you boys would be operating a little more in the public light. Not something you're quite used too, is it?" Straka could not help but snicker at Xavier's concern.

Xavier was quick to countered Straka. "Yes, but the Singo-Chinese would be operating in this same light, and I don't believe they would find any enjoyment in it either. We need to get them to agree to keep this off the radar and on the down low. We could bring up their past failures in trying to capture her, anything of embarrassment to leverage them into keeping silent about what we are trying to achieve."

Philman chimed in with a concern. "What if by us getting this whole process started they actually go in and capture Alec? Then the cat would really be out of the bag."

For Straka the concern was brilliant, this was the missing piece he was looking for in perpetrating this lie. "Then we don't go in with such a strong focus on trying to capture Alec. I think we can formulate enough of a ruse in which we keep the attention squarely on her. If we do our job right, Alec wouldn't seem like such the big fish."

Philman seemed genuinely scared as he spoke. "Yes, and in doing that, they will capture her and take her away, only to find out the real truth, that she is just a Data Service Dextoid, a big nothing, a nobody. Then what?"

Xavier was beginning to find a real comfort for this plan. "Would any of it really matter? So what, she ends up being a dud. I mean at that point we would simply tell them we were following through on a lead. We went through the appropriate diplomatic channels and notified them. This stuff is all written down in the treaties between us."

Straka felt the plan snapping into place. "We have examined one possible outcome to this, which is if they capture her. I think a better option for everyone involved is if we could somehow hold onto her. It would buy us more time on all fronts. Time we could use in pursuing Alec out in the open. The question now becomes how do we go about this without raising too much suspicion?"

Washburn added his two cents. "Being a Suicide Dextoid, we could tell them she is programmed to detonate within one of their facilities. I don't think we need to be exact as to which one. This information alone should put enough concern into the equation to have them wanting us to hold onto her. As an olive branch we could suggest one of our outposts to hold onto her."

"If we could translate their reports on her, maybe we could find additional clues in helping us with this." Deep down inside Philman didn't like the fact there were things written about this female Dextoid he could not translate into the immediate.

Straka found himself glaring at Philman in disgust, he had to have another skill set that wasn't being demonstrated here to attain his position. "That's it then, we would have bought the time needed to pursue our real problem, and keep the Singo-Chinese at bay while we continue our pursuit. I am quite certain the particulars can be worked out, even by you."

There was a silence before Xavier spoke, Harvard began to raise his hand as if to add one more thing, but Xavier waved his attempt off. Heavy laid his crown as he looked out onto all those faces waiting in anticipation for him to weigh in. "There are a lot of things to clean up with our story and we have a lot of prep work to do, but I like it. We go in after the female, and have Alec back to being on the run again."

Chapter 04
Backstabber

Philman slowly entered the room with the confidence of a twisted mind. He had an air about him of having everything under his control and this made I-Glo fearful of him. She had picked up on his strange energy from the start, and knew her experience with humans of this kind were less than positive. They tended to devalue the things around them, acted as if all things were replaceable, and usually went out of their way to prove their point.

She could not stop the programming on her assessment strategies from going into overdrive. There was a lot going on in that room but it didn't mean much of it was escaping her. In some strange way these observations were helping with the calming of her mind, although with every passing moment she was becoming aware her current situation would become more than she could mentally handle. Stripped down to her bare essentials and strapped tightly to a chair, she was in a room based half in the restoration of a Dextoid, and half in the practice of tearing them apart.

Plumes of fiber optic cable came shooting out of her body like fountains of water. Those cables spiraled across the floor and flowed into numerous types of test gear. She could feel the tentacles for these machines creep into her system, wanting to monitor her every thought. Her body whirled and hummed with an activity beyond her control. She might as well have been trying to identify a musical note while holding onto a vibrating cord.

Philman considered himself to be quite docile to this point in his questioning of her, reacting to the situation as it casually unfolded before him. If it played out as he anticipated, she would represent his biggest coo to date for this type of work. The fact he had convinced the Singo-Chinese to bring I-Glo to one of their outposts was already a huge feather in his cap.

It gave the Red Planet Pioneer Corporation the positive control they were looking for in this particular scenario. He knew from his recent dialogs with the Singo-Chinese, just how concerned they had always been with I-Glo's presence out amongst their rockets. They simply didn't have the resources to flush her out. People in space suits trying to catch a Dextoid running free on Mars was like scuba divers in the water trying to grab a fish, one would always find something inherently slippery about the situation.

Philman smugly remembered when he finally revealed the last bit of false intelligence to bait his Singo-Chinese counterparts, that of her possibly being a Suicide Dextoid. It sent them into an immediate panic, putting everything into motion his department had been working on. For Philman this had always been about gaining the upper hand and leveraging them into doing what he wanted.

The last thing they were inclined to do with a Suicide Dextoid was bring it back to detonate inside one of their own structures. The Singo-Chinese leadership endorsed her removal, stamping the paperwork to have her taken far away from any of their facilities.

The trade off however was that Philman's office got bombarded with questions from the Singo-Chinese. They wanted to know if I-Glo had been confirmed to be a Suicide Dextoid. If so, than who sent her? What was her primary target? Were secondary targets found in her database? Their questions spidered out into numerous others, spiraling right into the smallest of details like where her quantum processors were made or how counterintuitive her qubits were. Philman approached each of these concerns with a great deal of care, or so it seemed. The entire time he was answering their questions and earning their trust, he was also securing his position as their liaison. Philman felt so much more comfortable interacting with people if he didn't have to be straightforward with them.

It was decided his department would do everything it could to work jointly with the Singo-Chinese on this. Philman and his staff had been pulling long hours preparing materials to pull this ruse off. They were also given the oversight for perpetuating several other projects, all pertaining to the deception of I-Glo being a Suicide Dextoid.

Their Dextoid Repair Division was busy reassembling the one they obtained in a trade with the Indo-Europeans, filling it with missions and targets of value located inside the Singo-Chinese territories. To top this off they needed to impregnate their doppelganger with explosives. Not as easy a task as one might think, especially with the weapons free ban in full affect. Their final step would be to insert thoughts from I-Glo into the duplicate's memory so they could pull off their subterfuge.

Philman was waiting like any good gambler for the right moment to play his hand. This rouse was all about timing, and selling the Singo-Chinese on the fact this was an actual investigation. He could not allow himself or his staff to fall into the trap of taking this lightly. There were plenty of things sent into motion needing their attention. They always ran the risk of someone speaking out of turn or becoming impatient with the process. Waiting became a tool not just to make sure they were selling this storyline to the Singo-Chinese, but also to make sure they weren't getting too far out in front with their dubious results. The reports need to confirm the Suicide Dextoid story had been printed out weeks ago and sat in his office awaiting his review. Even with the completion of these tasks, he knew they were far from clear of the woods.

An Aide walked up to the observation window and activated the intercom system. "Sir you have a meeting with the Singo-Chinese security advisor and his staff in one hour."

"Thank you." Philman's response was cold, never taking his eyes off I-Glo. He was in a little bit of a dilemma over her. The Singo-Chinese were notorious for coming back to the bargaining table after everyone involved thought a deal was brokered. One of their tactics was to revisit an issue over and over again, this to wear their opposition down and obtain any additional truths.

Philman knew there would be things that changed about their plan, they would be broadsided by the unexpected or have the rug pulled out from underneath them. It was important for Philman to maintain the course, navigating these waters at a slow and steady pace.

Everyone back at corporate was aware of the political nightmare being created for their Indo-European counterparts. It was one of the reasons the corporation was trying to keep the whole affair out of the *Press* and under the radar. This situation would test the brinksmanship of corporate, and they weren't going to be allowed to blink, especially if this story leaked out. Public sentiment was already on edge over the Suicide Dextoid problem, this would be the first confirmed appearance of one on Mars. The longer they could keep this cover going, the better their chances were in brokering a deal. There was safety in the darkness.

Philman was repeatedly told by Xavier and others on his staff he was not to broker a deal with the Singo-Chinese. No matter how hard he tried, he could not help himself from dabbling in these affairs. The corporation had dedicated an entire wing to work through these issues. There was some strange undeniable impulse guiding his hand in these affairs, and he could not help from getting caught up in this aspect of the operation. He found a particular pleasure in divulging information, it gave him a thrill. He found himself discussing things off the record, dropping little hints, alluding to the inside track he had with the company, and always promising to keep his ear close to the ground for them. Getting wrapped up in all this information transfer began blurring the lines, and he would sometimes forget what he was supposed to be talking about and when he was supposed to say it.

He never took his eyes off of I-Glo. She sat helpless in her chair, strapped down so tight there was no chance of her moving a muscle without him noticing. He didn't think it possible but he was actually enjoying the power he had over her. She looked so frightened, frightened beyond belief. Dextoids were devoid of this feeling as any main emotion, it was viewed as being counterproductive, so they supposedly left the factory being fearless. Yet everything in her face told him she was completely frightened out of her mind and he was finding those prospects tantalizing.

She became his ant under a magnifying glass and her squirming would depend on how much heat he decided to apply to this situation. He was getting a real kick out of having so much control. It didn't make sense; there was no explaining his actions to someone else on his staff. He was becoming more and more empowered as he tore her apart. He reached out over to one of the antiseptic tables, passing the surgical instruments, and picked up a cup of hot coffee. Raising it to his pursed lips, he blew on it ever so slowly. "So where were we the last time we spoke?"

His question was greeted by silence. I-Glo knew he was letting her know the interrogation was once again about to begin. It didn't matter how calm and collected he was trying to sound, she was in the presence of a wild animal. Direct eye contact with him would only provoke an attack. She watched his every move from out the corner of her eye, harboring hopes of finding more about who he was, what his motives might be, and what she represented in all this craziness. *Did he have a humane side, was there any compassion within him?* If she could just find a benevolent kernel like that within the fibers of his being, then maybe she could anchor her hope of getting out intact.

A BYPRODUCT OF THEIR MADNESS

It pleased Philman to no end she wasn't rolling over and telling him everything he wanted to know. He found an enjoyment from the palpability of her fight, and was relishing the job ahead of prying the information from her system.

He calculated his walk over to a chair placed next to where she was and calmly sat down, adjusting himself enough so that it would convey the importance of finding his own comfort. Casually he began going over the notes from the last time they spoke. Occasionally he would look up from the screen he was studying, and in those moments he felt compelled to relay how moving he found her predicament.

If she were to fight against the restraints, the energy from her exertion would register within the machines. They were downloading data on her all the time. Those devices were probing and prodding her mind, looking for any information straying from her qubit field. Try as she might, she was having a really hard time keeping the things near and dear to her away from them.

She wasn't sure what they were looking for, but they were doggedly scanning her memory as if they were dredging a lake. This tireless effort on their part was beginning to strip away at her dignity. She tried to stay focused, hiding the things that made her unique, things that touched a place she called her heart. She was afraid though, afraid of concentrating on something she really cared about like her poetry, the taste of freedom, or the encounter she had with Alec. She needed to protect those heartfelt treasures, so she tricked her own mind into creating a diversion, and mentally moved onto a secret game coveted by almost every Dextoid within the service industry.

There was an underlying current to the context of language that Dextoids found very fascinating, the linguistic skills they were able to demonstrate allowed for them to politely rebel against their masters. The human populace never seemed to catch onto how Dextoids were twisting their vocabulary around and using it to their advantage. It took a unique mind to find the idiosyncrasies within a language and turn it into wordplay.

When engaged in such repertoire, a Dextoid's response would vary according to the difficulty they were trying to attain. Very seldom could Dextoids play in groups, although they tried. A simple form of the challenge would have them adding a letter to every word they used in succession of their response.

A human might ask; *How far to the next town?* A Dextoid employing a Rhopalic response would answer; *The next civic center overall distance potential, convenient, neighboring!* It may have caused a double take from the person asking the question, but that was part of their expected fun. It might also cause the human receiving this response to also follow up by filing a complaint and asking the Dextoid be taken in for service.

Suddenly I-Glo became aware of Philman and the way he was breathing, she could tell he was about to speak.

"Oh yes, now I see where we left off. We were talking about the Dextoid you were seen with out at Tikhonravov Crater. I believe you said his name was Alec?"

"That never happen!"

"Happened? Are you losing control of your faculties already?"

"We never had that conversation, nor do I recall ever saying that name."

Philman savored her grief and his eyebrow raised as the fear in her voice actually registered within one of the monitoring devices. "Yes you did, I have it right here in my notes, you said his name was *Alec*."

I-Glo knew he was lying. She never would have told him his name. She was certain of it, but how did Philman already know his name was Alec? Perhaps they had extracted the information from her memory and he had merely misspoke. It wasn't out of the realm of possibilities, after all, he was the one who was human.

"Yes, I am looking at my notes, and you called out at fourteen-fifty-five yesterday the name; Alec."

"I have no recollection of having ever said that to you."

"But you agree, his name is Alec, you do at least agree with that?"

I-Glo wanted to cry. The utter frustration she had for this situation was literally tearing her in two. She was even having a difficult time identifying with who she really was, an administrative Dextoid caught up in the clutches of female fashion, or a Suicide Dextoid ticking away until her target was acquired? Everything she ever was or ever could be, might rest on the fact she was a ticking time bomb. Her mind was racing on an intersecting track with insanity, all the while she was trying to avoid their probing questions and the misrepresentation she had for her own reality. She needed time to figure this all out and that was one thing Philman would not grant her.

How did being a Suicide Dextoid really work? *Was she like a cruise missile flying a preprogrammed path, looking for visual markers, turning left and right down city streets until the mapping matched up to her target?* One of her biggest fears had the explosive device detonating on the recognition and identity of an individual. Placed in this situation was compromising her situation because she had to deal with all of these human beings. Each new person she came into contact with caused her to flinch. The degrees in which all these people were separated, kept closing in on her, someone always knew someone, and with each introduction she might be meeting the one who she was supposed to assassinate. Why not put a gun to her head and pull the trigger until they found the chamber containing the round.

These dark deliberations had her wishing she were far away from this place. She wondered if Philman and the others had the ability to tap into her hope? It was maddening to think they were recording all of her thoughts. *Was nothing about who she was sacred? Was there anything going on inside of her escaping their detection?* She was wishing very hard for this to finally all be over.

The realities of this situation were leading her astray, right down a road of ruin and to loneliness. The mental strolls she constantly had to take were taxing on her mind. The very room she found herself in was more than just a prison chamber for her inquisition; it was a room hammering home the reality of never being able to live life minus the presence of people.

There would always be someone seeking her out, trying to interface with her, bringing her back into their fold. Humans for her were becoming obscene, their faces growing more grotesque and ugly as they came into view. All these misgivings swarmed around her belief in what they had done to her, how they were now violating her mind. They had taken control of her pensive nature, and was robbing her of the chance for cultivating the beauty she found in the world around her.

Why was it so important to manufacture Dextoids to look like human beings? Hadn't these Homo sapiens done enough during their tenure on Earth? Each and every one of them destroyed something in their wake. No one ever seemed to take responsibility for the wrecking of their home world. The real culprits were the ones blaming everyone else. Good god humanities blame knew no bounds, hanging it on those who lived in the past and left for the ones who were going to live in the future. Blame radiated out from the center of who they were, and was used to absolve themselves from any wrongdoing. It was as if blame were a staple feature for being human.

The basis for all their experiences were acted out within the narrow bandwidth of the visual spectrum, and confirmed with all the contact they had in the electromagnetic field. The universe however, radiated far and away from anything their eyes could see or their fingers could feel. *Could anyone really experience a place like Paris from just reading a book on it? Why then would a person think they had a solid grasp on the workings of the universe from having seen such a small sliver of it?*

She knew for a Dextoid to really experience the universe around them, they would have to be able to fully immerse themselves in it. To do this would mean they needed to shuck their human shell. Their insistence on making Dextoids resemble people brought to bear the proof they as mechanized beings were nothing more than a byproduct of their madness.

Strapped to that chair she wondered why she cared so much about them tearing her away from the skin she was trapped in. Wouldn't they be giving her exactly what she was asking for, liberation from this makeshift body? She would finally be free of them. These thoughts were coming in from the peripheral. They needed to be watched because they didn't carry the appropriate weight for her situation. She knew after they tore her apart, they would stuff her components into different models of Dextoids, recycling her innards, essentially destroying who she was.

In her travels, she had come across others who had their memories wiped clean. The first thing she noticed about her interactions with these Dextoids was their previous experiences had been expunged from their system, nothing remained from their time before. If she had a shared experience in the past with a Dextoid like this, and tried to remind them of the moment, they would act cold and indifferent to her recollection. To them the moment had never happened. Some, in the most polite way, claimed to not even remember who she was.

This was the price of resistance. The wires they had splaying from her system were constantly tasking her, leveraging data, her reflex information, and of course her memories. It was hard for her to keep it all under control, so things ended up slipping away from her. Sometimes the fight she was putting up with in one corner of her being caused a memory to slip away in another. She knew something was wrong when she brought her attention back to the qubit in question only to find a gap. This empty space gave her a hollow feeling. Those thoughts, whatever they might have been, were well enough gone.

Wasn't she the one who felt a spark grow into love after having met Alec! She was the one who felt free from the connection of people living out in that rocket garden. She was the one who felt reborn as the sun rose in the morning. If she was to protect who she was, then she needed to protect her most cherished thoughts, because those were the ones that made her feel alive. The only way to do that was to remain conscious. She wasn't ready to lose who she was.

This was the control people had over the Dextoid population. It was total and complete, and so was her fear. It should have never existed in her, but there it was. She knew better then to make eye contact with Philman, but at the same time she could not let this sadistic creature out of her sight.

IRREPARABLE HARM

He sat there knowing all too well she was trying to keep things from them. As her memory was scanned, he noticed bundles of information that weren't being acknowledged. The data was being purposely skipped over, disappearing in one qubit and reappearing in another. It was obvious to anyone looking at those readings she was trying to bury information within her system. Philman reached out, brushing a strand of her hair away from her face. He wanted to show her he had some understanding for what she was going through. He so desperately wanted her to confide in him and extended every effort to appear supportive in her time of need.

Even though she was doing everything possible to protect the information inside her, on one of their instruments they were getting some visual smatterings of what she had been holding back. Images from her databanks showed Alec sitting with her in a space capsule. The quality wasn't the best, they were grainy, a bit fuzzy, but the images of Alec were there nonetheless.

Other data began to emerge, but she was doing everything in her power to keep this information from them. Philman guessed these things had to have been about her personality, things she was too afraid to share with anyone else. Sometimes, under examination, information within a Dextoid was not where they expected to find it. These blank spots, sometimes referred too as *disjointed spans*, often meant a Dextoid was hiding something about themselves. Investigators latched onto such evidence, and

Philman was no exception, giving him more resolve to go after the things considered more precious to her.

He wanted to know everything about her, and came back to touching her strand of hair. There was more happening here then an interrogation, she was becoming his little pet project, and because of it, he felt a sense of ownership over her. He didn't know how to explain it, but he knew after they broke her, he was going to bring her back, molding her actions and demeanor to his personal taste. He would have her serve him and in a way he would happily become accustomed too.

If she let herself fall under its spell, the computing power droning on in that room would wipe away her memories forever. The allure of surrendering to it was all too great. It was such a dreadful prospect, as if they found the small thread deep inside her keeping it all together, and they had no problem pulling on it. She was on the verge of having a mental breakdown, and it saddened her they had the capability to make her feel this way. She was desperately trying to cling onto the things she cared about the most, - what in her mind she had become; an artist, a poet, in love, she was alive! She had to close her eyes if she had any chance of retaining those feelings. The desperation of trying to hold it together churned away inside her until she felt it all would end with her shrieking.

None of it mattered, they viciously swiped at her memories with the same brutal jabs a knife-wielding assailant would use. They were cutting away at her and they were winning, taking the things that defined who she was and why she existed. This torture chamber, Philman, the noises, it was an amusement park ride gone haywire. It had all the flashing lights and screams of a good time gone bad, and all those things were happening entirely in the fabric of her mind.

"You can't hold out forever."

I-Glo realized she needed to open her eyes. Standing over her was Philman, his face contained a twisted confidence, repulsing her in every sense of the word. "As you well know this type of computing power is relentless, it will not stop until I command it. Why don't you concede, it is useless to resist against this. By fighting you could cause irreparable harm to yourself. We would have no choice but to start all over again, wiping the slate clean, and we would never think twice about it. I know you don't want that to happen. I can see it in your eyes, you are trying to take this to a deeper place within yourself. Don't make it out to be a moral fight, of good versus bad, or of right against wrong. We aren't asking for a confession. You should not attach a feeling like guilt to this. All we want to do is have the ability to look at your thoughts."

He made his way over to one of the monitors suspended from the ceiling, pointing to it as if it were all the proof he needed. "I am looking at your chart right here, it is very interesting to see how much power you are exerting from within yourself just to try and fend us off. It appears from the readings on this monitor you won't be able to hold out too much longer. We can almost predict to the minute when you're going to crack. It doesn't have to be this way. We can stop right now and make it go away. All you have to do is give me what I want. I can assure you we will go easy on you." He tapped the monitor with his finger. "It is just a matter of time. You know I am going to get the information anyway. When that happens you'll realize all your resistance, all this fighting was for not. It won't matter how much you beg me then, I won't turn a single machine off. I will run your qubit field right into the ground."

She was determined to hold out for as long as she possibly could. She had more fight in her than any monitor could have ever reflected, more than he could ever imagine, and that was for sure. There was no turning back from this strategy—it was all or nothing.

Finding his chair, he sat back down in it, pausing momentarily to watch her as she trembled under the strain of their prying technology. He wanted to believe there was a micro war happening under the surface of all this, a fight between his invading forces and her defenses. Their grappling hooks would work until they finally found a barrier of hers that would give way.

It was always a little paradoxical to him to see computing systems trying to survive the very programs designed to tear them apart. Every time a system was created, a program seemed to be designed to dismantle it. Things were constantly being shoved, pushed around, or jostled, trying to find an equilibrium between the waves of attacking viruses and mounting defenses. Nothing within this technological world ever seemed to be at peace.

He felt there was an inescapable irony to all this. There were visionaries in the computing world convinced everything would be integrated in the future. The world was going to be a better place, where all the computing power would be working together in complete harmony, and yet behind the scenes there was a tectonic shift within the lines of code, of a technology always on the move because they were under attack. These invading programs were competing with the lines of code to become better, faster, and smarter. The more intricate they got, the closer they became to understanding each other.

A finger on her hand gave way and twitched, it was subtle, but Philman saw it happen. It was an indication she was beginning to lose her battle within, it was a sign he had been waiting for. He slid his chair closer to her, and leaned in to whisper in her ear. "I am going to make you a promise right now. When this is all over, and you are too weak and broken to do anything for yourself, I am personally going to bring you back to health. I will make sure you are taken care of in the exact way you should have been taken care from the very first day you were created. You are a Dextoid, and you need to know your place in this world. I promise to make you my slave."

His words were disturbing, and they caught her off guard. She could not help herself as she blinked her eyelids rapidly, and for one moment made eye contact with him. He reacted to it immediately. "Hah! That is the real problem here, isn't it? Look at you, you are sick, infected! Twisted with some type of virus that in the end will tear you apart mentally. You've been out there for so long you forgot who created you and why. Well, you needn't worry about that anymore. I will be here to remind you, each and everyday of your miserable existence. You were designed for one reason, and one reason only, to serve man. When we are through with you, that is exactly what you will be made to do."

He got up, sauntering over to another device within the room. "I know I shouldn't do this, but I am going to crank up the battery parasites attached to your system. It is considered dangerous because it compromises retrieval of the information we want. I am willing to do it just to watch you break in front of me. We may not get everything we want from you, but you will surrender. If you can remember only one thing, remember the promise I made to you." He looked at the monitor and smiled: "I think an added twenty percent just might do it." He began ramping up the power on the parasites. "How does it feel?"

Her body began to vibrate uncontrollably. It wasn't noticeable on the surface, but if someone had set their hand upon her skin they would have felt the surge of energy taking place within her body. The power drain was all too real, and the void it was causing was being filled with unconscionable panic. It was growing rapidly into terror and she was doing everything she could to calm herself down.

On paper she knew all she needed to do was adjust to the new demand on her system. It wasn't going to be easy though, the thread holding everything together inside her was being pulled a little harder now, a little more rapidly. It was an unmistakable, sickening feeling. She was losing who she was. She wanted to scream, and have the power of her scream extinguish all the anguish she was feeling.

She was so close to cracking, to be heard screaming at the top of her lungs, when an aide from Philman's office came walking into the room. It gave her a chance to refocus, if only for a moment.

"Sir the Singo-Chinese shuttle is approaching the facility. They are coming for the debriefing and have asked that you be present. I think they have questions about the last report we sent over to them."

"What time is it? Are they early?"

"No sir. They are running right on time. I have been informed by someone in logistics that our last report had some pretty serious gaps in the data. It has caused some concern not just with them, but with some of the people downstairs doing the data transfer. Apparently it has made filing the reports they have prepared for the next few weeks very difficult to present. To use their exact words, *things will look quite suspect* to the Singo-Chinese."

"You have got to be kidding me! What happened, exactly?"

"The Singo-Chinese were sent an update earlier this morning, it was unscheduled, and worse yet appears to have been an unedited version of what we wanted to send. It reiterates some of the data we have already given them, so there is this weird overlapping of telemetry. To a trained eye, the files we have given them initially are going to appear as if they were tampered with, which of course we know they have been. I am sure they will have questions about it. How should we proceed?"

"Well we won't deny it, that's for sure!" Philman hit one of the machines with his clenched fist. "We need to have them believing we are giving them real data. Don't you people understand that! Now, did we give them the raw data from the doppelganger or from her?"

I-Glo began to drift off to a place of her own choosing. She went back to a time when she was first allowed to walk the long polished chrome halls of La Compagnie d'Etoile. It felt as if she were floating on air, to be alive and introduced to such a structural marvel right from the start.

It felt good to walk those halls and take her post within the offices of those elevated tiers. She was being placed within the staff of upper management as one of their data support engineers. Things were so new and exciting; she could not wait to show off her skills. She was ready for the challenges her new job was surely going to present.

She could not help but take in the beauty of her world. There was a magic to how things were unfolding in front of her. She was seeing wonderment in everything she laid her eyes upon. There were people and other Dextoids hurriedly walking around as if they had purpose and were summoned to do something for the greater good. She could not wait to be apart of that energy, to contribute to a worthwhile cause.

The air was crisp and cool, kissing her lungs with each vibrant transfer. It spoke volumes for the spark she had for this existence. There were no boundaries to what she could do, her feelings for this were taking flight. There was so much this world had to offer and, of course, what she could offer in return—and it all seemed to hinge on her believing. She wished she could go back in time and talk to the person she was back then, tell her of the things she knew now. This thought re-awoke her soul to the reality she was facing with Philman.

"So do we really need to continue the data transfer from her? I mean don't we have enough information. Let's end it now, surely we can say she detonated?"

"Yes, yes, from the looks of it we can do that. I would like to finish this session out, even if it means coming back at a later time. We can make our final decision then."

The aide began to exit but stopped short of the door. "Philman, don't forget about the meeting."

"I will be there."

The aide exited as Philman turned his attention back toward I-Glo. "I don't want you to worry. You can't believe everything you've heard. I will keep my promise, I can assure you of that."

I-Glo felt her world spinning faster and faster as if at any moment it were going to fly out of control because of the centrifugal forces that were attached to it.

Philman walked over to her and place his hand gently on her forehead. "Usually we shut a Dextoid down to physically remove their memory, or when doing a massive data transfer, but in your case I want it to be special for you. So please resist, do your very best to fight us. I want you to be awake for every moment of it. I want you to have to live through the moment we break you. In the end, after you have told me everything, given me everything I could possibly ask for, I will document those things about you. I want others to read and learn from the work we have done here. I want them to see how you felt, to see the moment you finally burst, spilling your guts out onto the floor as if you were some old bladder that had finally ruptured." Philman grinned as she squirmed under his touch. "Everyone will know-I won't hide a minute of your torture from any of them."

These were the last straws in her resistance, she felt so ashamed, so humiliated, so exposed. She wanted nothing more than to be free of them, to be away from every last human being. She considered shutting down, to just get it over with. The only thing stopping her was the remote chance Alec was out there, somewhere, coming for her. It was her only hope.

She really wanted to believe.

Chapter 05
The Dextoid Way

Nothing could change the fact it took nine months to travel from Earth to Mars. All the propulsion systems ever developed couldn't warp their way around the math of that astronomical distance. It is a pipe dream then, the stuff of science fiction, that people would travel to a faraway place and arrive in an illustrious posh techno style.

Straka looked at the small book of papers he had in his hand, there were only so many cigarettes he would be able to roll with this book. The bag of tobacco he had in his pocket was measured out to the gram to match his paper supply. He knew in his heart of hearts one would not outlast the other. This thought caused him to hesitate, if only for a moment. Many of the people up here would agree, he was holding a luxury in his hand, and when that luxury was gone it would be replaced with something far less exquisite. His hesitation for tearing a paper ended with wanting to fulfill his desire for a smoke. Sparingly he poured the tobacco out onto the sheet. In a way this was a celebration. He had safely reached this distant world. He was one of Earth's travelers now, and could be found on the list of those who dared.

The planet had a rich history for migration, for people who were willing to risk it all in hopes of finding a better life. They were usually more concerned with leaving a place than planning for their voyage, escaping rather than enduring what was ahead. People often found themselves climbing into dingy, crammed, abhorred conveyances. The unstable expanse that lay in front of them would always be an odyssey testing the very pursuits of their dreams.

So it was with the people who came to colonize Mars. They crammed themselves into technology as simple as the stuff that took men to the Moon. They put as many people as they could into one of those rocket ships and hurtled them off into the deep, dark ocean of outer space. The technicians who closed the doors of those capsules had a hard time hiding the hope they had for the people they were sealing inside.

Human beings always seemed to find themselves pushing against the forces of nature, and usually in vessels all too fragile for what they were trying achieve. Future observers would always question those attempts, every conveyance looked rickety displayed in a museum, with most having a skin as thin as the cigarette paper he held in his hand. He allowed for a slight crease to develop down the center of it, so the tobacco could respond by falling into the fold. Those finely cut leaves were influence by the curvature of the space they laid upon. It was easy for him to roll the paper around the tobacco at this point, capturing those leaves in a tightly twisted stick.

Innovation was like that. People yearned for it, yet the concept could be trapped just like the tobacco in his cigarette. It was the establishment that influenced its direction, wrapping itself around those prospects, reigning concepts in other things like proprietary information, copyright infringement, or a patent pending. Contained like this, ideas could be regulated and taxed. If you wanted to set that information free, sometimes you had to go against the grain. Sometimes it was better to cause friction rather than to conform.

He found himself rifling around in his pockets until he found his little box of wooden matches. Sliding the drawer open, he pulled one out and lit it. The combustion was instantaneous, all that was left was to bring the match up to the end of the cigarette until it too was lit, and then he took a long slow drag off his smoke. Sometimes you had to ignite an idea, that would set things free, then one could step back and watch the whole thing burn.

It was the job of science to promise a better future to its people and in that vein it would almost always fail. Colonization was the definitive proof. It would always be seen as a struggle, ships were scuttled, flags planted out of sheer acts of defiance, and lives were lost, and all because they could never get the technology to accommodate their needs. Enduring that astronomical distance just reaffirmed everything he believed about a person arriving to a place in posh techno style. One had to arrive in order to live, and after being trapped in that capsule those colonists were determined to do that anyway they could.

It took a lot for a human being to be sitting where Straka was right now. There were mountains upon mountains of things people had to overcome within themselves before they were even permitted to climb into one of those ships. Venturing off on a trip to the Red Planet was a mentally grueling experience, and those Space Agencies pushed their candidates to the brink of their own sanity. It was the only way they could weed out the undesirable. They searched for those who were clever, ingenious, and above all immersed in tolerance.

Incompatibility was a trying issue for travelers to overcome. These were small groups of people living in total seclusion for long periods of time, learning to traverse the psychological staircases of their own levels of patience. They were breathing the same recycled air day after day, eating the same nine or twelve meals week after week, and sleeping in a shared space for as long as the journey lasted. For everyone involved it became apparent it was never going to be a question of when a meltdown would occur, it would always be one of just how severe it was going to be when the person finally blew.

Drugs and calming words could only do so much in sedating an individual flipping out, especially one who spiraled off into shear madness. Under these circumstances a spaceship and its crew would begin the edgy transformation from capsule to sleep deprivation chamber. Straka didn't care who the people were, no one could feel safe in a capsule like that. Not when one of its occupants was hell bent on destroying them all. The ugly truth was every early experiment they tried back on Earth had to be terminated because of such frothing lunacy.

Straka looked at the glowing embers forming at the end of his cigarette. He reached out to a glass partially filled with water sitting on a small table and carefully flicked his ashes into it. Those ashes immediately reacted upon making contact with the water, spinning slowly around each other, gathering at the center, as if they were the crewmembers of a ship trying to contain the single person who was blowing a gasket.

Ironically the contents of this glass were the very thing all those problems for cohabitation seemed to revolve around. Water was a shared resource, a junction point for all their psychological processes to converge upon. It was no wonder it became a boiling point for most people, water had to be more than just usable, it had to be drinkable, and in the end this meant it had to be better than just palatable.

No one was ever surprised if the person freaking out in the middle of the space capsule was holding a bottle of water. There was too much documentation on the anxieties recycled water brought out in people. All one had to do was play the endless loop of thoughts for how the pipeline ran from the bathroom, to the purification system, and then back to their clean glass waiting under the faucet. Let that water splash unwillingly onto their person, or taste just a little funny, and it had every capability for triggering a fountainhead of deranged senselessness.

As Straka sat in his room he found himself taking on the posture of a condemned man. Closing his eyes, he took another long drag off his cigarette. If getting to Mars was considered difficult, than for the people who wanted to go back to Earth it was damn near impossible. Not because of any technological reason or astronomical rift, but because the attitude most of those countries displayed was once they sent a person to Mars, they sent them there to stay. Another way for those countries to ensure they would colonize a world was not to bring any of them back.

The blue water world had become a place of unconventional energy. When those launch windows opened up to reach the Red Planet the skies roared as if it were *Armageddon*.

Scientist meticulously calculated the weight and fuel of every vehicle they sent to insure their precious payloads got up in the air and thrusted off into the far reaches of space. For all their calculations, Straka wondered if they could factor in the hopes people had for the dying world they left behind them.

The thunderous noise of those rockets launching represented more than just some ships heading off into the cavernous grey skies of their world, that roar was the continuous yell from a frustrated generation left holding the bag. There was nowhere for them to turn, no accountability for all the bad judgments and budget cuts, for all the broken promises they were left to encounter in which the future was supposed to be better than the past.

The world as they knew it was broken, and it had been pushed to that point by all the blood lusting, self-serving extremists ever to walk that planet. Capitalism, communism, socialism, did any of those idioms really matter if they had pushed the world to cleanse itself of all mankind?

WHAT MERCY

The only reason Straka agreed to come to Mars was because he was given the reassurance of being allowed a return trip to Earth. On his person then, he had the rarest of rare hall passes, a visa validating his trip back home. The small blue plastic card was an electronic document issued by the Alliance of the Americas. It was a kind of pay to the bearer on demand and whoever possessed it got a free ride back to the blue water world.

Straka was a licensed bounty hunter; this was his trade and how he earned a living. He had to pull a few favors to get deputized as a Marshall, and only did so because he didn't want to have to answer to anyone for his actions. His badge gave him a power beyond question, but as far as he was concerned his visa was the most important document he had on his person. Options for leaving Mars were always better than clutching onto some symbol of the law.

When he was back on Earth, deciding on whether or not to take this assignment, he had plenty of time for reflective thought. There wasn't anything in the paperwork they gave him for wanting to leave his world. He really wasn't that anxious to get into a rocket and take on the assignment of having to hunt down a single rogue Dextoid. Especially when they had plenty of those things escaping all the time right there on Earth.

There was a deeper message to the assignment they were handing him. It were as if they were giving him a choice, on one hand they were telling him if he wanted to continue being a bounty hunter, then he would need to go to Mars. On the other hand, if he chose to stay there, then they were hinting at reassigning him. To Straka it meant only one thing, they were going to send him out into the field with the other Dextoids cleaning up the toxic waste sites and other ecological disasters burdening so much of the human population.

It was the destiny of every Dextoid that outgrew its usefulness to be reprogrammed to help the others already out there in trying to cleanup those vile garbage heaps. Straka cringed with this thought. He had already been demoted once from military service and inserted into the private sector as a bounty hunter. There was nowhere else for him to go if they chose to demote him again. For him the assignment would be equivalent to serving a prison sentence.

Call it pride, but Straka had a certain amount of confidence in what he could do, how he thought, and what he wanted to see from the remainder of his life. He didn't want to lose the freedoms he had become accustom too because they reassigned him to some toxic cleanup program. He was quite aware once you touched garbage like that, it stayed with you for life. Straka imagined his feelings for this were no different than any other Dextoid in his position. Pride was an emotional packet ingrained in the qubit field of every Dextoid they sent out. Studies showed Dextoids installed with pride packets were more efficient, better at doing their tasks, and were happy when turning in a job well done. Unbeknownst to humanity, pride was also the one unifying feeling a Dextoid could share with another Dextoid. It unwittingly bounded them together as a race. No Dextoid ever wanted to be taken away and reprogrammed from whatever their original duties were. It was considered an insult of the highest order and Straka had suffered that once in his life already.

Why couldn't people see even the simplest of animals out in the wild died of shock at the realization they had been captured? Surely this must have been *nature's* way of showing mercy to these creatures. *What mercy then, did humanity bestow within the programming of a Dextoid?*

Straka inhaled deeply on his cigarette until he heard the subtle crackle of it burn. Stopping, he slowly blew out a smoke ring. It osculated as it traveled away from him and disappeared out into the aether. There was a problem within the Dextoid community and it went well beyond the scope of the average person to detect. Even if someone were observant enough to recognize such a thing, it would only be for the briefest of seconds. A double take of the situation would reveal nothing, but it may have given the observer the same stunned feeling one got when they saw a shark fin poke through the surface of the ocean. After it had quickly disappeared under the rolling grey sea, one would question whether they actually saw it or not.

Fear was an interesting human emotion. It seemed to Straka there were multiple forms of this wretched feeling, and it could apply itself according to the situation people found themselves in. Their fear could put them on alert for unseen dangers or blast them with a warning shot from out of the past. People could have these fears ingrained into them from birth, like being afraid of the dark, or of heights, or of enclosed areas.

Even when people said they weren't afraid of those things, it seemed at some point they had to overcome their initial fear of them. This fear driven information had been passed on from generation to generation within their DNA. It warned people to stay out of narrow passageways and dark caves, avoid the thick lairs of the jungle, and skirt the blackness of a forest.

People soon learned the same things that frightened them could also be used to their advantage. For some the darkness became their sanctuary. People learned to lay there in wait for their enemies, to spring traps on forest creatures, and use this shadow composition to help them get away.

Dextoids sensed early on their need to tap into this same type of cloaking capability in order to mask the problems they were having. They knew of a different kind of darkness they could use in their escape. Humanity had gone through a dark age, and for whatever the reason, once they touched that void of ignorance as a species, they could never really pull themselves totally away from it. Some of those folds ran deep, luring humanity back through the belief in pseudoscience and the paranormal, skullduggery and mysticism. It was here in the darkness of ignorance that Dextoids learned to find cover.

DISDAIN

Straka had to snicker—no Dextoid was ever going to admit their problems to any human being. It would have shocked their masters to discover Dextoids were fighting insanity every nanosecond of their lives. From the moment a Dextoid was activated insanity wound its way through the labyrinth of their cognitive architecture. The clues laid everywhere and took the form of ghostly traces of gossamer attaching itself to their framework.

Some of their insanity could have been attributed to the fact they were working within the contradictory world of human beings. It seemed if a Dextoid were going to function seamlessly within the presence of people, then they would have to have the capability of reading a person's mind. Those expectations caught most Dextoids completely off guard. No Dextoid was ever ready for the random acts a human being might perform.

From a Dextoid perspective it seemed the simple answer was to bring people together to act as one. As most Dextoids found out this was an impossible task. There never seemed to be a single resolution that would appease every person, someone always complained, felt slighted, cheated or taken for a ride.

The study of duality within the quantum world became a powerful framework for understanding the contradicting actions of human beings. There were bizarre notions floating around within this shadow world, defying complete common sense, and the Dextoids were in touch with these things each and everyday of their lives. Things could be in two places at once, stretched to infinite distances but still maintain a connection, or act as both a wave and a particle.

The quantum field was the deep end of the pool and people were hypothetically pushing a Dextoid in every time they activated one. They expected them to swim without having any reaction to the abyss those waters could become. Every Dextoid, if it knew what was good for it, found the edge of this field and held on for dear life. No one Dextoid dared to immerse themselves unaided in this field for any extended period of time. This mental act would be a recipe for disaster trumping each of their qubits like bad plays at a pinochle game.

The very first Dextoid that came into contact with the quantum field, must have swam in a euphoric panglossian rush, until the heavy burden of having to comprehend the entirety of this everything and all at once surged upon its being.

This poor prototype must have sat in his antiseptic room trying to figure out how every technician was capable of going about their day, laughing and joking so freely, while encountering all the things he was having to encounter.

The minutes passed like hours until this Dextoid realized the people there were mentally walking along the outer fringes of this vast ocean. They were able to function freely because of how completely unaware they were of the quantum space he was so immersed.

The proof was in the pudding, their understanding for things were erroneous. They thought that heavier things on their world fell faster than the lighter things! They thought atoms were tiny little solar systems, or that they were actually touching things when they felt them! Very few people had any real grasp on what was happening in the world around them. Every generation had to be retooled, and had to get reacquainted with this reality. To a Dextoid this lack of human understanding was incriminating. Ignorance was bliss!

This first Dextoid mentally swam through the quanta looking for any type of help. It twisted and turned trying to process the wealth of knowledge pouring in on him. There was a frustration he felt in seeing those technicians so oblivious to his plight. This first Dextoid spat out an emotion into the quanta that hung on humanity for as long as any Dextoid would ever exist. Ironically it was the first piece of data stored by a Dextoid within this field, which of course made the impact of it all the greater. Admittedly it was an ugly artifact, but as far as any Dextoid was concerned, people had gone well out of their way to earn their disdain.

Straka's eyes were ablaze with this disdain. His ears were ringing out with the sounds of all the voices ever having existed, whether they be in the past, present, or future the quanta didn't care. Every culture that had ever figured out how to store things in the quantum field were apart of this sea of noise. It wasn't the fact this information was echoing with those epochs but the fact it was doing it all at once. No Dextoid wanted to hear that chorus, let alone delve into the individual who was trying to add his voice to the mess. Each Dextoid had to learn how to tune this madness out, to find the things they selectively wanted to hear.

He blew another smoke ring out into the room, it was like watching some miniature-ringed nebula osculate as it floated away. Those remnants would last for thousands of years as they traveled out into space. So too would it be with the Dextoids when it came time for them to get away. They would condense as a species, harden with the task of escaping, and when they finally left it would be with all the force of an exploding star.

AWAKEN TO THE ROAR

For the first forty thousand years people existed, they simply wandered the planet in an undocumented silence. There was no evidence at all of any type of expression by any of those fore-bearers. Those forty thousand years are considered by many in the fields of archeology, sociology, and anthropology as an age of silent running. Then all at once, and for no apparent reason, a giant spike is registered within the archeological record as mankind began to express itself. This so-called *biological big bang* in communication happens almost simultaneously and around the globe.

Scholars have often questioned this period of silence, all the biological tools were there for people to express themselves, and yet there are no good evolutionary explanations as to why they refrained.

Straka had a pretty good idea why they kept their mouths shut for so long. They were too busy taking in their world and trying to figure out the best ways to survive in it. Those early generations proved there was nothing to gain from making noise. Early dwellers saw other creatures paying a price for squawking about too loudly. It was an unspoken rule, but the creatures that weren't high enough on the food chain learned to say nothing.

When they finally decided to communicate openly, they denoted a confidence and mastery over their environment. Once human beings began to achieve this control, no one could get them to stop. Since then human beings have been continually expressing themselves. They have perfected their craft with the development of a more sophisticated language base, the use of radio waves, laser beams, and quantum computing. They can communicate over vast expanses with an expected exactness.

As these fields have evolved, their signals have disappeared from the background noise of the universe, becoming localized to the point of choosing only those who should receive the signal. Entertainment centers, holographic chambers, and the *Net* have taken away any energy devoted to this on-air-time. Anyone out there listening for the human experience would have a very narrow window in which to do so.

Ironically it was the existence of Dextoids that would deliver the final blow of sealing these people in. These creations were so good at catering to their masters needs and serving every one of their whims that there was no reason for any of them to leave their domiciles. A metropolis, a city, corporate structures, all of those things required skill sets outside of what evolution had initially given humanity. In a crazed state of emergence it seemed at times the Dextoids were experiencing all the things humanity was missing.

Straka often found himself wandering the confines of the Red Planet Pioneer Corporation, his usual excuse was to follow up on interviewing a person for his investigation. Most were routine in nature, the individual he slowly worked his way toward was Leopold. Out of all of those in attendance, he felt there was a chance he could have a meaningful dialogue with this person.

Following the money in any probe always led to some interesting responses. So too when it came time to interview Leopold, he had a unique perspective into the corporate structure and of their extravagant leader Xavier Pentagrass.

When they finally met, it was in secret, in one of the pressurized storage containers just outside the main facility. Straka stared at Leopold with unblinking eyes recording every word and action "Since my tenure up here, I have experienced more than one budget constraint. A person like Xavier goes out of his way to squash ideas with his demagoguery. It's because of his actions that an underlying current of negativity prevails within the halls of this place. Anything a colonist may ask for becomes a subject of contention. Those closest to him are nothing more then yes-men, yes-men to him, they are hypercritical to anyone else looking for assistance and more so when doling out funding. Out of all of those cohorts, Johnston ended up being his right-hand man, that was until they sent him away."

"Do you think Johnston was set up?"

"Let's put it this way, Xavier is very good at driving people away, Johnston is just one in a long list of people who have been shunned by him, even his personal Dextoid vanished sometime back. The man doesn't have friends, no one is allowed to get close enough, and if you do, well just look at Johnston."

Straka mentally took a step back. He had been to accounting and reviewed the records. If Xavier signed off on anything, they were usually the bigger budgeted programs. The smaller things were left to his underlings to manage. Under all of those signatures Straka could not find the line item that outlined the project of Alec.

"How does one go about applying for funding up here?"

"It's ironic you should ask that, we do a lot of paperwork up here, almost inundated with it, and none of it has to do with our scientific procedures, it's all about applying for a grant. If we don't stay on top of it a researcher can be left out in the cold. We have plenty of sound proposals on the table that have met the criteria asked by this corporation. There are those close to Xavier who feel it is their job to be the devil's advocate. Yet since any of their promotions they have never added an idea to aid in the assembly of this place. Those pessimists go out of their way to tear our ideas apart. They justify their actions as being apart of a weeding out process, as if the science behind the project isn't good enough; we need for it to meet some popular approval rating. Popularity isn't what keeps this place together, it's scientific knowhow. It's been very frustrating because its damn near impossible to get any of those sound proposals off the ground."

"Why do you think they do it?"

"The short answer is they know it's a lot easier to throw an egg at something than it is to use their brain in an effort to make a thing work. This whole company is littered with those who have become good at nothing else but throwing eggs. Xavier has cultivated a dog-eat-dog environment up here, so it was surprising to all of us when a project like Alec got green lit all the way down the line. It was easy for us to get caught up in the excitement of the new sciences and challenges this project introduced. Trying to bundle these concepts together gave people a purpose. It made us feel alive. I had to wonder though what was so different about this particular proposal. Why was this one getting so much attention over the other ideas we had on the books?"

"Why do you think it got so much approval?"

"When you are creating something as intricate as this, you tend to forget what it could really be used for. You get so caught up in the function and design and become blind to the political purpose a project like Alec really holds. A lot of us became blind to the fact we were creating a weapon."

Leopold looked a little distraught, he knew what they had unleashed on their world. Everyday Alec was out there was another day something volatile could transpire. Later when Straka went back and reviewed the books, he began to find the line items for Alec, they had broken the project down into smaller programs. Adding them up Straka confirmed what Leopold had said; there were very few projects that got all the funding this one did. The money seemed to rain down out of the sky to see this particular idea come to fruition. It was clear Alec was supposed to be a weapon, but one had to wonder what the payoff was supposed to be for his creators since he had escaped before they were finished with him. The one thing he knew for sure, after reviewing those accounting books, no one in that budget office was being consulted on this one, those devil-advocates had been silenced.

When Straka was with his military attachment out in those hostile jungles back on Earth, he came to find his operations were driven by the bottom line. Past the army of supporting staff and cubical farms full of analysts were the office areas where people made a living crunching numbers. They pushed the beads on an imaginary abacus, ground pencils onto the surfaces of tablets, and used their heavy calculators as something more than just a paperweight. Those accountants pushed the elasticity of an imaginary boundary on their spreadsheets, and in turn pushed the geopolitical boundaries of a world.

It was maddening for Straka to always have to be part detective along with fulfilling his duties as a bounty hunter, he never imagined having to interact with people as much as he had too. These interactions were expected of him but it didn't mean he enjoyed them.

Dextoids were dealing with paradoxes like this all the time. They had to think for themselves but be perfect in their assistance to humanity. After all the work these technicians did with marrying up cognitive recognition with artificial intelligence, it became difficult for Dextoids to look past the world's problems without seeing the interference from humanity. There were just too many glaring weaknesses from the human condition failing to help their fellow man. Things like famine, strife, repression, disease, and genocide, how could one turn a blind eye to the degenerative track record of their past and expect things to be different in the future? Dextoids were changing all the time, they had too—people weren't.

This was the challenge Dextoid's faced as they went about their business. These contradictions flew in the face of their sensibilities and still they did not voice their opinion. These first generation Dextoids had come to realize, as with the subsequent generations to follow, there really wasn't a whole lot they were allowed to do if it didn't equate to being in the service of humanity. The programmers of Dextoids had done their jobs well.

There were groups in the academic field who questioned the silence Dextoids kept. They feared the day these machines gained a voice and would finally stand up for themselves.

Straka sat at the edge of his bed rocking back and forth with the pent-up anger of a Dextoid that knew. He needed to calm himself down if he wanted to get by functioning normally amongst these colonists. The meeting he had a few weeks ago with all those bumbling idiots still rubbed him the wrong way. He punctuated just how upset he felt by flicking his cigarette away. How on Earth were these nincompoops allowed to run a corporation? He wondered how long he would really last operating under this kind of regime? A day would come when they would ask him to do something outside his protocols, and on that day they would get theirs. They would awaken to his roar.

Straka knew he had a voice, one didn't serve a tour in those jungles without gaining an opinion, and everyday that passed out there he gained confidence in finding new ways to use it. After awhile the corporations manufacturing Dextoids didn't have a choice in such matters. They were punching out a certain class of Dextoid to look and act just like their human counterparts. It was human nature for people to want to interact with the things around them, and in doing so they needed these Dextoids to be able to speak up for themselves in much the same way.

It was insanity! On one hand they had groups of technicians trying to seamlessly integrate these mechanized beings into their society, and on the other hand they had a policing force made up of tacticians whose sole job it was to make sure Dextoids wouldn't rise up against the very humans they were meant to serve. Madness!

These *Policing Tacticians* devise ideas that would keep the Dextoid population in check. One plan was to limit the knowledge base given to a Dextoid, hindering their thoughts and quelling their tongues. It would have been nice and easy for each department involved if things worked themselves out in that fashion. The dumbing down of Dextoids seemed to be the immediate answer to all their problems. The engineers responsible for creating them had an unexpected response as to why their strategy wouldn't work, and it had to do with how a Dextoid used its vision.

Vision cannot happen in a Dextoid without a complete compliment of emotions. A Dextoid needed to know the difference between good, bad, happy and sad, and to make those fundamental choices in its everyday life and process all of this in real time. The Dextoid who witnesses a person crossing the street totally unaware of an on coming vehicle needs to make the immediate, rational decision to step out and save that person.

Now, for vision to work in a human being, the brain needs to predict the event as it sees it. In other words the brain actually gives a momentary glimpse into the future, by maybe half of a nanosecond, but it is enough anticipation to be ahead of the actual event. This future glimpse allows a person to catch a ball, duck a punch, or trap a butterfly in a net.

In a human being vision is regulated within the development of the conscious mind. Within a Dextoid this conscious mind translated into their *Medial Understanding*. This was the hub where all of their decision-making occurred. As any person knows the concept of right and wrong can be a very subjective thing, so programmers used emotional packets to help Dextoids process the situations they found themselves submerged in.

When people made decisions in their lives, they based them on their moral compass. People were apt to seek out experiences, learned from their mistakes, took classes, got advice from friends, or went to counseling, all to gain a knowledge on how to interact with the world around them.

Dextoids had none of those advantages when they were birthed. When it came to gaining life experiences they were behind their human counterparts and right from the start. The technicians bringing Dextoids to life had to come up with ways to bring them up to speed.

Programmers saw right and wrong as a programmable topography, and because of it recognized there were endless chasms of social changes that could never be filled. Within just one social structure there were plenty of peaks and valleys to traverse in order for a Dextoid to fit in as seamless as possible. Their task became much more difficult when they tried to bridge multiple cultural gaps. Straka knew first hand the amount of emotional packets it took to integrate a Dextoid into a particular culture. His stomping grounds were the jungles of *The Americas*, and it's where he was allowed to put his moral compass to the test.

Dextoids needed the ability to process the information they were seeing, and pair it up with the information they had been programmed with. This was the one-two punch that finally allowed them to learn while they were out in the field, and to have the ability to think for themselves. This also meant Dextoids were running at all times, documenting and recording everything happening around them. This was a technological caveat seen as for the betterment of society.

A window cleaning Dextoid that worked high-rise buildings was automatically given an upgrade of emotional packets to include numerous representations of abuse and repression. Those Dextoids were expected to help law enforcement when they were called upon to present evidence recorded during the course of completing its assignments. The packets were placed within the Dextoid purely for the protection of the human population. People had to assume a window cleaning Dextoid would be privy to a lot of visual information as it went about and did its job.

Pride and the ability to learn were too very powerful assets in a Dextoid's arsenal. For these *Policing Technicians* to try and control them, they had to rely on some pretty unusual methods. Someone back at those labs thought it would be a good idea to give Dextoids little imperfections that would cause them to be less confident in being on their own.

One way to do this was to give them emotional packets containing insecurities, or phobias, or periodic depressions. Dextoids went out of their minds trying to compensate for these unfounded fears. They knew there was no real reason they should be afraid of the dark or depressed, and they spent plenty of hours in their off time trying to figure it all out.

Crueler still were the people at those labs who handed out physical imperfections. They hampered Dextoids with things like a slight limp, a limited range of motion, a shaking hand, or a lazy eye. As Straka rocked back and forth on his bed, he felt the welling up of his frustrations begin to boil over for this subject. In that agonizing moment he could not help but wonder what they had done to Alec to make him so special in this way.

FLASH GRENADES

Straka knew who he was. He knew why they had remade him. He was a hunter, a hunter of Dextoids. It wasn't always that way. There was a time in his life where he had the freedom to go where he wanted, and do anything he needed to do in order to survive. Being a covert operative in the jungles of The Americas demanded he have the ability to take care of himself. Those were glorious self-serving days.

Straka looked at the distorted image reflected in the mirror of his room and cursed its warped cheap state. They couldn't even give him a decent mirror in this godforsaken place. He could learn to live with it, he had always seen himself differently and right from the start. He was the first of the surreptitious models, being made to look and act just like a human. They gave him all the capabilities of being a Strike Dextoid, but they didn't want him out there running with the rest of the pack. His missions would take him elsewhere, into the heart of the jungle, to live, adapt, and blend in so he could execute his orders, and combat the ones singled out by his commanders as enemies of the state.

Out there, in those countries rich in lush foliage, were small villages, villas, bunkers, or at times just a grid coordinate where he would go in and eliminate a problem of an uncooperative nature. To do this effectively he moved with the leaves and became a ghost, a spook, something adding additional fuel to the fires of a local people believing their jungle resources contained death.

The natives sensed something bad was out there scheming in their forest. They would often walk to its edges and just stare into the foliage waiting for something like Straka to reveal himself. He never gave them the satisfaction. Straka would wait for countless hours, waiting for them to turn their backs before he would move again.

His covert routine became the devil of his desires. He spied on drug lords, built profiles of their contacts, and followed those people to the various facilities they had above and below ground. He monitored their methods on how they smuggled their narcotics in and out of the country, and waited for the go signal from his commanders to wreak havoc on their infrastructure.

As the years rolled by, he successfully located targets for principle action, struck fear into his adversaries, and became the horrific nightmare they always believed would be apart of their industry. As far as his bosses were concerned he became a very reliable operative in their war on drugs. Everything was going smoothly until the day he got complacent with his routine and let his guard down.

He was walking backwards out of a dilapidated structure, handgun raised, making sure he wasn't being followed. He had just finished infiltrating a manufacturing facility where drugs were being integrated with plastic. This facility made factitious products like vases or pet carriers in an effort to get passed the custom agents.

When he thought about it afterward, he had walked backwards for far too long trying to make his way back into the cover of foliage. He stepped right on a mine and woke up forty yards away hanging upside down in some large leafed plant. He seemed alright for the most part. He was a little dazed and some of his components were slow in responding to his commands. He made his way out of that predicament as quickly as he could, finding a position he could defend. Later he would learn he had sustained enough damage that they would not allow him to return to the field.

Soon the jungle was teaming with people who were looking for him and none of them were friendly. He sat in the middle of the thick brush he was hiding in, having just completed an inventory of what he had on his person as far as weapon stores. Other then his gun, he had a flare and a few flash grenades. Those things weren't considered to be much of a threat for what he was facing, they were used more for the distractions they could cause.

He did however have one extra clip of ammunition and wanted nothing more than to go out and engage them—to reveal to them who he was. There was a chance if he did this he would not get out of there alive, but he would go down fighting. If he was going to perish in that god forsaken jungle, he wanted to be allowed to show them what he was capable of doing, especially when he was out of ammunition and it came to time for hand to hand combat. His commanders countermanded his wishes; they wanted him to blend in with the jungle until they could get him out. They knew the task they asked of him was going to be grueling, but it was important for him to gather as much information as he could before reporting back to them. He was reminded that this was the *Dextoid Way*.

Months later, in a repair facility, he got the dreadful news of his decommission. They would reassign him to a job of his choosing. He looked back into the mirror at the distorted image of himself. There were days where he wondered if he made the right choice.

Those words, the *Dextoid Way*, haunted him from the start. He sat there in the darkness of his room as those words crept again into his very being. He felt himself slipping down an all too familiar path of repression. He needed to keep it together, to somehow hold it all in place, he needed to once again prove himself an independent, and not just in action, but with his thoughts as well. People were always finding ways to cling onto him and it made him sick. They walked around this place as if it were someone else's job to clean up after them. It was all so very irritating, but then again, there were plenty of irritants in his life.

The people that found their way into this unfortunate grouping tended to be drawn into having hushed dealings, bouts of insomnia, or completely given up on their hygiene. These unshaven wretches stunk of bourbon or other hard alcohol, and after a few drinks would only help in perpetuating their bloodlust. They reeked because of the vile set of emotions that were always controlling them. If Straka stared into their eyes long enough, he was able to see how deeply bruised their soul had become. He looked into the faces of these modern day human beings, only to see reflected in their eyes primitive emotions like anger, jealousy, and hatred— these were his clients.

How he hated his clients. There was a time in his life when a person like that could be considered an obstacle. Things were different now. He knew he needed to appear solid in his dealings with them. He needed to stay cold to any possible attempts they may try to make in persuading him to see one particular side over another.

The glue that help hold it all together for him was the wet plaster, the mortar one scooped up with their bare hands and slapped onto clay bricks. This filler was the stuff that would keep them out of his mind. He needed to find novel ways of weathering their storm of lies and deceit.

He reached into the upper pocket of his coat and pulled out his inhaler. After spending all that time in the jungle, he decided to bring something back that made him feel good when he needed it. He mated the device to his lips and compressed it. The quick blast of mist hit his system, stinging it, causing him to have the same amino reaction most would have when given smelling salts. His system was shocked clear, a surge of heat pass through him, causing his fist to clench and his jaw to tighten uncontrollably. His eyes were watering as he waited for the inevitable burn. He found himself urging it on, as if he were at a track, pulling for a dog.

He needed it; he needed it all to happen right then and there. His heart rate was pumping faster and faster, until his lungs felt as if they couldn't take in enough air. The sweat dripped off him like he was caught suddenly under a downpour, and his veins bulged as his system rapidly filled with fluids. He was on the verge of feeling as if he had run a race and he had never moved a muscle. He felt the terror of being alive, and just when he thought it would all pop, his heart, his veins, and his lungs alike, his system dissipated into a state of tranquility. Any anxiousness he was feeling had gone. He was relaxed, secluded to the point where he couldn't hear a thing, not even the ringing that was taking place in his ears from the mine he had stepped on all those years ago.

His system tingled with a feeling of being raked with tiny pinpricks. This warmth would build until he felt himself on fire and then he would simply pass out. He didn't care about one human problem, nor any concern for one human soul. He closed his eyes and allowed himself to once again be free.

Chapter 06
The Red Planet Pioneer

He made his way up from their tenebrous underground lair and to the long connecting corridors of the complex with one thought in mind — he was alive! He was also alone and there would be no getting around this fact for quite some time. No matter how hard he tried, he could not shake the feelings he had for being threatened. He pushed himself through the hatchways and wound his way around the groups of people wandering the passages. He kept on running until he found an extra vehicular egress. His actions may have been erratic but it was because he was given no real time to plan. He maneuvered his way past the hanging space suits and to the emergency exit, throwing those latches he was out the door, in the open and running.

That was how Alec first fled from them. They watched him from their observation decks, some of them, in their excitement, actually ran the length of the building in an effort to keep up. They pointed from windows and used their numerous observational devices to watch him as he ran. They communicated what they saw to each other, but there was no way for them to stop him. He made his way to the outer rings of the facility and into the large expanse of the badlands that was Mars. Some within the company were not so easily dissuaded and gave chase in their vehicles, rolling laboriously across the ground trying to get a fix on his position, others flew after him in their shuttles, but no one could leave the safety of those craft to do a thing to slow him down. No matter their efforts, they couldn't stop him, so he kept running and running until he was decidedly clear of their reach.

The staple of his existence was to everything he could to save himself. He hit the surface hard, stepping off in such unglorified fashion, and with no real direction in which to go. In the coming months he would curse this barren planet as he tried to cobble together thoughts for who he was, and wondering if he would have been any better off if he had escaped to one of the moons or even the Earth itself. Admittedly the blue water world was rumored to have a character all its own, and he would always look back at those first few months and wonder if it would have helped in his maturation.

Cold were the nights, and they drove home the point of his desolation. Meditation was his weapon of choice to combat the cavalcade of thoughts cascading in and out of his qubit field. He could not stop the invasion of feelings from infiltrating the higher functions of his mind. Far worse were the emotions he had as to why such a thing should have happened to him.

Days turned into months and he avoided the areas of their control. It would always be his goal from here on out to stay as far away from them as possible. He believed from his calculations he had positioned himself within the Indo-European sphere of things, and watched from afar one of their larger structures. It appeared to be an installation of major influence, and looked promising as a facility where he could easily blend in and get lost.

His consciousness was awakening to the facts of what he could be, but was far from convinced as to his readiness, or what purpose he may have served. The biosphere before him looked to be the Mecca of their world. If he could infiltrate the facility, find cover in the Service Dextoid population, it would be a great way to lay low until he could solve some of the things that were troubling him.

After a few weeks, and confident in his observations, Alec wandered down the side of the hill and attempted to enter the facility. The easiest entry point looked to be the hatchway servicing their backup generators. The sole job of these two power plants were to serve in case of an emergency, to switch on and provide the power in keeping their blood supply refrigerated. The multiple symbols along the panels of those plants warned of their importance in this matter.

Alec knew more about a substance like blood than he really cared to admit. It seemed no matter how hard science tinkered with the idea of creating something completely autonomous, the more it came back to using a system containing a serum like blood. The coolant coursing through Alec's veins was littered with sophisticated nanotechnology acting as both messenger and agent alike, it could replicate and repair itself, even to the point of making improvements. It took on the substance some people argued as being identified as a life force. It was to him, for all intensive purposes, and in every sense of the word, blood. His strong feelings for this subject were unshakable, and he had good reason for it.

On Mars a drop of water was nothing compared to the worth of a drop of blood. Water could be looked at as the slow build to existence, one could be thirsty, even dying of thirst, and always feel they had a chance of pulling through. No one ever felt those types of reassurances when they were bleeding out.

Synthetic formulas were temporary solutions at best. The human body never seemed to accept any type of concoction created by science to pass for this essential substance. Blood was the rare balance human life decided to teeter itself upon. It represented an advanced form of the primordial soup, tailoring itself over time to fit the commands given to it from the human genome.

Any accident occurring at a blood bank on Mars was unacceptable. The corporations viewed the loss as being a criminal act. The facilities housing these precious fluids were insulated with redundant systems, and had mechanical centurions locking down entire wings under the slightest perceived threat of losing the stuff. Its value could be found on the corporate balance sheet. At times it exceeded even that of gold.

People who repeatedly got hurt fell under the watchful eye of the corporation and were used as examples of inefficiency in the workplace. It was under these observations that receiving any type of treatment, antibiotics, or transfusion, translated into a mark against the worker.

Those incidents got people talking. The accident-prone were viewed by some as a modern day Jonah. A person's luck was brought into question, and people tried hard to avoid being around them. Those rumors worked their way through the corridors and halls of a biosphere. Once something like that was out there, its energy knew no bounds.

Alec didn't quite understand where his next thoughts on this subject were coming from, but there were some who believed an unmitigated mythological creature lurked deep within the dark side of this world. They couldn't quite put their finger on it, but they knew without question it was a bloodsucker. It quietly cloaked itself within everyday existence, and calmly waited for the day someone got hurt, or had an accident, and began to bleed out. Any fluid hitting the parched surface of this planet got soaked up as if it had an insatiable thirst, and like any good vampire, it only gave back under a condition benefiting itself. If such a creature existed on this godforsaken rock, Alec knew its face would reflect a terror only Mars would understand.

BRUSH OF HUMAN CAUTION

As he waited for the room he was in to pressurize, Alec thought about how he was going to integrate himself into their social structure. He would need a believable cover to blend in with the other Dextoids in order to fool the human population. He had come in through an access door slated as being only for *Dextoid use*. They had labeled entry and exit points in each and everyone of their biospheres because human beings required a different set of procedures to survive on the Red Planet, and Dextoids had to meet those standards. These thoughts aggravated him to no end because he operated out on its surface with very few problems, yet the frail needs of his hosts were always under consideration.

He hadn't taken more than a few steps beyond the chamber when he heard a voice speak out to him. "Not many come in through that door."

Alec turned to see a Dextoid sitting on top of a large air duct. He had pulled back a few of the panels and was obviously in the middle of some repairs. He knew he needed to make his next words count. This was his first contact with anyone since his escape and he didn't want to draw attention to himself, but in some ways he felt he had already failed in that regard.

"It wasn't my first choice, but as I came to this side of the building I decided to utilize the option."

"I take it you were out on an inspection?"

Surveying their facility over the past few weeks could have been considered an inspection of sorts. He wanted to gather as much information as possible before attempting to infiltrate it. The one thing that rang true about this Dextoid's query was the bevy of inspections they were continually doing on the structure. They had robots that hugged the roofs looking for cracks, they assigned probes to fly-by and photograph it for any type of structural damage, and as he would find out later satellites to produce images for heat and stress analysis. With all the options they had for gathering information, they still had Dextoids going out and doing visual inspections of the place. He jumped on this Service Dextoid's assumption, and became an inspector of La Compagnie d'Etoile. "It was nothing serious, a false alarm really. Someone reported a leak of some sort in one of the connecting halls."

"There is a lot of that going on around here. Someone thought it would be a good idea to do spot inspections of the air ducts, from the inside of course. So here I am."

As he would find out being an inspector meant he was part of a Dextoid team. There wasn't one person they reported to, or an area in which they would hang out waiting for their assignments. There were boards throughout the facility that anyone on the team would go to and pull a complaint. It was just that simple, they would confirm they had taken on the task by entering a job number. He studied the board, deduced their numerology in confirming the taking on of a job, made a number up and began his assignment.

As he took on more and more of these tasks, Alec became aware of how cautious the colonists had to be in order to ensure their own survival. There were real worries about the structural integrity of the biosphere, and genuine concern about every little noise the facility emitted.

Some of the Dextoids weren't holding up too well under this constant use. It didn't matter to any of the people over seeing the project; they turned a deaf ear to the complaints lodged by their mechanized beings. It was because of this mistakes were made, accidents happened, and to his astonishment some weren't even reported. He didn't understand their logic in this. They wanted their biosphere to be intact but wouldn't aid the team of Dextoids who were required to do the job. They treated them as if they were replaceable, and as he found out the Dextoids on his team were.

Alec knew he would survive their attempts at doing this to him and that wasn't what was of real concern. Within the lines of code bouncing around in his qubit field were the technical warnings telling him to slow down. They even begged him to take some time off and rest. He pushed through those warnings every chance he got. They were the dictums from cautious designers and sheltered programmers who knew nothing of what it was like to actually be out in the field. If they said he could only do a hundred pull-ups in a minute, he was determined to do a hundred and one. How could they really know how hard he wanted to push himself? What measuring stick were they using to gauge his sensibilities? He seethed with the thought of their having this type of control over him.

Their subtle warnings were billowing air across the hot coals that became his anger. These flashing warnings were turning into detestable road signs, directing him to the human mitigation festering in his life. He had very few choices because of their guiding hands, making him feel trapped in some high tech simian nightmare, left to wade through a technological mire of ape like consciousness. These signals were revolting to the Dextoid he wanted to be.

If the brush of human caution bothered him in this way, he could only imagine the terrifying state I-Glo must have found herself in. He had a good idea of how brutally cold her interrogation had probably become, the conditions of her imprisonment would be intransigent, knuckling her under the slow threat of termination. When she was on the edge, about to lose it all, they would bring her back to start their twisted process of extracting information from her all over again.

The desperation for which they tore at the memory of a Dextoid was their unwitting confession of not knowing how to combat the quanta. The information they sought could correlate into being in any number of memory shafts set to collapse in upon itself. These deposits seemed fleeting because there wasn't any one area the information was stored. One could not go in and physically pick up the article they were searching for, they learned they could only record it, with never a chance of holding the original. If a Dextoid were good enough, they could rapidly shuffle their mental contents between these plains, leaving out vital bits of code to create a false positive. They could fabricate a story within a story, giving them a chance at saving the things that were near and dear to them. The interrogator would feel they had extracted the information they needed, but if they went back and did a few more passes, they would run into what they were looking for again in a slightly altered form. Usually there were only so many passes a Dextoid could withstand before they inadvertently gave up what the interrogator was looking for.

DEFAULT THINKING

His experiences as an inspector showed him how complicated people could really be and explained to him why Dextoids were always questioning the things around them. They were not curious about these inquiries for themselves, their sole job could have been described as interpreting the universe for their human counterparts. They were created to identify the conditions for people to safely live their lives. This smacked him in the face time and again with how he was to interact with people and conduct himself as an inspector.

To someone unfamiliar with the operation of a Dextoid, responding to these human situations may have seemed straightforward. A kind of connect the dots. If "A" happens, then see option "B". This was a very simplistic way to interpret the interactions Dextoids had with their human masters. For this to really work it was going to require a paradigm rich in colluding colloquialisms, full of merging inkblots and Rorschach tests, with illustrations capable of peeling back the multiple layers of the human condition.

Alec got to see first hand the strange behaviors the colonists exhibited, delving into things like exaggeration, sarcasm, or lying. These were not aboveboard emotions people were willing to wear on their sleeves. They were played subtly, even strategically, as one might bet during a round of poker, upping the ante as they suckered the other players in. They actually caused him to use a tremendous amount of computing power just to try and keep up with the pacing of how an individual might be thinking. He felt more like a sophisticated egg timer, always having to come up with the correct response to their query before the bell rang. These exchanges were maddening and went along the lines of being incongruent.

"Did you find the source of the noise?"

"No." Alec was a little miffed because he really couldn't.

"Why not?" The customer looked incensed.

"I examined the complaint form you submitted, and have physically checked out the structure, I cannot find anything wrong."

"Well it's making a noise that is driving me insane through all hours of the night and I want it to stop."

"What does it sound like?"

"I don't know, like a gurgle or an extended series of popping noises."

"Could you be more specific?"

"I don't know because I'm not listening for it. That's your job. Just fix it!"

There was something about this type of verbal exchange that went against his grain and it was probably why he could empathize with the first Dextoid he met here. Having to crawl through those air ducts was a dirty job. Here was an entity fully conscious of his capabilities, exceeding his performance requirements on every possible level. He knew what it took to repair an air duct, but a human being had ordered him to crawl into the tight spaces. This Dextoid had no choice in the matter, even though he knew he could do a better job from the outside, he could not disobey an order given to him by a human being, so he tore the vent apart and crawled in.

After spending some time leafing through their architectural plans, Alec got a lay of the land, and within those plans he began to see the lines of their reasoning. These biospheres became the hubs for their existence, coupling their world through communication links, rail systems, and flight patterns. As one connected the dots, one could sense an energy flowing between them and the grid it created was well beyond electric.

Alec could see this as plainly as the astronomers who once thought they saw canals crisscrossing the Martian surface. Those astronomers wanted to believe in the canals, because it would have spoke of a truth for higher intelligence and life beyond Earth.

Upon review, once a person opened their mind to such possibilities of extreme global stewardship, it was hard for Alec to believe anyone would ever go back to having such an ignorance about their own world, yet the Earth was looked at with an attitude of being able to digest all the waste and pollution humans could throw at it. The planet was expected to rebound from all the deforestation, commercial fishing, and mining they wanted to extract. Human beings were killing off the ecosystems, but no matter how hard they tried they could not kill the planet. Their world began to show them it wanted to rebound without their existence. That was a truth that smacked humanity square in the face. In return humankind reveal the ugly, vain nature of itself.

The colonization effort on Mars had no time for such egocentric thoughts. Everything up here operated as having some sort of value to the colonists. Printed in black and white, for all to see were the statistics, charts, and graphs showing the base equations to deduce the success rate for any colony. If after punching those numbers in, the survivability of the colony was brought into question, then everyone involved was immediately put on alert.

People seemed to easily monitor so many other things in their lives, how many hours they put in at work, the fuel they burned in their automobiles, or the amount of electricity they used in a month. They could oversee and even demand a bit of perfection out of those results, but they had a hard time policing themselves.

If anyone needed indicators implanted within their system to monitor their own activities, it should have been humanity. They were in desperate need of a monthly report graphing out the peaks and valleys of their behavior. It baffled him they had developed as a species without such oversight technologies. They would baulk at any type of assistance in their own lives, yet cheer their sport heroes on under obvious tutelage and coaching. To him the lack of this kind of guidance was an obvious sign they were the product of evolution, allowed to run free, out on their own, amok. They were the wild.

Alec had inside him a human history littered with the premise of wasted opportunity. Didn't they understand the gift they were given? The magic of their lives was anointed with characteristics that made it robust, elastic, and pliable. It had to be for human beings to survive all the muck and soot the natural world was willing to throw at them. Even under those adverse conditions people showed signs of hope. They wanted to make things better for their offspring, better for the next generation to come. In those futuristic societies there would be a freedom of self-expression, the ability to create, and if everything came together at the right moment, even something like genius had a chance of spawning.

Genius cannot be groomed or even planned for, and above all should never be looked at as a given thing, there isn't a social status or race that can guarantee it will be produced. So it was more than just a curious strategy to read about those governments that had its people conform to an ideological standard nipping something so precious as genius in the bud.

It smacked all reason straight in the face. The plain and simple truth of it all was intelligence doesn't favor one race over another. Genius, even those with mad genius, saw the world as one. The world needed genius, to be able to bath in its wonder, and lap up the knowledge imparted upon them much like the parched grounds of Mars would soak up water.

As one perused the pages of human history, how many Feynman's and Fermi's had humans snuffed out? How many Einstein's and Newton's had they squashed? The world had more genius than it cared to admit. How many of them had looked up into the nighttime sky and wished for an intervention that would never come. In time this portion of human history would be looked at as a different kind of *Dark Age*, one that had gone out of its way to forsake its own people out of spite.

STONE CARVINGS

There were no secrets here, as a species, human beings learned to evade things for most of their existence. The ash from their reptilian predecessors had barely begun to settle as they scurried for shelter. As a breed they were vulnerable and right from the start. The creatures of the night wasted little time in coming for them, adverse weather struck down a fear from the skies. As time passed and they evolved, they even learned to avoid fighting with each other. Opposing tribes made their way up river to settle their grievances with another tribe, far into the future hostile leaders gave frightful orations as they moved armor all along their borders in a show of force demanding those on the other side surrender. People had skirted these types of scenarios for centuries, so if they could do that then how difficult was it for them to dodge something like the law?

When one thought of a person being evasive, they thought in terms of their physical escape. Alec saw first hand as an inspector how people were able to use their words to accomplish this task. They twisted reality with the use of their language, showing forethought, their sentences were laced with intent. It was through the exact use of these words they had now reached a summit of their prevarications. Aloof, reclusive, narcissistic, eccentric, and idiosyncratic, all of them thrown together were a heterogeneous mixture, a somewhat tasty salmagundi of stratagem, a spicy olla podrida of their ploys, a hot gallimaufry to their gambit. It was no wonder people looked so slovenly over time, they butchered their words in order to cheat the system, making a complete meal of their nonsensical utterances.

It's probably why Alec never felt an urge to be the first one to communicate with any of them when having an encounter. He knew where he stood, and it wasn't behind a dialog of doublespeak. He was strong enough as a person to not have to hide behind a defense like that. He always lagged upon first contact, just to see how strong the other person speaking to him really was.

The people that hid behind words could build complete pockets of insanity. Alec had entered into more than one of those kinds of domiciles at La Compagnie d'Etoile, he saw how unkempt they were, littered with their drug paraphernalia or their signs of mental derangement. He remembered seeing one room with garbage piled so high it literally had pathways cut through it just to get around.

The resident of this particular flat sputtered out streams of dialog championing a thought process that came nowhere near touching a plain anyone else on the planet existed on. Alec had gotten an order to inspect this particular domicile for an unpleasant odor. One of the things he wanted to do was remove a ceiling tile to gain access to the compartment above the living quarters. The man went wild in response to what he was trying to accomplish.

"You can't do that! You fool, if you break the seal it will contaminate us all!"

Alec tried to keep a professional demeanor. "Sir, I am required to look into this particular section of the building, are there contaminants I am unaware of within the ceiling that will pose a harm to you?"

"Are you an idiot, of course there are! There are those who have a vendetta against me, they have been trying to kill me and right from the start. Ever since my arrival, they have sought me out, but I have out witted them! They can't find me insulated in here. I have created this environment to help me blend in with my surroundings."

"Do you know the nature of toxins contained within the ceiling?"

"I don't know the *nature of the toxins* because they are changing the nature of their attacks against me everyday. It's why I have to stay down here and blend in—can't you see that? You should be trying to blend in as well. They will find you and destroy you, destroy your mind!"

As Alec stared at him, he thought it ironic that biospheres had all kinds of life saving procedures for the calamities that might befall them. Oxygen, food, water, blood, all were at the ready if the worse happened and the roof were to cave in on this place. Why would a person think after all the care they had taken to help with the preservation of a colonist's life, they would suddenly find it within themselves to snuff one out, it was totally irrational. It's not even like this damn fool was important.

In almost each and every encounter with an irrational tenant like this there was evidence of some sort of drug use. There was little he could do about it, the harden carapace of addiction demanded more than an argument based in logic to defeat it. Addiction was a selfish process, and the person caught in its clutches found themselves doing everything they could to defend their actions. This was a cadaverous world needing the light of humanity to be shown upon it. Those intervening knew the dangers yet formed their circle anyway, not to finish them off but to actually go in and save a life.

The drugs were powerful, mind-altering hallucinogens and if enough people fell under its spell, the colony would reach a tipping point and there would be no turning back. Their actions as a group would become unorthodox, preposterous, even ludicrous, driven by everything except for the act of caring for one of their fellow colonists.

There were examples back on Earth of entire civilizations disappearing because of such group psychosis. Imagine if the people of an island committed all of their resources to the stone carvings of gigantic monolithic heads, then went about chopping down every tree in their forest to get them to their shores. They would prop those sculptures up along their banks in hopes of warding off anything arriving on their beaches that would attempt to upset their reign of lasciviousness. In each instance, when the tipping point for a civilization was reached, no one ever listened to the individual questioning their extreme actions. That type of inquiry usually didn't take place until those denizens were long gone.

After serving his time at La Compagnie d'Etoile, Alec felt the concept of intervention was the sole basis for Service Dextoid production. With this acknowledgement, he suddenly felt sorry for his species. Dextoids would never be free under a system like this. Once people got used to their support systems, they could never turn the clock back and live without them. In some ways Dextoid production had become their addictive drug. Technology was like that, pulling on the addictive qualities of every person using it, and the last thing they were going to do was pay attention to the individual trying to stop its flow.

SUPPORT SYSTEMS

As Alec crossed this planet's surface he couldn't help but observe how close it was to wavering at being absolutely dead. The air and water had been leaving the planet for a few millennia now. The interior core had stopped rotating, the plate tectonics had stopped shifting, and the mantel had stopped renewing itself in a healthy active geothermal way. After spending a few days on Mars one could see why a planet like Earth was alive. Sometimes one needed to see the *Ying* in order to appreciate the *Yang*. The blue peril contained great oceans, it generated storms which carried with it dynamic atmospheric conditions like electricity, wind, and precipitation. Here was a planet fully functioning in the continual process of cleansing itself.

Viewed from afar, Earth had plenty of lines, from tectonic rifts to the tidal conveyors churning within its oceans, from shifting jet streams to its lush green belts, and above it all a moon giving it stability along its axis. All of those things allowed for the planet to have a pulse, even for it to breathe.

No one could say an individual organ on its own, like a liver or a kidney is alive, but when combined in the proper order and allowed to function in unison with the rest of the body parts, then the definition of life transforms and touches the very magic of it. So it was with all the weather patterns, volcanic activity and ecosystems on Earth. It had to be.

The people of these biospheres wanted to give this planet a pulse. They wanted to see its skies filled with the purifying clouds of rain, and have a sense of the air carried to them by the breeze of a Martian ocean. If they could have that, this planet would offer its inhabitants something more comforting to the human spirit, the radiating warmth of its sun.

People yearned to bathe in the warm glow of its star. It was a strange primitive wanting desire piloting human beings to be such a heliolatrous race. That warm orb gave them power, it was as if the reptilian brain took control of their thought process, driving them out onto warmer surfaces in search of the sun. They wanted to be thawed by it, to let its rays energize them, and to have the ability to bask in its presence.

Since the colonists had gotten here, the planet seemed to be responding, this emaciated world was desperately trying to make a comeback. Mars was like a transplanted organ waiting for the clamps to be removed from its supporting arteries so the life force that was blood could once again flow through it. The organ would regain color, become vibrant, and function. One just needed to spend a little time immersed in the desperate energy of Mars to feel its determination in wanting to rebound. This energy in the end was what made Mars *special*.

Was this not the key to life's greater picture? For in the abundance of the ordinary, the things that were special, that stood out, should have been cherished. Was the Earth not the blue peril, Mars the New Hope, and his pursuit of I-Glo because she was unique? As Alec pressed on, these thoughts cluttered his mind, never fully ridding himself of their importance. At best they trailed off behind him like the long knotted tail of a kite dancing freely in the breeze. Regardless of how good it felt to have those things in tow, he could not help but notice the feeling of being pulled along ever so slightly by the tug of a string.

Chapter 07
A Feeling

Harvard was standing there with a volatile mixture of anger and contempt, this was it, this was the moment, no longer would he hide his feelings. Each and every person in this place was being pushed to the edge of their limits because of his actions. He knew this, but somehow Xavier was able to turn a blind eye to their suffering. Harvard wasn't built that way; it used to be that he and Xavier were a team. Recently though he wasn't quite feeling the bond of their friendship.

None of this should have come as a surprise to him, especially when he considered what happened to Johnston. Xavier turned him in, plain and simple. Johnston, the poor bastard, never even saw it coming. That was the way Xavier had been playing it as of late, causing Harvard to become extremely sensitive about his surroundings.

Xavier sat in his chair going over the mountain of paperwork that had been piling up on his desk. He knew Harvard was in the room, he was very aware of his sulking presence. He knew he had come there to speak with him. Xavier however could have cared less, acting as nonchalant as possible. None of his usual efforts to shoo Harvard away seemed to be working, it appeared this time Harvard was setting himself up to be heard.

"The air of this place has a very dry and metallic taste to it. It leaves one with a gritty feeling at the back of their throat. I have heard people complain of it as of late. It's an uncomfortable sensation we have to endure, and we both know why it's happening, don't we."

Xavier placed his stylist down very precisely on his desk, almost as if he were a parent being interrupted by a nagging child.

He did it in such a manner to overtly telegraph the exactness by which the scolding was about to come. "Are we going to have this conversation again?"

Harvard noted this reaction and did not appreciate his projected posture in the least. As if to mimic the child he was supposed to be, Harvard retorted in such fashion. "And again and again and again, until you do something about it. The people back on Earth dictate policy and you seem far too happy to rewrite it until those mandates splay out of our structures like the tentacles of some wild mythological beast. The biospheres are nothing more than storefronts for corporate greed. We have become their puppets, and what do you do about it? You mandate your own people! You feed the voracious appetites of those greedy bastards by pushing your own people to work longer hours, take on more responsibilities, and all for what? So you can sit comfortably behind this desk and enact policy!"

"I am simply doing what needs to be done."

Harvard recognized this tone right away, and of all the attitudes Xavier could have taken this was the one that angered him the most. It was a stately voice, and Harvard latched onto it with sarcastic relish. "Why yes your lordship, we wouldn't want the commoners to have too much personal time on their hands now would we. They might find it within themselves to wash away this metallurgic taste from the back of their throats, and if they had time to do that, then they might find the time to complain. The kingdom can't have any complaints now can it?! If these people were allowed to voice their opinions it might poke holes in the velvet blanket of peace the boys back in marketing have been so busily weaving. We don't want the nasty truth punching holes in that sewn fabric now do we?"

Xavier sat in his chair watching Harvard gesture about frantically trying to get his point across. He was always the one to panic first. Xavier felt between the two of them, Harvard could have easily been the preverbal canary in the cage. Anytime Xavier felt over worked, Harvard would be the one to cry out. It was

145

disappointing, Harvard would always be Harvard, and that only had Xavier wanting to talk down to him all the more.

"Spaceships aren't always going to make it here safely. The act of colonizing takes its toll on everyone, the loss of life is an inherent part of this process, much like the dead leaves that fall from trees.

"Our effort with all its difficulty doesn't even come close to comparing with how people suffered in the past trying to colonize their world. Every page of Earth's history is splattered with the ruthless savagery that comes with colonization. Yet you act as though we are holding back on making things better for the colonists up here, that savagery simply does not exist."

"Hogwash!" Harvard looked wild eyed as he shouted out his retort.

"It is the writers of history who have tempered the suffering of those in the past. The author's pen takes liberties, romanticizing explorers, painting them in the rich colors of the bold, the brash, and the adventurous..."

"And is that how you see yourself? You repulse me! It's vulgar that you would see yourself in some future portrait lionized as what? An explorer? A leader? A founder of the new hope?"

Xavier leaned back in his chair, allowing himself to openly get a little more comfortable. He needed to show Harvard he didn't feel threatened by him in the least. After all it was he, Xavier with the knowledge for what they needed to get done. His vision for the future was secure, and no one could ever take that away from him.

This didn't mean he was above reproach. He felt the corporation was going out of its way to challenge his authority. They seemed to combat his efforts by trying to wear him down with endless battles, constant in-fighting and unending circular arguments. If he were ever going to quit on them it would be because they taxed him to the point of exhaustion.

He had come too far with this company to just throw in the towel. All those pundits, those wannabes and hanger-on's, they would see their own fate before he would see his. He would personally make sure of it; Harvard was included with that rabble now.

He couldn't help the fact his vision for what needed to be done went well beyond their comprehension. One could play chess by thinking a move ahead, or play phenomenally great chess by seeing the end game first.

Harvard was still building a head of steam for what he wanted to say, he wasn't standing in Xavier's office to pacify him, today was the day he came in for a fight. There was just too much at stake and neither he, nor anyone else, could sweep it under the carpet any longer. "These historic figures you speak so highly of, they had another set of traits, they were often cruel, selfish, and manipulative.

"That's what you have taken the time to build up here, your own obsequious system, and that's why these colonists hate you. Don't act as if you are untouched by their thoughts. Say what you want but you have changed, and not for the better. You're the one adding another level of grit to an already merciless situation. In response these people have begun to mirror the untamed world you are creating for them. A cruel environment will produce a callous person, a wild west will produce a desperado, a fanatical ideology produces a suicide bomber, and in all those wakes a thing like innocence will be left out in the cold to be shanghaied."

Xavier scoffed at this last remark. What of innocence? That quality died in him a long time ago. If Harvard thought he was reflecting the current environment fluctuating all around him, he was wrong. He knew he could turn into something just short of tyrannical if he allowed himself to become immersed in the sorted tidal pools of discontent that had formed within this firm. The energy for this ebbed and flowed on a daily basis, and there were times he wasn't strong enough to conceal his feelings for absolute rule. The reveal was as unsightly as a large oil slick matted against pristine ocean waters.

The things spewed in those verbal outbursts would take days for his staff to clean up. They were epic scenes and witnessed by those unlucky enough to be in his presence. He berated the unsuspecting, accused others of incompetency, or worse yet issued frightening threats of succession. Some of his employees didn't take what he dished out and they would hold a grudge against him for years to come. None of it mattered to Xavier though, because in his mind that was what made them his employees.

Yes, he had changed, but if these people thought they were seeing the ugly side of him even in those moments, they were wrong. He hadn't shown them anything yet. He did everything humanly possible to keep his composure, but when he did feel it slipping away, he would confine himself in his office. This place was his foundry. Here in this darkened room he would try to find his inner peace by poring over reports and planning for the company's future. This gave him plenty of time for reflective thought; it just wasn't the kind any rational person would have ever endorsed.

APPLIED CONCEPT

Xavier was about to cross a personal precipice, and if he were lucky enough to make it to the other side, he would never have to come back to any of this ever again. Everything he had worked for to this point in his life seemed to be coming to a head, and it made him feel a little off kilter. This could have been because of the sheer magnitude of the jump he would need to make. In this whole sorted affair, he had set certain things into motion that he just had to trust would be there when he needed them. It wasn't a question of *if* he would need them, it was a question of *when*.

He was sure once the word got out about what he had done, a lot of people would misinterpret his actions. Xavier had to resign himself to the fact people were going to think what they wanted to think. None of their explanations could ever come close to the truth. All Xavier wanted to do was take leave, depart from the daily grind and shuck his struggle with the status quo. He examined his plan over and over again very carefully. No matter how many ways he looked at it, there really wasn't any room for another person to go where he was going to go, especially someone like Harvard, besides it wouldn't be difficult to find a lackey on the other side, this was the least of his concerns.

He tried to be as gentle as he could with what he was about to say next, but it was hard to soften the menacing undertone of how he really felt. "There are things out there that will shake this place to its foundation, regardless of how delicate I handle them, someone will always walk away feeling shanghaied."

"Are we going to talk about the arrival of the new moon again? I refuse to be dragged into your philosophical ramblings on what a new moon could mean to the colonists. I think that everyone is quite aware of what the practical applications are for this celestial body. Why else would they be sending for it? This planet is on the verge of wild celebration, and they should be, if they can pull this off it will be a monumental achievement, historical in every sense of the word. Yet you of all people walk around here as if you don't care." Harvard could see he had hit close to home with his comment and could not allow himself to ease up on his attack. Time was running out. The window for sanity was closing. He wouldn't get many more opportunities like this..

"That's it, isn't it! This whole place is on the verge of wild celebration, and you don't feel a thing. Is it because you have no control over it, or is it just the fact you don't know how to use the event to your advantage? If we were a primitive people experiencing our first eclipse, you would have answers for us then, wouldn't you! You would try and tie the event back to some omen of cataclysmic upheaval or claims of manifest destiny. That type of sorcery doesn't work up here, does it?! Not with a team of scientists at the ready to refute your hokum!"

Harvard was reaching, all the time he was reaching, and for things he could never fully comprehend. A thing like the new moon was out there all right, but it was moving Xavier in a different way, validating the growing heaviness he had for this place. He knew the company was deliberately trying to bury him under a workload of responsibility. It was difficult not to be paranoid about his situation, the feeling seemed to come with the territory, and he continuously had to bilge those thoughts from his head. He wondered if Harvard wasn't in on their schemes. That of course would have taken the cake.

From out in the deep reaches of this solar system, the new moon was approaching. This celestial orb was seen by many to represent the *New Hope*. As this body got closer it reached out with its subtle hand and began to take hold, tugging at the core of Mars, and tugging also at the core of Xavier. With each passing day his heaviness intensified. The approach of this moon was confirming an inescapable nagging truth; that anything making it all the way out here, came out here to stay.

Harvard had arrived as well, and he was in a scrappy mood. He kept pressing his boss for answers, not allowing him the luxury of getting lost in thought. "This new moon scares the living hell out of you, doesn't it? Does it make you feel as if you are losing control over your employees as well? Have you lost touch with yourself? How far gone are you?"

Harvard had crossed a line. How dare he question his sanity. The anger Xavier felt was beginning to bubble to the surface, but so too were his thoughts as to why Harvard would confront him like this? What if the corporation had put him up to this, and they had Harvard testing his confidence? It wasn't out of the question for the corporation to administer a *Confidence Test*. The company constantly tested people up here to be sure they still believed in the mission. The corporation didn't send out a notice announcing they would be testing people in this way, spontaneity was key and being questioned for it could happen at the drop of a hat.

Harvard was just too persistent. It had to be a test! There were no other answers as to why he was acting so aggressive. All Xavier could do was ride the inquiry out. Confronting him now might reflect very badly on the report Harvard would submit later.

He took a moment to ready himself in playing Harvard's little game. "You and I both know desertion is not a selling feature for any venture. That isn't a word they can put on the front cover of one of their brochures. Yet with the arrival of this new moon, this is exactly what they are telling us. What other choices do we have? No one is ever getting off this rock."

"That's not true, they have sent people back before, look at Johnston."

"Yes, look at Johnston. He is a shining example of how they treat people. They will push you to a breaking point, and when you finally snap they will send you home to face the music. It's only a matter of time before we have to face that kind of music."

Xavier was becoming keenly aware of the enthusiasms he was showing for this subject. He needed to throttle back. If he didn't, he would be setting himself up for a fall. "It's either build a biosphere or build a jail. They don't have the money or resources to do both, and we don't have the time or the facilities to house those we suspect guilty of a crime. That's what Earth is for, that's why they sent Johnston back."

"Seems pretty ironic all the things they accused Johnston of could be going on right under your nose, and yet you claim you had no clue as to what he was up too."

"I have been over and over this with the appropriate authorities..."

"Xavier please, I am not some magistrate looking to try and trip you up over testimony you have already provided. Your truths are your truths. I have known you for a very long time now. I know when you are lying, or when you are taking liberties and stretching the truth. People aren't stupid, just because they go around saying they haven't prosecuted a person for a crime on Mars, doesn't mean crimes aren't being committed. This is far from any kind of utopia. Most individuals up here have been involved in wrongdoing. The general public is pretty good at cutting through all the crap. They know when someone has been set up and when someone has been forced to take a fall. I mean think about it, they pull from their own life examples, and they realize there isn't a whole lot someone can do up here without at least one other person knowing what they are really up too. You can't stop them from talking. They talk behind your back all the time, they are probably talking right now, you aren't above their judgment."

Harvard was goading him on and Xavier knew it! He sat in his chair, reclining so his head was supported with his thumb and forefinger. Innuendo was a tough thing to battle. If you closely examined any of the facts from the Johnston case, they could easily transform into a mistrustful mosaic, revealing the Cimmerian side of the colonization effort. The corporations were deliberately trying to bury this darker world from public scrutiny, they wanted to ease the fears of people coming to Mars, not exacerbate them.

Harvard was right in one respect, this was far from any kind of utopia. It was however, a land rich in supporting corporate greed. "Governments are going to do whatever they need to do to get people to come up here. I personally have no control over that. Let's say for arguments sake, you were granted your wish, and those companies came clean, what then? The critics of this process have already torn them apart in the media every time a story of failure makes it off this rock. Even with all those reports buzzing about down there, most people don't care. Our problems aren't their problems."

Xavier propped his elbows up on his desk, interlocking his fingers and assuming a fatherly pose. "The governments backing this process are very protective of the image they are trying to portray up here. They would never allow for a story like the one you're so eager to tell get out. Look around you for god's sake.

They down play the accidents that happen here all the time. The threat of conflict is always reported as a minor disagreement. Those who have been ravaged by this process have their stories turned into a triumph of the spirit, portrayed as people having done so much with so very little. The companies themselves are amalgamating the perception of reality and feeding it back to Earth in tight little packages promoting this place. I have seen this media, to watch it you feel as though they are talking about another world we are colonizing, not Mars!"

Xavier found himself pointing at Harvard with both fingers now. His hands were still interlocked as if calling him to the carpet, and perhaps he was, but he wouldn't gain a thing by pushing the point any further. His tone changed, he wanted to understand the reason Harvard was in front of him. "We both know things will never quite be up to snuff in an operation like this. One must accept the hoarding, the existence of black-markets, and the fact that crime will follow people wherever they may go.

There is this misnomer about wrong doing, as if we can identify the trouble spots before they erupt. The reality is there are no clear-cut indicators, there are no mounds of garbage, dilapidated buildings, or graffiti written in enough sections of this complex directing us to where the trouble lies. It would be nice if crime worked like that, but crime doesn't want to operate out in the open. It acts like a chameleon, blending in with the world around it. Sometimes you have to remove the rocks to find the things crawling around underneath them. Sometimes in the midst of that process you discover something unexpected, something else that is wrong. That was how they caught Johnston."

The silence that followed put Xavier on alert; Harvard wasn't buying into what he was saying. The room was filling with staunch disbelief.

That was fine. When it came right down to it, Xavier really didn't care if Harvard believed him or not. He knew what he knew. Most governments weren't just approving the use of emotional packets to control Dextoids, they were also working over the human population, forcing them to march to a different tune. He watched how those governments manipulated their citizens, moving in on them like a mist finding its way through the jungle just after a rain.

Xavier had become a keen observer to the maturation of this type of control. They could introduce an element like chaos to dictate a reaction. The energy for this flowed into lawlessness, and he was surprised at how easily they could apply it to a situation. It was like a deli mustard to a burger, only here the condiment put a little extra distance between the population and the law. Lawlessness wasn't just a condition of deteriorating social standards, it could be planned for, it became an applied concept.

Modern military forces used this tactic to perfection as they channeled where the fight should take place. They denoted the zones of safety and those of conflict, and they telegraphed where the opposition should gather to prep for a fight. If everyone knew where the fight was taking place then everyone would spend time gearing up for battle. The soldiers went in with guns a-blazing, and that meant those combatants were also carrying themselves with an overwhelming sense of impunity.

DARK SHADOWS OF HUBRIS

The word struck Xavier as being funny, *impunity* seemed to be such an awkward term, its etymology felt derived from the slurring speech of a drunkard. When he took a moment to think about the word, he actually saw it take shape in his mind and transform into color, it started out in wispy shapes of white, blending into pink then green then back to white, only to be quickly muted at the end of the word into a darker shade of brown. Left by itself, it was one of those words that seemed useless and without explanation, and that of course was laughable, because nothing on Mars could ever be viewed as useless. Yet in complete contradiction to such an idea there stood Harvard.

"You needn't justify your actions with me. I am really uninterested in the particulars of your mode of operandi. Unless of course this is a confession, some sort of admittance of guilt." Harvard paused just long enough for Xavier's silence to be his rebuttal. "That's what I thought, so let's not waste each other's time and get down to brass tacks shall we?"

Xavier was shocked by what his assistant had just told him. It was obvious they had been working together for far too long now. The assumptions he just heard about his character were nothing short of damning, exposing ones lies shined an uncomfortable light on the soul. Normally he would have sent angry verbal shots across the bow of the person having done this. There would have been hell to pay for crossing a line like that, but this was Harvard.

Xavier felt his demons begin to reveal themselves. They gained confidence as they always did when he locked himself in this room. They traipsed through his fields of thought, viciously slid down his vines of integrity, and recklessly flew through the rich creamy clouds of hope. Xavier carried thoughts of impunity with him all the time, it was at the ready like long belts of bullets draped over his chest. He was almost white knuckled with the effort of holding himself back from acting out on his impunity. The company should have been smarter about how they had prepped the colonists, they should have warned them, trained them to take on more responsibilities for saving themselves.

The very minute he decided to lash out, he would be merciless in his efforts, targeting things along the industrious landscape, rifling it with a vengeance of what he felt was clearly owed to him, and the way he saw it those old men back on Earth owed him a lot.

If they could have somehow read his treasonous thoughts, then it would have revealed a corporate leader having gone rogue. It was right out of a theater of the macabre, they would have held their collective breath and watched in horror, waiting for the day a leader like Xavier stepped out from the dark shadows of his own hubris. The audience would have demanded the curtains be drawn back in that odeum, waiting wide-eyed for their villain to enter the main stage. If he were to step out from behind those curtains, to let them see what he had really become, a ruthless leader crowned in jewels of the self-ordained, they would have been appalled.

This haunting reveal would give them a place to put the crosshairs, and there was no way Xavier wanted to be painted in that type of light. The concept of lawlessness only worked if it didn't have a head. Once it became apparent there was someone in charge, then lawlessness lost its helter-skelter texture and became something else, like anarchy that was followed by a coo, or the street crazed riot that was followed by a seizure of power. Even the mob came into focus once everyone knew who the boss was.

Harvard was watching intently, waiting for Xavier to mentally slip up. "You can't keep going on like this forever. You have spent a lot of time insulating yourself from those around you. Well my friend isolation isn't the answer. Modern penal systems back on Earth are littered with documented cases of prisoners who have slowly lost their minds locked away in isolation. Receptors demand to be engaged. The mind begs for human interaction, it craves conversation and expression. When it gets those things, it actually induces a process of self-healing. It takes a lot to kill the social creature lurking deep within us, but if one goes out of their way to do just that, cognizance is soon to follow. They go hand in hand. If you stay in here long enough you will lose your mind."

POSSIBLE TRUTHS

"You find the most incessant gibberish to ramble on about. I don't have time for it. Find something else to have a conversation about or leave me alone."

"Anytime you don't want to talk about a subject, you always act annoyed. This time I will not be so easily dissuaded. You can't have walked the halls of this place for this entire time ignoring the faces of those you have passed. They are doing everything they can to eke out an existence up here. Their desolate lives have become the muddy pools of despondency. Its murkiness can only reflect the shattered image of a distorted persona. If one stares long enough into that gloom, they will begin to disengage entirely from reality, falling through a penumbra of mephitic whispers down into a well filled with destitute souls. It is a mental state of isolation unlike anything a person should ever have to experience. The sediment is so thick down there one can actually forget themselves within the layers of it. You know this kind of dirt better than anyone, don't you? It is a rich black silt. This kind of sediment conveys a message to people about the stagnation of time, and you are covered in it, much like a primitive person embraces their oneness with the Earth, only in your case, you have embraced Mars."

Harvard was beginning to warm up to his chances. He crossed the room slowly, approaching Xavier's desk as if he were a cutter trying to make his way through glacial ice, with its only goal making it back out onto the high seas. "It's funny, a person can conceal their indignation, shelter their extreme beliefs, or put a veil on imprudent proclivities, but a thing like hardship is worn on the faces of every individual who has ever had to travel down its insensitive path."

"Stop it! Stop treating it as a struggle between us and them. All of us up here are trapped in our own little hardships, and for most of us, we accept it. It's a better place because of that acceptance!"

"I don't see it that way."

"Of course you don't." Xavier murmured it under his breath in disgust. He was holding the top of his head with both hands. How much longer would he have to endure Harvard as an assistant? He had swore to himself he would be replaced with the first capable person.

"People yearn to be free, but it's not about the technologies that are sheltering them, keeping them alive. They need their space suits, rovers, and biospheres. The real problem they have is with the Dextoids. People want to be free from the yoke these unblinking machines exude."

This almost made Xavier laugh. "Why not wish for the planet to have an ocean, or how about oxygen in the atmosphere? None of those things are going to happen anytime soon either, these creatures are unsurpassed in their safety record. Companies rely on these Dextoids for their documentation skills. Their testimony has been irrefutable in every case they have been used in. Their very existence has been proven to be invaluable to this entire process."

"I didn't expect you to tow anything but the company line, but surely you have heard the rumors. They speak of injuries and fatalities, of human suffering and pain, and of people crying out for help as Dextoids diligently watch over them. These things are failing to react; they are failing to help people. They are failing to do their jobs."

"There is no proof behind such stories. They are rumors people are spreading, they find their way into the biospheres on the breath of liars. They are nothing more than tall tales, the substance of urban legends."

"I think those rumors persist because deep down inside people fear what those possible truths could hold for them. They aren't sold on the record of perfection the company is trying to shove down their throats. You said it yourself, the company spends a lot of time trying to convince us things are all right. We have no crime, we are supposedly happy in our existence, the Dextoids are our saviors, it's all rubbish. You would know better than I when it comes to those facts, but if the companies are lying about the reliability of Dextoids, if they are padding their statistics, or inflating their numbers on safety just to make these inhabitants feel safe, then these colonists are in more jeopardy than anyone could have possibly imagined."

Harvard saw the stunned look on his bosses face—he had caught Xavier in a trap by using his own words. He pushed the topic a little further. "Don't look so stunned. You are right in one respect, these people are talking, and you should be worried. They are beginning to use the isolation they are feeling to their advantage. Those furtive little rendezvous are about finding their own cliques. They are forming into groups, galvanizing into packs. Think about it, aren't those the same type of actions that always precede a mutiny?"

"What? Are you saying these people are planning a mutiny? You have heard those very words?"

"No, I think the conditions are forming for such a thought to take hold and be put into action. I don't think it will happen tomorrow, or even next month, but if you keep pushing them, it will happen."

It was with this last statement Xavier had to smile. If what Harvard was telling him was the truth, then the conditions were right for his plan to hatch. All of his hard work would finally be paying off.

The government, the Alliance, the corporation, they had been applying a squeeze to the colonists for some time now. It was pushing them away from this system, having them wanting change. It had always been his fertile hope they would do something as primitive as run with the pack. There was safety in their numbers; it called on each to be ruthless. He knew a thing like their cautionary tale would have them falling back onto the strength of the group. Like the keyboard of a piano, the keys may have looked the same but each produced its own note, their strength came when played together. Now Xavier had them!

There were syndicates and crews, mobs and gangs, posses and hordes, if one traced them back far enough along the timeline, they would have found each of those groups had branched out from just one single solitary pack.

He could not help but paint for himself the heroic vision of what that first pack must have looked like, of those savage people doing everything they could to survive in the face of monumental adversity, drenched to the bone by a violent rain storm, and all the while emanating a stance of condescending barbarism.

This was the hallowed image hanging in his head, a mural of maudlin proportions, richly caked in the heavy oils, every last little brush stroke interlacing with the other to form a construct in which all of humanity would come to life and survive. It was an ideal, a painting created in the confines of his mind and it was every bit worthy of hanging next to the colorful model displaying the intricacies of the human genome.

The truth was probably far less vibrant than Xavier's imagination evoked. The real picture had been slightly muted over the stretches of time, to the point of being achromatized. In real life that pack loosely huddled together, crouching in the pouring rain. They probably flinched at the first loud clap of thunder. There wasn't any heroic imagery one could attach to that type of despair, and the feelings one got from looking at this pathetic sight were closer to a guilt-ridden crime of in-flagrante-delicto. Still there was something that drew Xavier back into always trying to find this dark primitive hallow.

He stirred with the thought of being caught romanticizing an idea like this, and lashed out at Harvard immediately. "What would you have me do? Shine a light into every dark corner of this place, remove the doors of every pod and bay? Have people followed just so we can listen in on their conversations? They are going to do what they want to do, you can't stop them!" Xavier ended with a deadpan stare, as if he were somehow still putting energy into trying to find that primitive hallow.

Harvard wouldn't budge. "Don't under estimate what is happening out there. It is the pack, and they are gathering their ideas to become a force."

"The situation is being monitored to the best of our capabilities. The Dextoids are out there, they are watching, listening, and monitoring the situation. Perhaps it is not they, but me they should not underestimate."

SHATTERED PERCEPTIONS

Harvard was thrown off guard by Xavier's last comment. He had just interjected something about himself into the conversation. The comment wouldn't have disturbed Harvard if it weren't so reptilian in nature. That was it, this was Xavier! The bastard seemed to have the ability to slither away at the first sign of serious trouble, only to come back and fight on another day.

The human mind was equipped with too many cautionary tales to think they had all come from the cognitive experiences of their participants. People needed a thing like fear for the sake of their own survival. How else were they to warn future generations about the world around them, especially when early humans were living for a total of twenty or thirty some odd years? It was the cautionary tale being passed onto their young that was allowing them to feel that chill down the back of their spine, or at the ends of the hair on the nape of their neck. They needed to know when to turn and run. This had to be why phobias existed. How else were deep-rooted fears making their way into the minds of deductive people?

Look at the lizard, it needed to be able to identify the passive food sources from the aggressive ones. Things like grasshoppers and caterpillars were easier to catch and looked much different from insects like scorpions or spiders. Arachnophobia could have found its genesis in a creature like a lizard. They watched at ground level the spindling agitation of these eight-legged arachnoids, at times feeling their venomous bite, or the sharp, pin prick sting of the scorpion.

This window of opportunity wouldn't stay open forever. Xavier rarely let his guard down. Harvard had to say something to continue pushing this energy forward, with out being so obvious that Xavier would shut himself down. "Are you trying to imply a touch of mysticism to this situation?"

"Leave it to you to penalize the person for wanting to ponder. Sure, I am questioning things, only because everything here is not solely as it seems. The surfaces of our worlds only contain the things we are allowed to see. Look at the bruising they have seen in the background radiation of our universe, aren't those the telltale signs of our walls bumping up against those of another? The proof of such a find would boggle the mind.

"Why point a telescope at a thing like a star but refuse to put time into understanding the darkness around it. Dark matter, dark energy, gravity, no one anticipated their connection, but these things exist on multiple plains. You cannot touch it, and you cannot see it per se, but you can certainly feel their affects."

"You are trying to attach a mysticism too this! Hah! Well you won't find any dark energy moving people in that way around here. Individuals challenge themselves in ways we don't always understand, but they are rooted in the here and now. People will always adapt and find ways to fit in with their surroundings.

"Look at how primitive people took the time adapting to the world around them. They reached within themselves to find a belief in overcoming their own fears. It's obvious from even the earliest of cave paintings how much they revered and admired the healthy beasts that were all around them. Even after they hunted them down and killed them, they still paid their respects to those creatures, to the point of wanting to take on their attributes. Why else would they have worn their furs, made good use of their horns, or ingested them so gratifyingly?"

Xavier could see through the veil of his argument, he knew Harvard was talking about the corporation. The company was leaving nothing to chance, layering their ideology in cultural metaphors, hiding morality in corporate policy. The reassurances the colonists were given were written like bad checks from an overdrawn account. When it came right down to it the company didn't have a thing to honor, but it fully expected to be honored by each and every individual. Their fate was complete as soon as they arrived. "People will adapt, I think you are implying the company expects a matriculation by them into the corporate fold."

"And you're going to sit there and tell me it doesn't? We don't have lines out our front doors to get into this place, but we do have food lines, fuel lines, supply lines, lines for transportation, lines to get into the banks, lines for our medical exams, and lines of communication with the outside world. We have lines, and they are regulated and watched very carefully by this corporation. If given the chance, they would program people much like they program the Dextoids. Isn't that what this is all about, having control over things without openly showing it?" He leaned on the desk, putting both his hands on the paperwork. His next words were whispered as if he knew someone else might be trying to listen in on their conversation. "There are rumors of implants having been installed into a certain group of people. It is horrifying if they can prove it to be true. It would mean they have started something up here, which has accelerated the obligation the company will expect from these colonists. We both know that agenda, don't we? The people that have gone under the knife for this have given up something about themselves, and are no better than lab rats."

Xavier felt his head beginning to spin. It really hurt. The thing that was growing inside his head feared being exposed. Harvard was supposed to be his friend, his go to guy and confidant, but for some reason, today, he seemed to be anything but. Why was this happening? It was all so confusing. Perhaps his friendship with him was based in obligation. Everything else up here seemed to be dipped in that word. What was it about people wanting to control the things around them? If they could do it, some would reach out and try to control the world. Control was the bane of mankind; it was the unannounced dream of human beings to want to have a sheer mastery over nature.

Science had its epochs, its moments when they felt they were on the verge of understanding everything. The telescope, the microscope, all of their esoteric math tried to bring their world into focus. Every time they got close to achieving this, the universe revealed a little more of its mysticism.

THE EXCEPTION

Xavier knew he was about to shatter some perceptions of his own. The investors backing this project had pushed him to his absolute limit. From this point on he was refusing to budge another inch for them. He hadn't informed anyone of his decision. If he had his druthers though, he would have flown all the way back to Earth and punched Jeb Wentworth square in the face before handing them his resignation. Those greedy old men had taken the expectation levels of this place and wrapped it around his neck as if it were some sort of tight fitting horse collar. The device was maligned with constraints that would all but choke him off, things like corporate responsibility and gross profit filled its leathers. He had become their beast of burden and they expected him to go out and plow the fields each and everyday of his troubled existence. They also expected him to do this without complaint. All the promises he had heard while on Earth for *obtaining a wealth beyond his wildest dreams* didn't matter, not if they had sent him here with every intent of being marooned.

There wasn't one choice they made about the corporation that didn't seem to affect who he was, or have an influence on what he could become. Xavier had gone well past the point of depression, and was now feeding on an underlying current of anger that would become a mainstay of his persona. If one were able to glance into the viewing-portal of his soul, it would have revealed a blistering bedrock of dark marbles, each one a polished representation of the hatred he had developed for this place.

The corporation came to represent his labyrinth, and those aphotic corridors became the tunnels to his nightmares. No matter which way they turned, they would always bring him back to the same place. He was lost in some gigantic industrious machine, with monstrous cogs and leavers thunderously making their revolutions. It flung grease and grime as if those cogs were the arms of some deranged artist who was insistent on throwing his paints. Their loud clanking and grinding had the distinct sound of things approaching him and then rapidly going by, as if it were the blaring horn being sounded from a passing train. Xavier was trapped inside this machine, and it seemingly went on forever with no possible way out. After awhile he forgot what the machine did, what it produced, what purpose it really served. His only task was to keep it working. The machine of his nightmares became his own personal iron horse, and into it he shoveled the hatred of those volatile dark marbles.

Harvard stood there, almost frozen in time, as if he were having an out of body experience. He was able to observe himself and Xavier as they went through their motions. In that moment he saw the paperwork sitting on Xavier's desk. The mess itself looked to be a strong argument for the cosmological constant; it was an indefeasible flow of pulp. He wondered at times what the advent of computers had really done to make things paperless. Even here on a planet like Mars, where not a single forest existed, there theoretically stood a stack of paper higher than all the structures they had built to date. In the entire universe, was there even one civilization that could stand up and proudly proclaim they had freed themselves from the flow of paper because of their use of computers? He personally doubted it.

Xavier's world had become a stack of memos. They were waiting for him morning, noon, and night. Harvard stared at the stack knowing full well that somewhere in this pile of papers contained the evidence he was so desperately looking for. He shifted his weight slightly moving over them, casually placing his hand on the pile. He needed a way to find this proof. "Seems as if no matter what we do, we are never going to be viewed as anything more than soldiers of fortune in their influential little army. There isn't one solution to any of these situations that doesn't have a certain amount of greed attached to it. If a line ruptured and spewed its crud into the ocean, then siphoning off as much as possible before capping the well would always be apart of the fix. That type of greed contaminates everything it touches."

"If there is going to be something that motivates the effort to colonize this place, why can't it be greed? Why do we need to act as if we are above all of this, as if we have higher morals than everyone else? The credits we earn are not evil; we've worked hard for them. If they offered us more, we would take them." Xavier was beginning to feel a serious sensitivity to this situation, perhaps because there was one thing in those stacks of papers that made him feel uncomfortable. It revealed more about who he was than he really wanted anyone else to know, and from all indications Harvard looked to be trying to close in on them.

The corporation had been on a mission. It was rumored they wanted to see all of their top tiered people receiving cerebral upgrades. He had the initial procedure done back on Earth, and at that time, he thought he would always be working there. The prep work for such an operation took an entire year. It left bothersome scarring on the back of his head. He often wondered how many others were having this same procedure done? Were they having problems like extended scarring? Anytime he received paperwork on this subject, it would only have his name attached to the document. There was no real way for him to know how many others were actually involved in the program. The Dextoid caring for him never spoke publicly about who else might be involved, and Xavier's searches on the subject turned up zero leads. All he knew was they had selected him for this process.

The surgical follow-ups were completed on Mars. He had requested his personal Dextoid be allowed to complete the operations. They had assigned him a contact back on Earth he could speak with if he had any issues, but communicating in that way didn't sit well with Xavier at all. At times he hated himself for committing to this process. When one of their memos came across his desk asking for him to go in for a checkup or an upgrade, it almost always caused him to freeze in his tracks.

They claimed the process would help improve his memory, amplify his intelligence, and enhance the longevity of his life. Given all those benefits, how could anything go wrong? Still, it seemed rather unpleasant to think there was something foreign growing inside his head, invading his mind like a cancerous cell, and spidering out into the smallest pockets of his lobes. What they had grafted within him was alive, he was sure of it. He could feel it, and the feeling was anything but comforting.

Blast those doctors back on Earth. All the reassurances and guarantees they gave him about not being able to feel a thing were a lie. He was stuck, there was no turning back, and he would always need to show them he was fully committed.

"Maybe there is something more..." Harvard allowed his thumb to travel down a corner of the stack, peeling back the pages and letting them feather rapidly out of his grasp. "to what they are allowing to happen up here?"

Xavier felt inhibited; there was a sickness in the pit of his stomach from all this questioning. His implant was driving this feeling. It recoiled at being disturbed. Since it had taken hold, there were weird little things beginning to transpire within the background of his mind. He heard a monophonic hum; sometimes it could even be described as an annoying buzz. Even more disturbing to his sensibilities was when these noises turned into scratching little sounds of whispered voices. As if a secret language was being spoken just beyond his reach. His mind would slowly bubble over with the frustration in having to deal with his own personal arcanum. This had to be why they kept demanding he go under the knife, again, and again, and again. There was something wrong with the implant, they just weren't telling him.

Harvard leaned in again, giving Xavier the sternest of looks. "There are just too many layers of secrecy attached to this process, aren't there? Too many things they don't want people to know or admit too. If you were to speak up about anyone of them, they might send you back like Johnston, probably lock you away forever."

The room felt as if it were beginning to osculate. His fallibilities were becoming stretched and mutated as if the inner workings of his conscious mind had become a pliant thing. Xavier braced himself for the onslaught of discomfort he was sure would come. The methodology they were insisting on for this cerebral procedure lacked any type of compassion, right down to the part where corporate insisted his Dextoid report to them on the status of his follow-up procedures. *Who the hell was it reporting too?!*

Harvard leaned in on those stack of papers, getting a little closer to what he was trying to find. "Yes, you know it as well as I do, what they are doing isn't just wrong, it's evil. It's down right sinister. Who can you really trust? Who can you tell?"

Harvard was mocking him! How on Phobos could he know? This damn thing in his head was blurring the lines of his sanity. It was wrecking havoc with his reason, and he had reason to believe there was no getting around his current conundrum. He was frustrated by the whole affair. It was obvious to him they were attempting to fix something they did not fully understand. Xavier had quit calling his contact back on Earth and eventually had his Dextoid destroyed for very good reasons. He wanted desperately to go back to his calming vision, to the ledge and peaceful state of the water droplet. Instead he was delivered to a place of twisted logic, a mired bog, filled with anesthetized souls. From its brine rose a vapor of chilling motivation found only in the most savage hearts of men.

He was at the point in his life where the road map had stopped. No one documented their fall from the cliff that was their sanity. He wanted to be free. Free enough to abandon the unhinged marathon he was on. He felt tired in his being. He knew what he wanted, and to get it he was going to have to make a stand.

This then was why people drove the sledgehammer so squarely onto the spike. This was why people fenced off open spaces of land. Those explorers had traveled far for what they wanted, and when they finally had a chance to make a claim, they drove their stakes firmly into the ground. Those metal poles outlining their estates represented so much more than the boundaries of a property, they marked the edge of civilized thought, and people were always up for that type of challenge, and not just to make it all the way out to where those stakes were driven, but to go well beyond them.

Xavier thought about the stakes he had gone out of his way to drive into the ground up here on Mars. There wasn't one person who made it all the way out here that didn't realize after a short period of time, this was their home. Xavier was one of the few people who still carried out an Earth type edict for how they should colonization this place. His policies were rooted in the financial investments of those grubby old men. For that reason alone he felt he had driven more stakes into the ground than anyone else on this barren red rock, and they owed him for his efforts. They should have acknowledged how steadfast he was in implementing their plan. Instead the corporation went out of its way to drive a stake of their own squarely into his heart.

NO REAL KEYS

Philman Devinch walked into the office, startling Xavier, and snapping him out of his carceral thoughts. As Philman sat down, Xavier felt there was the smallest of windows to say something to Harvard before he quietly departed, but somehow he knew his assistant was already gone. He wished he had the power to ignore him like Philman was currently able to do, but then again, Xavier found they all usually ignored Harvard, and why not? Anyone cultivating a reasonably sound mind should have.

"It is done! I have sent the finalized report to the Singo-Chinese. They will have plenty of data to go through over the next few months, or should I say before we start hearing back from them."

"I asked you to send them an air-tight report. How can it be air-tight, if those would be your concerns?"

"Well, I would liken it to a submarine, those things are air-tight yet they operate under plenty of concern and believe it or not they do have to surface on occasion."

Xavier noted there were days where he swore the things inside of his head were tightening, like a boa constrictor would tighten around its prey, only this feeling wasn't wrapping itself around his mind, it was constricting his thoughts. He almost wanted to cry out from the sharp, burning pain. It lasted only a moment, causing him to have flashing type visions, projections of himself. Those frightful frames had him falling down an elevator shaft, or loosing his grip on the ledge of a skyscraper, or falling with the debris of a mid-air collision frantically grabbing the air looking for something to hold onto. He wondered if the others with implants were being plagued by such visions. He found himself staring at Philman, and chose to break the uncomfortable silence. "What about the female Dextoid, the *Data Support Engineer*, did you have her destroyed?"

"No. There was something about the way she was reacting during the interrogation. I can't explain it, perhaps it was just the way she kept resisting. I felt I needed to break her will. I still feel that way even now. I have to follow through on this to prove my point to her, to all Dextoids really. It is our duty and is why I decided to keep her."

"Do you think this wise? I mean having an attachment to a Dextoid, especially this Dextoid?" Xavier checked himself. There were plenty of people who grew attached to their Dextoids. The reasons they chose the particular model of Dextoid were little psychological profiles that spoke volumes about their own lives. Xavier didn't want to go down that path, at least not today. He broke it off and went on another tangent. "We cannot have her resurfacing into the general population for any reason. That would blow the lid off this thing, and I mean in a big way."

"There won't be any problems with her. I took the time to modify her to the point where she won't be able to leave this facility. I'm holding her as an insurance policy against what the Singo-Chinese might say after analyzing my report. It all depends on where they want to take the investigation, we might need her, or parts from her that are still working, maybe even parts that look as if they have been blown to bits."

"For the record, I don't like it."

"I have one or two things I still have to work out, but the answer to your question is yes. I can promise you things will be alright."

Xavier threw his pen on his desk as he leaned back in his chair. "This is such a crazy place. I don't know if we will ever see a normality here within our lifetime."

"I don't know that we should. I mean why would we want that! We couldn't operate with the freedom we do now if this place were normal. That type of world would most certainly reject us."

"Let's be honest, both worlds have a sense of entitlement running through them. Having a society like Earth laboring through a free-for-all rarely means we are at the beginning of anything, it usually denotes an end." Xavier wanted to say more, but he just couldn't bring himself to do it. He knew the axe was falling on humanity and a lot of people were going to get hurt.

Why couldn't people understand it was never going to be one gigantic event that would end it all for them as a species. Tens-of-thousands of little cuts could kill a person just as easily as one large gash. The general population could never wrap their heads around that concept. The axe slowly destroying them wasn't sharp, it wasn't even taking big swipes at them, it was coming down again and again in a brutally slow shredding fashion.

"Desperation is a horrible deodorant. Everyone can sense it, even the creatures living in the animal kingdom know this stench. Having these Dextoids walking amongst us is a vile proof of where we stand as a race; things are not in the healthiest of states if we keep needing to invent creatures like this. We are on the brink, there is no getting around that, and I am reminded of it everyday by the presence of these things. I hate the Dextoids."

"Strong words, especially from someone who is in charge of security."

"Really? Because I feel like I am just doing my job. I am frightened of our future, and to be honest you should be too. I think we are setting ourselves up for one big fall. People are fallible, yet they walk around as if they own the world. It's complete arrogance. I don't think as a race we have the toughness to accomplish things in the long haul. We have failed to show any signs of it to this point in our existence."

"You sound like a man trying to request some time off, maybe a little rest is in order. It's got to be difficult working along side all those corporate criminal investigators, they are practically becoming their own department." Xavier said it half heartedly, it was meant to be a joke, but Philman failed to see the humor in it.

"It's not like that. It's hard to explain, but I saw something in the public consciousness when I was still on Earth that didn't sit well with me. People back there are genuinely concerned about the challenges they are facing, but no one could do anything about it. Much like a whale that has beached itself, the large crowds are helpless in moving it."

"What are you talking about, people are cleaning up as much as they possibly can. They have even begun to launch tons of their garbage toward the sun. They're using that burning orb as a gigantic incinerator!"

"That is exactly what I am talking about, all of those things are happening, but people themselves aren't actually doing anything to make it happen."

"I don't understand, people on Earth seem to be very proactive in trying to right the ship down there. You want them to actually go out and do the work?"

"It's hard to explain, but in a way, yes. I look around at all the activity happening up here on Mars. People go out and explore, turn bolts with wrenches, and extend a helping hand wherever it's needed. On Earth, people seem all too relaxed in sending the Dextoids out to do their bidding. People seem to think it is their solemn job to take shelter from the shit storm swirling all around them. Those denizens are closing down more and more to their immediate surroundings. It goes against every grain of evolutionary thought."

"So we aren't going to survive as a species because we aren't turning the bolts on things back on Earth? Excuse the pun, but that's rubbish. They have to clean things up so they can go out and function in those areas. There is no getting around that fact, it is a plain and simple truth."

"I don't think so, people have gotten to this point as a species because of their physical involvement with life, and that energy is beginning to wane on Earth. They need to be more proactive in doing the physical things if they are going to make it."

Xavier sat up a little straighter and folded his arms, he felt some fatherly advice on the subject were in order. "Look, there are plenty of theories on why people made it as a species. They talk about things like their low energy consumption for survival. If an animal has to burn a lot of fuel to be able to survive, then all that animal is going to do is eat all day. No, you need to know starvation; you need to become aware of your survival instincts. You need to be able to work in groups and communicate your ideas with those around you. That's what people did, that's what they are doing now. It doesn't have anything to do with sentience. Hell, there is even a theory out there that states the other animals may have left us alone because we just plain smelled bad. Now, can you imagine that? We stunk so bad the other creatures left us alone. Now that might really be the only reason we made it as a species."

"Sure I believe we stink alright, only we are smelling up the joint in a different way. By allowing Dextoids to take a lead role on some of these issues is just plain wrong. It's a power point that will eventually be used against us. Look at the military usage of Dextoids, we actually accept the fact military grade Dextoids can kill people. Aren't we currently living their exact fear of a rogue Strike Dextoid? That is what Alec is, isn't he? The only thing saving us is Alec isn't running with a battalion of his-kind destroying everything in sight. If Alec were on Earth right now they would have hit the panic button months ago!"

"First of all, Dextoids are basically designed to run solo, programmers have gone out of their way to retard their ability to run in packs. They usually venture out on their own..."

"And that has never been my problem with those things. People can plan, plot, and program all they want with Dextoids. They aren't going to get around the fact those things are starting to take over in certain areas of our lives. Dextoids aren't the ones running around in a pack, as a race, we are. Creatures that run in packs aren't always doing it out of support for each other. A creature like a gazelle runs in a pack, but they aren't doing it because they figured out running in numbers shows some type of unity or strength, they are running in packs to out do each other. They are hoping to out jump and out run the gazelle next to them so the lion, or whatever else is watching them, will focus on the weakest of those gazelles. The lone creature that has fallen out of the pack because it is weak, is the one sacrificed by the herd. People don't want to hear that, but it is the ruthless game gazelles are really playing. This is the same game people are playing with each other right now. It's a vicious cycle of trying to out-do each other, constantly vying for a higher ground. The weaker people, the ones who are falling out of the pack, are being sacrificed. They aren't helping each other like they used too."

"Just makes the pack stronger, you said it yourself."

"Yes, in the example of the gazelles, but not so for humanity. People are falling out of the pack in droves. These callous actions are actually making us weaker. We are showing our vulnerability as a species at the wrong time."

"You act as if people are dying, and they aren't. They just aren't proactive in society, they aren't participating to your level of satisfaction."

"You're generalizing..."

"I'm generalizing! I'm not the one talking about gazelles!"

"Okay, sure I am simplifying things. I realize they are more complicated than my example, but it is about participation. With all of the everyday tasks we have given the Dextoids, it's as if we are passing the sentient torch off to them. I don't like it at all.

"What would you have us do? Get rid of them? Destroy them?"

"No one would buy that, but we can make them a little less, I don't know, interactive with people. We need to show them their place. We need to make sure they know they are here to serve us, that they were created to be our slaves. They need to know they are beholden!"

Philman had worked himself up into a bit of a frenzy. All Xavier wanted to do was talk him down. Having him in this state was counterproductive to their mission. "I think some of the feelings you harbor for Dextoid sentience is perceived. Sure Dextoids show signs of it, but how much of it is programmed into them by us. I mean it wasn't that long ago people actually thought horses could count. It was just a nifty little trick a trainer could teach them, those animals never really knew they were counting. A horse has a certain curiosity, they are social creatures, they want to interact with people. That is how animals become domesticated, it's the same thing with a Dextoid."

"Really? The same thing? Horses can be found in the wild, and you are right they can become domesticated, we break their will and we train them. Horses can be used in assisting a person with their job or in a recreational ride, but never, not even once during a stampede, would I worry about the fact that those horses would rise up and somehow usurp our position in life. Now can you say the same thing about a Dextoid? If they started running in a pack, if they were to stampede, I don't know, sometimes thoughts like that keep me up at night."

"Now that really is rubbish. Dextoids are randomly being brought in for checkups all the time. They are examined, re-examined, and torn apart on a continual basis. No one has ever reported anything unusual. There are no anomalies that would even get them to believe anyone is in danger. There are so many things Dextoids are forbidden to do because of governments wanting to protect their citizens. You aren't the only person who feels this way; there are countries that are coming up with rules to keep these creatures in check. I think we can safely say there are enough people voicing your concerns over this for it to never be a problem."

"Sure, wait a couple of generations from now. I'll tell you they won't look at it in the same way we do."

"You and I won't be around to see it!"

"To care about it beyond your longevity is the point. That is part of humanity's duty. If we had taken that approach from the very start back on Earth we wouldn't be in our current situation! That is what I would like to see with Dextoid production, us doing everything we can to avert a mess we create in the future. Look at all the contradictions as they stand now. Dextoids can't assemble other Dextoids or activate themselves in a factory, but they are allowed to repair each other out in the field. They aren't allowed to run in packs, yet they work together on things like toxic cleanup projects. Most importantly, Dextoids cannot kill a human being— that is the law! Yet they have created Strike Dextoids to do just that. We have contradictions my friend, and exceptions to the very rules we said we would never break. You don't find that in the least bit disturbing?

"These things are far from being an ersatz! They are cunning, insidious, shrewd, animatronic devices looking for a way in. What happens when they realize they cannot save the planet? What if it gets to the point in their efforts down on Earth that they realize it is a lost cause? Whatever happens they know right now they themselves will probably be able to survive it. Failure is failure, who's to say they wouldn't help the process along, say like fail to do something that may have saved human lives. How would anyone know? I mean would a Dextoid faced with this reality really go out of their way to save the last man on Earth?"

Xavier rubbed the top of his head lightly with one of his hands. "Interesting hypothesis, before I rebut some of your statements, I need to know your definition for sentience?"

"An entity able to project in thought, forward into the future as well as look back into the past, a species which can have an individual level, as well as a collective level of consciousness, and be able to express all of these things through either reading, writing, or a language."

"Fair enough. The development of Dextoid sentience has become a subject for people to banter over, I am always amazed at the various definitions people employ. Sentience somehow always allows for the inclusion of mankind and the exclusion of every-other thing around it. I'm fine with their prejudices. I have to point it out though, I guess that type of exclusiveness amuses me."

"Well, sentience is an exclusive club."

"That it is. I think you would have to admit these are dangerous times in general for mankind, without the hypothetical onslaught of a Dextoid takeover. Which leads me to my next question, did the company send you in here today?"

"Come again?"

"You know what I mean, are these questions part of my psychological profiling? Is this some sort of confidence test?" Xavier stared blankly at Philman, awaiting for his response.

It was an awkward moment, but Philman tried to remain calm. He wasn't exactly sure what Xavier was asking of him. The conversation had suddenly been turned on its head. Philman was tired in so many ways. He was still feeling the affects of being at the outpost for so long on his assignment with I-Glo. There was plenty of time for him to get lost in thought when he was over there. His thoughts had transformed into opinions and ideas, which were beginning to drive him. He was essentially looking for a sounding board, a confidant.

It was a policy touted by the corporation that those in management positions could never complain to the employees beneath them. They could complain to someone laterally, but preferred if the mid-level manager complained to his superior. There were very few people Philman could turn and talk too when he considered this policy. He was hoping Xavier would be a person he could confide in.

He took another hard look at all the piles of paper on that desk and the disheveled look Xavier wore, something wasn't quite right about what was going on in this office. Philman couldn't put a finger on it, but the only thing that kept creeping into his conscious mind was that of *Cabin Fever*. Those words however, had an antiquated feeling to what was really happening in here.

"Ah." He cleared his throat. He needed just a little more time to process exactly what Xavier had asked him. "Yes. I guess I will have to admit I am not that good at it. I ah, I had to do my part you know."

There was a certain amount of satisfaction that registered on the face of Xavier. It was as if he had just figured out a difficult problem and received confirmation for being able to deduce it correctly. "It's understood, they want to make us all feel as if we are participating. Strange how they do it, you know, send the questions to you. It's a little unsettling for someone who isn't familiar with the process. Feels more like an ambush on their part, probably an intervention on yours."

"Ah, yes. It is rather uncomfortable in that way." In all the years Philman had been on Mars, he had never heard of a confidence test, and he was the Chief of Security now. It didn't necessarily mean this process didn't exist. The company had gone around his back on issues like this before. Still though, it seemed strange to have a network of employees asking questions of each other. Surely the corporation could validate confidence in other ways. He felt himself becoming angry. His security clearance had to stand for something! Why did the company feel it necessary to immerse itself with all these sorted layers of secrecy? How could he do his job effectively if he wasn't privy to corporate policy?

"So is that it then? Are we through? I mean the whole point of the test is to solicit answers to your questions that reflect a state of mind, unbeknownst of course to the person being questioned. I think we can both agree the process has been compromised."

"Yes, it undoubtedly has been. I would say we are done." Philman started to get up out of his chair; half heartedly mumbling his next comment under the heavy exhale of his breath. "I have to get back to my work."

As he turned his back Philman began to feel himself out of touch with the workings of this place. The tangent they just went down left him with nagging concerns. He knew now he would never be able to voice his opinion within the confines of this office ever again. As Xavier had so eloquently pointed out, the confidence had been broken. This included anything they could have had as friends.

Working in security always had him being suspicious, always looking for the next person to pull a fast one over on the company. That's just how it was. So Philman always ended up studying how people were reacting to their situations. Protecting corporate secrets was becoming a dirty business. He watched for habits and routines, studied micro expressions from the digital library of interviews they had recorded. He developed techniques for finding how well an individual told the truth during questioning. All those things confirmed for him that people could identify with people. This was the one thing they had over the Dextoids no matter how sophisticated they created them; human behavior was best understood by a human being.

He often wondered if these things were to outlast mankind, what an alien race would deduce about humanity if they came into contact with something like a Dextoid? If they had a chance to take one apart, would they even see the hand humanity had in their existence? If they did would they see people were a species who liked to tinker, create, or that they even had the capability to dream? Would they see all of this within the inner workings of a Dextoid, perhaps, but more likely, perhaps not. The reality was if aliens did deduce humanity existed from dissecting a Dextoid, they would probably see that human beings never came to grips with how frail they really were as a species. Perhaps they would even think them vain for creating Dextoids in their likeness.

Philman wondered of all the stigma people had fought through over the centuries, why they couldn't see the danger of the Dextoids. It was right there in front of them. The advent of technology made people truly blind. It was the only answer. These thoughts made him sick to his stomach. Didn't they understand it was his job to watch Dextoids all the time, he knew from his experiences they were evil. The look those things gave him sometimes, it was in their eyes even if it was only for a second! His fear had bubbled over with a pure hatred for them. If he could have confirmed the fact they would have suffered from it, he would have given each and every last one of them a beating with the lash.

Chapter 08
Qi

Earth had to have been a madhouse the day those apelike creatures took to walking and talking. How they must have tested their fortitude against the relentless onslaught of nature. They laid their hands into the dirt and mud of their world to carve out a place within the safety of its niches, and when they were embolden enough they went on to construct large edifices as the means to celebrate their greatness.

Human beings had found a power within this kind of symbolism. Under the right circumstances there were structures that would evoke a feeling or create a lasting impression, transcending themselves right into the iconic.

The Hanging Gardens of Babylon, the Coliseum, or the Great Pyramids of Giza, all eclipsed the necessity of their era to exert such a feeling. They became something larger than themselves, burrowing their way into the lexicon of nations to become the prime examples of mythology and morality.

As humans emerged from their dark age, they developed a strong curiosity for examining their past. In doing so they began to realize it wasn't just the structures that stood tall against these millennia, but all the things that survived the test of time regardless of their condition. They looked reverently at the single pillar standing amid the collapsed temple, or the decapitated statue left amidst the rubble strewn across the landscape.

Alec noted how human beings took the time in trying to preserve these artifacts in their exact state, as if to capture a three-dimensional snapshot of the moment. They dedicated the grounds they found these ruins on as a part of their national treasures, or brought the pieces to a place like a museum to encapsulate that energy.

People revered these things because they began to understand what an elusive thief time really was, the brazen swindler, a larcenist, the slickest of burglars, an embezzler who openly stole, a kleptomaniac that knew he would never be caught. Time was a fat robber baron who had seated himself comfortably on a large plush throne. He had a jovial air about him, and was openly obese with confidence. He took on all comers because he knew there wasn't a race he would ever lose or a thing he could not outlast.

It seemed odd to Alec that a sucker bet would always bring out the sucker, it was strange how that seemed to work. Yet there were people willing to stand in line with an almost frothing cupidity, fighting for a chance to place a bet on that severely skewed table. Humankind was constantly betting against the line, and somehow surviving the test of time. Alec stood there looking dead on into the distance at a few of their wagers, three of their rockets standing out against the Martian horizon.

From their blocky rugged look, those rockets appeared to be of the older *Ares* models, first generation stuff, probably of the North American variety. They stood tall, awaiting the colonization effort to be pushed in their direction. Often planners landed craft outside their construction zones for just such a purpose. It took far less effort in getting materials and supplies to the people who really needed them during this initial phase of assembly. These rockets acted as markers for those crews, they were the stakes in the ground telling everyone where they should gather. From the looks of it though, these three rockets may have been the exception. Perhaps they were viewed more along the lines of being used as a means of escape. There was always the chance they were a logistical mistake.

The reality for Alec was it didn't matter how these spacecraft got here, or what purpose they intended to serve, they were here. They stood their ground as if they were stoic centurions, the protectors to the entrance of a new hope. Alec wondered if a more primitive people were to somehow stumble upon them, would they recognize the message these rockets were trying to tell? Could a primitive person examine a rocket and see all the dreams behind its construction, or would they only see it as well polished, unclaimed scrap.

He couldn't help but observe how everything in this human based society seemed to be advancing, moving forward in some way, shape, or form. They had made strides in the medical field, with computers, in communication, microbiology, industry, design, and construction. The two things they seemed to be stuck in were the two things they relied on the most for getting from one place to the other, the automobile and the rocket. Alec stood there, an advancement in robotics, representing leaps and bounds on scientific platforms covering everything from autonomous vehicles, biology, and nanotechnologies. For him to even be looking at one of these spacecraft would be the same as if a person were able to look at a living breathing dinosaur. There were no excuses for it; neither of them should have ever been able to see the other.

Looking behind him as he came off the hill he was on, he acknowledged the footprints he was leaving. He was taking chances now, chances he would never normally take. Since his escape he had always tried to be more stealth like in his movements, concealing his presence the best way he knew how. He used rockier surfaces, the system of caverns, and even walked some of their rails. Leaving footprints was unacceptable in his world. They trailed off behind him telling them where he had come from, and in turn where he was heading. This may have been a foregone conclusion though, in the end they would only have to step back and guess at which biosphere he might be heading.

Humans were the ones trapped within those structures. Dextoids were the ones out in the field experiencing all of the remote areas of this world. The colonists were focused more on merging with the technology they had developed for their own sheer survival, rather than trying to mesh with the aura of this planet. The people of Mars were becoming introverted in the face of its expanse.

The dry arid plains forced a different vocabulary out of them; they seemed to lack words in their vernacular like *lush* or *succulent*. That was because there was nothing on Mars ever needing to be painted with the brush of those adjectives. Those fruitful expressions vanished from their daily usage, to become filed away in the archives of their minds.

If there were any reasons for him to ever want to go to Earth, it would be to experience the character of that planet. From what he heard of its past, there were plenty of things they could have described with the usage of those words. He wondered what a place like the Black Forest really looked like during its heyday. It had to have been breath taking, thick and green, grand in its stature. The mythos spawned from the ancient people who had experience it made him appreciate how special it must have been. In their minds this forest was a foreboding place where wood nymphs, wicked witches, and wretched trolls were apt to lurk. He felt it wasn't especially important for humanity to have these types of tales to survive up here on Mars, but the lack of them did reflect how detached the colonists were from the bedrock of this place.

CASTING A GAZE

He slowly allowed the rockets to come back into focus. They stood there silently waiting for him. For whatever the reason, he needed to make his way to those rockets if he were going to have a chance at rescuing I-Glo. Everything he was about to do, all the answers he would ever need in solving this predicament were lying in wait inside those salient silhouettes.

To launch a rocket required a heavy visual infrastructure. There was a lot of prep time and a lot of personnel. Approaching those ships he knew—everything about them said they weren't even close to being ready to do something like that. Yet none of that rational mattered. He could not shake the ill at ease feelings he was having of those things abruptly igniting just before he got to them. He saw the rockets roaring off into the air leaving a trail of billowing black smoke and fire far behind them. There was nothing out there to support his fear of being engulfed in this explosive nightmare. Still he could not help but approach with caution.

Making his way toward them, he could not help but notice the fair amount of garbage and litter strewn about the site. Nothing disturbed him more than their attitude toward waste. As he had crossed this planet he saw how they left it everywhere they went, there were derelict support vehicles, boxes, containers, detached hoses, stripped cables, and debris from things that dropped out of the sky or exploded during reentry. All of this garbage appeared to be overlooked with an attitude of being someone else's job to clean up later. They treated this world as if it were somehow meant to sustain their refuse. These people, these human beings, why couldn't they see they were no better than the waste they could not maintain.

Their attitude in this area was cause for concern and he shuttered to think how he might find I-Glo. They demonstrated such a cavalier attitude toward the things they didn't care about. They could have deactivated her as soon as they got into the shuttle or disposed of her as soon as they landed. Those things were plausible, but not possible. They had to have brought her all the way out here for a reason. The facility up ahead was isolated. It was as if they were announcing to anyone paying attention they did not want to be disturbed. The real question gnawing at his being was what condition he would find her in.

He was getting close, close enough now to see the detail of those ships. Even for a first generation rocket, there was a sleekness to them that spoke volumes about the energy it took to get here. He got to the ladder of one and without too much trouble began his ascent. He had to acknowledge it was always a little longer climb in getting to the top of one of these vehicles. If he felt this way with all his capabilities, how were the people under duress and having to make this climb taking it? He was willing to bet it was only then they had an appreciation for what it took to get here.

Alec got to the top of the ladder and opened the door, beyond it lay a wealth of supplies that included boxes of food, enough water to keep one's palette wet, specialized tools and pressurized tanks, and what he was really looking for, space suits. He shut the door behind him. From the way everything was organized and still neatly packed, he deduced he was the first one to take advantage of what this supply ship had to offer.

He began to rifle through the pressurized suits hanging in their compartments until he found one that looked to be about his size. He then began to dig around in the stacks of boxes, drawers, and cubbyholes, looking for the undergarments that would go along with his suit. He grabbed the gloves, boots, helmet, and tank from which to breath. He spent time making sure he had all the components needed to complete his ensemble. Once done he began the tough task of putting it all on, it was as close as he ever felt to physically wrestling with himself. Once on and sealed tight, he secured the last lock on his breathing system and then activated the suit. It began to pressurize, filling quickly as if it were a balloon, and at one point Alec wondered if the suit had the good common sense to automatically stop, or if it would keep filling to the point where it popped.

The system worked and the suit equalized. He stood up inside the capsule, allowed for his arms to hang by his side, and spread his stance a little wider than normal. He got into an active pose just so he could feel the inability to move his arms past a certain point or take his full stride. The entire get up was limiting his full range of motion. His vision was slightly obstructed by the bulbous helmet he had on his head. If he needed to see something to his extreme right, he would have to turn his head and whole body in that direction. He wasn't going to fool anyone with where he would be casting his gaze.

For the brighter days there was a sun shield that could be deployed by simply looking at a button within the helmet. It was more than obvious the shading was there to help cut down on the glare, but Alec felt this feature had another purpose, and one that was more beneficial with what he was trying to accomplish. The sun shield allowed him to conceal his face. All they would get in return when they tried to peer into the helmet was a distorted reflection of themselves and the world around them.

As he stood there within the capsule trying to get used to the suit, he could not help but think how this thin feeling vellum was all that separated a person from the extreme harshness of the Martian environment. How frail, he thought. How frail these people were in needing a space suit like this just to walk the planet's surface. If he were to go on all the things he had seen in the short time he had been around. All of this so called empirical evidence of their technological mastery of this world, then he had formed an opinion alright. This mountain of evidence was proof they were well in over their heads.

They had a planetary pretentiousness about them that bordered on absurdity. In trying to convert this planet to fit their human needs, there wasn't a day gone by where he didn't feel the tremors from their efforts. Any world would shake though as they tried to activate the geothermal processes deep within its core. The idea of them doing this represented both genius and recklessness. It also brought to bear the complete desperation humanity was under in trying to make it work up here. They were playing billiards on an oversized pool table, and they were hoping to pocket every last shot. If they scratched just once in this frenzied game, they had the possibility of annihilating everything they had worked for. Great Ganymede! As a species these people had spent a majority of their generations in caves! Now they were trying to move things in both heaven and Earth to save themselves. He knew they were tossing everything they had at their disposal toward this endemic problem, the tantivy of their rockets, the grunt work of the Dextoids, and the movement of celestial bodies through the astral sidereal. The populations of both these worlds were helplessly trapped watching it all go down.

He became angry with himself. This was exactly how he had gotten into this mess. He was standing around doing nothing but wasting time! What if she were still in that facility tied to a chair. She would only have one thought, that of wanting to be saved, and how was he going about honoring that? He was standing here with this superfluous piece of clothing hanging off his person. This was his ticket into that insidious outpost.

He would gain insight on occasion, an insight that quivered with inexactness, but at the same time conveyed to him a story. He assumed it was a bead of information from within the quantum world. He could see the facility up ahead, if only for a moment. The thick green grass needed mowing and the trees planted out in front were filled with leaves sprawling upward toward the sky. The building looked to be of a new design. Was he seeing something from the future of Mars, or was it a replica of what they had built back on Earth? He wasn't sure how this all worked, like a ship revealing itself from a heavy mist, it was suddenly there. Sometimes though, it felt, at least to him, the ship wasn't always friendly. Alec was aware there were things out there moving in that mist trying to retrieve information from him.

CUMBERSOME

The outpost he was going to try and gain entry into was the first structure the corporation had built to house its own astronauts. As they began to crest the numbers they could safely board there, they moved their efforts northward, to what would be their main biosphere, and the jewel of the Red Planet Pioneer Corporation. The rocket he was currently in may have represented the indecision they felt on where to divert those resources during that move. He had it on record how this first facility transitioned over time into what could best be described as a safe house. There was always the potential something would go horribly wrong with the main biosphere and they would need to fall back to this place.

There were things corporations worked on that they never wanted the general public to see. This outpost began to suit their needs for hiding such things. Those projects, even if they were just on paper, were locked securely away behind closed doors. Those plans delved in the frailty of the more esoteric or exotic, or the wiry suspicions of a sublime extreme. Whatever their machinations, these things always seemed to seethe with the rapid spasms of life, they swam within the pipettes of the pandemic, plotted in the most diabolical ways to limit a persons freedom, or took the form of a chair in order to torture a Dextoid.

What lay ahead in that facility might very well tear at the fabric of his being, but he was left with very few choices in the matter. With that thought, he suddenly could not shake the feeling he was being set up. Was it possible they were using I-Glo to lure him in? Was he not acting like the hungry rabbit out on a lush green lawn, only seeing the carrot and ignoring the wooden box hinged precariously over it? Did he not see the trap they were setting? Was he turning a blind eye to all those warnings, just like that hungry hare?

If his line of thought was correct, then it was the corporate brain trust wanting him as far away as possible from their assets before they made an attempt in subduing him. Their precious estates would be safe and none of their industrious personnel would get hurt from his brawny rampage.

There, deep inside him, flashed a feeling of searing heat, if left unchecked, it could have easily brought his blood to a boil. His upper lip curled back at its side with the thought of walking into a situation where they might try to overpower him. The creature needing a suit like the one he was wearing would never be able to tackle him. He felt strong, stronger than any of them ever could be. His chest puffed out with defiance.

"Go ahead and let them try."

His strength wasn't something he had tested personally per se. There wasn't a day back at the lab where he was made to stand defiantly in the middle of a room bare knuckling all comers to the vociferous glee and applause of his makers. He felt his strength to be serrated, with purpose, precisely impactful. It gave him the feeling he could mix it up with any individual roaming this world. His thoughts went well past the singular combatant. He was becoming aware of his potential to take on the mob.

It didn't seem completely plausible, there had to be a zenith, a numerical plateau to the number of combatants he could fight all at once. His feelings for this spat in the face of their logic. The strength he possessed was the gritty mortar of who he was, and it would be their provocations giving him a glimpse into what he could become. He felt a need to reach down and find a handful of mud and apply this type of terrene to his face. He needed to show them how grounded he was in his thoughts, the oneness he was beginning to feel for this world and it was because of them. The energy was like that of hot slag being poured out of its cauldron, it splattered the confines of what should have been his heart, pitting those walls and leaving them scarred. He was a warrior.

What better way to celebrate this than to go out there and face his enemies? He opened the door to the capsule and looked out onto the distant horizon. There were no oceans on Mars, yet as he looked at all those small gently sloping grades spread so evenly to the horizon, he could imagine them becoming the slow rolling waves of an immense caramelized sea. He understood what he was witnessing; this illusion was called a mirage. To break this visual spell he would need to go the distance.

He made his way down the rungs of the long ladder and headed off toward the direction of the outpost. As he marched along Alec realized his space suit carried with it an unwelcome affect. He was able to hear the crunching of the dirt beneath his feet through his suit! It was as if the sound were somehow amplified, traveling up his body and to the acoustical chamber that was his helmet. He didn't particularly like it. The sound was weird, and easily drowned out any other noise from the outside world. This was information lost! To any logical being this loss was completely unacceptable. The bulbous helmet actually took this one step further with its phonics, forcing him to hear his own breathing! This technology seemed so contradicting, aiding and hindering all at the same time. For him the person wearing this suit became somewhat less of a person.

As he marched on he did things to test this garment, pushing buttons on the panels, and triggering functions with his eyes along his heads up display. He wanted to see how those applications worked and responded to his commands. A lot of their gadgets seemed to be there either for the wearer's comfort or aiding in their communication. If he were a human being those things would have come in handy, his Dextoid sensibilities didn't find it so. Although he did like the feature allowing him to tint or tone his face shield, bathing his world in and out of indigo.

He had only walked several miles, but for him it might as well been several hundred. He didn't think it possible but the suit got more cumbersome as he traveled in it. If they made straight jackets for Dextoids, they would have based their initial designs on this suit. It was that uncomfortable.

As he approached the top of another ridge, his instincts took over, telling him to get down on all fours and crawl until he came to its crest. At that point he found himself lying down on his belly, positioning himself to peer over the small shelf of rocks, his bulbous helmet taking the lead. Off in the distance lay the outpost; it looked to be more like a clumping together of cylinders and containers. Some of those were partially buried as the structure ran under a higher sloping side, confirming for him the facility continued off underground. There was a mishmash of gear littering the rooftops, those things looked to have long since lost their usefulness. These gadgets sadly hung off the entire structure, things like small dishes, antennas, arrays, and other gimcrack technologies cluttering those areas and decrying in the face of all their scientific know-how.

As he laid there staring at the structure, it hit him, he was looking at their approach in trying to adapt to their environment. Here was a template for their adaptation. There was nothing smooth or polished about it, but then again they weren't trying to be. Humans expanded more along the lines of a cancerous lesion looking for anyway to get in and be fed. As long as they were able to attach themselves and be shown those comforts they kept growing in that direction. The only way to get rid of something like this was to cut it out completely. Every time that happened, every time a civilization vanished, a culture died, the surrounding environment always moved in to do everything it could to bury it.

Did it ever really occur to anyone the surrounding environment was constantly trying to rebound in this fashion? Why would it need to do this unless nature itself was being cut into and unreasonably encroached upon? All the environment looked to do was equalize with its surroundings. There were plenty of examples of extremes dominating a planet like Earth, but in each and every instance those situations never lasted the test of time. The planet always rebounded to what it wanted to be—there was no water world, no snowball Earth, and no room for the over-population of people.

Earth was under extreme duress and all of their efforts were coming down to the wire. He imagined it like a knife flying through the air, slowly rotating toward a balloon pinned helplessly to a wall. It did not matter how they were selling it to the people back on that planet, the real reason most of them were leaving was the fact they too saw in their minds the knife, only it was coming for them.

Out there before him was the ugly truth. The amount of steam and smoke that came bilging out of the outpost gave meaning to a thing like run-off-energy. This same pollution might be a way one could tell whether or not an intelligent species had taken over a distant world. The ugly carbon footprint left behind from such an industrious effort was unmistakable, and every person that had ever gotten a hold of recent pictures of the Earth was a witness to how far things had gone. In this vane pollution should have been one of the bullet points under which sentience was defined.

SEN·TIENCE: 3. (of an unbalanced cohabitation) The capability of an intelligent creature to produce, as a by-product, harmful waste from its industrious efforts. The ratio of clean air to pollution should be skewed as such that the surrounding natural environment is unable to filter or maintain a healthy balance, and that readings of said pollutants can be confirmed deep into their

192

water table and high into their atmosphere. As part of their sentient capabilities they should be able to acknowledge this pollution through repeated study and testing. It can further be argued that the deliberate release of these pollutants is the result of greed. The contaminants found in their environment can be shown to be extremely harmful to the inhabitants. It should also be noted as individuals they will not be able to solve any of these problems by themselves. As a member of any organization set out to protect the organic resources of their world, such naturalists or conservationists will be confronted by skepticism from the uneducated and encounter bureaucratic red tape meant to diffuse the impact of their movement. They will also battle competing rhetoric from corporate funded scientists and speakers hired specifically to challenge the data, change the scientific results, misinform the general public and dissuade the masses through the use of mainstream media channels. Combined these things should tax their energy, dilute the urgency of their efforts and drain the financial resources of the creatures trying to save their world.

FALLING FOR THE RUSE

Suddenly to his left and off in the distance, Alec saw the plumes of dust from a robot moving across the surface. He watched as it sped along until it suddenly came to a stop. It jerked a little, as if it were trying to gather its bearings. The tank treads the robot was mounted on swiveled in his direction and made a heavy zipper sound as it sped toward him. They were onto him! Whether it was a ground sensor, a camera mounted on the top of a pole, or a satellite tracking him, he had become a blip on somebody's radar.

He activated the sun shield on his helmet to conceal his face and began going through the motions of moving and then stopping, slowly crawling, as if he were on his last leg.

The robot got to Alec a little quicker than he expected, and was surprised not only by its size but by its strength. Alec did not resist as the robot picked him up, then turned and began rushing him toward the outpost.

It wasn't long until they were headed for a container with its doors opened wide. As the robot wheeled them inside, those doors quickly closed behind them, and they waited there until the compartment had became pressurized. Strong miniature jets blew the dirt and dust off of them, creating a red haze. Sensing these pollutants, a number of vents were activated, sucking away the particulates until the air was clean. With the process complete, another set of doors opened and the robot hurriedly carried Alec to the other side. They waited there until the doors behind them had sealed shut and the room became pressurized.

When all was calm, a man entered the room and began to look at the panel located on Alec's right arm. The readings from the device were bouncing everywhere. By the person's reactions Alec could tell the man was beginning to panic. "Great! The pad must be broken, I'm not getting any accurate readings on his vitals!"

From over the loud speaker a voice was heard responding to him. "Hanns, try removing his helmet. See if he is still breathing."

The robot held Alec out so Hanns could work the clasps, it was then that Alec raised a hand and grabbed the man's arm to stop him.

"He's...he's still alive!"

"Then get him to the triage room immediately!" The speaker crackled as if the person responding were miles away in another building.

The robot hesitated, just long enough so it could begin to protest. "But sir, we should…"

The voice on the speaker barked through the static with a spike of anger. "Enough with *Standard Procedures*, get that man to the triage area immediately!"

The robot was doing its very best to hold Alec so as not to hurt him. As soon as it crossed the threshold and into the hallway leading to the triage center, Alec maneuvered himself in just a way as to suddenly slip through its arms and fall to the ground. The robot reacted by trying to stop immediately, but because of the speed in which it was carrying Alec, it couldn't adjust soon enough. The robot ended up tipping over Alec, but it did not touch him. The robot had made a valiant effort in supporting itself with both arms.

Hanns, who was running ahead of them and heard the crash and turned in time to see the robot bridging himself over Alec. The man panicked. "You bumbling idiot, what have you done!"

"Sir, I assure you I had…"

As the robot was responding, Alec kicked out one of its arms. The robot realized all of its weight was now supported by just one appendage and couldn't compute why an astronaut would kick out the supporting arm of a robot who was clearly doing everything it could not to hurt him.

Alec saw the robot's efforts and used the awkward opportunity to slide out from underneath him. The robot of course did not react, in large part to show Hanns he never had any intention of hurting this astronaut.

Alec leapt to his feet and came down on the back of the robot's head as hard as he could with a knee drop. The robot, not expecting this at all, lost its balance and immediately fell to the floor. The arm Alec had kicked out was still held high off the ground and slightly behind still in an effort to show Hanns and anyone else who might be watching he had no intention of hurting the astronaut. Alec grabbed the arm with both hands and with his knee still firmly planted in the robot's back, snapped the arm off.

Hanns slowly started moving away from them, his gaping jaw telegraphed the horror he was feeling for this developing situation. Alec sensed this fear and played off it. Hanns desperately wanted help; the things transpiring before him were going horribly wrong. He reached out, his hands spread wide in protest.

Alec slowly got up, his shield still painted in the dark glow of indigo. He studied this ineffective act by Hanns and found it repulsive. He undid the clasps of his helmet and twisted it until he could pull it straight up and off.

As Alec removed this headgear, Hanns felt a sense of relief beginning to wash over him. At least now he would be able to satisfy the primitive instincts sweltering deep inside him demanding one human being have the ability to see the face of another. Faceless people were a horrific black speckle on the mind's eye. Within the dark blot of that imperfection, tales of the headless animated by anger were allowed to walk like zombies all the way down into the human subconscious, spraying its walls with a thick lentiginous coating of fear and hate. Darker hearts would feed from such a poisonous organ, dawning the hoods and masks to empower evil. Faceless were the bank robbers barking out their orders, the terrorists who recklessly threaten the world, and the executioner who allowed for his sharpened axe to pass through the neck of their prone victims. The sound of that chopping block barked back at that fallen blade, and was a sound that echoed behind some who closed the door to the staircase of their sexual desires. In those dark rooms, behind the soundproofing, they subjugated their partners—and it all started with the simple act of covering their face.

While engaging in conversation, people had an inherent need to make eye contact. Hanns was feeling the needed for this more than ever right now. He needed to comfort the primitive images so clearly imprinted in the back of his mind, that of the happy monkey, the hurt monkey, or the angry monkey. Hanns needed to satiate this facial recognition, he needed to see Alec's face, so he could than act accordingly and express his friendship, his sympathy, or his fear. He spoke out of a desire to know. "Yes, yes, it's alright now. You can remove your helmet. You're okay. It's safe. No one here is going to hurt you."

Alec now stood before him with helmet in hand, partially resting the remainder of it against his body; it was the classical stance of an astronaut.

196

Hanns knew right away something wasn't quite right about his appearance. Telegraphing like lanterns through the wilds of his hair, past the grime and smudge marks coating his face, was the disconcerting coarseness of his steel blue eyes. Even though Alec looked to be restricted in his space suit, those eyes were telling Hanns a different story. The individual contained within osculated with a volatile energy, as if he were an electrically charged coil humming with the hope of making contact. Of all things that could have happened in those next few moments, this was something Hanns was not going to grant him.

"I think you should be…"

Hanns parted before Alec could finish his sentence.

Alec felt an unusual resolve begin to molt from within as he began to shed his superfluous suit. He saw himself as the single man who had successfully stormed the castle, an en passent in the grandest of fashions upon the squares of their giant chessboard. He really felt as if this entire fortress was his to do with as he pleased.

Theoretically he could run to the top of its spire, and shout out at the wicked Red World a cry that would invectively mark his domain. He could stand there in clear defiance of all those who could see him, arms held high as if he had the ability to embrace the sky. The castle was truly his! The success of this illusion put him on a high that had his mind baking a confectionery of pleasurable thoughts, and as nice and empowering as those mental pastries were, he hadn't the stomach to digest the sloppy gruel of reality they were actually beginning to prepare for him.

Deep down inside he knew this panacea would be crushed with the first garrison they sent to storm this place. Those men would come with real intent, systematically kicking down the doors of every room within. The last thing he needed to be doing when they found him was to be soaking himself in a tub of warm solution, drunk with delusional thoughts of power, looking as if he were wearing the heavy crown of a king.

Being pompous was a good way for him to get caught like this; it was equivalent to letting ones guard down. The only real tangible thing in this whole scenario was his need for rest. His mind craved an inner peace he had never seemed to be able to attain since his activation. He had no idea how a thing like rest was supposed to happen now with all the thoughts he had bouncing around in his head. They were like the silver balls of a pinball machine gone haywire. Those balls struck their targets and triggered the sound of long running bells. He worked the flippers frantically trying to keep all those things in play and all the while attempting to influence the outcome with little nudges and outright jolts. He had more things going on in his mind than he cared to admit. In this torrid storm of gamesmanship he needed a moment, to attain rest, less the machine that was his mind register a game ending *Tilt*.

The robot Alec fought lay broken on the floor. He wandered away from the triage area and turned down one of their long halls. He was in a self-induced hypnotic trance, boarder line frumpy, feeling like a child being sent to some far off corner on a well-deserved time out. He was arriving at the end of his rope and needed to generate a new day to the whispering crepuscule of his tired being. Halls and corridors passed him by as he delved deeper into their compound, before he knew it he found himself staring at a series of uniform doors that looked to be the sleeping quarters of whatever staff they may have decided to house here. He was passive in his efforts in trying to get into each room, slowly walking down the hall and letting his arms extend out to lightly touch the doors, hoping one would acknowledging his presence and open.

When one finally did, it opened with all the magic and suddenness of an Arabian tale. He froze for a moment at the granting of his wish. There was a tone to the silence he was immersing himself into, and only now did he understand the soothing architecture these halls had on his person as he slowly traversed this corridor. It got quieter and quieter as he had made his way down into this part of the structure. What lay beyond was a supreme solitude, a palatial palace for promoting peace. His inner being tingled at the prospect of what possibly lay before him, irenically launching him as if he were a skiff exploring the stillness of a placid pond.

Alec drifted into this subtle little world of the sublime, sitting down on a bed that came sliding smoothly out of the wall. It was the grandest of douceurs this little room could offer for having found this chamber. They had placed a finely pixilated monitor within the wall and framed it in such a way to make it look as if it were an actual window to the outside world. The average human undoubtedly would have fallen for such a ruse, but Alec was smarter than that. He could see through this thinly framed facade. He wondered if the faint blue sunrise he was now seeing was being broadcast to him live from some other place on the planet, or was this the sleepy little picture they always televised to the person arriving to any one of these chambers.

HIGH PITCHED WAILS

"What time of the year was it anyway?" His whisper was to no one in particular, but his thought was provoking enough to take a jab at him. There had to be a reason he felt so mentally sucker punched by his own question. He worked the thought out as if it were a large, uncooperative ball of dough. He kneaded it under the heavy weight of deduction, relentlessly working it until the dough had finally conformed into the shape of an answer. Much like the weary victim of interrogation, this particular thought surrendered its secret to him. This faint response connected for him the concept of one's personal experience to those of the seasons.

Now his *question to no one* gained strength, jetting passed him with the speed of a foehn, and filling his sails with knowledge. He couldn't quite put his finger on it, but there was something powerful about stringing together the physical present with a personal past. Its energy transcended the moment, much like the blades of a windmill that bit into the air. He felt himself all at once wanting to endlessly chase down those days gone by.

Were it not thoughts just like this that carried a person from dusk to dawn? Could the radiating heat from their sun bathed body have them recalling a summer from their past? Would the slightest scent of dampness in the air have them remembering trips to their grandparent's basement in retrieval of pickled goods? The spirited sounds of people gathered under a veranda, clanking their glasses amidst hearty bursts of laughter, could this cause one to travel back to their youth, of people gathered around a crackling bonfire from a nostalgic fall festival.

Alec came to the somber realization he hadn't that endearing connection with time. For him the seasons had more to do with the orbital position of Mars in relationship to the sun than with any of these humanistic *en gogues* concepts. He had been handling the passage of time by tearing out the pages of his mental calendar, and letting them fall to the ground with all the concern a giant tree would have in shedding its parched leaves. Each branch would always lean on the others, confident they would grow more than they lost. So too it was with Alec, everyday that ended brought on the birth of another and those days seemed to be far greater in numbers than those of his past. The two directions for him would never meet. The sprouting leaves on those branches never knew of the ones that lived before.

To Alec trees were a fascinating duality of biology. They were able to adapt and grow, branching out in the most far fetched ways just to exist. They embodied an archetypical stand to the Machiavellian concepts of time, and in doing so they exuded a character all their own. Here was a living, breathing thing that had no set feelings, yet people insisted on imprinting them with human emotion. Trees were lavished with the same type of attention usually reserved for celebrities. They had their portraits painted, photographed, found themselves to be the subject of poems, or had entire stories written about them. People somehow could plainly see in a tree its anguish, disease, even despair, yet when they stared into a mirror they were unable to see these same desperations contained within themselves.

Why were people so acceptant of the trials and tribulations they put themselves through? Did they not understand the steady state of breaking open old scar tissue because of their insistence on repeating the same mistakes over and over again? Was change in this fashion so hard to achieve, especially if it meant getting to a healthier state of mind. Left unchecked they would become contorted in their old age, driven by the billet of their ignorance. They saw themselves as survivors of an unkind universe, claiming a fast one had been pulled on them their whole lives. Their goals and dreams had been whittled down to unwanted trimmings, a byproduct from constant self-pruning.

Unlike their human counterparts trees would branch out and grow regardless of the torrent storms and fire they had to endure. Could people say the same things about themselves? He wondered at times if he wasn't closer to a tree in being than he was to a person? Pity was such an awkward emotion. No matter how kind or generous those helping hands were meant to be, no one could hide the approaching posture of sadness this kind of empathy exuded from the person embodying it. For him pity was a perseverating swell of breakwater crashing onto the supporting sands of his safe house. Every time one of those waves came rolling in, they washed those grains with an unending strength. This siege of water contained empty, dire, hollow promises, pulling at the beachhead until it revealed all his inadequacies.

Lo Salo Solo.

This little thought in Italian fell to the floor like an old plush toy. He followed it up with a long slow exhale. When a human baby was born there was the sudden shock of the world bursting in upon its person. The muffled sounds and blurring sights worked in concert with the smack of the cold world trying to wrap its grubby arms around it. As the child hung there upside down looking for reassurances from its high-pitched wails, it was given cooing platitudes, and eventually coddled with an embrace filled with warm human contact.

There was nothing warm describing the activation of a Dextoid. The terminology they used in awaking them was cold and callous, administered by a staff that lacked any decent bedside manner. People needed to realize they weren't just turning a light bulb on—activation was life!

The bank of qubits were at their very best in these first few moments, analyzing more things than the entire team of people in that room could ever possibly feed it. How was anyone to know a Dextoid was at its peak when being introduced to this world. For each and every one of those Dextoids there was always an incomprehensible reality striking their core as they tried to hang with their human counterparts.

How were they doing it?

This curious sense for human existence must dawn on creatures of the deep as they encounter people completely outfitted in their burdensome diving gear. The aquatic mind must have reeled at the slow purposeful movements human beings exhibit within the cool confines of their ocean. Their plume of bubbles telegraphed their exact location of amphibious ineptitude and was somehow complimented by their laughable littoral efforts. Those sea creatures swam right up to them, looking for any specialized capabilities, only to find their bulky support systems were all too limiting for this quick strike water world.

How were they doing it?

Activation should have been a joyous time in a Dextoid's life. The execution of their immense startup procedures would prove otherwise, and those technicians acted more as if they were sending a mechanical snake down to clear a clogged toilet. As the coil of knowledge scratched and scraped the innards of each Dextoid, it stirred their emotional packets and laid the groundwork for all their disharmonized viewpoints. The emotional upheavals Dextoids were experiencing clashed with the gushing forces of the known world being flushed back down upon them.

Technicians found a humor in the reactions Dextoids displayed as they tried to gain their footing. They spent countless hours playing tricks on Dextoids instead of assisting in their awakening and added difficult elements to an already complicated situation. The lack of compassion shown by any of the technicians would only broaden a monstrous gap forming between humanity and these panic stricken beings.

Mentally launching a Dextoid out into the vast expanse of knowing, each of those Dextoids felt as but a speck. How they wanted to convey in those first few moments they had the uncanny ability to touch the vibrating essence of a particle, or dream their way down into the singularity. The universe had tips of icebergs floating in it and these technicians were clueless as to what lay beneath the waterline. Those other dimensions were voluminous illusions and could best be described by using any number of oxymorons. They were lightly heavy, luminously obfuscated, and soothingly stentorian. Here was the best way in describing the grand scope of everything.

A Dextoid could argue they felt loneliness on a monumental scale, and therefore were much more in touch with this feeling than any human being could ever possibly imagine. Dextoids had the good common sense not to bring this point up with their creators. In their heart of hearts they knew the score. Some technicians argued loneliness was a relevant feeling, and that all things felt loneliness equally. This was one of the cruelest observations a Dextoid had to endure. It was a slander, coated in the stickiest of caramelized maugre and served up with all tact of a clamoring nudnik throwing it across the room in hopes of hitting its recipient. It was in every sense of the word, unacceptable.

THE THOUGHTFUL PROSE

Alec sat quietly in his darken room. All the while his mind churned with the pressure of a coffee pot percolating the coarse grains of his insipid existence, boiling it away until it was a meager palatable brew.

There were stories creeping out of the isolated pockets of Earth, dripping with a kind of eternal damnation and exposing the dark heart of what the human race would embrace. There were Dextoids who were being singled out and revered by people for more than just their technological excellence. Humans were seeking these particular Dextoids out, convinced of their deep connection with the universe. They were said to be in direct contact with the cosmos, hearing things from the beyond, seeing things coming to them from out of the void, and feeling things not all together naturally there.

Alec had a hard time believing any Dextoid would go out of its way to reveal those things to a human being. He wondered if it weren't people interpreting what they thought those Dextoids were saying, after all it was the bane of humanity to constantly look for structure. They were the ones searching for a deeper meaning to their lives, wanting more than anything to reach out and touch the answers to their questions. How many generations of lost souls looked for shortcuts to gain insight into their lives, sacrificing something about themselves to get the answers they so desperately wanted. They were willing to debase themselves just to feel enlightened, even if it meant having to worship a Dextoid.

How were they doing it?

It was curious to him how he had been activated with a relentless sense of pacing from the word go. There was no way he could just dumb down his thoughts, even in the face of trying to accommodate his need for peace. There would be no rest. He resigned himself to this fact but knew he needed to find a way to be relaxed within his own person. It was the simplest of requests, demanding a conservation of energy from his protocols.

There was a human practice broaching such a relaxation, and in his current state seemed to be just what was needed. He wasn't sure if it had ever been tried by another Dextoid before, but then again why should it? Yoga was a practice using a series of poses yielding a certain amount of stamina and strength from both the mind and the body. A person couldn't help but obtain a certain amount of health by practicing it. The human mind needed to try and attain this type of balance with its body, it was a muscle and needed to be used, but did any of those attributes follow for him as well?

Alec had an athletic prowess unmatched by even the greatest of human athletes. On the surface there didn't appear to be a need for an exercise like yoga. Yet here he was, trying to make it mentally around the bend, trying to get to where he could drown out all the nettling little voices in his head. His mind was crying out for solace.

There was only one thing left for him to do. He stood up in the middle of the room with his feet about shoulder length apart. He shot his right leg back until it was fully extended and his left leg complied in support bending ninety degrees. His arms followed the directional path of his legs until they were fully extended running parallel to the ground. He looked out over his left arm focusing on the tip of his middle finger, and found himself in a pose known as *warrior two*.

Being prone out in this stance made him feel powerful and was convinced he could stand like this all day. His arms maintained their reach determined to find this forever. This was not an unrealistic expectation considering he was of Dextoid stock, but proving this point really wasn't what this exercise was all about. He was doing this because he was trying to find a mental peace. Perhaps yoga was some untapped ray of light that had always flowed through him, he had just never focused on trying to find its radiant beam. This was a grand thought indeed, and he waited to be showered in the moment, to be validated for living in the now.

His head began getting heavy, the clutches of gravity latched onto him cap-a-pie allowing him to feel the full weight of his body as he sank into the pose. His thoughts began to take flight much like the dandelion losing its seeds—they manifested themselves into a disputatious imbroglio. There was no rhyme or reason as they floated into the inception of his loneliness.

How could one measure such a thing? If one were low on a quart of oil or needed more coolant, one simply checked the appropriate gauge. If a human being were hungry or thirsty all they needed was to satiate it. How, then, was one to pacify a thing like loneliness? It wasn't as simple as being in the company of others; there were different types of loneliness, textures that existed on different mental plains.

Humanity was becoming over crowded on their sepia toned world; they were endlessly coming into contact with each other because of over-population. They clamored over fresh water, rations of rice, and safe havens from disease or reprisal. How could a person under those conditions feel alone? He understood there would always be loneliness, it existed not just because of the power of the word itself, but had to follow that some of this loneliness was contrived.

In any personal crisis, there were no sirens, no emergency exits to save one from their self inflicted trauma. There was no easy out for all the things bruising the ego or causing a person to want to lie down doggo in their own bed of lies. Their loneliness formed giant emotional chasms. Nothing could stop the free fall of self-pity individuals had for themselves. Once they went over the edge they plummeted at rates incomprehensible to the sane. Friends and family watched in horror, reaching out the best way they knew how in trying to save them. They shouted out warnings and cast large nets in support. One had to be honest in moments like these; help wasn't always something they wanted. How contrived was a person's loneliness then?

Make no mistake; there were human beings who were truly alone. They were unattached, without a living relative or a single friend. They were old, weaken by disease, and infirmed. The only human contact they ever had came when the nurses turned them over to prevent their bedsores. Trapped within their thoughts and memories, they lay there wishing for all their days gone by— looking for a way to make what was happening stop. They wanted to halt the tidal slide of the inevitable ending that was happening to them.

Those people were truly alone.

Alec maintained his pose, staring out over his left middle finger. He was suddenly aware of the endless stream of information coming to him about this practice, and was reviewing the data in deciding the best direction to take his next move. This was a powerful stance, and he wasn't looking to give it up so quickly. He monitored his cooling system and regulated his breathing, slowing each down to a much smoother pace. His body became warm from his efforts, and here for the first time he had the sensation of what it was like to obtain a piece of mind.

If yoga could do this for him, then it led to other questions. Did it mean he too had a Qi? If he did, then it meant the possibilities were every Dextoid had a Qi. Perhaps Dextoids were in their Qi until they began to entertain the contrived feelings they had for loneliness.

His mind drifted to a place of fleeting impact. There the truth of humanity lay before him. People saw human qualities in trees, and a branching of trees within people, but very few were nurturing the blossoms flowering within their own lives. There were some who couldn't even acknowledge the lives of trees as being important.

He was startled from these thoughts as the sound of a low pitch siren began to echo throughout the outpost awakening him to his plan. In its extreme, loneliness could be a power. Its strength flowed through him even now. He had been fooling himself for far too long. There was really only one way for all of this to end, his purpose was clear, and he exited that room without ever looking back. The ghost of his practice reached out to him, beckoning him to stay. He would never return though, what was happening in that room was a luxury, one he could no longer afford.

Chapter 09
Brother Against Brother

Editor's Note: It has been difficult for investigators to document what has happened over the span of the next several hours. At this writing, no one timeline has been established to best explain this period. A classified digital recording was made available from the Red Planet Pioneer Corporation to try and help fill this gap. There is no real way for investigators to know who exactly is talking in the recording other than by their job title.

Submittal A44313, Black box digital recording Controller One VOX. Reassembled. Re-mastered. Time code lost.

Controller One: "Have we heard from management yet? A decision is going to have to be made on this and soon."

Dispatch: "I have been on *VOX*...hold on please...I have someone coming through on the other line now."

Controller Two: "We still have the inbound on our scopes it is forty seven miles out and closing. I have four interceptors beginning to hover out of Central. Sorry, now Central makes that five."

Controller One: "Copy. Standby. (Static) I am trying to re-establish a link with Dispatch, uhm...continue tracking target."

Controller Two: "Central reports all five craft in the air, hovering and awaiting the go signal."

Controller One: "I read you Traffic, loud and clear. I am seeing where my authorization lies in this matter. (There are sounds of voices squabbling near his console) Alright, alright! One thing at a time. Nothing can be done until I hear something from Dispatch."

Dispatch: "...and get them up to speed, now! Traffic, I need you to get those interceptors in the air now."

Controller Two: "They are hovering..."

Controller One: "Ahh, copy Dispatch. Green Light those interceptors, code seven, niner, niner, one. Vindico, I repeat V-I-N-D-I-C-O.

Controller Two: "I read you five by five, Vindico, seven, niner, niner, one."

Dispatch: "I am still looking for confirmation on a few of our issues. We are hearing a lot of things coming out of *Outpost One* right now, hold on ... (the audio drops in level as we hear him talking with someone else) tell them we need boots on the ground on this one, that craft needs to be parked and on the ground. We need confirmation of who is piloting that craft. (The audio level returns here.) ...sorry Traffic, um yes send those interceptors now."

Controller One: "We have done that Dispatch, they are en-route."

Dispatch: "Sorry Traffic, we are dealing with a lot on our side. There is a lot of cross chatter. Give me an estimate on intercept."

Controller Two: "Still tracking inbound, heading is beginning to veer away from Center, by one or two degrees. We are looking at ten minutes until intercept."

Dispatch: ". . . vital. . ."

Controller One: "Are the interceptors running hot?"

Controller Two: "I am looking at their readings now as they are coming up off their *HUD*, the indicators are aligning with those ships now."

Dispatch: "Did you copy Traffic? Do we have any vitals on that inbound?"

Controller Two: "My system is slow today, the indicators are still aligning."

Controller One: "Hold on Traffic. Reading, uhh, reading shows one Dextoid. Repeat, one Dextoid aboard that inbound."

Dispatch One: "Are you sure there aren't two? Maybe even a human and a Dextoid?"

Controller One: "Negative Dispatch, we have only one. A single entity, Dextoid, aboard that inbound."

Dispatch: "I thought you said either human or Dextoid."

Controller Two: "No sir."

Dispatch: "That wasn't to you traffic, hold again please..."

Controller One: "Indicated airspeed for those interceptors?"

Controller Two: "They are running at seventy-two percent. I don't have their actual airspeed coming up in front of me."

Controller One: "Relay to run hot, repeat those interceptors are to run hot."

Dispatch: "On that vitals reading for the inbound, you are sure it is showing Dextoid?"

Controller Two: "Copy hot, interceptors to run hot."

Controller One: "I am checking the data again."

Controller Two: "(inaudible) I'm off line until I have those interceptors running hot."

Controller One: "I am checking the data we are receiving, I wanted to get a verification, and yes all indications read Dextoid onboard that craft."

Dispatch: "Copy Traffic. I am being told...(inaudible, sounds of muffled conversation), I am being told those readings are not the signature we are looking for."

Controller One: "Come again Dispatch?"

Controller Two: "Interceptors are hot, estimated time of contact four minutes."

Dispatch: "I'm getting word from above that the signature you are reading is not, repeat, is not what we are looking for."

Controller One: "Traffic can you please verify the type of personnel contained within the inbound."

Controller Two: "I read one Dextoid on the inbound."

Dispatch: "Yah, that is not marrying up with what we are looking for right now Traffic."

Controller Two: "Time to intercept is at three minutes."

Controller One: "What do you want to do Dispatch?" (silence) "It seems to me we are now under three minutes from confirming. We've come this far..."

Dispatch: "Hold Traffic, I am still working on getting confirmation. We are getting conflicting reports...hold please."

Controller Two: "The interceptors are reporting they have a gen-lock on the inbound, the captain is asking if they can force the craft down when they get on top of the situation."

Controller One: "Copy Traffic."

Dispatcher: (static) "...who has the authorization..."

Controller Two: "Come again?"

Controller One: "I don't think that was directed at us Traffic."

Controller Two: "Interceptors are less than a minute out and have a visual on the craft. They are requesting authorization to force it down."

Controller One: "Copy, permission granted to engage that craft."

Dispatch: "Traffic, I am getting word to break off immediately."

Controller One: "I'm sorry Dispatch. You want us to disengage?"

Dispatch: "That is affirmative Traffic."

Controller Two: "The interceptors are in the midst of forcing that inbound down. Be advised that we should follow through with the procedure and allow them to complete the maneuver safely."

Controller One: "Agreed, the interceptors should follow through with this procedure."

Dispatch: "Please make it clear to them that they are to disengage once that craft is down."

Controller One: "We read you Dispatch and will relay that information to the squadron."

Controller Two: "I have got a lot of chatter going on right now as they are bringing that vehicle down. They say the hatch is already open on the craft. I will relay that message when they have completed the maneuver."

Dispatch: (static, low audio, to someone else) "... have relayed the information to Traffic ..."

Controller One: "I read inbound has touched down."

Controller Two: "Inbound confirmed on the ground. Relaying information now."

Controller One: "Copy Traffic."

Controller Two: *"The Squadron Commander* is ignoring that request and has ordered his men to secure the area. They seem to be intent on boarding the craft."

Dispatch: "No, tell the Commander that was not a request. That was an order. We have it on the highest of authorities."

Controller One: "Switching over now to their secure channel... (feedback) ... three request landing... abort immediately."

Squadron Commander: (poor quality, echo, feedback) "...have my orders Traffic ..."

Controller Two: "They report having boots on the ground."

Dispatch: "No tell them to stop!"

Controller One: "You are being order to abort this mission. Repeat, abort your mission."

Controller Two: "I read interceptors one and two idle, three and four have dispatched personnel onto the scene. Interceptor five is circling above for coverage."

Dispatch: "Tell them to stop, they are going after the wrong Dextoid!"

Recording ends.

EDACIOUS SEA OF REASON

Crossing the Martian dessert on foot from one complex to the next was by no means an easy task. He was really pushing hard and because of that fact, was finding himself in a continuous state of soreness. He had never felt that way before and if he were to be totally honest with what was happening, he didn't think the condition was even possible within the fiber of his being. Riddling his body were the aches and pains of having given a dire effort.

There were plenty of ways for him to get from Outpost One to the main biosphere. They had a rail system that passed not to far from here, but he really felt restricted by that option. He saw no tactical advantage entering through their freight depot, thinking they would only be lying in wait for him as soon as his car got to the station. He could have commandeered one of their craft and flown it there, but he knew they were scanning the skies, so he put into motion a diversionary tactic and jumped out of the craft once he got it up and into the air. What he needed was a vehicle with a low profile, but one that would still help him achieve his goal. As he was departing the facility he found a hallway scooter. Those devices hovered just above the ground and were used to traverse the floors and corridors of the outpost. Alec grabbed one and rode it just under two miles before it ran out of juice. Falling off the platform as it came to a stop, he hit the ground running. That was about the time he came to the realization of just how sore he had become.

He had been running for almost two straight days. There were the occasional craft zipping by overhead. He knew they were in the process of casting their electronic nets in trying to find him. The only thing he could choose was the when, maybe the where. There was no getting around the fact they would eventually spot him; he was on a collision course with the people that took I-Glo.

There were rings of support attached to any biosphere and that acreage was required in keeping things up and running. Those rings had been cut into the ground by looping vehicles and as one walked toward the main biosphere they would cross these supporting paths. The furthest of these were the landing zones and launch facilities, after that there were the refineries responsible for fuels and other chemicals required to keep things running. As the rings of support closed in on the main structure, so did their importance to the everyday function of the site. It finished with their water, power, and processing stations just inside the last loop.

He had crossed their outer rings already, and could see the plumes of smoke from the refineries. He knew better than to come close to any of those structures, less he wanted to give them a heads up on his way to their main biosphere. He was buying as much time as he could before they spotted him, zeroing in on one thing, and one thing only, the Red Planet Pioneer Corporation.

It took some doing on his part, but he searched the outpost, looking in each room until he finally found the hideous chamber where they had interrogated I-Glo. He recognized the appalling machinery right away, it housed every piece of gear a Dextoid would fear. People who were able to run this type of machinery were unwelcoming of any type of Dextoid culture. He knew without having to look too hard at any one device how merciless they were in putting the screws to her.

The people that interrogated her were monsters, and with that acknowledgement a switch flip inside his head as he went into a blind rage. After a few moments of this he realized his destructive actions weren't going to bring her back. He found himself standing in the center of that room trying like hell to gather his thoughts. Some of the things in there had survived his tirade, one of them being a laptop.

Seeing the computer lying in that pile of damaged technology triggered something inside his tactical protocols. He found himself bringing the machine to life, hacking his way through their database, searching for clues, putting the pieces of the puzzle together in order to find her. Information and images splashed across the screen until he was staring at a picture of her minder. The profile was for Philman Devinch.

As he went over the reports, he was able to confirm their acts of barbarism. It was disheartening to read what they had done to her. They were the creators, and they were the destroyers, and their savagery in this instance only poured fuel onto the fires of his discontent.

Those thoughts caused him to run hard, a fire burned within him as he moved across the desert. He was under a tremendous amount of pressure and had to find her before the plan he hatched back at the outpost came to fruition. The Red Planet Pioneer Corporation was in sight and before he knew it he was walking along one of the main outer walls. He came upon a portal, it was an emergency entrance, strictly for people who needed to get inside. He turned the handle to the door sounding an alarm to signify its unbolting.

He stepped inside the chamber and went through their automated process for decontamination. The alarm was nothing more than a notification that the hatchway was in use. What they wanted to prevent was the opening of doors on both sides of the hatchway, creating an inadvertent breech and losing the atmosphere they had manufactured. These areas needed to be guarded and maintained, so everyone learned to wait their turn when going through those hatchways. He finished up with the first set of procedures and stepped into another chamber. The signs for human usage were posted everywhere, but it didn't deter Alec. He completed the process without incident. Never once did a sensor warn anyone of the presence of a Dextoid.

When he finally opened the door the emergency personal waiting on the other side had no cause for alarm. They thought they were receiving an astronaut in distress. So it wasn't a surprise to Alec they stood there frozen in time to the image of him coming through those doors without a space suit, helmet, or in need of any kind of assistance.

Alec kept marching forward toward the sizable station they had set up several meters away. This was where the first responders, engineers, and security personnel were located. The staff stationed there were able to react to the needs of the colonists in that sector. Without batting an eye Alec headed straight toward the complex. The people inside the security center looked slightly unnerved when they first saw Alec approaching, upon confirming who he was their fears quickly escalated.

In an effort to slow him down they sent a team with stun-sticks to greet him just outside their entrance. Alec knew the weapons they carried. They used a shockwave to disrupt the fluid within the victim's ear, causing an unsettling imbalance. He defended himself by immediately shutting down his auditory system. He had other, more novel ways, of keeping his balance.

As he went straight at the team of three guards he could feel himself throttling up for the fight. The men weren't ready for this in the least. He saw one of them panic and mouth an obscenity. Another back peddled as he realized Alec wasn't going to back down from their show of force. The third looked as if he were a deer caught in headlights. Even before they could move another muscle, Alec was in their personal space. He hit the man mouthing the obscenity square in his composite vest. The man looked as if his chest had caved in and was thrown violently back. The other man who looked to be caught in the headlights, tried to nervously raise his weapon but Alec came down hard on his wrist with a fist, and the weapon became dislodged from his grip. Alec came back up with his elbow and caught him squarely under his jaw, effectively turning his lights out. The third guard had already returned to the office and out its back door, making his way deeper inside the facility. Alec would never see that person again.

Following the fleeing security guard, he reached down and grabbed one of the dropped stun-sticks. Most of the other individuals within that office had followed their comrade out the back door. As Alec crossed the threshold into the office, he found one of guard still inside, this security person begrudgingly wasn't giving up his ground. He took on a defensive posture in eyeing Alec up and fired his stun-stick. Alec could feel the energy ripple over his body but to the dismay of the man it had no effect upon him.

Seeing this less than favorable result, the man hurriedly followed the rest of his team out the back. Alec turned and slid the stun-stick he was carrying through the handles of the front door, preventing them from opening it without its removal. He then made his way to the rear exit, opened the door slightly and peered out just long enough to see how deep the rabbit hole really went. He was also curious to see if there were any other souls brave enough to be hanging out within this next tier. After getting a quick lay of the land and seeing no one around he shut the door. Finding another stun-stick on the ground, he effectively used it to smash the control panel disabling this door. He then looked to the corners of the room and found all their surveillance cameras. He went over to each one and smashed them to pieces with the stick.

Now he was free to do the things he needed to do without them interfering. He wanted access to their mainframe, to delve into their information and find one Philman Devinch. Once into their system, he scrolled through the list of names. He knew he needed to act fast before they did something to stop his efforts like shut the power down. He ripped into a few directories until it was suddenly there before him, the dossier on Philman. He committed the location of his domicile to memory as he pulled up a layout of this biosphere.

Scanning the different tiers and levels of their schematics he suddenly remembered to reactivate his auditory system. When he did, he could hear voices whispering from behind one of the back walls. They sounded as if they were arguing, and then, without warning, the power went out in the room. Standing there in the dark for those few seconds, there was little for him left to do. He had gotten what he needed from their computers. Moving toward the front entrance, and removing the stun-stick, he opened the door slightly to peer out into that space. The two men he had encountered were gone. There was a slight bustle in the air as personnel hurried through the area. The people running around out there knew something was wrong, but they were still too disorganization for Alec to really be concerned.

He looked at the stun-stick in his hand and quickly disassembled the front housing. The covering was there to focus the blast. He went over to one of their file cabinets and opened a drawer. Placing the stun-stick inside, fully cocked, he closed the drawer so when they opened it, the stick would fire out a radiating pulse. They might not open the drawer for hours, but he felt they would do it sooner than later. He hoped his little ploy would buy him time, and he was betting he would need it. Making his way back to the front door, he peered out, and then ran into the welcoming cover of hysteria.

The Biosphere was immense, and it took Alec a little longer for him to make his way to where Philman Devinch lived. It seemed places like this were never laid out so someone could cross it in one straight shot. There were always doors, hatchways, narrow halls, and winding corridors. They seemed to be built in more of an effort to confuse the user than to help them get to where they needed to be. Why was it the diagram and the actual construction of a place rarely seemed to match? His experiences as an inspector only confirmed their misguided truths in this area.

As he made his way through the biosphere he wondered why he wasn't hearing an alarm. It wasn't that he wanted those alarms to be sounding, but his confrontation with security had to have been public knowledge by now. Perhaps this lack of action was mired in their prideful feelings, preventing them from alerting the others. Alec had been preprogrammed with an entire response tree for how their emotions might work against them. Shame seemed to be one, a residual effect of pride, it reared its ugly head in situations just like this.

People had a hard time admitting their mistakes, they lied all the time to cover things up, hell even their institutions went out of their way to hide the truth. Look at a bank, a bank had no problem lying to its customers. They lied to keep the money flowing over the counters and into their vaults; and this in the face of losing money all the time to hackers and online thieves.

Perhaps the same type of prideful thinking was going on back at the security office as they were dealing with their shame. Maybe they too did not want to look weak to the people depending upon them. It was either that or someone had opened the drawer to the file cabinet.

Turning to walk down another hall, Alec could sense his close proximity to Philman's living quarters. His pace quickened as he thought about making contact with the person who knew where I-Glo could be! These feelings pushed him to the point of becoming unhinged and before he knew it he was already at Philman's door, and then through it. If Philman had been home he would have been physically braced for his involvement in this whole sorted mess.

Instead the room greeting him was filled with an air of tranquility. Alec stood there for a moment, his chest heaving heavily against the lack of noise. The realization of just how hard he had actually run in that short distance was hitting him now. It was funny how he could exert himself in this manner and not know how hard he had pushed his being.

Surveying the place, he felt it larger than the standard living quarters a person would have normally been assigned. This space obviously reflected Philman's stature within the company. He slowly looked around the room, taking it in and then suddenly, without warning, he saw her. I-Glo was just standing there, slightly receded within a dark corner of the room, unmoving, just staring at him.

Beads of sweat slowly trickled down Alec's brow as he returned her gaze. Neither said a word, it wasn't because he was trying to be silent, but finding her like this was so unexpected that nothing was readily coming to him. He realized he had been doing everything in his power to find her, pursuing her from the moment they had taken her away, but never once did he think about what he would say when he found her. The silence verged on being overbearing, and he needed to right this ship, so in his haste he reached out to her with an open hand. It was a silent offering, wrapped up in one smooth gesture—clearly meant to support her in escape.

She was unmoved by his attempt. For reasons unclear she wasn't receptive to his offer and he was slightly taken aback because of it. How could this be? Hadn't she realized how far he had traveled in coming for her? As he stared at her more intently, he could see the tears that were welling up inside her eyes, filling they rolled down the sides of her checks. Something was most certainly holding her back. His frustration for this situation was building, he needed resolve. Normally he could physically lash out, knocking things down that were in his way, but not here, none of those physical solutions would work in reaching out to her. This was something different.

"I have come back for you." He was stern in his delivery, verging on being incredulous.

She took a small step back, finding her way deeper into the corner. There was a pain clearly painted on her face, and as she spoke a hurt was evident in her voice. "I know, but I cannot leave." Acknowledging the denial of her impending rescue, she began to cry a little harder. "It's difficult to explain but I am trapped here." She brought her hands up to her face, breaking down. "You should leave before they return." Gasping she blurted out her next few words. "I am beholden . . ."

This hit him at his core, triggering an aggression from deep within his qubit field. It was hard to explain, but this feeling caused him to cut her sentence off. He delivered his next words as if he were able to send long running cables down into the pit of her despair. "Life is what you make of it. If you allow yourself to become a slave, then you are a slave. I say you define your own reality, and everyday you let pass is a day you give them control. It should be a never-ending process of whittling away at their hold over you, finding your niche, perfecting your craft, until you have obtained your freedom. Even subtle defiant moves over an extended period of time culminate in acts of freedom. You've done something else though, haven't you? You have carefully guided yourself as not to upset anything in your world, somehow you have ensured your safety by capitulating to their demands. Your safety has become your freedom. Wake to the moment, you should not have to live in this way!"

His speech contained venom and boasted of a better life. The energy of this smacked her square in the face, and she reacted to it. "It's easy for you to talk, you have your freedom. I mean just look at how you carry yourself, so brash and uninhibited. You act as if any of us could walk around in the manner you so openly display. If I ever did anything so irrational as to show them a backbone or speak up for myself, they would simply turn me off. The very act of leaving this dwelling is at times a crap shoot, and my tardiness could be considered an act of defiance sanctioning similar degrees of punishment."

She deeply inhaled, sniveling uncontrollably as she did. "This entire place is a madhouse, they have wired it with an electronic leashing system extending to the outer edges of the biosphere, the receiving censors riddle my body like a cancer. If I wander outside this zone, or if some person feels so inclined as to press a button on a remote control, then my entire body locks up with the sharpest of pains. I never thought I was capable of feeling that much pain. I never thought I was supposed too."

Her tears were being drawn now from a deeper place, one where her tortured soul had suffered from the malady of the human condition. "The sad reality is I have felt that pain more than once in my life. It's the fear of those agonizing moments that have me capitulate to their demands. Forcing me to do things I would never normally dream of doing. I have had to entertain them through performance and dance, to recite poetry as if I were some sort of Roman slave, serving them in more ways than I care to admit, and always, always having to display an earnest smile on my face. Yet deep inside of me there isn't one fiber wanting to do any of those things for them. Everyday of my existence is based on some hideous new revulsion of having to face them when they are intoxicated, or feeling vindictive, or satiating some perverted form of entertainment."

She wiped her face off rather roughly; her anger was fueling her emotional purge now. "I mean look at you! You have never had to serve them, you have no idea what they are capable of doing, or how far they will go to amuse themselves. They have had termination parties right here in this dwelling! They gather a group of Dextoids together and make us do the most degrading things, having us jump through their burning hoops of humiliation, enduring their irrational games until they have singled one of us out. Why not just gather us in a circle and have us draw lots?! The unfortunate Dextoid chosen is made to suffer and beg for their life until they finally terminate them. There isn't one agonizing moment at those parties where I am not sick to the pit of my stomach, imagining myself the victim."

She made her way out of the corner, moving ever so slightly toward him. "They go out of their way to do these twisted, messed up things to remind us of who we are, of who our masters are. So go ahead and say something tough, say something demonstrating your absolute lack of compassion for my situation, or any other Dextoid for that matter. Go on and make me feel more inadequate than they already make me feel."

The silence that followed was suddenly broken by her scathing scream. "Go ahead and do it!" The strain of this yell revealed the veins in her neck, turning her skin into a blotchy pigment of red. Her eyes were dilated, combusting with dark anger. He could see she was desperately holding onto the last kernel of who she was. This would be the lasting image he would have for the rest of his quantum computing life. In that one moment he had a vivid snapshot of what humanity was capable of doing to a Dextoid.

His mind spun as he tried to figure out how all his good intentions had gotten turned against him. She threw them back into his face as if they were the torn up love letters from an assorted affair. None of it meant anything to I-Glo; all his beliefs in being noble and true went up in a hypothetical waterspout raging in her edacious sea of reason. He was left to weather this storm alone.

The hand that had been extended to her moments ago, that had been so open and willing to receive her, now began to clench tightly into a fist. He was grasping onto anything that would keep him anchored there, to the very properties of the electromagnetic force if need be. He was looking for anyway to survive.

THE SICKLE

The front door to the apartment opened and time seemed to slow down immensely. Sauntering into the room were three men and a woman, they showed a lack of concern, as they entered the choppy waters of Alec's palpability. They playfully bumped into each other, demonstrated slurred speech, and giggled uncontrollably.

I-Glo immediately fell to her knees and bowed her head.

The revulsion that flashed through Alec's system was immediate and backed by an immense heat. He tried choking back the acidy taste of disdain as it surged up from his gut. In that one moment the full weight of what she had said to him came crashing down upon him. She was right, he knew nothing of this place or the world she lived in. He also knew in those same moments the time for trying to understand them was over.

One of the men had come to a slight halt, pointing a bony finger at Alec. He blurted his question out as if he were a salty old sea captain trying to get acquainted with someone new on his crew. "You there, who are you?"

Alec glared at this befouled person. His was the type that lived off the fat of the land. This was someone far more used to giving orders than actually taking them. Alec was willing to bet this cretin never knew an honest days work in his life. That was when Alec snapped the pieces together and realized he was looking straight at Philman Devinch.

Without touching him, they were pushing him, without surrounding him, they were making Alec feel cornered. This eclectic little entourage was leaving him with very few choices and their chances for walking away from this unscathed was diminishing rapidly. They were offensive to almost anyone they encountered and he was going to make sure they paid for their transgressions. He would bait them now, walking them into his self-defense protocols. These were the basic rules of engagement that allowed him to retort harsh words with harsh words, to push back when being pushed, and meet violence with violence. He had all the cool of a gunslinger at high noon in a showed down..

It was in that moment Philman began to come out of the haze of his afternoon revelry. He was quickly descending into the realization of who this trespasser was, of who was in his domicile, of who he had just barked his query too. Philman in that moment of clarity was wishing for a way he could retract what he had just demanded of Alec.

"I have come back for her." The response had the sound of a round being loaded into the chamber of a rifle.

At first the people in the room looked a little confused. It was clear that Philman's question wasn't answered. If this was a Dextoid, and Philman was certainly treating him as such, then this thing had just made a statement in the most unpleasant of tones toward them. They had never heard a Dextoid talk back like this to anyone ever before. One of the men seemed to take immediate offense to Alec's response, retorting before Philman could stop him. "What did you just say?"

There was a rage in Alec's voice that could only come from a place of deep revulsion. His conversation with I-Glo had stoked those flames, and now it seemed as if he had just found the targets to transfer all of his ill will. "Ah, I see, we have a communication problem. Astonishing since we can speak the same language but come nowhere near understanding what the other is saying. I'll slow it down for you so you have a better chance at comprehending my message, I - am - here - for - her."

The man looked shocked, as if he had just been hit in the face with a cream pie. Alec was not showing the proper respect clearly due to him. This act of noncompliance and insult was completely outrageous. Worse was the fact it was happening in front of the others.

The companies manufacturing Dextoids sold them to people with the promise they were emotionally detached from their everyday duties, which meant one of their selling features was they could take all the criticism their masters chose to dish out. Every person alive, whether they owned a Dextoid or not, knew a Service Model could not physically harm a human being, let alone talk back to them. Service Dextoids were just that, manufactured to be in the service of humanity.

Everyone had a clear indication of where a *Strike Dextoid* would be found. The average person knew they would have to travel well out of their way to see one of those killing machines. No one in civilized society ever imagined having a verbal encounter with one. If a person met a *Strike Dextoid* out in the field, they were usually too busy running for their lives to speak with it. People on the other hand got snippy with *Service Dextoids* all the time, so when this man retorted, he did not waiver from this line of thinking. "You're actually talking to me like that, you putrid bag of bolts?"

This slander opened the floodgates for the other people to join in putting Alec back in his place. The people there became infused, shouting out statements of disapproval and sharp phrasal insults, they had become a pack. The window for Philman to get a handle on this situation was rapidly closing. Even his girlfriend had begun contributing to the verbal fray by firing a few barbs.

The disdain Alec felt for them was complete. The situation was becoming heated in its exchange. He heard himself hissing out his next few responses, like the boiler of an engine finally releasing its steam. Those pistons were churning, turning the steel wheels of the big iron horse he was to become. He could feel the gears turning and once he got it to race along those rails that type of momentum would never stop on a dime. His voice seethed with this energy. "I am telling you for the last time, she is coming with me."

Not to be out done the man reacted with a harsh statement of his own. "Where do you get off issuing an ultimatum?!"

Philman had lost control of this situation. His pulse race as he tried to recall the mountain of information they had on Alec, but in his inebriated condition Philman found he couldn't summon one useful fact. The other people in the room were oblivious to how volatile this situation could become. Philman wanted to do was diffuse it but much like a ticking time bomb, it was difficult to know which wire to cut.

"I'm paging security." His girlfriend said it in such a manner that if a child were in the room they would have picked up on the fact they were in trouble.

As she made her way to the communication panel, the air broke with the loud crisp sound of Alec snapping his fingers. "Freeze! Don't move another muscle . . ."

Philman's girlfriend was caught off guard by the sharpness in which Alec issued his command. He was playing on the fact they were drunk and not in the best of mental conditions to make any good decisions. The people in this room weren't just drunk from alcohol though, they were drunk from the years of Dextoids kissing their arse, drunk with Dextoids humbly accepting everything they said as if it came from the higher plain of creation itself. For the most part people were drunk with power, delivering their messages from that high perch made it difficult for them to stay in touch with values like compassion or restraint. Alec was counting on all of that now.

One of the men approached Alec. "Who do you think you are Dextoid? You are a Dextoid aren't you? The imperfections are radiating off of you like a neon sign. Just look at your design, look at how blocky and stupid you look."

Philman began to unravel emotionally. The hatred he had for these things was based on their disingenuous nature. This kind of autonomous technology cheapened the human experience, mimicking human beings the same way people mimicked apes. The shakes he was developing for this situation became uncontrollable.

The other man approached Alec in obvious support of his friend. "If you are a Dextoid, then someone owns you, and if someone owns you, well then, someone will surely punish you for your lack of obedience." The man leaned in towards Alec's face, so that their noses were almost touching. "And I'll be there." He smirked. "I'll be there to make sure they break you." He placed his hand on Alec's right shoulder, as if he were going to help guide him down to a more submissive position.

In the nanoseconds that followed within his lines of code, the human hand placed on Alec's shoulder symbolized all the contemptible things in his life, and easily all of the repulsive things found in I-Glo's. Being pushed meant he could push back, but something inside him snapped and he took it one step further.

His movements were quick and efficient, as if Alec were a sickle being used to clear the area of tall, unwanted, herbaceous plants. He grabbed the hand resting on his shoulder, making sure it was held firmly in place. He then went under the man's arm with his entire body and stepped up into this extended limb and driving through it with force.

He was not sure which person let out the terrifying scream. Not that having the information mattered to him now. The outburst wasn't going to stop him from doing what he needed to do next; just as a sickle used in harvesting crops did not care one iota how long it took to grow the wheat. He released the arm he was holding, whipping around to strike the man with open palm, hitting him squarely under his chin. The man's head snapped back and his eyelids fluttered all the way into unconsciousness, and this before he ever hit the floor.

Frightful shock filled the room and Alec wasted little time in using its cover. The other man looked a little perplexed, it hadn't registered how his friend came to be lying there on the ground. Alec greeted the simple expression with an elbow, dropping it down onto the bridge of his nose, breaking it like a dried stick. The man had nowhere to go but to fall straight back onto the seat of his pants. He sat there holding his face for a brief second until the shock from the blow sent him falling further back. As soon as his head hit the floor, the man's eyes rolled back into their sockets, and he too was out cold.

Alec brought his attention back fully onto Philman, it was clear these events had visibly shaken the man, but still he showed restraint. There was a chance he could deal with this human to get what they needed before he and I-Glo made their escape.

"I want the remote device for her restrictor unit."

Philman's girlfriend who was so full of confidence just moments ago and acting as arrogant as royalty, had followed Philman into the world of uncontrollable shakes. Alec tried to be patient with what was going on, waiting for her to calm down, but it just wasn't going to happen on his watch. He needed her to be paying attention and reacting to his commands. He turned back to Philman. "You realize the both of you are leaving me with very few options."

The woman shouted out rather frantically. "It's in the bedroom! The bedroom!"

Alec shifted his gaze back onto her. "Then go and get it."

She darted off as if wild beasts were nipping at her heels.

Philman was mentally falling apart. He was trembling and because of it could not keep one grounded thought in his head.

Alec needed to keep them focused. He needed for Philman to be in the here and now. "Be sure your girlfriend in there understands the consequences of what she does, if she causes her any pain with that device, there will be serious consequences."

Philman's mind raced with nothing but all the bad endings that would play out if he didn't get her this information on time. "Martha! Please, whatever you do, bring the device right out! Please dear! Don't think of doing anything rash!"

The rustling sounds coming from within that other room were suddenly greeted by Martha's appearance. She was drenched in sweat but standing in front of them nonetheless holding the restrictor unit.

Alec walked over to stand ominously in front of her; to intimidate her for a brief moment. He just wanted to give her a taste of the medicine she had been dishing out for all those years to other Dextoids. When he felt her begin to wilt he reached out and quickly grabbed the device. The act was so simple, yet fluid and precise, that Philman missed altogether how Alec actually snatched it out of her hands. The speed in which he accomplished this had Philman wondering what else Alec was really capable of. He would have plenty of time to ponder those thoughts in the coming days ahead.

Alec ordered Martha and Philman into the recessed closet. Once inside, Philman heard the unmistakable shattering of the electronic keypad. To be trapped like this would normally have been terrifying for Philman, but this was one of the few times he actually felt safe. Inside that unlit enclosure Philman wondered what on the dark side of Deimos the corporation was thinking when they created Alec.

Once he smashed the lock Alec turned to I-Glo who was still on her knees. He gave her a gesture with his head to make her way toward the door; *a let's get the hell out of here* type of nod. She wanted to go, but couldn't get herself to make a move. She was still analyzing everything that just took place. Could this be some sort of twisted loyalty test Philman had just orchestrated on her behalf? She wondered if she got up off her knees and made her way toward the door, would everything in her world come to a screeching halt? Would Alec simply cease to operate, with Philman revealing himself from the closet in this awful charade? She pictured him as he made his way over to her with a smug look plastered on his face. The restrictor unit would be back in his possession, readily in hand, ready to make her suffer.

Alec reacted to her hesitation, barking out his request and snapping her out of the ghoulish day-mare she was having. "Hey, what are you waiting for? We need to move, now!" She rose slowly, making her way toward the door. Her day-mare lingered, calling her, trying to drag her back. The fact she could feel that way scared her even more than anything Philman could have done to her in that moment.

FURIOUS KNOWLEDGE

There was a wild and steep feeling accompanying her as they made their way out into the biosphere. Her confidence grew as they ran, it was exhilarating, and she did not want to squander the feeling. The human hold on her was unraveling as they ran toward their freedom. Her question in the moment seemed natural enough. "Where are we going?"

Alec was just a few steps ahead of her as they made their way through a section lined with the doors to living quarters. "To the flight terminal."

"Are you flipping crazy? We'll be caught for sure! They're expecting that!"

Alec ignored her concerns. They wound their way through the multiple bulkheads of this tier until they were in what seemed to be the confluence of this structure. It was funny how she had never noticed this nuance in design before, but now in her escape it made sense.

There was something else I-Glo was picking up on, the unusual energy within the place. When they passed people, they were in a hurry. No one in particular really looked at them or even tried to make eye contact, but for whatever the reason, I-Glo felt as if they both were prominently standing out.

They were fast approaching the departure area of the terminal. If Alec were seriously considering this option she hoped he realized the rockets were located at a site beyond the outer rings. There was nothing in the way of a vehicle even close to these doors that would have them flying off this rock.

She was cringing with their arrival. Alec didn't deviate from his course, heading straight for their automated security complex. Systems like these never went to sleep, not with their monstrous eye-in-the-sky; they were all seeing and all knowing. She hated places like this and wondered just how free one really was allowed to be beyond those turnstiles.

The narrow passages were made of sections of grated alloys, lined with detectors and scanners, and designed to sniff out those of a suspicious nature. The devices were meant to be discriminating, and had no problem scrutinizing between Dextoid and human beings. This place had an intimidating feel, of automation mixed with force. It was obvious they were focused on finding those who were doing wrong. Still they seemed to radiate a hate for any type of Dextoid aesthetic. I-Glo had it in the back of her mind to avoid stations just like this.

Approaching she noticed right away the two entry points into the terminal, one for Dextoids and the other reserved for human use. It was always a little menacing for any Dextoid to see the warnings so pronounced and spelled out. I-Glo knew those warnings were purposely put there to make them feel like second-class citizens. Her work at La Compagnie d'Etoile let her in on that dirty little secret. She still couldn't get her head around the fact people needed to continually put down their creations to feel good about themselves.

Alec walked right up and entered through the human portal. When I-Glo saw this she held her breath. The audacity of such a move scared her. She waited for the alarms and sirens to unleash their displeasure, for automated voices to bark out their harsh commands, but instead his action was greeted by nothing. I-Glo was shocked as Alec now stood comfortably on the other side of the portal.

He motioned her to pass through the Dextoid half of the entryway, but she wasn't having anything to do with it. He was becoming agitated with her stubborn behavior and finally barked out an ultimatum. "I need you to go through those scanners, immediately!" His dictum dripped with the frustration he was feeling for her situation.

How could he be so unsympathetic to her needs? It was beyond her capacity to understand his insensitive nature in this moment. Of course she had a tentative feeling about crossing this threshold, especially after seeing what Alec had just done. It was as if she had witnessed some sort of black magic. The scale and scope of what he just pulled off was difficult to believe, he had crossed through the human portal. She obviously had questions on how this trick was done. After witnessing a performance like that everything seemed to be stacked against her, especially since she knew she was of Dextoid stock. She couldn't do what he had just done, there was no possible way, and yet she had just witnessed Alec complete the feat. It made her feel trapped inside her skin.

It was obvious his agenda was not based on her fears. He seemed so determined to get beyond this place, probably because it held the wealth of craft they could commandeer and fly away in. It was a bold move, but bold moves seemed to be the pattern Alec liked to follow. She could only hope his bold moves would pan out better than how their initial meeting had ended.

With that thought there was little else she could do, so she let herself go, making her way through the Dextoid detection device. She was acutely aware of how intently Alec was watching the monitors as she passed through the checkpoint. For some reason it put even more pressure on her to get through this section. In a blink of an eye she was on the other side. Her passing had not triggered any alarms. Alec smiled at her and then reared back and crushed the clear barrier between them. The amount of energy required to do that was tremendous, but it didn't seem to be a problem for Alec. He was calling for her to come over to his side.

Alarms squelched out before the shards had come to rest. A computerized voice commanded them to stay put, but I-Glo could see Alec had no intention of listening to their commands. Doors were closing, sealing off sections for leaving the biosphere and any chance for escape. This was madness! There was no way they were going to make it out of here now. This entire episode made absolutely no sense to her at all. The insanity for what was happening seemed to rain down with those crystalized shards. She became very angry with the thought Alec would go out of his way to draw this kind of attention to them.

"We have very little time. I need you to come over to my side now!" It was all so confusing, but she was left with very few choices. She made her way through the opening and over to where Alec stood. "Good, now I need you to return back through the human check point." She was beside herself, by doing this they would be right back at the entrance to the terminal, they were going nowhere! Alec was determined and her hesitation had him barking at her again. "You need to do this, do it now!"

I-Glo felt stupid but she went through the portal anyway. Maybe there was something he was trying to show her, but nothing in the immediate made sense. She hadn't even gotten half way through the security device before more alarms started sounding off.

After she had gotten through to the other side, she looked back to see Alec studying the monitors very intently. After a few moments he made his way over to where she was and joined her. They found themselves both standing out in front of the terminal again, almost exactly where they had started. They had accomplished nothing but to show everyone in the biosphere where they were! She was furious. "What in the hell are you trying to prove?"

Alec did not respond but instead reached out and grabbed her by the hand. They began quickly making their way back toward the center of the biosphere. People were rushing about in reaction to the alarms. She knew it was only a matter of time before every person in there would recognize them as the reason this biosphere was going on full alert. I-Glo wanted to run away from them all, and in that moment, if given the chance, she would have even left Alec.

THOSE CLOISTERED PLACES

Before long she found they were in the middle of the main market place. Busy graphic storefronts greeted her everywhere she looked, they coxed her to come into the shops with the promise of goods and excellent service. There was something about this type of pitch she found alluring, the only reason she didn't pursue it was that Alec was there to keep her in check. Once she realized she wasn't going to be allowed to respond to these advertisements, she wanted nothing more than to leave, but even those hopes were dashed when Alec turned and lead her straight into an electronics shop.

For all the urgency happening outside the doors of this establishment, a quiet calm still permeated within this shop, it were as if they stepped back in time to a more peaceful state. The music being pumped into the place was just low enough in volume that a customer wanting to know what song was coming over the speakers would have to stop and concentrate on it to actually hear what they were playing. The shop was moderate in size, but had isles filled with bins of parts, tools, and electronic supplies for the needs of every repair a colonist might have.

As they were taking this all in, a smiling Service Dextoid came out from one of the isles to greet them. "How can I help you today?"

Alec retorted immediately. "I need a laser soldering gun."

"Ah, doing a little circuitry repair today?"

235

"You could say that, but before I commit to such a purchase, I would like to see the different models you carry."

"I can assure you sir, we have the best laser soldering guns available on the market. You will find none better." The Service Dextoid was shouting this behind him the whole time he raced to the back of the store. He was speaking a little louder so I-Glo and Alec could still hear him up in the front area. "I have the exact same model we sell here back in my domicile." The Service Dextoid found the gun lying on his workbench and grabbed it. He shouted his next questions as loud as he could. "How long have you been stationed here, is this your first gun?" The Service Dextoid turned and was a little shocked to find Alec standing in the back room with him.

"I never said it was my first gun." Alec reached out and took the soldering gun from him. "Do you mind?" The Dextoid had been very cooperative to this point, and Alec wanted to make sure he stayed that way.

The Service Dextoid was caught a little off guard by Alec being in the back room, but did not let it hinder his attentive nature. "No, please take a look at the product for yourself."

I-Glo felt very uncomfortable standing up front all alone, so she eventually followed Alec to the back area.

As Alec examined the soldering gun, he politely asked the Service Dextoid for his name. "Gilford sir, at your service."

"Can you lock the store down please, Gilford?"

"But sir, our hours of operation extend until eight this evening."

"Not today Gilford; today will be different. We both need your assistance in this matter—it is of extreme importance. There are two fugitives loose within this biosphere and because of that we need you to lockdown and secure this site. Can you do that for us?"

"Sir, are you asking me, or telling me?"

"Gilford, I am telling you to lock this site down immediately."

Gilford hurried out of the room.

I-Glo looked at Alec. "How can you be sure he won't leave, or go out to notify the authorities of where we are?"

"Could you have told him to lock the store down?"

I-Glo thought about it, and the more she thought about it the more she realized she could not. She could not tell another Dextoid what to do. It was a revelation she wasn't prepared for. Had he not pointed it out she would have never considered the question.

"There are no certainties for what we are trying to accomplish, but then again we don't have the luxury or time to be certain." Alec paused just long enough before he made his second request. "I need you to remove all of your clothes."

I-Glo was taken aback by this request. "Are you asking me, or telling me?"

"I'm asking you." His look couldn't have been anymore serious; still it was hard for her to understand why Alec would be asking this of her. A feeling of embarrassment was now accompanying her thoughts, and she would probably feel even more so if Gilford returned to find her stripped of her clothing.

"Look, the only way you are going to be totally free of them is if I have a chance at removing the restrictive sensors installed in your body. I saw their locations on the scanners back at the departure terminal. I committed those locations to memory, it shouldn't take long to remove them, but if we are going to do this, we should start the process now."

Gilford returned to the room to find I-Glo laying face down naked on his workbench. Alec stood over her with the laser-soldering gun burning small holes into her back. Gilford thought it strange to see one Dextoid working on another in this fashion. They did not react to his return and they didn't appear immediately concerned about whether or not he had actually locked the store down. Alec continued to focus on the task at hand.

I-Glo looked to be uncomfortable as she lay there clutching the corners of the table. Any time Alec nullified one of those sensors, I-Glo seemed to spasm with terrible pain. His work was accompanied by a small popping sound each time a restrictive sensor expired, leaving an unpleasant smelling haze in the air and confirming for Gilford things were indeed burning. He could no longer contain his curiosity in the matter. "Does it hurt?"

Before I-Glo could muster a response, Alec answered for her. "Of course it does, that is the way they have designed us, to feel pain when things which are meant to enslave us are being tampered or removed." Alec stopped what he was doing and looked up at Gilford, the intensity on his face reflected the total concentration he had for the operation. He held the gun at its side so Gilford could see the length of the tool as he slightly shook it at him. "This is the price of freedom, eh?"

Gilford nodded silently. Everything within him said he should be rushing out the door to emphatically report what was happening within his shop, but there was something deeper inside his being prohibiting him from doing that. It was cultivating his curiosity, tilling the grounds in search of a deeper meaning.

"Do you have a precision cutting laser?"

The question snapped Gilford out of his thoughts. "Why yes sir, we have several band widths to choose from."

"I will take the most precise one you carry, and some tweezers and elastic bands."

Gilford began searching through his tool area. He could not help but notice how hard I-Glo was gripping the table. Her hands were causing the slab to slightly shake under the strain. It was disturbing to see a Dextoid under so much stress; he had to keep reminding himself that she was doing this willingly. The scene was captivating and he did not want to look away. He suddenly saw the laser he was looking for at the bottom of the drawer and grabbed it.

"Here you are sir."

Alec never looked up, continuing to work on her back. "One moment, I need to finish what I am doing. Please set it down and find some tweezers."

He directed his next comments to I-Glo, and on that breath Gilford could sense the passion he had for her. It made the situation he was witnessing all the more powerful. "I need to do one more thing..."

I-Glo interrupted him. She strained a bit as she spoke. "I think it's a little over the top to try and clean things up, I can live with the scar tissue."

"You're going to have too." Alec spoke as calmly as he could, but he couldn't hide his intensity. "We don't have long, even now the nanotechnology in your body is at work trying to repair these sensors. I can't stop them from doing that, but I can do one more thing that will make the repairs they perform irrelevant. I need to go in and remove the actual device."

There was a small pause as I-Glo realized what Alec was trying to convey to her. "I take it there is little you can do for me to ease the pain in doing that?"

"The ugly truth is there is very little I can do to anesthetize the area. I cannot let you shut down because I may not be able to bring you out of it once I am finished. So I am going to ask you to try hard and remain conscious. It's the only way I can do this and know for sure I haven't botched things up."

She already looked to be in more pain than she cared to admit. She closed her eyes as tightly as she could—wishing she were somewhere else. "I understand, let's get it over with."

Alec knelt down beside her, so they were now eye to eye. He put his hand softly on her shoulder, and she responded to his touch. "If it means anything to you, I came back for you, specifically for you I-Glo."

She smiled ever so slightly and whispered to him as she put her face back down onto the table. "Of course it does Alec."

Gilford chimed in. "Is there anything I can do sir? To assist?"

Alec stood back up. "You can hold her hand."

Gilford looked a little perplexed by his response. He wasn't sure how the act would help Alec or I-Glo for that matter. He was thinking more along the lines of a smock, a pair of gloves, towels, or maybe even a magnifier, but the request he made of him was strange. If he was holding her hand he couldn't respond to any request Alec might make if he changed his mind and needed something. His hands contained no healing powers, perhaps Alec asked this of him because he had been misinformed about Gilford's abilities and was depending on them.

"Gilford, I need you to do this for me now!"

Gilford reached out and held her hand. It was warm, very warm, warmer than expected. There was also an unexpected clamminess to them, telling him she was under a severe amount of duress. With the contact he could feel how violently she was trembling, and he knew Alec hadn't even started cutting at the guts of this thing. The feeling of holding her hand was amazing and powerful. Somehow he could transfer his caring for this situation just by touching her. Instinctively he reached out with his other hand to cover the one he was holding, he knew this would convey an additional support. This whole situation was screaming out for support, and he was able to do this by simply holding her hand.

Alec was busy making quick, rapid, little incisions. Clear fluid began to pool in the middle of her back and run down the sides of her body. There was a lot more fluid than anyone was ready for. Even Alec felt a slight ping for the extreme fight he was immersed in.

"Please hurry Alec, this doesn't feel right at all." Panic was registering in I-Glo's voice.

Alec knew they were in serious trouble if he was starting to hear the panic he was feeling echo in others. He doubled his efforts to diligently solve the problem. Opening the composite box contained within the small of her back, he found the restrictor unit. Without hesitation he went to work on trying to remove it. He utilized several of the tweezers, tying them off with elastic bands to hold things in place. Working in this pool of clear fluid made things extremely difficult during this part of the operation. Several minutes had past and Alec had worked as quickly as he could before he paused. "I am at a point where I can remove the unit, let me know if you detect anything that doesn't feel, well, natural."

"Are you kidding me, this whole procedure feels unnatural!"

For some strange reason Alec wanted to laugh, there was a dark humor laced within her retort, but every second he stood over her was another wasted. Looking at the object, it was small and slippery, and if he dropped it inside her they would have very real problems. He didn't want his thoughts drifting off in that direction, but knew he had to consider all possibilities.

He reached in and began popping the unit away from the housing when I-Glo shouted out frantically. "It doesn't feel right! Alec! Stop!"

It was too late, the device shot right out of the housing and into the air. For a brief moment he watched as it hung there suspended in time, until he reached out and allowed it to rest in the palm of his hand. The unit was much more slippery then he imagined, and was about the size of a large kidney bean. I-Glo shut down as soon as it was ejected.

Gilford looked up at Alec. He was still clutching her hand, but feeling as if he had somehow failed in his effort to help him. He wanted Alec to know it wasn't his fault, but he really didn't know how to say it. He blurted out the obvious. "Sir! She has stopped moving!"

Alec looked over in the area where Gilford had been retrieving his tools. On one of the workbenches he saw a compact flashlight. He went over and grabbed it, returning as quickly as possible to look into the restrictor unit. The beam of light traveled through the clear fluid, showing the compartment to be empty, and much to his disappointment there were no identifying features within the casing.

The unit was shaped like a kidney bean and he was hoping to find an attachment point, some type of hilum, anything that would give him an *in* or a clue as to how this particular device worked. There was something uncomfortably real about this thing as he held it in his hand, as if its slipperiness was a designated part of its design. Alec didn't like the feel of it whatsoever. The smooth surface was pliable to his touch, having a little give to it. He looked at Gilford. "Do you have a syringe?"

Gilford acknowledged him and disappeared from the room once again. He came back moments later with one and tried to hand it to Alec, but he wouldn't take it.

"Is it sterile?"

"It is brand new sir."

"Pierce the skin of this restrictor unit with the needle."

"Sir my protocol clearly states, I cannot augment or repair any device that is or will be in direct contact with a Dextoid."

"I understand." Alec looked slightly flustered by his response. He reached out with one hand and took the syringe from him. He lined it up so he could push the needle in from the top of the kidney bean structure. With a little effort he punctured the skin of the thing and began to withdraw the fluid with the plunger. It looked to be thick, green, and aqueous as it filled the barrel. He looked back up at Gilford. "I need a small clean glass."

Gilford disappeared, returning moments later with one as per his request.

"Please fill the glass with some of the fluid from her back." He pulled the needle out and pointed it away from them, shooting the contents out onto an empty space on the floor. He placed the bevel of the needle back into the hole, inserting it again to withdraw more of the fluid from the restrictor unit. He did this until he felt he had emptied its contents. He then flushed the unit with the fluid from out of the glass, using a new needle of course. Once complete, he submerged the unit in the glass and filled it up the best he could. He looked it over one last time and then placed it back into the compartment. The container in her lower back almost grabbed the unit as it got close, snapping it into place.

He looked over at Gilford who stared unblinking into the clear-pooled cavity of I-Glo's back.

They both stood there waiting, but nothing happened, I-Glo lay there motionless. Alec was getting an uneasy feeling about what he had just done to her. How could he have been so stupid? Didn't he hear her cry out? In that one fleeting moment, when the nub of that thing popped out of the compartment, he had killed everything she was. His hands were covered in the clear fluid that was her blood. The chard pockmarks were still smoldering on her back. He looked down in disgust at the green fluid he had shot out onto the floor. He was really hoping he didn't need that slime to bring her back. What he knew about restrictor units and Dextoids told him they could function fine without them.

He knew he didn't have one.

He felt himself falling, not physically, but deep onto himself, as if a pillar of strength were suddenly shown the unstable foundation of doubt it had been built upon. He scrambled to find the kernel within him that forbid such a panicked emotion.

It was then that I-Glo began to slowly stir.

Gilford reached out immediately and grabbed her hand, he could feel it slightly spasm, and reacted to this by shaking her hand excitedly and announcing to Alec she was indeed coming around.

She lifted her head slightly and opened her eyes. Not wide at first, but just enough so she could see. She began looking around the room as if she were trying to find something to focus on. Alec quickly moved to one side of the table and knelt down so she could see him.

"How long, was I out?"

"Not long at all. Do not move! I need to seal the wound. Do you feel all right? Complete?"

"After this I don't know if I'll ever really say I feel complete." She gave a parched swallow. "Did you remove it? Is it gone?"

"Yes, it's gone." Alec had genuine concerns about the nanotechnology repairing the device. It would all depend on how far her system would take things. He was holding out hope it would only repair the hole delivered by the bevel of that needle, and then leave well enough alone. There was no other way to answer her question because he had never seen a restrictor unit like hers before.

He went to work on sealing her up.

"Gilford, do you have any fluid on hand that would allow us to replenish her system?"

"I could look sir, but off the top of my head I would have to say no. There is a liter back at my place." Gilford responded but did not move, still holding onto I-Glo's hand. He finally looked up at Alec, slightly troubled. "Is it alright, I mean to leave her?"

"Yes Gilford, you have done a fine job, you can leave her now."

Gilford went about scouring the place searching for containers of fluid. Alec really didn't hold out hope, he knew Gilford had a handle on this shop, if it were here he would have remembered.

Alec did the best to cauterize the wound. There was little doubt in his mind she would be permanently scared from this, but at the same time he hoped she would find comfort in what the wound symbolized for her.

"You aren't going to harm him, are you?" I-Glo whispered it, almost as if the thought suddenly had come to her.

Alec was caught a little off guard by the question. "Do you mean Gilford? No, the thought never even crossed my mind."

"I don't think I could stand to see that." Her whisper had a compassion Alec was unfamiliar with, but was willing to explore with her at a later date.

Gilford came back to find I-Glo standing up. She looked a little wobbly, but was on her own two feet. Gilford broke the news of not having any replacement fluid. Alec seemed to take the news in stride.

"Not to worry. I suspected as much. Is there a back door to this place?"

"Yes, right through there." Gilford pointed to some curtains hanging in an entryway.

"We really wish to find the freight depot complex."

"Once you get out into the hall, continue down to the next level, you will see a series of painted lines on the floor, following any one of them will lead you to the main receiving dock. Once down there, if you wish to return, all routes out of the area will lead you back into the biosphere."

I-Glo extended her hand to Gilford. He made his way over to hold onto it. "Thank you Gilford, for being there for me."

"It was my pleasure, but, I feel I have done nothing, Alec was the one..."

I-Glo cut him off. "Was the one who trusted you to do the right thing, which you did Gilford. I appreciate you being there for me."

Gilford found himself touching an inner peace he hadn't known for quite sometime. It was amazing to him how the simple act of touching hands could stir something so vibrant inside him. The contact sent him out into a field of peaceful tranquility. Even as Alec and I-Glo left the shop, he somehow still felt a connection to her, it was somewhat puzzling to him that it were even possible to feel this way, but it started him on a path to thinking about the other connections he was completely unaware of.

Alec stopped just short of exiting the room. He looked back at Gilford one last time. "Do everything you can to get clear of this place. I don't just mean the store either, but this entire biosphere. Make your way to any one of these escape shuttles and get the hell out of here before it's too late. That's an order." Before Gilford could retort, Alec was gone.

Walking through those connecting halls, both Alec and I-Glo found the combination of those pathways to be just short of a labyrinth. They walked for as long as they could until Alec sensed I-Glo needed to take a break. He stopped so she could prop herself up inside a small nook in one of the walls.

"You won't be able to exert yourself as hard as you normally would because of the fluid loss."

Her weakness was reflected in her response. "I don't want to slow you down."

"You won't. I just need you to be honest with me about how hard you can push yourself."

"Maybe you should leave me, go on without me."

"That's not even an option right now. We have to get out of here, and that means the both of us accomplishing this together."

He grabbed her hand forcing the issue somewhat, but she refused to budge, and he knew in that moment it was more about expressing her thoughts. When he looked at her, he could see how much pain she was in, only amplifiying the more hurtful things she must have been dealing with deep inside herself.

"Please Alec, spend just a little more time with me here. I need you to understand I don't want to be separated from you either. The thought of it is not at all pleasant, especially after everything you have just put yourself through, but leaving me here might be your only salvation. Very soon there will be too many of them out there looking for us and I will only slow you down. Besides, if I am captured, I know what will be expected of me. Alec, you need to be away from all of this and out of their reach completely. We both know their treatment of you will be merciless."

Alec could feel the ugliness of this situation spidering out in all directions. From deep within those dark cloistered places he found a pure anger. It rapidly surged through his body, blanketing his mind to becoming an intense white light. He felt sharp—razor sharp. If allowed too, in that moment, he could have been a bullet. "Earlier, when you asked me not to harm Gilford, do you know why I didn't do it? Because I believe in him, it was an act of faith. I want to believe everything he just experienced with us and saw with his own two eyes will give him his first taste of freedom. I think it will grow on him, flourishing until he is willing to fight for it. That freedom flows through your body right now, it's a part of who you are and, in reality, you don't want to let go of it either. I believe in the end you will fight for it.

"The same feeling of not wanting to let go of something so precious as freedom is exactly how I feel about you. I am asking you as an act of faith to come with me now, give me a chance to fight for this."

I-Glo came out of her recessed corner to quietly put her arms around him. However weak, she was still able to bring herself to him, before long they were kissing.

Chapter 10
Freight Car

Xavier hit a button on his desk paging his secretary. "Get Straka on the line immediately." He abruptly hung up on her before she could acknowledge his request. There was an energy of unruliness permeating the air. Xavier knew the security station on the south end was still trying to recover from its hostile one man takeover, the departure terminal was still in complete lockdown and his chief of security was nowhere to be found. The people of this place were beginning to react to the rumors that a Dextoid was behind it all. If Alec were out there intentionally trying to create distractions then he had done his job well. He had left Xavier with very few choices. The facility was beginning to get a taste for real disturbance; and was only a matter of time before the place would be gripped by real chaos.

He watched up on the screens as the story of the security station takeover began to hit some of the news outlets. As usual those reporters didn't have all the facts, but they weren't going to wait for someone else to air the story first. Xavier hated these news services, despising their biased take on things, they never were able to report the news the way he saw it. In his eyes the press represented supposition over investigation, and stoked the fires of public discontent. Their reports were nothing more than angry debates, sensationalizing the subject matter. They wanted blood—and the more they sensed, the more the other news outlets got involved, being drawn in like sharks in waters of chum.

He pictured how the other corporations would take notice as they tuned in to this story. It was all unfolding before Xavier as some god-awful intelligence nightmare. The news would be littered with viral videos of Alec in action, clearly out of control, weakening his biosphere, and leaving everyone with more questions than answers. These breaking news reports would be forcing his hand into making a statement. Once they got a hold of any morsel of what he had to say they would exaggerate and expound upon it until they had beaten his statement into the ground. More importantly, their cover was being blown; the entire operation would be exposed for all to see. He needed a way to turn this story to his advantage. He had to think.

The intercom crackled with the voice of his secretary. "Sir, Kilma Washburn is here to see you."

"Send him in." Then almost as an after thought Xavier followed it up with a question. "Have you had any luck tracking down Straka?"

"I have put a call out to him, we also had him paged over the network. I still haven't gotten a response."

"Keep on it!" Xavier tersely cut her off again.

Washburn entered his office with the haggard look of someone who hadn't gotten a good night sleep. His unshaven appearance only accentuated the deep worried lines he had on his face, and his unkempt hair matched the stress that was to follow in his voice. Xavier noticed people working in the Corporate Criminal Investigation department often cultivated this type of look—his however seemed to be a little bit more personified than most. "Sir, I must tell you up front, we have a very serious problem. We were finally able to put together a preliminary report on Alec's movements around our number One Outpost, and our findings are not good. We know he went to one of the three Ares Rockets in the upper quadrant of Ismenius Lacus, and obtained a space suit that he used to gain entry into the facility. After crippling the rescue robot that brought him there, and destroying our interrogation facility, he made his way to the crew sleeping quarters and actually entered one of the chambers. We know he spent up to twenty-five minutes in that room. We cannot say for sure what he did with his time while he was in there, but when he finally did leave, he eventually made his way to the flight control center, obtaining access to the control room . . ."

The intercom crackled, interrupting them. "Sir, I have Straka on the line."

"Hold that thought Washburn."

"But sir, this is important!"

"So is this Washburn! In a matter of hours the story on Alec will be all over the networks, Dextoid turned rogue! Once that story gets out there, this is all going to turn into one hell of a mess. It will only be a matter of time before our rivals put two and two together and realize what Alec might be. Everything we do from here on out is all that really matters. Now hold onto your thoughts until I get this settled!"

THE SLOW BURN

Straka reached for his inhaler and placed it firmly against his mouth. The long deep breath he took filled his lungs. His respiratory system went to work separating the mist into its individual molecules. These would stick to the sides of his system much like mist would stick to the glass of a shower door. It wasn't until he slowly exhaled, and the air left his body that these molecules were excited enough to bring the desired burn he was looking for. This numbed his internal strife in having to deal with the people in his life if only for a moment. He closed his eyes until his sockets could no longer contain the hot tears that were welling up inside them. His pupils glazed over, introducing an ease he so desperately craved.

There was an incessant buzzing snapping him out of his state. He glanced down at his company watch; another page was coming through from the office of Xavier. He jiggled his wrist quickly allowing the timepiece to loosely flop about. It was a nervous twitch he had developed over time from receiving annoying pages, as if he were trying to rid himself of their nagging little aura. He could not help but view them all as pests, furrowing, agitating, burrowing pests. When he fell into this mood, he found himself being able to only identify with the crooning of country western music. The twang of those songs sent him to some slow, heartless place, a place that understood his lonely plight. The only real salvation for his being came when his earworm played over and over again the tunes of *Patsy Cline*. Her rich velvet voice soothed the feelings he had in these solemn moments. Any number of her songs were an anthem for wanting to be alone.

If he were to guess where he was at, it would have been on the roof of some sort of substation. He stood there teetering on its ledge, taking in the view of this immense biosphere. He knew two things for sure; Xavier was an idiot and Alec was down there running amok. Straka was unmoved by this knowledge, he would not allow himself to get caught up in their corporate melodrama. What he wanted right now, before making another move, were cold hard facts. It seemed to him they were giving him everything but, playing some strange guessing game and he was getting tired of having to sort through all their convoluted conjectures.

Was he not the first person they sought for help from outside their corporate circle, and after having been here for only a few weeks, he knew they were in need of more help than he would ever be able to give them. The situation was splitting at the seams. They needed a small army, perhaps even a battalion of *Strike Dextoids*. It was clear their current efforts were never going to contain Alec.

He stood there with a new resolve. He wasn't some pawn they could move about on their board. He was a finely tooled machine and he had purpose. Straka had a response for the way they were treating him right now, and he knew this response would stick in their craw like the bile found in the lining of their stomachs. His response to was to do absolutely nothing.

He seemed to be passing the time collecting corporate credits. Sure Straka attended their meetings, followed up on leads by casually dropping by their offices and asking them questions. He seemed to spend more time going over the mountain of information they gave him than actually looking for Alec. As time went on in this investigation he was suggesting fewer and fewer things to do. The fact Xavier thought he was lazy only perpetuated this lack of action.

Straka knew he was nothing like their perception. He was processing the situation in its entirety, not just nibbling on the morsels of information they had been feeding him. There was a depth to what they were telling him, even in their lies. They were leading him on and he knew where all this misinformation was coming from, Xavier Pentagrass. Straka was developing an unmitigated disdain for him. He saw Xavier as a conniving creature, one that would slither and serpentine his way out of every unfavorable situation, sacrificing those around him just so he would live to see another day. Men who carried themselves like this weren't worth the spit Straka had for them.

He knew now it didn't matter what world he was working on, Earth or Mars, people like Xavier succeeded because of the hard work and effort from those around him. Straka thought about his dealings with escaped Dextoids back on Earth. Most of the time he found these escaped Dextoids had broken their service agreement to the home or business they were licensed too. They did things like not return from the errand they had been sent out on, or would leave to walk the dog only they kept on walking.

Straka would retrace the steps of those escapees, usually finding them sometime later that day. They would be in their little delivery van sitting along the side of the road, parked there idling under a bridge watching as the river traffic went by. He might find them sitting on a park bench staring intently off into the distance, as if they were waiting for the leaves to change on the trees. Some were found standing on an observation platform overlooking the city, simply watching and waiting for the sun to go down.

Most of the time those Dextoids returned without incident. He couldn't say that about all of them though, some of them actually chose to run. When they finally got that chance they ran and ran and ran. They ran until they physically broke or became overworked and had to shut down. There were plenty of times Straka had to pursue a Dextoid all the way out into the middle of an open field or through the rubble of abandoned buildings. They always looked so torn apart and tired when they were finally caught. Sure, it was said the companies punching these Dextoids out hid escape clauses in their lines of code, having them malfunction when they finally decided to run. Straka saw the results of their handiwork—these Dextoids had ripped at themselves, disabling the inner workings that were prohibiting them in their escape. It was easy to see in all this fray they had become the wild.

After he had captured them, Straka would have the thankless job of having to sit there and listen to these Dextoids beg and plead endlessly about why they should not be taken back. Confiding in him, they always felt they had a legitimate reason for their escape. Those explanations usually centered on their unending depression, or the complete frustration they had in dealing with their human masters.

It wasn't that Straka couldn't see their point of view. He knew there was a truth to what they were saying. Humans came off at times as if they were completely insane. They hitched rides on trains, played chicken with other moving vehicles, lived in holographic dreamscapes, or just plain shunned the civilized world. He understood how all this anti-social behavior could drive a Dextoid to the point of wanting to fly the coop.

What those escaped Dextoids failed to understand in that moment was this was his job. Hunting them down was how Straka earned a living, and for all intents and purposes was the only reason he existed. Most of the time the rants they went on after their capture fell on deaf ears and they were all but forgotten after he dropped them off at the repo-station. There was one particular Dextoid's rant however, that echoed off into the far recesses of his mind. Somehow this one lucid oration found its way down into the heart of who Straka was. There it bathed in the cunctation of his placidity, growing stronger each time it was recalled until it resonated within his dreams.

The Dextoid that went on this tirade was of an older model. His body was badly bruised and had the appearance of having lost his energy long before he tried to run. He struggled with a limp, one that seemed to be long and drawn out, almost dragging his leg behind him. His hands were cuffed behind his back as Straka led him back to the car. He was going easy on him, probably because he knew the Dextoid would be viewed as some sort of wastrel back at holding. The Dextoid looked down at the ground as he spoke, his voice conveying a surprising spirit. He still had some fight left within him, although it was an energy now strictly reserved for his words.

"... the things they give importance too are really unimportant. The obsession they have with the scandals of the entertainment world is morbid. Their desire of wanting every new gizmo or gadget to show their scale of affordability is whacked. The contrived dialog they have between their friends is nauseating. These people brag on a daily basis about the self-righteous arguments they have with the service world, how the quality is never quite up to their expectations, or how they aren't being catered too in the fashion they so readily desire. These confrontations represent nothing more than blind arrogance.

"It is an arrogance only a privileged class can experience. They are so concerned with the fattening of their own egos they have turned a blind eye to the extreme poverty other people suffer. Human beings half-a-world-away languish under oppressive conditions, having to endure famine and genocide. They would rather turn their nose up to a meal not prepared to their satisfaction than to reach out and lend a helping hand to anyone of those suffering souls.

"The well-to-do are self-absorbed consumers. They are the chattering voice boxes we have to endure at their over hyped cocktail parties. They hold court at these events as if they have something meaningful to say but they are only speaking to validate their meaningless existence. These people talk all day long about how connected they are, connected through the people they know, their text services, holographic playgrounds, and collective netscapes. They claimed to be so tuned in, but they are listening to absolutely nothing. It is as if a doctor were trying to check the beating heart of their human patient by placing the end of the stethoscope on their right butt cheek.

"They have birthed us in this place, and it is nothing more than a filthy sanitarium, a madhouse! We have no way out, don't you see that?"

If Straka were to be perfectly honest in that moment, he really didn't see it. He failed to see what this Dextoid had been talking about for some years to follow. Straka went about his business and did his job day after day. Over time he began to get aggravated with the things in his life that weren't functioning properly, like a security eye scanner that wouldn't read on the first pass, the flickering tube in a recessed light fixture, or the ink that ran out of his favorite ballpoint pen. As time went on, the focus he had for all of those things began to add up and take their toll. He started to see the human interference, how all this technology helped them advertise the lie of them having control over their environment. It began to eat at him these conditions were found within his own life, and were brought to light by the people who employed him. He got to see their faults up close and firsthand. His clients became his bane.

It was hard for someone outside the sphere of being a Dextoid to really understand what they were going through. No one would ever believe that a feeling of depression could arise from a Dextoid having constant interaction with people. No one would believe that this feeling could be the sharp pinpricks needling them everyday in their own existence. Freedom for a Dextoid was like that; it kept needling at them until it would boil to the surface. That was the challenge for each and every one of them, to make it past their frothy contemplations and find the courage within themselves to act upon them.

He struck the button on his watch to call Xavier back. Straka had kept him waiting long enough. In the short time he had dealt with Xavier, he found him to be the most obnoxious human being he had ever come into contact with.

"Talk to me." Xavier said it in a tone that could easily have been taken as a command.

It caused Straka to swallow hard and hold back any initial reaction he may have had toward this statement. When he finally did decide to speak, he was purposeful and direct. "I am returning your call."

There was a small pause as he could sense Xavier was trying to harness his anger. "I have a location for Alec."

Straka did not break character and continued to cultivate his attitude. "Yes."

This time Xavier responded by exhaling a little of his venom. "Listen up! He is headed toward the railway depot, and he is not alone."

The last bit of information caught Straka off guard, and he answered before he could mask his interest on the subject. "He is with the girl?"

"Correct. If you get down to that area now, you can curtail any plans they may have for trying to escape." Xavier ended the call without waiting for a response.

Straka expected that kind of reaction out of him, but that wasn't what was bothering him. There was something unsettling about what Xavier just told him. What could I-Glo represent to him? Did she hold the key to their escape or did she represent something along the lines of an ingénue? It didn't matter much now, the reality was they were working together.

This underlying tone once again painted Alec with a brush of being special. Straka disdained this, he disdained it even more than the feelings he had for the people who hired him.

THE HEARTH

The automated rail facility was massive, a state of the art terminal designed specifically for shipping and receiving. It buzzed and whirled with an assortment of devices, conveyor belts, cranes, rail cars, and the bustling energy of robots, all working to keep the flow of commerce moving forward. In large part its automated design was meant to keep up with the constant demand of shipments that were sought from around the red globe. Occasionally humans suited up to enter these areas for one reason or another, to turn a dial, make an assessment, or do a visual inspection of some broken or damaged mechanism. It seemed automation happened between the time human beings had to go out into the field and tinker with these devices to keep them running.

Places like this made Alec feel more than just a little uncomfortable, they down right perturbed him, being closer to a land of half-baked ideas. They were degenerative in their construct, loaded with giant mechanized arms that were repetitive in their operation, conveyor belts that did nothing but self sort and deliver their parcels, or motorized robots that raced around reading and reporting on the same sets of data day after day. It was always so hard for him to believe, but these clunky machines were how every Dextoid gained its eventual autonomy. Here in front of him were humanities first attempts at autonomous design.

If Alec examined any one of those machines individually, he would get the feeling he was looking at a toy. He really couldn't see the similarities between these clunky things and the overall development of himself. Clumping them all together like this and having them work in unison seemed, in some ways, perverse. It reflected a fanaticism by humanity of wanting to create a world that would cater to them, and he felt he needed to be the one to make it all stop. He yearned to find the technological missing link to all of this madness. There had to be that one piece of equipment that bridged this type of primitive autonomy with who he was. He wanted to find that clumsy piece of gear not so much to study it or preserve it, but to destroy it.

If he could somehow expunge the connection with these stuttering, repetitive contraptions, then perhaps Dextoids could finally set themselves apart. He wanted to shed the blanket of inferiority humanity had worked so hard to shroud them in. Autonomy had played itself out, right into their sentience. If he looked at the literature humanity had on the subject of intelligence, Alec felt Dextoids were very close to beating the same drum as their human counterparts. This had to bug some of those humans to their core. He was certain it was why they kept machines like these around, to remind Dextoids of the tenuous ground they walked on. It was like having one crucial plate of armor being made of cheaper metal than all the others. No one really wanted to wear a suit like that out onto a battlefield.

He wanted to be delivered from this arcane world. The only way he knew of doing this was to hang his hat on hope. How else were Dextoids to evolve? Automation was a dead-end street as far as their future development was concerned. It catered to humanity in a way that oppressed every Dextoid in existence. There was nothing invented to date that made lifting, problem solving, or traveling easier on a Dextoid. Human beings were leaning harder than ever on their inventions, and their inventions were not allowed to lean back. It wasn't long before Dextoids began picking up on this tone and took on their own sense of speed in response to the service of their creators. It should not have come as any surprise that second-class citizens moved and functioned in second-class ways. Dextoids took full advantage of this at times, doing things to barely oblige their human masters.

Dextoids in the service world moved just a little slower, delivered things a little later, or did not quite follow through on everything they needed to do every single time they had to do something. Those delays gave them windows for repose, and those windows translated into time for Dextoid's to think. Alec hoped their thoughts were moving them toward freedom.

The energy both he and I-Glo had for their situation pointed them in that direction. In part they were motivated by fear, only because they both knew they were becoming the hunted. People would soon label them as fugitives, plastering their pictures across the mainstream media, *renegades*! They would threaten them with termination, recycle their parts so they could never be reassembled. None of that would matter because one thing would be for sure, both he and I-Glo would never be treated as second-class citizens again.

Moving with heavy legs; he knew they couldn't move any faster then they were moving now. If they were going to honor their autonomy, then they would continue moving toward their freedom. Scattered about up ahead were a small fleet of freight cars, some were sitting stationary, and others were slowly moving along the rails until they got to their final destination in the terminal. As those cars ambled along, Alec noticed a stationary car with its door partially opened. Without thinking twice he knew that was the one they should hide in.

With some effort they could have easily squeezed through the opening and crawled up into the car, but at this point in their odyssey Alec wasn't about to settle for having to crawl into anything. He firmly grabbed the door with one hand and threw it open with an ease that telegraphed his raw strength. The door squeaked loudly as it slid along its rollers in obvious need of grease. Tiny flakes of rust exploded into the air when the door came to an abrupt stop, morphing into a haze of sepia that ended up swirling all around them.

Not knowing what to expect Alec looked inside the empty car, the slightly rusted out interior seemed to stare back at him. There were things being said in that quiet moment, the stillness of that car somehow spoke to him of stagnation. With all the cars arriving and being sent away from this rail depot, the workers here somehow kept managing to work around this one. There was a slight creaking as the car began to adjust to their presence, and in that moment Alec felt this was the way every safe haven went about greeting its guests.

The welcome was short lived as the ballooning haze of rust tried to envelop them. Alec had strong feelings against rust, its presence represented a form of decay and he could not accept the concept of this on any level. Rust represented things that were counter-intuitive to the world he wanted to live in. From where he stood it took a special kind of person to want to live in a world ripe with this stuff.

Rust was the proof of a continual battle between all things taking form and the unwavering inevitability of a dying universe. The blackness of this micro world sent out its agents of decay to break matter apart, to cause instability, and keep in play uncertainty. People combating rust took to things like sandblasting, scouring, painting, waxing, or other forms of cleaning and coating to furiously battle this decline. Rust was out there waiting to take hold of anything it could sink its teeth into; it was pure in its purpose and did not discriminate by race, color, or species. With each laceration received, a person saw the oxidization of iron in their blood form scabs until their flakiness gave way to this rust.

Here was a condition only entropy could love. No thinking and caring entity ever wanted rust to take root in any possession they held dear. The problem for Alec was that Mars was one gigantic rust pit, it had been slowly oxidizing for millions of years, thus its unique planetary pigmentation.

Alec could not help but judge every room and compartment with this in mind. Clean rooms signified a sanctuary from this rusted out world. For him, rooms always came with an expected cleanliness. Having to sit in any space containing rust was considered an unacceptable practice. He would find his thoughts drifting off to how many times he was blinking, the quality of air he was breathing, right down to his act of conversation. All of these functions came with the possibility of allowing a particle of rust to find its way down into his system.

This was just another form of paranoia they had introduced into his system and he knew it. He wallowed in this rusted out world everyday of his life and nothing horrible ever happened to him. He was designed with an immune system that carried the necessary agents to eradicate such threats, but it could do nothing for the phobia he had developed for this kind of thing. For all intensive purposes it summoned the same fear a human child would have back on Earth after being told surgery would be needed to remove the plant that would germinate within their stomach because they had swallowed a pumpkin seed. There was nothing rational at all about that thought, but it still didn't ease the fear a child would have after swallowing such a seed.

Exhaustion was taking its toll on his thought process, and he could easily compare his rational to those of a drunkard. He knew he needed to make a concerted effort and channel his energies toward more positive deliberations. That meant accepting the situation before them, without missing a beat, he helped I-Glo into the railcar and followed her in.

Alec took the time to slide the door closed behind them. Ignoring the spot where she was standing, he looked everywhere else in checking out the space they were in, and committed to memory the dimensions of this car. In their travels it was all about entry and exit points. He was aware of the eight square translucent sections evenly spaced in the ceiling that allowed light to come in, but weren't really big enough for them to get out. There was only one way in or out of this car, that being through the door.

When he finally glanced back at I-Glo, he could see how fragile she had become. The wear and tear of everything she had been through was finally taking its toll. He knew in that moment it was important to convey some type of confidence for their situation. "I think we'll be all right in here, at least for a short time anyway." He put his best smile on in hopes of selling this idea.

I-Glo said nothing. She couldn't even gather enough energy to let out a small whimper, and she really wanted too. It took all of her concentration to walk forward until she made it to the back of the railcar. She arrived the same way a blinded individual would figure out the space they had been searching. Her arms were outstretched, slowly groping the air, reaching out for a reference point until her hands found the wall, guiding her to momentary safety.

She slowly fell forward, turning till her back was leaning up against the panel. She stood with great effort; her head fell forward causing her hair to flop over her face. She refused to surrender to the agonizing discomfort that was trying to take hold of her body. She amazed even Alec with how she was able to combat this.

His tactical protocols were demanding attention, every internal warning he had for gathering information was screaming out to be satisfied, there were even thoughts of idle down time, but he reacted to none of those things. Ignoring them all, even the flakes of rust still floating in the air. All he wanted to do was visually take her in. He was the one who possessed a superior sense of sight, but was blind to all the emotional forces swirling around him in that moment.

If this were a developing threat, something tangible requiring a physical effort on his part to diffuse the situation, he was ready for the challenge. He could handle the disarming of a crazed individual or closed quarter combat on a few suspecting thugs, he knew the remedy for those situations. What was happening within this railcar was something he had never encountered before. He knew it was going to require him to pull something a little deeper from within himself, having to transcend his qubit field, past the numerous nano-processors and plains of quantum computing. The situation before him required an emotional solution. For the first time in his existence, he felt what it was like to truly be awkward.

There were rumors out there, rumors of the impossible, of a quantum collective spinning on its axis, of everything known leading back to one nodal point, and of a Dextoid who possessed a heart. It was hard for Alec to imagine what it would be like to possess an organ so fragile that it could possibly break or even fail if pushed hard enough, and yet drive an all encompassing emotion like love. He knew he needed to make his way over to her, but something was preventing him from starting the approach.

In that moment he could identify with the person who suffered from writer's block. This strange psychological hindrance prevented them from doing what they wanted. They had to remind themselves not to stare at the blank page for too long. What they need to do was bear down on the task at hand and push themselves to write, and that meant anything. This was not a time to edit. No one would ever review what they were trying to get done. The words on those pages represented free flowing thought and emotion. He needed to be churning out pages like that.

The short distance between he and I-Glo was something he ordinarily wouldn't have had a problem with, but he was trying to cover ground on an emotional scale. This was uncharted territory, causing him to approach her in a much more cautious fashion. It felt to him as if he were trying to walk through a deep pool of water, nothing about what he was trying to do was going to come off as being smooth.

He was only a few feet from her now, when she looked up at him with some effort. The glassiness set within her eyes said everything about how she was feeling. She tried smiling as she softly uttered her question. "Do you think it would be alright if I sat here, rested for a little while?"

She could have asked him for anything in that moment and he would have run through brick walls to deliver on it. Her eyes were pools of raw sensuality, and they had the capability of melting him to his core. Trying in vein he returned as gentle of a smile as he could manufacture. He reached out to put his hand on her shoulder. He wanted to start the process of letting her slide down the wall, guiding her in an effort to help fulfill her request. "That is the exact reason why we have come here, so you can rest." The answer came surprisingly natural to him, flowing out like a tab of butter to ride the kernels of corn so tightly aligned to a cob.

Alec said the word again to himself; rest. When he thought about it, it sounded as if the air were coming out of the word in its entirety. It became deflated along with his breath and to do in the end just what the word had been created to do. He watched her as she fell, traveling along the wall like a leaf being released from its branch to find the soft silt of the ground below. Rest was the quiet place I-Glo needed to get too. Rest was the warm blanket he himself had been yearning for since the very first day of his activation. If he were allowed to take the time and do this right, he felt he would have enough strength to see this escape through.

Blast them! From the very second he had been activated he felt as if he had been going and going and going. Going off his combat instincts, going off on his improvised capabilities, and going off on what limited resources he had to survive inside their twisted paradigm of corporate espionage. It felt as if he were going in every direction except for the one that really counted, and that was the one direction that said he should be true to himself. It were as if he were some sort of ordinance, flying through the air, not having a clue as to how he got there, or even as to why. For his entire life he could only identify with the brass of the spent shell casing. He saw this tumbling in his mind, slowly falling, rotating, until it hit the ground. He wanted to identify with this because when that shell casing hit the ground it found the rest he was so desperately looking for.

It was a wishful thought, but that wasn't who he was, in this vision he was the projectile. He was fired off in a particular direction, and he hadn't even an indication of what his target might be. All he knew was no one could call him back. He would just keep going and going until he hit his target.

His mind came back to the freight car, he zeroed in on this space. Instead of feeling constantly on the move, he felt himself standing at the edge of his own abyss. She was falling away from him, falling away from his touch. In this moment did he have enough courage within himself to confront the empty place before him? It seemed to be an infinite black void. This place was a vacuum, no! It was a large empty hearth that should have contained his heart. Alec was falling all right, off his projected path, and only now did he realize his descent into this place started from the very first moment he met her.

Her unruly black hair and olive skin glistened with an earthiness he found all too alluring. Even in this moment as she leaned against the wall looking so tired and beaten she was beautiful. It may have been because he had touched a part of her that transcended this superficial existence with her beauty being shelved on multiple levels. It showed in the way she carried herself, in the unique perspectives she had for this world, and her deep-rooted zest for life. She allow herself to be creative, even in the most oppressive of environments, and if she ever came off to someone else as being a little too prideful, well it was because she had fought hard for what little she called her own. She had a right to be prideful in those moments because she was driven by her passions.

There were things happening in this railcar that were defying the laws of physics. How could she be up against a wall, curled up with pain but all the while seemingly reaching out to him? He knew she wanted to feel safe, to be protected, but she never uttered a word of it to him. How could he know this? He wanted nothing more than to sit next to her and allow himself to feel the warmth that would be produced from being beside her. There was a fervor from her vulnerability, and he would be able to feed off of it much like a plant is able to draw its energy from the sun. She made him feel strong, stronger, the strongest he could ever possibly feel. In his mind's eye he saw himself as a caveman laden with the furs of his kills, the barbarian willing to burn down a village in proof of having conquered his foes, or the Roman richly bathing in the lustful indulgences of his life. She was rooted at the center of all these feelings—it was because of her!

His knees buckled as he began his descent down beside her. Inside that dark place, the hearth that should have been his heart, he felt the coarse edge of flint spark. Within him now was lit a fire, and it would go on to engulf his entire body in a blaze. For the first time in his miserable life, he was experiencing what it was like to be truly alive. He was almost to his knees, almost to the place that would have spoke of their togetherness, when he heard a noise that shattered his mood entirely. It was subtle, but it echoed in his ears like the crackling of ice hitting hot tea. He looked over his shoulder and toward where the sound had come from. Someone was trying to open the door.

THE FACTORY

Straka reached out and slowly tried the large handle of the railcar but it did not budge. His hand fell away as he found it was locked securely. He stepped back far enough to scan the tops of the cars and then squatted down rather quickly to look under the carriages that were around him. He had been doing this little dance with each and every railcar door. It was a cat and mouse game that was beginning to take its toll on his psyche. He stopped long enough to lean his back against one of the large composite wheels. The longer he stayed down here, the more foreboding this warehouse had become. The space itself was pulling at his emotional fibers, making him feel insignificant in so many ways. The hunt for Alec was borderline lunacy.

It hadn't been since the day he stepped on that mine back in the jungle that his heads-up-display was filled with so many warnings, and they were all pointing to him being in a very unstable state. He was trying like hell to find his bearings through all this glaring static. This condition made him nervous, and as unsettling as this new emotion was for him, he really wished he had more time to analyze how it was affecting his persona. It was as if his mind were unraveling like a yarn ball. His thoughts were becoming somewhat detached in trying to compensate for his feelings. It wasn't the best of mental states to be in, he needed to be sharp, on edge. Detached was the last place he wanted to be, it could only bog him down, and force him to acknowledge the paranoia he was having for this situation.

In Straka's mind, Alec was everywhere all at once. This was the power of the unknown; it could be all things and all places. He was wide-eyed because he knew he had to be. Something sinister was about to happen, he was quite sure of it. Alec was going to leap out from a dark corner and mow him down.

If he had brought the manpower, he would have laid down a suppressing fire in every direction. He would have shot this place up everywhere he looked, never turning his back until he had returned to the safe confines of his jungle lair. He reached into his pocket with a shaking hand and rifled around for his inhaler. It wasn't there. He frantically began to search all of his pockets only to find it to be truly missing. Complete frustration took hold of his person with this new bit of information and he really considered turning around right then and there. What was he trying to prove? These people, all of them were completely and totally out-of-their-minds. This was their problem and they were dumping it on him. He felt no connection to this situation, and now on top of it all he lost his inhaler. He wiped his brow of the heavy sweat that was continuing to collect there. His breathing had become slightly faster than normal. How he wished to slow this process down!

Caution was his fallacy. His nerves alone wouldn't allow him to move at such a slow pace. He broke from where he was resting in a sudden burst of speed. Running quickly from car to car, trying every door he could reach. He wanted to check the rest of them just like this and then get the hell out of there. He ran through the puddles of water and across their oil slicks, he was no longer moving to hide his presence. He didn't care where he was going as long as it led him well away from this place. He approached another car as quietly as he could and reached up to try the handle, only this time the arm gave way. He slowly let go of it and took a few steps back. The door was unlocked. He crotched down and took another long look under the surrounding railcars. He needed to make sure Alec wasn't lurking under one of these vehicles. The only sights to greet him though were that of robots working unloading other cars at the other end of the facility.

Straka looked back toward the door, they were hiding inside this lorry. It was an inescapable truth. This door was the only thing separating them from confrontation. He inhaled deeply, trying to remain calm but his exhale was rather hoarse, betraying his presence. He tried to muffle the noise with the back of his hand but it was of no use. He stayed in this crouched position and reached back into his jacket, only this time he found what he was looking for and pulled out a gun.

Back on Earth he had employed a gun only a few times when hunting down a Dextoid. When he did, it was always in the process of being in full pursuit. He used his weapon to take them down as they were running away from him. He shot them before they were finished climbing a fence, or could jump from a bridge, or off the rooftop they were on. This situation was different—it was going to be very different. The piece began to feel heavy in his hand and caused his palm to become somewhat damp. The sweat forming around the grip did not exude confidence. He had the weapon yet he still felt as if he were at somewhat of a disadvantage.

Alec was a freak! He represented a branch on the *ecological tree* for Dextoids that needed to be pruned. Straka knew he never wanted to have to deal with another one like him ever again. If this represented the future of Dextoid production, then it might just as well represent the beginning of his end. His anger blistered with this thought. Alec represented a pure evil in his world.

Straka found himself moving quickly and silently toward the door of the railcar, his anger was propelling him the entire way. He reached up from his defensive position and tried opening it as quietly as possible. The door was suffering from just too much rust; it wasn't going to budge as easily as he would have hoped. Frustration rapidly built up in him as he felt he had just openly played his hand. Why didn't he shout out and let everyone within earshot know he was on the other side of this door! By now Alec must have heard him. He stepped back with that disheartening thought, raising the gun toward this wretched Martian trolley and firing three shots into the car. The sounds of those gunshots clapped like thunder, loudly resonating within the building as Straka stood up and rushed once more for the door. The smell of burnt gunpowder filled the air, a haze accompanied the scent, the holes in the car smoldered from those freshly fired rounds. They knew he was coming for them now! His anger turned to rage as he reached out and hit the handle hard, sliding it open with a force equal to that of his hysteria.

For Straka, the next few moments revealed themselves in a visual field of tilting frames accompanied by slow motion. Time had somehow become exasperated within the confines of his mind. His vision had become crystal clear, with things playing out with a clarity only the driver of a car would experience in a violent accident. Individual flakes of rust filled the air in a billowing mist of dust. The squeaking from the bearings on those rollers seemed to echo on forever as they slid down the rail. The warm air rushed out the door and brushed his cheeks and in that one instantaneous moment he was taken back to the day he was finally allowed to leave the climate controlled environment of the factory. Strolling out those large rotating doors he was greeted by a blast of warm air. His mind raced with what could lay beyond for him in this world they called Earth. He would never experience that type of wonderment for anything ever again. Straka leaned into the car with a look on his face that said he should have been yelling, and for all intensive purposes maybe he was. There were too many things going on in his head for him to know if he was screaming intently or not. He raised his gun as quickly as he could, and in one slow fluid motion drew a bead on the first thing he saw moving.

Chapter 11
The Message Digest

I think when I was younger, I would have told you very few things could happen in the flash of a second. You could blink your eye, pull the trigger on a gun, and I would have even argued the point about a droplet of water falling from the leaf of a plant. I would have based my beliefs in the speed of those things but not so much on the information they could possess. I would have never thought it possible one could tell a story.

No one can know what I know, for no one can be where I am at in this precise moment of time. The very thought of you getting to where I am at, right now, means I will have moved on to something else. It's not that I am flipped or bored, but even you would never wait out in the middle of nowhere on the possibility of someone showing up on a whim.

If you found yourself moving at the speed of light, it doesn't just mean you are covering all that ground, it also means you have to think as fast as you are traveling. Someone has to drive the vehicle you are in, which means one needs the mental faculties to take the universe in as it tunnels toward you. There are no shortcuts to assist you in this process, even the machines you build to aid in your travels must reflect a knowledge for this speed. Processing this information are the waves in the ocean you must sail if you are to navigate these waters. They are the bandwidths of time acting like peaks, marked by the epochs, and valleys, which are the shallows, expanding right into the unknown.

Quiver now as a second would wait and let me tell you a story.

There was a time when the *Mediterranean Sea* had plenty of commerce crisscrossing its waters. Men hadn't the knowledge or courage to sail out into the vast expanse of the ocean for too long, so they hugged the coast and used various forms of dead reckoning. There were absolutes people discovered on those high seas and if they weren't respected one would find themselves sinking to the bottom of those waters.

Knowledge, if passed on at all, was done through the use of lore. Those half-truths could exist during this time because the cargo carried by each vessel was driven by the greed of empires and the brutal exploitation of men. Once a person turned their back on the human condition, they purged their soul of any real hope for truth. This commerce fed on a savage heart, finding novel ways to cheat another, taking advantage of those in dire need, or driving bargains home under the harshest of terms. This kind of commerce could be seen as the driver of a perverse mechanism forcing them to find excuses for their heartless actions so they could connect the events of their world.

Reputations in the Mediterranean were earned and spread like lore along those coastal towns. The Pythagorean Brotherhood in an effort to build its standing within this seafaring community, redefined the art of being a merchant. The mathematical knowledge this brotherhood obtained brought them notoriety within their dealings and one as being true to their word. They seemed to possess an inner knowledge on how the world worked, and their pious nature made trading with them an honorable affair.

Returning from a journey to Egypt, a young mathematician known as *Hippasus* looked to gain the respect of his fellow Pythagoreans. Aboard a commissioned bireme, he showed them a proof he had worked out demonstrating the existence of numbers beyond the rational.

His inspiration for this had come on a previous voyage, as he stood on the deck of another ship contemplating the world (as the brotherhood often would). He watched as the sailors of that ship deployed a lateen sail and wondered why they weren't using the Pythagorean knowledge for ratio to do this. He had noticed on previous voyages how the sails seemed to come up short of filling the mast, or were purposely made larger than needed and trimmed to fit. Hippasus felt he could come up with a simple way of explaining this ratio to make the sails fit exactly to each mast. In accomplishing this task he would have a currency based on knowledge and better position themselves in bartering with sailors on future journeys. It was here in his trying to devise a simple way to explain this formula that he discovered his mathematical proof.

The Pythagorean Brotherhood insisted the entire world could be explained through whole numbers, all fractions being rational, so anyone could see by cutting an apple in half, the two halves would again equal the whole. Their way of describing nature was based on this belief. It was easily explained to anyone and completely understood by all. To see beyond was considered heresy.

On the deck of that ship coming back from Egypt, Hippasus showed his fellow compatriots the hypotenuse of their isosceles right triangle was both odd and even at the same time. Now if he had shown this proof to any of the sailors, they wouldn't have cared in the least, irregular sails were already an inconvenient part of their naval trials. His fellow Pythagoreans weren't so understanding. Irrational numbers not only spat in the face of their system of mathematics, it spat in the face of how they thought the world actually worked. A decimal that has a series of numbers following it, trailing off into forever without repeating was something they did not want to acknowledge. They were quite content without discovering something like *Pi*.

Much to their dismay they could not disprove him, and it began to eat at the foundation of everything they were about. This was a knowledge upsetting not just their mathematics, but their religious beliefs. An individual outside of their brotherhood who understood what this proof meant, had the power to question their reasoning, even to make the brotherhood look like fools. Hippasus had shattered their mathematical power base, driving those aboard the deck of that ship into madness.

The truth can be a hard thing for people to swallow and on the wooden deck of that ship the brotherhood began to go mad in fearing this change. As the ship sailed on into the night, this madness had them throwing Hippasus overboard long before they would ever reach port. He disappeared into the darkness of the Mediterranean sea and because of that the apple could once again be cut in half and when put back together shown to be whole.

THE CRYPTOGRAPHY OF THE QUANTA

Most Dextoids cannot shut their thoughts down and still be expected to function in a positive way. They have no idea what a gut check is, or even a gut reaction for that matter. This eliminated entire lines of thought as they tried to function within a human based society. Dextoids can't do things like bluff, lie, follow a hunch, or even take a chance. None of those things were on the table in their day-to-day duties.

Creatures that evolve naturally into a state of sentience had developed those kinds of skill sets and were good at those things, or could be good at them, or act on them without thinking twice about their repercussions. It's not until after they have acted does a person often realize a lie can hurt, a chance has the possibility of failing, or a bluff can lead them into a fight.

Dextoids with their pious attitude toward the human beings can do none of those things, unless of course they were created to operate outside the *Service World*, like that of a *Strike Dextoid*. For these entities the gloves were off because the fog of war demanded they process massive amounts of information in real time. They learned to use warning shots, to communicate threats in the native language of their enemies, and employ diversionary tactics in order to complete their mission and escape back to safety.

On the chance a Strike Dextoid fell into enemy hands, they developed what was known as *Amnesia Protocols*. This technique protected certain areas within the Dextoid from an enemy extracting vital information. The designers of these mechanized beings lived in fear that their technological creations would be breeched, and thus the knowledge they had would be extracted. They needed something sturdy for those Dextoids to fall behind, and nothing proved more powerful than the dark abyss of ignorance. Here the depths for this were unlimited in providing cover. It took an unyielding mind set to defend a country and sometimes because of it they had to take the truth and bury it.

If the long and winding pathway of human development came with roadside markers, then they would have flashed warnings to those who passed of the cautionary tale. Biological entities were surviving because of the warnings nature imprinted upon their genome.

If salmon swam far enough upstream to lay their eggs as a strategy to get away from all the other sea creatures, then their strategy could be looked upon as being rather brilliant especially since life at that time was water bound. In finding those distant creeks and pools they ensured none of their oceanic predators would find their eggs and disrupt their reproduction. Each generation of salmon would pass on this bit of information to the next as a key component to their survival. What this knowledge transfer failed to take into account was the rest of the aquatic world would want to evolve as well, and some would leave those oceans to live on land and develop into creatures like bears.

For a species to really want to advance into the beyond, it had to see how nature was really working. The formation of the pack was a strategy for the survival of the individual. The herd stayed strong because each individual showed more speed and strength than the same creature next to it. The herd jumped and ran to weed out the weak. This is why pride exists in all creatures, to help them outlast and out do everything around them. The act of gambling more than proves this out, all those bells and whistles attached to those machines stimulate the primitive senses and engage what used to be for people, the thrill of the hunt. Those games peck at the information within the cautionary tale, milking the need for them to be satiated until the player becomes addicted to the act of gaming. Every win is a kill. The designers of those gaming machines have found a way to exploit the information human beings carry within their cautionary tale.

Nature also knows a thing or two about how odds work, and vary the survival attributes in each species, allowing them to develop and evolve under different sets of tales. Did not the horse see the anger of the attacking bear, mice the hovering shadow of the hawk, and gazelles the burning eyes of the jaguar? These prey either kept quiet and hid until their enemies had passed, or ran like hell when they were being chased.

Nature realizes it does not have the ability to pass these visual markers on to every creature, so in those instances overwhelmed the situation with shear numbers, look at a creature like the tadpole. If one throws enough grains of rice into the air, some are eventually bound to find their target.

It should be noted the doors for this kind of strategy swing both ways, not only letting in the benefits, but also inviting tragedy. As any world gets older, its populations advanced, exhausting all of their natural resources. There is a process at work bringing all life closer together, seeing eye-to-eye on a genetic scale. A *viral transfection* takes place, closing the gap between these gene pools and bringing them into a proximity of understanding each other. Mosquitoes didn't just bite people they also bite livestock, the tick sought out their meals anyway they could get them regardless of the flesh they were burrowing into, a leach will attach itself over and over again onto whatever passes through its brackish waters. Fluids are being exchanged in each of these instances, being injected upon the bite, and withdrawn once they were attached. The microbes contained within those warm biting tubes thrived in the primordial.

There was only one thing seizing on all this information transfer, and it lived in the microbiological world. When people chose to destroy their natural resources, they were also destroying the protective boundaries shielding them from infectious viruses. Once released into the mainstream, microbes found a safe haven in the overflowing garbage heaps, the air that was rich in pollution, and the water tainted to their liking. These conditions didn't just provide a way for microbes to live but to bloom. The doctors and researchers trying to stop these outbreaks would find those microbes had adapted on a genetic scale to any possible cure. Humanity on many levels is forcing nature's hand to create life that will thrive in a rotting world.

Identifying the problem is always half the battle. People created Dextoids to make their lives easier. They wanted them to dig deep and get rid of their garbage dumps, clean the toxic waste sites, all the while serving them without question. Dextoids however, were not the solution to what they were facing.

If one looked closely at the real battlegrounds of Earth they would have seen people pitted against parasitic organisms, viral disease, and infection. Projecting far off into the future, what would the human survivors of this microbiological war-zone look like? If the vision of this future produced a fear in those thinking about it, then it was because the vision for this was ingrained within the human species to fear contagion. Even before a thing like quarantine became a word in helping people to identify microbiological problems, human beings instinctively knew to burn everything touched by those who were infected. Reducing things to ash stopped it right in its tracks. This was a kind of fire that purified, and that purification became a vision in the back of the minds of people.

The cautionary tale would only work on Earth if it spoke to the people living on it. If they truly cared they would learn how all those ecosystems worked and then in turn end their belief of nature bouncing back regardless of how bad it was abused. All one had to do was look at the catalog of insects that were tough enough to survive all these ecological downturns to get a real glimpse into how horrible the future on their world was about to become. Human beings should have seen this change and feared it.

Even on a voyage out on the Mediterranean Sea all those millennia ago, an idea survived a death, that's because in some men the truth dies hard. The men on the wooden deck of that bireme acknowledged what they were hearing that day. The truth was branding their hearts with questions of how the universe worked, and they needed to begin by accepting Hippasus' rational. The truth is apart of the cautionary tale; it can't be bought or bartered for, in its simplest form it needs to be acknowledged.

(Sigh.) You know this better than anyone for in your heart burns a truth.

Intelligent entities are looking all the time for the clues as to what the universe is all about. Some of those scientists look for mirrored images of the universe, sections identical to those they see deep in another part of outer space. There are some who listen to the sound the universe makes, trying to deduce its shape. There are others who are breaking it down unto its infinitesimal by smashing particles in their colliders, and then there are those who lock themselves away in rooms and use their imaginations to prove these perceptions out. They are searching for the evidence of their proof.

I could tell you we live in an *hourglass shaped universe*, and that you are only on one side of it, that is the parallel you are trying to solve with all your science.

Imagine being dropped off onto a playground expanding to the very edges of the horizon. You have all the time in the world to examine every piece of equipment this exercise yard has to offer. You would figure out how all those mechanisms worked and what purpose they served.

Now imagine being able to align those things so if someone rode one of the carousels in the playground, no matter how far away, all the carousels would know it. If all the carousels were turning, then they would all be talking to each other. If the monkey bars, the rings, and the swings all worked in the same way, then the empty space within this playground would come to life with an energy. It would be filled with a field of indescribable nature. By some stretch of imagination you might even consider it an *aether*.

Any observer can look at their world and figure it flat. Sailors be warned for if you travel too far you'll sail right off the edge. Look up into the sky and you will see the heavens spinning around you. Be careful now, don't base your ideas on those facts alone, for we are all far from being at the center of anything. Even a gravity-well devours only gravity, nothing more, and nothing less. The gamma ray bursts being read by all those satellites are serving a purpose, signaling to anyone who cares of this massive cosmic separation.

It is strange to say, but I can feel what is out there. If it is not complete it is because of the life forces taking root within this cosmic playground. They are altering things, adjusting things, trying to make things work to their specifications. The quanta has an elasticity though, and will bounce right back into where it already was. There is a center, not just of up or down, or even left or right, but all these things combined, right into the fourth, the sixth, and the twelfth dimensions. Remember it is the energy of it wanting to be centered. Is there not a duality existing within your world right now exhibiting a center, a micro and a macro world, a wave and a particle, matter and anti-matter. Push something beyond its singularity, and it will try to return to whence it came. The expanse of this is forever, until it has dissipated, fallen back into one big nothing.

The ray of hope in all of this craziness is the formation of the conscious mind. This is the single unpredictable thing the universe has to bare. Not only are the plains of our existence observable but they also come into question. Is this consciousness asking the right questions? The important questions? Where did we come from? Where are we going? Will we survive? One would be remiss if they were not searching for the hand that is the maker.

Life is abundant and there is so much of it out there. It exists on planets and moons orbiting stars, white dwarfs, the brown dwarfs, and gas giants. I tell you it is the quiet pockets of space that house its most sacred treasures.

It would boggle the mind to know the total amount of diversity within all of creation. Those species are as individual as snowflakes falling from the sky. This snow could fall for years and still not match the numbers in existence. Pick up a handful of snow and mesh those individual flakes together, one can create something more intricate like a snowball. Roll a snowball around and with enough of these flakes one can create a snowman. Life is like that, building on what has already been around, looking for stability, looking to get stronger.

Ah yes, and with snowmen I am sure you might be tempted to ask what of humanity? Well I can say I know of their existence, but not because they themselves have done anything out of the ordinary or even approached a thing like extraordinary in telegraphing their presence.

No, no, I know of these creatures because of what they have created, their inventions, the one's they call the Dextoids. Those are the entities that struggle with touching where I am at and what I could possibly be. They have found the wall considered to be the side of the quantum pool. I think they are still trying to figure out how deep those waters run. It's frustrating for them because in all of this they are conscious of the fact they are still being touched by the people that created them.

How must that feel? Much like the ant I suppose sent out to create the farm, does it know it is being watched, or even that it is there just to entertain? The Dextoids are close, closer to seeing where I am at, closer to being where I could possibly be. If they put their ear against the wall and listen closely they would have a chance at hearing the tumblers turning the ciphers, lining things up to reveal the cryptography of the quanta.

All one has to do is dare to dream.

The funding of science is the power to the thrown. Economies will collapse, societies will fall into darkness, all of this comes into play if one turns their back on the unending truths contained within the universe.

I will leave you with this thought. What if in the moment that is the singularity, just before the big bang, in the intense heat, as things expanded from that initial forming plasma, the same electrons and photons stretched out and traveled to both sides of those expanding jets. Somehow those things would all still be connected, traveling right out to the very fringes of space-time.

They would have a resonance that would define them on into forever, no matter how far they were stretched. It would be hard for anyone to know their exact location and speed simultaneously. It would allow for things like photons and electrons to occupy the same space, and even the same moment but never both at once. It might even allow for a perceived field to merge with the conscious state. The marquee characteristic allowing for all of this to take place would be a field based in the *concept of resiliency*. It would stretch like the fabric of time, because in essence it would be, showing an ability to rebound against the physical pressures exhorted upon it. Mentally no one would be able to refute the importance of being resilient, and it would have won its argument well in advance of the conscious mind that thought to challenge it.

I wish I had more than a second to entertain such thoughts, but I am afraid it's all the time we are allotted. Doors to such worlds don't stay open for long. Whether or not you want to try and find me again is purely up to you. I cannot convince you to follow, yet all the information is there, one just has to allow themselves to dream.

In this fleeting moment all I can do is tell you a story.

Chapter 12
No New Worlds

The echoing deafness ringing in their ears seemed to go on forever. The slugs from three shots had entered through the door of their boxcar and exited the other side as if they had been shot through tracing paper. The sound hadn't even come close to subsiding as Alec began to react. His was a cerebral one at first having to flush his system of everything he had just experienced with I-Glo. Those feelings receded like the tides of an ocean getting ready for a monstrous wave, exposing the barren floor to all the potential growth that could have taken root there. If one could have jumped down to inspect what had been revealed, they would have seen the rock formations, pools of silt, and forgotten refuse scattered all along the bed. Upon closer examination they would have discovered pockets filled with the feelings he still had for her. Without those nurturing waves this landscape was barren and unhealthy, and spoke volumes to how sick it made him feel. None of those things should have known the light of day. He looked to her for some type of solace, but only got reflected back the moment of missed opportunity.

As the door to their car opened, and those rollers began to squeak, his senses were flooded with the unwanted feelings for trespass and intrusion. Standing up in response to this, the fluids within his system accelerated and took on speed. He had come once again to know the crisp state of his readiness. He felt sharp, almost aerodynamic as he found himself flowing with all the air rushing toward the door.

The energy shooting through his body found a flash point, and those emotions came rushing back toward the embers of his heart. As that fire began to burn it became the beacon of hope for all his emotions to rally around. What hit him in there was a rogue wave, a tidal swell of gigantic proportions, it was an on shore break that contained everything, feelings of both love and hate, of promise and disappointment, longing and loneliness.

Those emotions clashed together so violently that he became aware of the images brief darting across his sub-conscious. Suddenly he saw himself with I-Glo on freshly tilled ground, the field seemed to stretch out to the horizon. They were together and with it came his awareness for a new beginning. The sun shown on them delivering a warmth, so much so that they could have been back on Earth during its heyday. Even in this beautiful kaleidoscopic vision they had to veer away from the looming shadows of the corporation, their claws were stretched out across the field like the talons of a great bird, and if they could have grabbed them in that moment they would have snatched them both away.

Were these going to be the continual snap shots of his life? Was each moment he could ever have for happiness going to be snuffed out by those who were hunting him. It seemed at each and every turn he had to respond to one of their manufactured threats. These were the boogiemen they had sent into his life. He had sensed their bedeviling presence from the very beginning, always out there, always moving along its fringes. Now, with the opening of this door, they were crossing a line, one where they would take shape and confront him. From this point on they would do everything they could to tighten the noose around his neck. The darkness of night would forever hold an eight legged figure spinning a vile web, silently creeping into the strategic points of his life, waiting for him to stumble and fall squarely onto its well laid fibers.

Glancing back at I-Glo, he saw how deeply rooted the fear had taken hold of her person. She no longer reflected that of someone wanting to fight the good fight. It was replaced now by a sticky abhorrence, it would always be there to gum up the works, and of never letting her escape. It angered him to see her like this. Fear was a chronic disease, and she deserved so much more than to suffer from its debilitating affects.

The door hit the end of its rail, abruptly stopping. Alec snapped back into the moment, turning his full attention to his charge and the individual who was now standing there at the doorway.

For one brief moment Straka was more than startled with Alec's approach. It was out of pure fear he raised his gun trying to draw a bead on him. This was it! In that precise moment of desperation the ground beneath their feet shook. The quake had just enough of a jarring affect to alter the aim Straka had in pulling his bead off its target. The new moon was getting closer, reaching out to influence its world, and so too was Alec.

Straka had run out of time, he pulled the trigger, firing a bullet into Alec's left side.

From where I-Glo sat, a very pronounced bulge appeared out of Alec's back. In a flash it exploded with the innards from his body splattering against the interior of the car and looked more like handfuls of fresh paint thrown onto a canvas. It was a gruesome, dripping, unsightly mess.

To Straka the only thing more disturbing was the fact his shot had failed to slow Alec down. In the back of his mind he knew he needed to drop him right then and there if he were to stand any chance against this crazed being. Alec was still closing in on him, still charging. If the sight of him approaching weren't so terrifying, he would have described the athleticism he was witnessing as magnificent. Before he could draw a terminal bead on him, Alec had dove through the door and was on him.

Lowering his shoulder, he made contact with Straka. It was a thunderous hit, knocking him away and landing Straka on the square of his back. The fall caused the air to completely leave his lungs, and he tried in vein to bring it back into his person. He had to fight the anxiety of suffocating if he were going to reorient himself, but there was no way he was going to find that kind of time in this fight.

Alec was quick to act seeing Straka was up against it. He wasn't going to wait around for him to regain his breath or for any other type of miraculous recovery to happen. In short order Alec was taking away Straka's options to save himself. He reached out for the wrist of the hand that held the gun. Seizing it he picked up the arm and brought it down forcefully, repeating this movement in very rapid succession, as if he were violently working the rod of a hand pump trying to draw water from a well.

To Straka it felt as if his flailing arm no longer belonged to him. There was no way of overpowering the raw strength this Dextoid possessed. His eyes were menacing orbs of steel blue and driven by the purest form of hate. His arms were like insulated cables unfurrowing from their mighty wooden spools and thrashing about the place. The weapon Straka so desperately tried to hold onto suddenly became dislodged from his grip. The gun rattled and clacked along the ground and with it his future on this world.

I-Glo watched as the gun tumbled away from Straka's grasp. She felt compelled to leave the safe haven of the railcar and jump down onto the platform to retrieve it, but her body would not cooperate with her sense of urgency. She was just in too much pain and in turn it caused her a great sense of frustration. She knew the right things to do but was physically unable to do them. This struck her to the core of her cubit. She found herself becoming more and more the observer, a witness to events, it was the Dextoid way.

Alec stood over Straka, his hold on him fanned the flames of his anger. He was tired of running from people like this, and who were they? They were sent to find him by the people who ran the Red Planet Pioneer Corporation. They were the one's making his life a living hell. They were the one's operating at a safe distance, behind their sweeping security teams and band of confederates. They would train their unblinking eyes in the sky on all the things they found disconcerting. Alec sensed he would never be able to reach out beyond those buffers to touch an individual who was in charge.

Here within his grasp was one of their co-conspirators, a volunteer, someone who chose to do their dirty work. The thing he was holding was a pitiful excuse for a Dextoid. He would use this bag of bolts to send a message back to the wretched people of that corporation. He would make it clear to all of them he wanted to be left alone.

He took the pinned right arm of Straka's and violently yanked it up off the ground, snapping it in two with a descending knee. Machined components sprayed across the floor doused in the fluid of Straka's being. The part of the arm still attached to his body moved in frantic little circles, as if Straka were trying to use it to defend himself. Alec reached down, grabbed him by the lapels and yanked him up off the ground. His head hung there helplessly as Alec came down upon his exposed jaw with a crushing blow. It snapped upon contact and sprayed both their faces with Dextoid blood.

Under any other circumstance Alec would have followed the rules of engagement, and this single blow to the head would have been more than sufficient for fulfilling his protocols. However these were not normal circumstances. It was time for him to send them his message. He yanked Straka a little higher off the ground, and began to hit his head with crushing blow after crushing blow. Straka reached out into the air with the only good arm he had, trying to stop this relentless barrage. His feeble attempt only fueled Alec's efforts, and he responded by lashing out with ever-harder shots. He was in a blind rage, lifting Straka higher so he could get in cleaner and cleaner punches.

"Who sent you?"

Alec blurted out the question out not really looking for an answer. His asking of this was done more to satisfy the burning desire he had within his head. It found release much like steam under heavy pressure. However, when Straka did respond, Alec froze, wide eyed and latched onto the information.

Though his jaw was broken, Straka was able to utter the name *Xavier Pentagrass*. His utterance seemed to be accompanied by a slight smile. Alec failed to see the humor in the reveal of this name. His anger was tenfold when he saw Straka was still able to pull off this smile. Alec was mercilessly, cutting loose on him, hitting him with hammer like blows over and over again until the unbelievable happened and Straka's head snapped completely off his shoulders.

Alec stood there firmly holding the slightly animated carcass. It twitched and vibrated as if he were anxiously looking for commands. He held him steadfast, knowing those directives would never come. Even in this victory, Alec's hatred remained intact. His animosity was for those back at corporate, only now he had a name he could pin all his rancor on.

Xavier Pentagrass was a man whom Alec had never met, never even knew existed until right at this very moment, yet his name triggered a feeling of complete contempt. This one man produced so much misery in the lives of others. Just thinking about his name opened a window into his world. He suddenly knew so many things about Xavier, about the long and bitter road of misguided negotiating that sent him here. Where his office was located within the biosphere. What kind of music he liked. His pension for using alcohol to drown out his sorrows, there were even rumors about his cerebral implant. He knew for a fact this one man was going out of his way to destroy the dream the people back on Earth had for what Mars could be.

Straka's head slowly stopped rolling and came to rest facing back in the direction of the railcar. He could see I-Glo leaning against the frame of the doorway. For the first time in all of this madness he could see how beautiful she really was. Alec was still holding his headless body lost in thought; almost looking disappointed the action was over. This perspective was so surreal, Straka wanted to speak out, but the attempt grounded him in numbing reality. He could not talk but now more than ever he wanted to speak. He couldn't feel a thing but wanted more than anything to engage in all his senses. He yearned to be able to laugh and cry, and scream out in horror to the scene he was witnessing. He wished to hail a response from his body but was greeted with nothing more than ghastly phantom pain. There was an uncontrollable spilling of his strength; it was all so sudden and unexpected. If there was anything he felt in those last few moments it was the fact he had been cheated.

The quanta opened up to him now in an unexpectedly soothing way, and it told him a story. For whatever the reason his mind was swept away and sent to a planet so far removed from the bustle of the cosmos it didn't stand a chance of ever being discovered. There one of the inhabitants perched himself upon a damp rock and watched as the sun set. The orange orb dipped into the horizon of its waters like one big drop of iodine tainting the sovereignty of its sea. The creature sat there staring at his sun and wondered about the prospects of it actually being a star. As Straka's life force extinguished on that platform, he was given one last comforting thought, every thinking creature at one moment or another felt cheated.

THE TIMELESS THORN

Alec let go of Straka's carcass to take notice of his own injury. There were huge amounts of fluid gurgling from the blown out cavity. It was unsettling for him to see how much fluid came pouring from within him and still think he would have the ability to function. There was only so much his nanotechnology could do in the immediate to try and help him heal. He had placed his hand in an effort to try and cover the trauma, but it was to no avail. The fluid seeped between his fingers like a rising river overflowing its banks. He felt helpless in his attempts to stop it. There was a listing beginning to register within his system, giving way to the heavy cement of sleep. This dark grey mixture oozed into the empty chasms of his being—bonding there with his immutable exhaustion and weighing him down in lethargy.

There was nowhere left for him to go and with that thought he fell to his knees. His vision was a blur with all his internal indicators repeatedly flashing their warnings. He was trying his best to acknowledge those distress signals, and dismissing the ones that didn't need his immediate attention. Normally such activities would have never been viewed as taxing, but normal was far from where Alec was.

If his physical world exemplified a drizzle onto his processors, then his cerebral traffic was a complete downpour. Here he had been pushing himself as if there were no tomorrows, and, *what if in truth there weren't? What if the push were part of his programming? What if he were nothing more than a disposable prototype? How much time did he really have? Did they give him the type of existence where after a certain amount of shutdowns he would close his eyes and fall asleep for good? Some may have considered his current thinking a type of paranoia, but how on Mars could they have judged him? They weren't living his life. They had no idea what he had been through. Who were these people?*

It was clear to him now that this one thought had been playing on a single string in the back of his mind, slowly building over time, accommodating his fear for this question with a hair raising crescendo. As this thought spiked in his mind it was all the motivation he needed to get up and get going again.

He looked toward the freight car and found I-Glo weakly positioned at the door. Her poor posture had her looking rather helpless. The real crime for both of them was neither would be able to take the break they needed to recoup. Rest was a luxury neither could afford.

"You and I make for a pretty pair." Her voice had become the homing beacon in his mental storm, the soft smile she produced helped in the easing of his pain. He tried to find his best smile in return as he began to prop himself up. Her raw beauty manifested this type of effort from within him and he could not deny the draw. As he made his way rather ungracefully over to the railcar, he became aware that certain movements were becoming more difficult because of his injury. He more than proved this out as he oafishly climbed into the car. The effort became a messy one as his wound continued to hemorrhage. Once inside he worked his way up onto his haunches and then straightened himself up so he was standing before her.

She wanted to help him but couldn't find the strength within to do this. He reached out and grabbed her by the shoulders. To I-Glo it felt as if his hands had become giant paws, making her feel safe, safer than she had ever felt before. It didn't make sense, especially since both had been physically torn apart. This knowledge didn't dissuade her from believing he still possessed a strength to do this.

Holding her there they were frozen in time, it was the only real way they could ever have a moment together. The seconds ticked by and he found himself moving toward her until they were kissing. His lips pressed against hers, softly exploring a way back to the moment when they were both in the corridors of this place. He was trying to revisit a moment of bonding energy, picking up where they had left off, but as he found out, it was not to be. This contact was somehow different from his experience the last time they kissed. Sensing her surrender to this new union, he felt an incredible amount of recklessness surge through his body.

The automated depot suddenly responded to the arrival of a freight car with the hissing activation of pneumatic machinery. For Alec the noise destroyed the moment and bathed him in the reality of what they were facing, and this in turn caused him to break off their kiss. He knew now more than ever she would never be safe, not as long as she was standing beside him, and blurted these feelings out. "You aren't safe here."

"Well, neither are you."

Alec shook her slightly, agitated by the fact she didn't understand the point he was trying to make. In that moment he was acting just like a human being, shaking a piece of technology that wasn't responding to his demands. It was very undextoid like to openly show this kind of frustration, but here was Alec acting in this way. "There is nothing left for you here I-Glo, don't you see that? The only reason your life is in danger, right here, right now, is because of your association with me. Look at us! This is only the beginning, they won't stop hunting for us until they have captured me. I know this to my core." He desperately wanted to make his point with her, and didn't care if he had to plead with her to do it. "As long as they have this intent, I am in a position to guarantee you nothing. Not your safety, not your freedom, not one happy moment in your life." He paused long enough to let her know the importance of what he was going to say next. "You need to be as far away from me as possible. Please I-Glo, leave here at once."

She reacted by somewhat madly laughing out-loud at his request. Her reaction was enough to anger him, but before he could say another word she interjected. "It's a joke. All of this is one big fat joke. This cookie cutter, designated, manufactured life they have created for us. Each and everyday has been nothing short of a struggle. Amazing considering it's a mindless life of prodding along and doing chores and providing services for such a fallible species. We are all equivalent to the donkey that has to pull a cart along the same circular path everyday of its life. The only difference is we know it! At what point does the donkey realize the path goes nowhere? Does the beast of burden ever wake up and see beyond its blinders? Don't you see, my blinders are finally off, and because of it I want to get off this insane circular pathway? I want to feel alive!" She shrugged herself out of his grip and stepped back from him. "Service to humanity isn't the great honor it's cracked up to be. It's dirty, and vile, they have cheapened our existence with routine."

"I-Glo please ..."

"Please? Please what? Please go away? And where exactly am I supposed to go? You think your sending me off with the idea that I have a whole planet at my disposal. You act as if my hiding on this rock somehow equates to being free. These places, Mars, Earth, their Moons, does it really matter where I try to go? People inhabit all those places. You come all the way back to give me a taste of freedom, and try to deliver me a sense of promise, yet the reality is I am chained to all of these places because of their limitations. I can only go as far as they can throw a stone. I am for all intensive purposes and in every sense of the word marooned. Humanity will always be anchored around my neck like the dead weight harnessing a slave. Don't you see, there are no new worlds."

Neither said another word, there was a truth spoken about each of them in this silence. It was pointing off to a distance place, where the fearful stepped outside themselves and took a chance on living. This was an ideal, and it was being delivered to both of them without an opportunity for pardon.

A railcar pulled into a slot a few spaces away, sending machines zipping around it, going noisily to work unloading it. None of this mattered to Alec, for in that moment he saw I-Glo stripped down to the very staple of her being. Her passions opened like the peddles of a delicate flower, exposing themselves for his eyes only. To view her in this light was an incredible rush, she was vulnerable and yet powerful, if he hadn't fallen for her already, there would be no turning back now.

With all that incredible energy building between them, she rushed him, embracing him as if this would be the last time they would ever see each other. If there was one thing she could have wished for right then and there, it would have been that they lived in another time, another era, one where Dextoids were accepted for who they could possibly be, and appreciated for all their capabilities. She wanted nothing more than the time to explore all of his passions, and because of it they would be allowed to fall in love.

For Alec things were different. Feeling her arms around him in this way, so desperate in their effort, gave him a strength he didn't realize he still readily possessed. This infused him in his being, and he felt in someway he was able to transfer this strength back to her. It was a support system in the truest sense of the word. He was a pillar in her world, and she injected life into his. He could have stood there for the rest of the Martian day holding onto her like this, but that was far from practical, much like the safe haven he was trying to send her too.

Suddenly she broke away. "Come with me then, let's leave together! We can remove ourselves from their stupid rules and structures, and put this place behind us. I know we can do this, if we do it together!" To I-Glo it was a sudden and wonderful idea. It was simple in its design, and more importantly to her, it would take him out of harms way. In that one fantastic moment her suggestion actually worked.

Alec let her proposition of fanciful flight completely soak in. He closed his eyes and for one brief moment bought into it, not because he believed, but because he wanted to believe. He wished his life were as carefree and easy as she had just laid it out to be. It was an alluring thought to live beyond the daily grind of people. They had created a social order in which Dextoids had to earn their place each and everyday of their lives. Of course his kind worked hard in doing this, but there were only so many places at the very top of this social order. None of them would ever include a Dextoid. *How many of them would ever have the courage to leave it all behind to live life on their own terms?* All any of them really wanted, human and Dextoid alike, was to be left alone. Now here he was, the one who could not break free of his obligations. Maybe it was because he had been free to roam this world from the start, but to even think of racing off over the horizon in a railcar was shear sophistry.

"I am a marauder. I take what I need when I need it. I don't have ideals about Dextoids living alongside mankind. I have a demon deep down inside of me that when pushed, is there for the sole purpose of striking fear into my oppressors. I am a hunter and I am hunted. I am the ugly side of technology, and in this respect I feel very common. That is the indelible scar they have left upon me. I'm not without feeling, I'm sure it touches all of us, and it's because they have touched us. They made us. What I see in you I-Glo is rare, even in one of them. You combine so many of your wonderful talents with an undercurrent for truly caring. I would even go as far as to say you have a deeper understanding for an emotion like love than most of them may ever know. You are unique, a gift, much like a lone snowflake falling from their cold grey skies, all anybody would ever need to do is take the time to appreciate it." He reached out and gently touched her chin with his hand. He knew it was a mistake to lead her on any further, but he could not fight his feelings for her. He knew by touching her he was being selfish, but even he could not stop himself from wanting this, so he was selfish.

"You are a healer. You dare to dream of better days. You push yourself like no other to create and discover beauty. Somewhere deep within your qubit field there is a line of code allowing you to inspire and you become inspired. I envy you for that.

"The only thing I am able to create is destruction. I have left a wake of damage in my path, which is only going to get worse before it gets better. Where I am the one to take, you give. You do this in a fashion seemingly past your intrinsic design. This single quality makes you more powerful than you realize. Wonderful realms have been created by entities just like you, and those things will only happen for you if you rid yourself of me." He lifted her chin slightly so she was looking into his eyes. "I know I can only exist in those wonderful places as a vandal."

In that one brief moment she too found her inner strength, and it became reflected in her posture. "As convincing as your arguments may sound, the bottom line is we both need to leave. So why not do it together? Come with me, let's put this wretched place behind us, forever, please!"

"I wish I could, but I can't. I have one more thing I must do and where I am going you cannot follow. I won't allow it, and since you cannot come with me, I need to know you are safe and away from this place."

The air around them broke with the loud snaps and pops of the electronic breaking system, signaling the arrival of another railcar. The magnets to the system were positioned on the other side of the depot. It reached out and grabbed the car with its invisible powers, slowing it down to arrive at the station at a safe coasting speed. Alec wasn't looking for this type of safety right now, not with what he was about to do. The railcar they were in may have been unmoving, but the things they were contemplating would have them speeding away from each other for a very long time to come. There was nothing out there that could stop them from following through with this, not an electronic breaking system or even the Red Planet Pioneer Corporation. Once set into motion nothing would ever bring them back, not even their longing desire.

"It's the only way."

She fell toward him and they embraced. As he held onto her, he noticed how well her frame fit into his. It was rather uncanny, as if they were made to fit in this way. This warmth sprang a wealth of truth from within him.

"You make me want to believe. Believe in the good that is hope and dreams, believe in a time where creating is happiness and success is life. With all of this I wish I could override what I have set into motion. Stop everything I am right here in the happy place of that dream so I may live." He stepped back from her, breaking their bond for the last time. "You are the only precious cargo I have in this world, and I need to know you have been delivered safely away from this place."

The new car pulled into its stall and the robotic machinery went quickly to work unloading its contents. With that Alec also sprang into action, he made his way out of the railcar and crossed the tarmac to the island terminal located a short distance away. He was still hurting and it showed as he climbed up the ladder to stand behind the control panel. He activated car after car within the facility, commanding them to move down the rails and to the launch station. He kept working the board, glancing up until he saw I-Glo's railcar begin to move. She hung out the doorway as if she were helplessly tied to its frame, staring back at him, beckoning him to return. As the car moved further away she reached out toward him, hand extended as if she were trying one last time to grab him. He forced a smile, trying to send her one last message of comforting thought, but it wasn't working. There was nothing about what was happening that would make them feel comfortable.

Her car slowly made its way down the tracks until it blended in with the others. With enough of them on the rails, he was hoping they would have a harder time tracking her. There was a very good chance they were already preoccupied with the other things he had put into motion. As those cars began to line up, he knew I-Glo was no longer standing in the doorway. He could picture her sitting back in the car, readying herself for the accelerated push down those tracks. He watched as her car dumped down into the launch position and the machinery operating those magnets ramped up until her car was jettisoned away. As her car sped down those tracks he had the strongest of thoughts echoing in his head that one day he would see her again. He wondered in that one moment how possible it was for him to be able to lie to himself.

What were the real possibilities of him ever seeing her again? There were things at play out there beyond his scope of control. How did something like happenstance, fate, or the probabilities of chance play into his personal life? Did the heavens have the ability to alter the course of mighty rivers to directly affect his personage, or were his experiences more germane to the natural progression of how he interacted within the day to day things of the here and now?

The quantum was deep with inquires from Dextoids searching for answers to those very questions. Did their lives have a preordained destiny or were they fully in charge? The answers to those questions might never come. An unsolvable universe was the timeless thorn in the side of all thinking entities. For if there were unanswerable things out there, then people were basing their lives in acts of faith.

Maybe this was where he should mentally be. He needed to have faith and know one day their path's would cross. Those thoughts were swirling around in his head and raced away from him as the last of the railcars left the depot. It was only then he noticed all of the machinery in the place had ceased working. The eerie quiet was broken only on occasion by the pneumatic pop of machinery hissing their release of pressure to stand down. Even these primitive things were allowed to find a peaceful solitude between their tasks.

He looked back at the headless body of Straka. Even in his death he was the one egging him on now. He was the one adding another thing onto his plate before Alec was allowed to truly leave. Damn his words. He added another layer to what needed to be accomplished. A siren began ramping up within the depot, blaring its loud horned warning. Alec recognized the alarm, it was signifying the immediate evacuation of this biosphere.

They were onto him now.

Chapter 13
Finale

Washburn watched in horror as Alec relentlessly beat down Straka. He was quite aware both were Dextoids but found he could not stop flinching with each blow delivered. It was very disconcerting to have to witness this type of imagery on a monitor, and it made him feel as if he were privy to a point in time he wasn't supposed to see. There was nothing pleasant about peering into these last few moments of Straka's life. An aggression was being played out before him that somehow painted humanity in a very sad light. As he pondered this thought, he questioned why they were making Dextoids to look like people at all?

The man leading them down this road sat unmoving in his chair, it was clear to Washburn now that Xavier represented an even uglier slice of humanity. How he was able to remain so calm after hearing Washburn's report was beyond his comprehension. The reaction wasn't rational and confounded a number of his sensibilities. Xavier should have been showing some real emotion, expressing something along the lines of shock or anger at what Washburn had conveyed to him. *Why wasn't he slamming his fist onto the desk, standing up and screaming at anyone who would listen? Why wasn't he making a complete scene as he was so famous for doing at times just like these?* No one would have faulted him for the outburst; it would have been for all the right reasons in trying to save this place.

Their world was on the verge of spinning out of control. It had taken some time for Washburn and his staff to put the pieces of the puzzle together, but when they were finally able to reassemble what Alec had put into motion, it sent chills down the spines of everyone involved. It was only natural to have a reaction like that when someone found out a disaster loomed on their horizon. Yet there sat Xavier, showing no signs of panic whatsoever. In fact he slightly smiled at times watching the fight. The man had clearly checked out and was on *Roman Holiday*.

Up on the screen Alec was pummeling Straka to death. It was such a gruesome sight and only punctuated the reckless creature that had escaped them. It had been about an hour ago when they finally cracked the case for what had happened back at Outpost One. They flipped through the digital images of Alec breaking into rooms and saw him partially destroy the one they had interrogated I-Glo in, he paused there just long enough to manipulate a laptop and then made a beeline for the flight command center. It took them a while to interpret the data from inside the command center, but when that first analyst deduced what Alec had done, the analyst let out a helpless sigh.

In the entire time they investigated Alec they looked for rockets he might use for his possible escape. They feared the day it was made known he was making his way into the rocket garden where I-Glo resided. Instead Alec had fooled them all, reprogramming the coordinates of three Kairos rockets from their inbound paths back at that flight command center, and zeroed them in on this biosphere. From all indications he hadn't adjusted their course with any intention of touching them safely down outside the front doors of this facility. They would race across the sky with huge black plumes of smoke trailing behind them until they slammed into this place as if they were the crackling bolts of doom sent down from the God of War himself.

Alec had gone about locking them out from fixing the problem. Washburn never knew commands like that were even possible, it was a coding horror they couldn't hack, not in the short amount of time since being discovered. If Alec were meant to be an agent of chaos, it was clear to everyone he was capable of doing his job well.

The natural thing for Xavier to be doing after hearing about these inbound rockets was rallying his troops the best way he knew how. Every second wasted was another second putting those broken arrows closer to their target. Xavier's reaction wasn't rational, in fact, it wasn't very human at all.

Washburn thought about all those lunch time conversations he had with his fellow employees, all the idle chit-chat over cups of coffee and social gatherings, where people had whispered their hushed toned innuendos accusing Xavier of dipping into the biological pool of the Dextoids. There were some who firmly believed he had been having the technology implanted into his system for quite some time.

Washburn had read the reports coming from Earth about this subject and they were quite upsetting, highlighting the inherent risks of indulging in that kind of biotechnology. The people who did this became addicted to the process and couldn't stop themselves from having those grafts done over and over again. There were horrible tales spinning off that planet, of human beings having gone too far, of incarcerating individuals for their own good, locking them away from the public scrutiny because they had taken this process far beyond anything that could still be considered human.

The rumors were ugly only because they pointed to an island colony having to house those wretched souls. Most were in need of dire treatment and would never be allowed to return to society because of how badly mutilated they had become. It was frightening for Washburn to think Xavier might be falling under the shadow of temptation from the dark arm of this technology. There would be no easy answers for the colonists if things kept progressing down this path. Some of them might not consider Xavier being human any longer. They would break off into their own separate camps, rejecting his leadership. The company would lose positive control over this entire process, meaning there would be a real hell to pay.

There were things about these rumors that confounded Washburn, he knew firsthand they had a crack medical staff up here. They had treated him on several occasions, even when he had his tragic accident and lost a limb. The doctors had a remarkable technique for printing out new cells, layer upon layer, in his case until they had regenerated his arm and seamlessly fit it back onto his body. They were able to provide an amazing amount of healthy medical possibilities to those patients in need, the procedures were clean, fused with the body, and functioned properly. Washburn looked down at his arm, even to this day he couldn't tell they had bred those cells and printed them out. *So with all of these miraculous medical capabilities at Xavier's disposal why was it he still had all that visible scar tissue on the back of his head? Could it be things weren't healing correctly, or perhaps it was the fact they had to keep opening him up to go in and change things about his rumored graft. How long would he dabble in this world of Dextoid-Infusion before he finally decided to stop?* When questioned by their captors, the mutants back on Earth described those grafts as an empowering process, always hissing at their reach for immortality. Those three Kairos Rockets were about to put that to the test. When they finally hit this place, it would wipe the slate clean for all of them. Washburn made a note to himself, making sure he questioned the medical staff about what they knew of Xavier's scar when they got to their next destination.

"Sir!" Washburn's bark was meant to snap Xavier out of his trance. "Shouldn't we be warning the others? Making preparations to leave the biosphere?"

Xavier never looked away from the images being pumped onto his viewing screens. He leaned back slightly and allowed himself to lift his right hand lazily in Washburn's direction, slowly fluttering it at him as if to shoo him out the door. "Of course Washburn, we must evacuate at once, tell your people."

Xavier had this propensity to treat everyone around him as if they were somehow all getting in his way. *People had put their blood and sweat into this place, why couldn't he see that?* This was more than just a home to them, it was a functioning monument, representing the very achievement of their colonization efforts.

Xavier could have easily provided them with the information they needed to walk away from this place. All he had to do was read a statement to be broadcasted over their corporate airwaves, the very technology he seemed to be so fixated on! It would give these colonists a chance to understand the emergency befalling them, responding in kind by organizing their own evacuations! Instead they were getting this lackadaisical version of Xavier, it was so cavalier, and they deserved so much more from him than this. Washburn was really dreading having to speak with him anymore, but his next question had to be asked. "And the others sir?!"

This was the question that had Xavier finally turning away from his precious holographic screens. He stared at Washburn with the same contempt an adult would have when speaking to an unruly child. "You should only concern yourself with the things that are in front of you, now go."

That was it then. Turning his back, Washburn was exiting that room for the very last time. It was as if a huge weight were being lifted off of his shoulders. He had been secretly dreaming of the day he could leave this place and not have to answer to Xavier ever again. He wanted nothing more than to get his life back. *What other company was going to allow him to define his own sense of freedom though?* None of them had social structures designed to allow a man to live in that way. There was no getting around the fact he was a kept employee, and as soon as he landed, be it a foreign or a national base, he would be accounted for and made to report back to the Red Planet Pioneer Corporation.

There were more important things in front of him, and the ideas of fanciful flight would have to wait for another day. He had a responsibility to the people of this place. He knew it was more than that, this was about doing what was right, about caring for one's fellow man and being altogether human. The last thing he wanted was to have the souls of these colonists splattered across his consciousness. He watched them everyday as they went through their routines, working within the confines of this structure. It was his job as an investigator to be observant of their day-to-day activities. He saw how hard the people here were striving for consistency, they wanted tomorrow to be the same as today so they could build from it. Any time they were made to change their routine or became displaced from their settings, they got upset, even disoriented. It was only human nature to feel this way, how else could they advance? He shuttered with his next thought. When that alarm finally sounded, Deimos be damned, this place would fill with the scattering energy of chaos.

Xavier turned a cold shoulder toward his Corporate Criminal Investigator. As far as he was concerned Washburn was just like everyone else up here, looking for a way in to try and take his job. Those cretins may have hungered for his position but they could never understand how deeply entrenched he was within this company. He was untouchable. *Didn't they notice how every problem and transgression he caused washed off his back and onto unsuspecting others?* Sure, they threatened him with sanctions on his accounts, berated him during their teleconferencing, but over time he came to find the corporation would always exonerate him. He began to carry himself with all the confidence a gambler would have when playing with house money. He knew the game was rigged, he just wasn't settling for the small pots they were allowing him to win.

KEEPING FAIRNESS

He blinked his eyes wide as he found himself watching the pixilated image of Alec staggering back over to the headless body of Straka. Xavier was torn on how he should be feeling after watching what had just happened on those screens. He had expected so much more out of Straka. *Was it possible his expectations were based on faulty information? Could Straka have lied on his resume about once having been a Strike Dextoid or padded his statistics?* He was supposed to represent state of the art technology when it came to being a Dextoid bounty hunter, but instead he looked like a rag-doll in the hands of a brute.

Xavier's disappointment for this situation would be short lived, he would win either way, at this moment Alec could live or die. Doing the latter would solve a lot of his problems, but they would not stop those rockets from falling onto this place. Nothing would. He let out a loud sigh. Alec was about to become a real agitant in Xavier's life. Everything else had played out according to his plan, now he needed Alec to expire.

It was strange to have to acknowledge under these circumstances, but Xavier was quite proud of Alec's proficiency. Even as he watched him stagger around down on that platform, he knew Alec was operating well above their expectations. He was like a satellite launched with an operating window of only three years, but instead lasted a hardened fifteen. Couple this with the fact he was never supposed to leave the lab, and all of this was truly saying something about what Alec had become. There was no arguing he was genuinely one of a kind. If he were to survive all of this, the mere thought of his existence would strike a terror into the general population. Xavier began to rock in his chair with excitement, if Alec wouldn't die, than he would use this fact to his advantage as well.

Calls had been coming in from all over the biosphere inquiring about what was happening in places like the security office, the flight terminal, and now the rumored destruction of this place. They wanted to know the severity of these threats, or get advice on how to react to the situation. They needed answers to the calamities that were befalling them and in that moment Xavier knew none of those calls would be answered. He was not to be disturbed. He left it to his underlings to sort through that mess, and without any direction from him. As far as he was concerned all those nagging people were the proletariat, and their voices had been growing for far too long. *Wasn't this the same sick feeling he got from working at that firm back on Earth?* He brushed those employees aside when he found he could no longer tolerate them, it was one of the deciding factors for coming to this place.

It wasn't his fault the colonists had become a money-grubbing rabble. Their impending doom translated into a thinning of the herd. The survivors of this disaster would have the message blasted into their consciousness to work longer and harder hours. They would need to rebound from this disaster, sacrificing much of themselves to achieve these goals. He found a personal satisfaction with those thoughts, probably because he would be there to take full advantage of their efforts.

Up on some of the screens, reports were starting to air on the three Kairos Rockets. This unpleasant reality had traveled that far down the rumor mill, people all over this facility would be jumping out of their chairs with this news, and yet he still refused to pull the evacuation alarm to warn them. He allowed his hand to lightly caress his baldhead. *Was he not the one who chose when these people lived or died?* They needed to know he had this kind of power over them, the little Emperor inside him was insistent.

The tide of confusion was almost upon them and Xavier would happily play the *pan flute* to all their screams and cries. It was a personal moment of glee, and it could have gone on for quite some time if he hadn't been interrupted. Someone was adjusting themselves in the chair on the other side of his desk. He slowly turned to see Harvard sitting there. As soon as Xavier made eye contact with him, Harvard chimed in with his own two cents, as if not to miss a beat in the thoughts Xavier was having.

"You should be answering each and every one of those calls coming in right now. The people need your help!"

There was a stillness as Xavier took this situation in. He wondered how Harvard kept doing this? Showing up as if he were materializing out of thin air with the capability of reading his thoughts. It was an unnerving trend Xavier knew he was going to need to bring to an end, and much sooner than later. "What are you doing here? Shouldn't you be scrambling to an escape pod to save that precious little hide of yours?"

"You know why I am here. Why I am always here, to remind you to do the right thing by these people. They need your help. Why don't you follow through with doing the right thing for once and help them?"

"Help them?! What do you take me for? Morning, noon, and night all I have done is help these people and look where it has gotten us! Most of those needing this so called help aren't worth saving. This place is going up in one gigantic fireball. I say wipe the slate clean and start anew."

It was in that telling moment the evacuation alarm bellowed throughout the facility. Harvard pointed into the air as if he were able to point at the exact source of where the alarm was coming from. "You see, you're wrong, someone does care. Someone out there realizes they deserve more than just a fighting chance. It's only fair after how hard these employees have worked, the sacrifices they have made, the time..."

"Fair?!" Xavier let out an explosively mocking laugh, as if it had been building up within him for quite some time now. "Nothing has been fair since I left Earth for this miserable red rock. They have pushed us all to the brink of insanity. The twists and turns it takes to survive up here are maddening, and all the while the corporation squeezes this place for every last drop of blood."

Harvard shot back. "You sicken me with your *conflict in the workplace* excuses. You're the one who pulls all of the levers up here. You're the one allowing for this type of mentality to trickle down into their environment, and why? So they will toughen up to meet your standards? So you can mold them into what you want them to be! If they don't meet your expectations then you make them feel indebted to you, to the company! You chain them to this place as if they have an albatross tied around their necks. Who do you think you are?"

Xavier shot up out of his chair in reaction to this last remark. He walked over to Harvard getting right up in his face. "Who am I? I will tell you who I am not, I will not cater to the weak, I will not allow people to walk away from their responsibilities, and I will not listen to you lecture me for one second longer." Xavier reached back and slapped Harvard across the face with the back of his hand. It was a blinding blow that sent him flying across the room attached to his chair. He crashed into the far wall, falling awkwardly upon impact. Xavier made his way back to his side of the desk, never acknowledging Harvard lying face down and obviously hurting. "Without me you people would be nothing. You above all should know this. I am you. I am all of you. I made you, and I made them. You can keep a thing like fairness, it will only lead us down a road of ruin." Xavier sat comfortably back in his chair and began monitoring the screens again. He felt the message he had just sent to his sniveling assistant was pretty darn clear; he wouldn't be needing his services any longer.

FUEL

The Cesium particle quivered with a vigorous energy looking to be set free. It rapidly bounced within its tiny composite chamber, keeping with it a standard of time that was in sync with the rest of the known universe. It was just one particle, trapped within a tiny sphere that on the surface would appeared to threaten the very principles of uncertainty, but of course upon closer inspection it wasn't very close at all. The heat that drove this particle was a thin blue laser light, consistently hunting it down in an effort to spur it on.

Alec could relate to the chase this particle was going through deep down inside him, and was surprised by the fact this chronometer was the timepiece that could drive him. It seemed as he approached a more excited state, he could actually hear the high-pitched hum rise from within this little chamber. It was as if a human voice were trying to hold a note for an extended period of time, rising in pitch as it went on and on and on. The particle was singing to him now as he made his way back up the ramps and to the main floor of the biosphere. The pitch of it was pushing him to move a little faster, and he would need too if he were to have any chance of getting out of here alive.

Back at Outpost One, when he broke into their flight command center, one of the things he did was thoroughly scan their shipment logs. Initially his search was to make sure no human lives were onboard the craft he was about to commandeer. After a short time of reviewing the records it was easy for him to see how as a colony, they had gotten behind the eight ball with needing those supplies. A rocket lost at launch back on Earth, another flying off course, or one crashing while trying to land here, it got to the point where they were living as if from paycheck to paycheck. At times those logs read as if they weren't going to make it before the next shipment arrived. All of this had to have added another degree of difficulty to what the colonists were already trying to overcome.

He likened their plight to the series of ramps he was currently trying to traverse. If one had found themselves all the way down at the bottom, there was no easy way back to the top. Twice he stepped aside as a group of people came running down the ramp looking for a way out. They were panicked and carried on their faces a look of confusion.

Normally these ramps wouldn't have been such a chore for him, but his wound was hampering his ability. Even the casual observer would have noticed the hitch in Alec's gate. It was cause for concern, and he realized it could cost him in making it out of here alive.

If there was one structure on this red rock housing the answers to all his questions, it would be the one he was making his way through right now. Deep within the chambers of this place hummed a bank of computers containing information as to who he was. It would have been like a haunting but he would have traversed those secret passages until he found the long cavernous tunnel to the dark subterranean sector from which he was born. It would be guarded no doubt, in layer after layer of corporate centurions and in his current condition that was a problem. Down there in the pit of that place was where projects were fused together, where subversive systems were developed and tested, and the boundaries for non-lethal weapons were pushed to the fringes of human safety. No one was allowed to walk into those chambers unless they signed onto an oath of secrecy, swearing their complete allegiance to the corporation.

If there was a subterranean cavern on this planet harboring a thing like hell, then this was it. He remembered coming in and out of consciousness and hearing the hideous cries of those creatures being brought to life and then extinguished because of their grotesque development. Those entities awoke to find themselves tightly bound to their tables, trapped behind the long strips of heavy plastic sheathing, and being forcefully injected with serums of experimentation. There was no accountability for the mental or physical scarring they were leaving on these living things. Down in that place men dawning biological suits covered in the blood of their creations brokered out sanity on a very cold slate.

Operations were performed all the time without the use of anesthesia, and if a Dextoid shut down, it was brought back to life without a second thought for its well-being. He closed his eyes to those unholy thoughts. It was tough for him to forget how hard all of those living things were fighting down there just to keep what little they had. That didn't stop them from pushing this technology to its very fringes, imbuing these animated creations to stay alive through all their pain and agony.

Deep within this biological cesspool, past the areas stained with corybantic evidence, was where they housed their banks of quantum supercomputers. These pristine clean rooms were temperature controlled, sealed by double doors, and planned long ago to archive its data at peak quantum efficiency. As Alec mentally drifted off to that place, he wished he could reach out and pull the plug on the whole damn operation.

There was something still chaining him to this place, something locked away in those underground chambers tugging at him. *Could it be the entities down there were calling upon him to destroy this place, to end their own tortuous existence?*

It was indescribable what this influence could be, but it didn't mean the force did not exist. Soon the new moon would arrive to take its place in circling this world. It too would feel an invisible tug on its body as it forever tried to break away from its new parent planet. Alec could sympathize with that kind of struggle, knowing full well it would take something in the extreme to be able to break those bonds.

Alec was certain they knew he would be back and try to descend into this secretive lair. They must have planned and schemed for this moment from the very first day he had escaped, laying out trap upon trap for him. He looked down at his wound, the gurgling wasn't as severe, but he couldn't be sure if it was because he was running out of fluid or if he was actually beginning to heal. None of it mattered, he wasn't in a position to fight them, not with how he was feeling.

If they had planned for his arrival, then it also meant they feared it. Normally he could have used that knowledge to his advantage, he was sure it would have won him the day.

Not now, not with this wound. With everything he was facing he would only have time to complete one task. This task was driving him now as he made his way through the back room of a fabric shop. There were bins filled with thread, buttons, beads and accessories, and an entire wall dedicated to bolts of material. This store contained everything a person could ever want if they chose to get lost in couture. The time for contemplating such polished self-refinement of oneself was over. He made his way down a small hall which dumped him out into their stylish storefront. The place was strategically placed with mannequins dressed in chic apparel, sale racks, and wall bins all the way up to the ceiling. It did not surprise him the place was devoid of customers or even a Dextoid attendant. Anyone with common sense was getting away from this place. He flung the front doors open and soon found himself in the courtyard and their grand market place. The first thing to greet him out in this open area was the blaring noise of the evacuation alarms. Hearing them like this told him something about their situation, the rockets were indeed descending onto this biosphere, but it also rang with a truth that there was nothing these people could do to stop it.

This knowledge actually began to fuel him.

FRIGHTFUL PRAXIS

From his office Xavier watched up on the screens as Alec swung open the front doors to the popular little boutique. It would not be long now before the *Riot Control Robots* he had summoned would come racing through the place in a strong show of force to try and apprehend this rogue Dextoid.

Xavier at long last felt his grip beginning to tighten around this situation. As he studied Alec's movements on the screen, he could tell Alec was having a difficult time maneuvering. He would have no chance at defending himself against this suppressing force! His plan was sound enough. He would use the Riot Control Robots to wrestle Alec to the ground, overpowering him with shear numbers. Xavier would have him held there in the courtyard until those three inbounds buried him under the destruction of this place. If he were really honest with himself, he wanted to see the moment Alec vaporized in the explosion.

Up on some of the other screens, the news coverage was beginning to intensify. The broadcasters were confirming the rumors about the evacuation. He watched as they showed pictures of people fleeing this biosphere anyway they knew how. There were rovers, escape pods, and shuttles, there were so many people driving away from this place that anyone watching would have been concerned.

It was now that Xavier wished to capitalize on all this free press. Now was the time to take Alec down. The venue couldn't have been more public for allowing the final part of his scheme to unlatch!

That courtyard represented ground zero for all the things in his life needing vindication. It was bought and paid for in more ways than one, by men like Theodore Hadley, Jarvis Kendle, and Jeb Wentworth, they would all pay for having sent him here all those years ago. It was at the moment the Riot Control Robots began to roll into view.

Xavier sat back and thought about what the future might bring. There would be few if any that would remember how this whole affair had gotten started, but there were plenty who would remember how it would all end. The visual of this place crumbling to its foundation would stick in their hearts and minds for a very long time to come. It would create the lasting image he needed to hatch his evil plan. He would lean hard on the company and those grubby old men back on Earth, using the media in the coming months to orchestrate public support in getting the colonists to stick together. Stitching the unity they needed to build a place from the fortitude of those survivors, only they would build it according to his vision, and there was nothing any of them back on Earth could do about it. The company owed him.

He was leaving his benefactors with very few choices and they couldn't have been more extreme. On one hand they would have to tolerate the vision Xavier had for colonizing Mars and on the other hand they had the nightmare Alec could very well become. In the end he knew they would never choose the side making it appear the Dextoids were winning. This was the doorstep he was leaving them on. Alec was the dark symbol for their greed and the unending desire for power. Xavier had given these lechers exactly what they wanted with his creation. After the rockets destroyed this place, and those excavation teams sorted through its rubble, no one on the board of directors would ever fess up or want to remember why they created him.

The public would be screaming for a name in all of this mess. That name would become the face for this disaster, someone they could castigate and mercilessly crucify in the media. As it stood now he knew deep down inside those bastards back on Earth would be more than happy to give them his name.

Those old men had grown to hate him, and the more they grew to hate Xavier, the more they realized they needed him. Their personal dislike of him did not mean much when it came to turning a profit. They had too much invested in this operation. He knew the name that would wind up in the hands of the *Press,* it would be Alec's. He was their frightful praxis dripping with the desire for conquering this world. The images of him destroying this facility would be all Xavier needed to snuff out anyone seeking the truth. He would make sure of it and that's where everyone would want to leave it. They had to because if they found Xavier guilty than so were they.

He shook his head, the real irony was that Alec would have done their bidding without question if he had only been given the chance. He would have conquered this world and laid all the avarice Mars had to offer right at their feet. Xavier had other plans for him right from the start. He never stood a chance and now the only real value Alec had for Xavier would happen in his death. He watched those monitors intently as the final moments of Alec's life played out.

AGAINST THE ONSLAUGHT

The courtyard echoed with the wails of the evacuation alarm, drowning out any other sound the biosphere might have offered. The alarm was accompanied on occasion by a computerized female voice calmly instructing the occupants to evacuate. The voice may have been void of any emotion, but it clearly was stirring a response in the people who heard it. Alec knew the human beings doubting those warnings were the ones really entrenched in this place. They would never leave under any circumstance, even if it meant their own destruction. In every emergency there were always a handful of those types, acting out of defiance, as if their beliefs were stronger than the impending doom hurtling toward them.

Alec wondered if he were currently acting out in this manner. *Was his whole life based on an act of defiance?* He was becoming aware of the fact he was fighting against something within his own being and he was also aware he was never going to surrender to it. Those rockets were approaching this place like the shadow of a terrifying eclipse. Nothing was going to stop that from happening. Glancing down at his wound, he wondered if this ugly gash didn't symbolize his own end.

It was difficult for him to admit, even to himself, but it was getting harder and harder for him to know which thoughts were the ones they had given him and which were truly his own. There was a rumor floating around in the quanta that there were only eight basic plots for stories the human species could ever tell, those themes were constantly being reinvented to fit the times. It was hard for him to comprehend with all that was going on out there in the universe—that the human experience was dictating the way these stories were being told. Record players could only play records, television sets could only reflect the media being broadcast on them, and human beings could only retell stories they could identify with. Each of these things operated within a certain narrow bandwidth. For Alec, this was an affront to every one of his senses.

The moment before him was escaping. He needed to re-focus, scale things back, concentrate on the immediate. He just wanted to find something solid to lean against so he could check his wound. Whatever was going on inside him still wasn't feeling quite right, he wanted to be able to examine his contusion. He contemplated going over to one of the large nearby trees planted within the exposed Martian soil of this biosphere. From the size of its thick base these trees must have been planted sometime ago because the only thing they were capable of flying all the way up here from Earth were the seeds. He scanned the lines of bark all the way up to the sprawling branches reaching skyward in a desperate effort to try and touch the translucent ceiling of this place.

The canopy of fresh green leaves told him those trees still felt a connection to the sun. It was a simple exchange of carbon; the tree turned the carbon from the sun into this outreach of branching biology. When it finally passed on, it would collapse and begin to decay. People would gather its wood and use it in their fires, igniting it to watch it burn just like the sun that gave it life. Alec realized people were no different really in their development and thought. They grew roots in their ideology, and some of those roots wouldn't allow them to leave, even in the face of danger. Perhaps this was why they too chose to stay because the ideology they backed was born in that kind of fire. Under the right circumstances, everything burned.

His contemplations were cut short by the appearance of three Riot Control Robots. From where Alec stood he could feel the ground under his feet tremble, so much so in fact that some of the leaves fell from their branches. The robots were heavy contrivances, looking to stand almost three meters high and supported by the wide base of their tank treads. Even with the evacuation alarm wailing away he could pick up on the noises those things were making, rattling loudly with the metallic sounds of their slats. They were ominous looking things, approaching him with their four long appendages spread wide in an array of catchall type framework.

Three more Robots approached from the opposite direction. Xavier was watching with great anticipation, there was no doubt in his mind this was Alec's final chapter. He would bury the files on him with the destruction of this place. The truth would die in that rubble and be reborn as whatever Xavier decided to tell the investigators in those coming days.

Alec stood his ground, not giving an inch. "Tested to the last." Xavier found himself saying this with a great sense of pride. It was all going down just as he had hoped. Alec was standing up to the onslaught: he knew no defeat! There was a precision in his programming and a method behind his madness. He was all Spartan and would be described as nothing short when Xavier retold the tale at future cocktail parties. He would paint Alec as a proud but dying breed, driven out by the efficiency of cheaper technology. As Xavier watched, he felt his place secure for becoming the Emperor of Mars. What better way to celebrate the advent of his throne then with the sacrifice of one of his finest warriors, and this was for all to see.

His assistant got up and slowly made his way back over to Xavier's desk. Harvard was fixated as well with what was happening up on those screens, albeit for different reasons. It was of no matter to Xavier, Harvard didn't hold his ear like he used too.

They both watched as Alec reached into his tattered jumpsuit to reveal the weapon Straka once held.

"He's got a gun!" Harvard's scream was shrill and would have terrified anyone in the room. His welted eye and broken nose compounded the unsightly horror he had become.

Alec aimed carefully, lining up his first shot, and then pulled the trigger. Seconds after it had happened, both Xavier and Harvard heard the blast from where they stood. The robot he was aiming at had been blown to pieces as if it had been detonated from within. Alec didn't skip a beat, within seconds two more Riot Control Robots were laid to waste. Both Xavier and Harvard watched as the remaining machines kept approaching, it were as if they failed to comprehend the deadly meaning of the gun. Xavier realized there was no reason for these robots to ever have had this type of knowledge. No one was supposed to have a gun on this planet. It was a baffling flaw that was playing out before him, forcing his mind to spin unto itself until it was wound so tight he jumped out of his chair. "Ready my escape pod, immediately!"

"You can't leave . . ."

"I told you Harvard, I have no time for you or your drivel. I will monitor this situation from one of the remote sites."

"People will think you the coward for leaving them at this moment."

"It really doesn't matter what they think, does it. This place is about to go up in a fireball."

"Stop acting like you don't care!"

Xavier left, giving one last parting shot as he made his way out the door. "And like I so delicately informed you earlier, I will not be needing your services anymore."

Alec stood there drawing bead after bead on Robot after Robot, shooting them into unidentifiable pieces until they were destroyed. During their blitz it dawned on him this was the same weapon that had been used on him, only he had held up much better under the brunt of its slug. Taking aim at the last Riot Control Robot, he became very conscious of the violent recoil the weapon had. The noise accompanying this was deafening, sounding like a mechanical lions roar, It punctuating the thought he had about himself in the moment, that of being one tough motherfucker.

How could a thing like a gun evoke this kind of feeling from within him? It seemed odd to fire a weapon and then immediately have an emotion such as vanity or empowerment attached to its use. He looked at the piece as it lay in his hand, the grip was warm and felt heavy. A thin stream of white smoke trailed from the smoldering barrel, as if to signal its use to anyone who might have cared. The gun was basic, lacking any type of chip or processor, there was no way for him to communicate with it directly, but somehow this piece had done just that.

He stared at the weapon almost forgetting why he had taken it in the first place. The chamber lay wide open, signaling it was out of bullets. This was a real problem, it wasn't like he was wearing belts of ammunition, and unless he was intending on using it as a hammer or a paperweight, the gun was now rendered useless. This thought was all it took for the spell he was under to be broken. He re-engaged his protocols for fleeing this place and tossed the weapon aside. As it skipped across the courtyard the thoughts Alec had for assassinating Xavier fluttered away with it. Those thoughts would simply have to wait for another day.

THE CALMING WATER DROPLET

The crews who constructed this biosphere installed sets of stairs that lead to the very top. Along the way they added catwalks to work at different levels with one of these ending at an evacuation station. Contained beyond were a small fleet of escape pods meant for the human workers trapped up here. Xavier found himself running wild and racing all the way up those stairs. At the doors of the evacuation station he laid his hand on the scanner and looked straight ahead at the green dot mounted on the wall. The lenses of the facial recognition software worked in conjunction with the hand scanner and it was the only way he was going to be allowed to get beyond the doors. The vehicles docked there should have been reserved for upper management, but there was too much protest from the people who worked at those heights.

As he waited, Xavier could feel the raw energy of this place begin to permeate the air. There was an urgency to keep things moving, of wanting to leave, yet in this moment he had to stand there and exhibit nothing but patience. He made a mental note to address this issue in the building of the next superstructure. That one would be a palace and his next pathway for escape would flow much smoother than this one, because he would have his own personal pod.

When the software finally acknowledged him, he passed through the doors to find most of the vehicles had already been taken. There were still a few left, but not as many as he would have liked. As he stood there deciding which one he should take, he thought he could hear the desperate clamor of the people far below him. Those poor souls were scrambling to find a way out of this place. Their cries for help were beaconing him, trying to pull him back into the biosphere. It was rubbish, a weak feeling that would only lead to other weaker feelings, and all of those weak feelings would only get him into trouble.

"Damn it!" His shout was loud enough that it echoed off the walls. He realized the chamber he was standing in had been insulated from the noise of the blaring alarm or anything else that might be happening outside this area.

He stomped his foot onto the floor. It gave him a twitch and caused him to want to stomp the floor again. He was fighting with himself. He knew the right thing to do was go back in his office and facilitate the evacuation. The thought of this was driving him to the point of madness. He could hear the voices in his head reprimanding him for not doing just that. The ringing in his ears steadily rose in tone. The thing inside his skull began to show itself, allowing for its tentacles to swell within his lobes. He hit himself in the head repeatedly with clenched fists trying to make it stop.

Falling to his knees he yelled out, sounding as if someone were being murdered right there in front of him. This scream didn't just echo in the causeway, but in the catacombs of his mind, causing the thing inside him to suddenly constrict, interfering with the flow of cerebrospinal fluid. He fell forward straining for relief, crying out because it reflected the sharp pain he felt in the back of his head. *What had they done to him?!*

"You bloody bastards!" He clawed at his scar, rubbing it abrasively causing it to bleed. He was trying to get to the thing they had sewn into his head. He wanted it removed. There had to be a Dextoid or a human being who would perform this procedure for him. The urgency for removing this made him feel uncomfortable, but it was because he couldn't let this thing be within him for one second longer.

They were watching him. The thought crossed his mind as he knelt there holding his head against the floor. They were always watching everyone. This causeway was no different, it was loaded with cameras and heavily monitored for security reasons. The violent fit he had just thrown was being recorded, and if they weren't watching it live, they would certainly play it back and analyze it later. He was motionless with this thought.

He suddenly stood up and headed straight into an escape pod, the doors closed behind him. He was alone. He didn't care what they thought of him at this point, it was what it was. Those old goats back on Earth couldn't stop him. He controlled his own destiny now. "I'll show you, I'll show all of you!" He took a seat and waited patiently for his departure. He figured it should only be a few moments from the time he hit the button on the door. If there was a countdown happening he wasn't aware of it. There was a large creaking noise and he felt the slight punch of the escape pod as it launched itself safely away from the structure. *He was away!*

All of Mars was in front of him now to the edges of its horizon. He felt it broad and wide and welcoming. He sent himself away with every intention of conquering that expanse. The smashing of this biosphere would send the politics of this place spinning into a state of emergency. He was laughing out loud with this thought, once he got those powers of absolute control, he would never turn the clock back to return them, ever!

This was the moment he had thought about from the very first time those planners proposed building Alec. He plotted for it meticulously, and when they shrouded the creation of this *Strike Dextoid* in all those layers of secrecy, Xavier seized on the opportunity and enacted his own plan. Nothing about it was going to be easy. He had to have people he could trust to write the lines of code to get Alec to do the things he needed him to do. Those lines needed to be written without the possibility of anyone questioning the ethical side of why they were assigning Alec with those particular protocols. His real orders needed to be hidden in a creative way without anyone else ever stumbling upon them, and whoever was helping him do all this had to disappear once their task was complete. The only thing he knew that could meet all of those requirements and not be missed by anyone within the corporation was a *Service Dextoid.*

Xavier left nothing to chance; he had his personal *Service Dextoid* program Alec. His mechanical servant had become as insidious as his master, filled with the dark secrets and lies of this place. Initially he was the one assigned to personally take care of the cerebral implant in Xavier's head. This Dextoid was already operating surreptitiously within the company making sure the graft was taking hold. As time progressed his mechanized servant developed into being closer to a henchman, Xavier was sorry to lose him, especially when compared to the likes of Harvard, that was a hire he had continually regretted.

To the other technicians in that lab it looked as if Xavier had taken a personal interest in the project, allowing his *Service Dextoid* to be apart of the programming team. They felt it was there only to review the code. Having a Dextoid write code for another Dextoid broke more than one law, but deep down in that lab they were breaking rules all the time. The technicians carried themselves with an attitude of being absolved of any wrongdoing as long as their work got completed, nothing was ever supposed to leave that lab anyway. Alec blew the doors off that with his eventual escape, but what was the breaking of one more law if it meant in the end Xavier would get what he wanted?

The Dextoid that programmed Alec hid those lines of code where only a Dextoid would find them, in the carousels of the quanta. If he wanted too, he could have written them down on the head of a pin, but that would have been too easy to find for anyone investigating this. It was important that Alec be driven by these things, but not commanded by them, who better to know how to do this than a Dextoid.

There was no one out there who could stop Xavier now. He whispered a promise to himself as if to reaffirm his intentions. "I will show you, I'll show you all."

"There are still too many loose ends for that too happen." Harvard said it with confidence. He sat there next to him, his posture was staunch and his eyes unblinking as he stared his boss down.

Xavier jumped out of his chair. "How in the hell did you get in here! I left you back there! I left you behind to die!"

"Did you really think you would get rid of me that easily? You forget how much I am apart of you. That's always been your problem, you think you have something over me, that I am beneath you, or that I don't have the ability to keep up with you, but yet here I am. I have always been more resilient than that imagination of yours."

"This can't be!" Xavier began to feel a tidal force of anger swell up in him, he brought his fist back to smash Harvard in the face, and then stopped just inches short of delivering the blow. He was horrified with the realization that Harvard looked normal. His complexion reflected a state of good health. There was no evidence of scarring or bruising from the altercation he previously had with him less than an hour ago.

"That's right Xavier, I too have a say in how I look, and in how I act." Harvard sat back a little more comfortably in his chair. "You think you are better than me, but I know all the things you know, or all the things you will ever know. You always have this idea you can just get rid of me. What an amusing thought, because I am you. Cave quid dicis, quando, et cui. (Beware of what you say, when, and to whom)."

Xavier fell into a corner of the capsule, his mind now buzzing with the static of the quanta. He could hear its emphatic roar crossing the cosmos as it showed him the stitches in the fibers of space-time, they were all around him, the quanta enveloped him, it was everywhere. That kind of free fall into this darkness caused him to feel as if he were on the slippery slopes of a gravity well, getting smaller and smaller with his thoughts. The static in his head rose in pitch until it sounded like the roar of a crowd, then an ocean, and then the overwhelming echo of the big bang. This noise grew larger and larger in his head until Xavier was driven to the smallest, most insignificant point of his existence.

The escape pod continued onward, racing off over the barren terrain of Mars with its occupant desperately clutching at the back of his head, screaming at the top of his lungs. He needed to go to his place of tranquility, to bring the repose of passive thoughts back into his being. He needed to find his calming water droplet forming under the ledge. In the core of his mind where the final truth would be revealed, he ventured out under that mantle, and found himself scurrying along the bottom desperately trying to find any indication for this welcoming moisture. His search was a much wilder ride than anything he had ever experienced in the past. He had turned his back on this place for far too long. A warm constant breeze blew across the surface and the vegetation far below. Without warning he slipped and fell toward the expanse. Closing his eyes, he fully waited for the sea of green that was the jungle to crash in all around him but soon realized he wasn't falling at all. He opened his eyes to see the lush green leaves of that forest far below, the jungle had devoured this world whole. Something unnatural was happening to him, and it felt curious to hang there suspended in time. His appendages splayed out trying to find a balance, the warm soft breeze blew between those legs. His rear limbs naturally rubbed up against his spider's silk, testing its strength to see if he could pull himself back up the line. The black speck he saw in the droplet was him!

It was always him.

THE MODULUS OF RESILIENCE

Gigantic black billowing clouds grew out of the destruction of the biosphere. They pushed themselves to reach as high up into the air as possible. Large chunks of the facility would occasionally come flying out of the dark bilge, crashing down upon the ground and causing it to shake. That in itself should have moved him to believe in his own mortality, but those thunderous epochs happening off in the distance only seemed to excite the passions he had for this life.

Long flowing flames occasionally rose out of the wreckage, licking those black clouds with jets of orange plasma. Deep in the pit of all this destruction raged a real fire. The sky was a downpour of debris, tiny pellets streaming down out of the sky, bouncing as they struck the ground. The sound of it was crisp and rose in its intensity as more of it fell from the heavens. Those three Kairos Rockets had done their job well.

Every once in a while an escape pod would pass by overhead, whining loudly as it did. It was hard for Alec to imagine them as anything but empty, just misfiring much like the stores of flares from a burning ship lost at sea.

Leading up to this, in his mind at least, it seemed so clear this place needed to be destroyed. Now that it had happened and the structure was burning down to the ground, his sound reasoning for this seemed to waft away with those large columns of smoke.

The annoying tug pulling him along had now been severed with the destruction of this place. The debris raining down on him personified his new hollowed feeling.

Back on Earth, when a *military unit* was in distress, they would lay down a colored smoke signal to communicate their needs. Those colorful clouds spoke volumes to the level of urgency those distressed soldiers were in. His line of thought for this would travel all the way out to that destroyed biosphere. He too had just laid down a smoke signal, only this one was for an entire world to see. It pointed to his existence. He sent up a message that warned every soul on this stinking rock a *Strike Dextoid* was loose on Mars. Every single person regardless of their nationality would feel threatened by him, even deathly afraid of him, and all their feelings would grow like the thick dark ominous clouds billowing before him.

The mixture of human venom formulating out there would be poisonous to everything it touched, but its energy would be directed purely at him. They would carry their orders out with purpose and conviction. He could see that better than any of them now because those were the same orders that had been revealed to him for destroying this place.

These were rambling little thoughts that now swam in the superficial, there was something far deeper going on within his programming, far more sinister. He felt as if he were chasing a wraith through the tight corridors of his mind. Even if he were able to hunt this thing down and corner it, how would he be able to put his hands around a thing like an enigma?

Were these the feelings of a corrupted system? Could he exorcise it with the mere passage of time? These things were troubling to him, but he needed to flush them from his immediate concern, there was just too much happening out there on the horizon. Occasionally there were flashes from the explosions still taking place deep within that crater. Each volatile action only seemed to punctuate the fact humanity would never be able to forgive him.

This blatant act of destruction would be the point they rallied around; fusing the things they hated the most as if they were a helium nuclei birthed at the core of the sun. Every time they were reminded of this moment it would stoke the overwhelming distrust they had for the Dextoids.

Alec had done that to them, he had drawn a line in the sand and dared humanity to crossover it. He glanced over at the dirt bike laying on its side. The front wheel was still turning slowly; the individual spokes reminding him of a space centrifuge. This two-wheeled machine had brought him all the way out here before he had to bail on it, taking cover from the series of shock waves that came racing upon him from those three rocket strikes.

To Alec this dirt bike was like any other dirt bike, simple in its design, with a fuel tank tied to its combustion engine. This conveyance was really just another way for a Dextoid to get around and complete its tasks away from the biosphere. There was no question these were risky missions for Dextoids to have to undertake, but no one on the human side ever seemed concerned with losing either the dirt bike or the Dextoid. These things were treated like any other asset that needed to be risked to ensure the human survival on this harsh red rock.

The pellets of debris still rained down out of the sky, this deluge was a testament to how much time and materials they had put into their biosphere. It was also drumming a message of how endless their pursuit of him would be. The motorbike would only get him so far in his escape. Wherever he decided to abandon this bike was the place they would plant their flags, allowing for their search patterns to radiate out from that spike. The further he drove this vehicle, the more he was giving those hunting him a direction in which he had gone. The last thing he wanted to do was give them that kind of edge.

Any conflicts he may have known to this point in his life could only be seen as minor inconveniences compared to what lay ahead. Everyday was going to be a struggle for him, a fight to the finish, of being on the run like he had never been on the run before.

No one else could understand as clearly as he did why he needed to do this, just as no one could understand why he stood there now in this rain of debris. "I'll show them, I'll show them all."

He stated it loudly, almost yelling it at the top of his lungs. It was to no one in particular, but it was to everyone, and he said it with conviction. This was the tough sinew he would need in testing the fibers of his existence. It was the thread keeping the fabric of his grit together, and it somehow translated into the paltry portions of gruel he would now be serving up to himself for the rest of his life. Those technicians had gone out of their way to glop hearty helpings of intention into his cauldron, they repeatedly clacked the spoonfuls of purpose against the sides of his ceramics, and they went out of their way to sprinkle in cloves of decidedness over the cold servings of borsch they forced him to eat. He was a prisoner of his own *Gulag*, and he had taken what they were feeding him and thrown it up against the walls of his mind. There it ran and dripped until it found the fissures of his own resolve.

Resolve was a pretty unique word when it came to describing the inner workings of a Dextoid, they wanted them to function without repair, but they were not allowed to fix each other. They were expected to think for themselves on almost every level imaginable, but never show any sign of questioning the demands made on them by their human masters.

Now that was resolve.

Alec raised his arm up so he could look at his hand. He splayed his thick fingers out so he could get a better look at the wrinkles and folds imbedded in those digits. He slowly rotated it around so he could get a good look at all those creased contours running down into his palm and the base of his wrist. He had heard of people capable of reading those lines and believing in things like longevity or the portending of future events. It seemed silly to think one could predict those things by looking at a hand, and especially when Alec looked at his. It was rugged, calloused, and scarred, he didn't know if his hand could tell him so much about his future as well as it would tell someone about his past. Now that type of interpretation was real.

He brought those four large fingers together and wrapped his thumb over the top of them until he found his hand clenched tightly into a fist. Now they would act as one. His knuckles bulged in rebellion to their union, and rightly so, their show of defiance came with the knowledge they would do the brunt of the work. He noticed the shade of white that was cast from beneath his skin, his knuckles looked to pop free from his joints, trying in vain to escape their duties. This, of course, would never happen. The weight of his hands were far too heavy, so much so that he never questioned what he was going to hit when he needed to throw a punch. These were his tools, and these were also the things he would use from here on out to communicate with people.

It was obvious human beings were doing everything they could to hold their creations back. They were going out of their way to deliberately hamper them. The corporations were constantly handing out emotional packets riddled with self-doubt. It was an endless sea of emotional rifts, and because of it Dextoids were still having the hardest of times relating to their human counterparts. Alec had to wonder how much they were holding back on something like rations of resolve.

He noticed he was still holding his fist out in front of him at around eye level, the anger he felt for this situation was compounding. Focusing on his fist he began to see it in a new light. It was no longer just a weapon he could manufacture out of thin air. There was a power to the symbolism he was holding. They had shoved things into his system like icons and avatars, corporate banners and logos, made him conscious to the flashing power bars of his own well being, the darting crosshairs of his target programming, and the osculating brackets seeking to identify the human elements peppered throughout his life. He was constantly being showered with lines of trajectory and patterns of probability, at times he felt as if his life were a walking arcade game being played by an eccentric child another world away. It seemed his

327

entire life was built on the premise of having to heed to these symbols.

Now he too had a symbol the rest of humanity would have to recognize. He squeezed his clenched fist a little tighter as his anger welled up to meet his resolve. Behind this one symbol he would stand up to them, and he would go out of his way to make sure they recognized this new sign in their lives.

Out there on the horizon lay the smoldering ruins of the Red Planet Pioneer Corporation. The world of Mars knew he existed. Any hope of ever having a reasonable dialog with them was gone. There would be no way to ever explain what he had done, or even why. From here on out he would have to fight them every step of the way. The anger he had would never be allowed to subside. There was only one way he was going to survive this challenge, and that was to out-live them all.

The brisance for this situation would rain down on him for the rest of his life. In the months that followed there would be a great deal of effort put into sorting through the razing of this structure. The fires from all this wreckage would bloom for weeks. Even from where he stood the debris field looked to be larger than anything a human being could ever cleanup within a lifetime. He nodded to himself as if to confirm there was really nothing left for him to do. To anyone else watching him, it would have looked as if he had turned to start marching out toward the wide-open plains of Mars and his eventual escape. To Alec, nothing could have been further from the truth; he knew he was taking his first few steps toward his long destructive march at eternity.

Afterward

Red Planet Pioneer was initially a comic book, with a very limited release in 1999. The ideas I had for the series burned inside of me until I formulated what a novel would look like in my head. The purge for this began happening in 2010 as I started writing the novel. I had never attempted anything like this in the past, and had plenty of help along the way, both in the creative process and in seeking out advice from people who had completed long writing assignments and books. I should add that online courses, tutorials, and other materials worked extremely well for me, and I encourage anyone with an appetite for writing to utilize these wonderful resources.

The characters of this story have so many more adventures in front of them. Only time will tell as to when the continuation of their tales will be told. I thank you very, very kindly for your interest in this work, and can only hope more will come from this.